JASON ANSPACH **NICK COLE**

DARK VICTORY

SEASON 2 **BOOK 2**

GALAXY'S EDGE

Copyright © 2021
Galaxy's Edge, LLC
All rights reserved.

This is a work of fiction. Any similarity to real persons, living or dead, is coincidental and not intended by the author.

No part of this publication may be reproduced, stored in a retrieval system, or transmitted in any form or by any means electronic, mechanical, photocopying, recording, or otherwise without the prior written permission of the publisher and copyright owner.

All rights reserved. Version 1.0

Paperback ISBN: 978-1-949731-56-9

Edited by David Gatewood
Published by Galaxy's Edge Press

Cover Art: Tommaso Renieri
Cover Design: Ryan Bubion
Formatting: Kevin G. Summers

Website: www.GalaxysEdge.us
Facebook: facebook.com/atgalaxysedge
Newsletter (get a free short story): www.InTheLegion.com

EXPLORE ALL PRODUCTS AT

GALAXYSEDGE.US

PROLOGUE

Years ago.

The man was late. That didn't bother Hunter Ferguson, who sat alone at a table, deciding whether to finish the meal set before him. Poached white fish, always fish when dining because he couldn't stand the smell at home, and this one with a tangy sauce he couldn't possibly reproduce in his own kitchen. Something he took on faith, having no desire to learn if it was true. Thick green stalks of imported *loppu*, undercooked and left untouched on his plate because *loppu* was a vegetable that chefs loved to serve despite their customers having no desire to eat it. Quartered baby potatoes fried in some exotic oil and spices the names of which he'd forgotten almost as soon as the waiter had proudly presented them. Those were good.

The other man's tardiness... was not.

Hunter looked around the restaurant. A place where being late meant something. Where staff worked furiously to avoid the stain of late. Too long. Forever. Words that mean death to a place like this meant to be the best. One of the finest in Utopion's River District. An exclusive establishment paying a preposterous rent and asking patrons for even more preposterous menu prices. Yet customers waited months on end for a table so they could boast to their friends about the hour they spent in the district where the rich and powerful sat among the mortals. They called it a privilege to pay those prices and considered it a blessing to see a House of Reason delegate or a well-known senator walk by.

Hunter hadn't chosen the meeting location, though the potatoes were excellent. That had been the other man. The late man.

More fish was eaten. *Loppu* was prodded with a silvene fork. Hunter checked his watch, mostly for the sake of the wait staff—all of them human, for the place was too important to rely on bots—who were no doubt searching for some cue that they ought to remove the sturdy menu sitting across from the lone diner. It would be a delight to remove the menu. A thrill. Proof that the ridiculous location and ridiculous prices were justified by such acute, devoted service. It was for them that Hunter checked his watch. He knew what time it was. Only ten minutes had passed since he'd last checked.

He had never been the "on time is fifteen minutes early" type. That was fine in a world where things operated on rails. Hunter's did not. Nether Ops did not. He had been told that as a field agent. Began to believe it as a field director. He now lived it as a department director.

Lateness was a thing that mattered to others. It was a sin for others. For those working their shifts in the restaurant. For the deluded politician with schedules neatly filled in five-minute increments. But not to a man like Hunter, who had made those important men and women wait. Because he had to. Entanglements happened. Reports came early. Missions went sideways. Assets were burned. There were reasons to be late. And so, usually, Hunter didn't mind waiting.

But the man who now arrived—the slim, professorial man with a kindly, wise face, gray and silver hair, neat mustache—it bothered Hunter to wait for him. Because this bastard was only late because he *could* be. He was late for no other reason than to make Hunter wait.

Hunter sat stone-faced in his seat, napkin in his lap to prevent the apron-wearing vultures from descending on his table and carrying off what remained of his meal. The potatoes really were excellent. He might wish to finish them after this was all said and done.

The late man looked about the restaurant as if he was unsure if he was in the right location. He, who had arranged for the meeting and made the reservation under a pseudonym. He clumsily removed a thick tweed jacket and hung it on the hook, then fumbled about in the wrong direction until a youthful hostess kindly pointed him in the right direction. He, who had surely scouted the location, memorized the layout, and had his own Carnivale men verify that Hunter was on site before even leaving the confines of his office.

He approached, not meeting Hunter's stare until he was right next to him. Then he rapped at the table and said, "I see you've already started."

"Starting is the only way to get back at someone who's late."

"Aside from leaving," said the man.

"If I could leave, I wouldn't have come."

The man smiled and sat down. A server appeared at once. The man waved her away. "Thank you. I just ate." He looked across the table at Hunter. "The food here is average at best. And if I'm going out for lunch, I prefer something sweet. A sticky bun or two."

Hunter shook his head. "You'll ruin your heart eating like you do, X."

X *tsked* and patted his chest. "Men in our position, we've no use for hearts. How was the fish?"

"Better when eaten alone. What does," he fluttered his fingers in the air, "the Carnivale need from my department?"

"You wound me, old boy. Is there anything wrong with friends simply catching up?"

"We're not friends."

"Colleagues, then. Surely you won't deny me that affiliation."

Hunter sat back in his chair and lowered his head. "I might." He searched the room and leaned forward again, quiet now. "The *Chiasm?*"

X looked down dolefully. "Regrettable. But... sometimes it is necessary to remove a man's head to see if he truly was a monster. We found our monster in the MCR."

"More like you created one."

"Shades of gray, old boy."

X removed his pipe and struck an old-fashioned match. Hunter suppressed a scowl. This, too, wasn't something the man needed to do. He was doing it because he wanted to. Because he could.

A waiter teleported to the side of the table. "You can't smoke inside, sir."

X regarded the thin blue wisps rising from the pipe, the aroma of burning tobacco filling the air. "And yet I am doing the very thing. How curious."

"Put it out," Hunter admonished.

X winked. "For you." He turned the pipe over and extinguished the smoldering leaf between his fingers. The anxious waiter retreated to his place along the wall, ever vigilant, ever eager to serve.

"I took my lumps over the entire ordeal," X said, pointing the stem of his pipe at Hunter for emphasis. "And yet I remain director. What does that tell you?"

Hunter splayed his hands. "Powerful friends."

"No more powerful than yours."

"What, then?"

X drew a slow, satisfied smile across his face. "That the game is still afoot. The hunt is still on. And the prey—the *real* prey—is still out there." He leaned back in his seat, his smile vanishing. "I'm taking her."

"Taking who?"

"The girl. Broxin. Your agent."

"Like hell."

"Like hell." X chuckled to himself. "I misspoke. I've *taken* her. It's done. She's with the Carnivale, may it live in infamy."

Hunter sat stunned, unsure if the old man was goading him or serious.

X winked again.

"She's our best agent," Hunter said.

X nodded wholeheartedly. "I know. Perhaps the best in all of Nether Ops. *And...* a true believer. And you and I both know what those are capable of. She cleaned up our mess remarkably well. All that business with the corvette set to ram the House of Reason. Wonderful girl."

Hunter shook his head. "No. I'll fight you on this, X. Her place is in Sec-4. I went through great pains to bring her in from the Legion and—"

"You have no idea the pains undertaken for that woman," X said calmly. Matter of fact. An academic correcting a student.

"Her father—"

X held up a hand to stop Hunter mid-sentence. He smiled, and Hunter found himself wishing that the man would rage at him. Would show some outburst of emotion. Anything to suggest that this was something more than a *fait accompli*.

"She was never yours or your department's. Only for a time. Stieg Broxin had a way of making things difficult. The man is dead now." X looked up at the exquisite, modern lighting, his expression wistful. "We're starting to go now, you know. Those who fought on Psydon. Our time has arrived. It comes in spurts. Starts and stops and then we all go down the drain—like the generation before us. Make way for the generation yet to come."

X centered again on his fellow director. "There's nothing left for you to do. This is a courtesy. Andien Broxin is where she was meant to be well before she'd had the opportunity to become a blemish for the House of Reason in its little shove-fight with the Legion."

Hunter glared.

"You haven't finished your lunch," X observed.

"I find my appetite missing."

"Well then, the check." X raised a finger and was presented with the bill. He whistled at the final amount. "All that for half a fish."

Hunter removed his own credit chit. "That won't be necessary."

X examined the man sitting across from him. "Tell me what you think of me, Hunter. Tell me what you really think."

"I haven't the vocabulary or the time."

"You'll find, Hunter, that we are the same. The distance you feel is one of years and experience. Nothing more. What you are, I once was. What I am, you will become.

Should you live long enough. No guarantee in our line of work, old boy."

Hunter stood, tapped his credit chit against the bill, and paid for his meal. "The same. No. We both hunt for monsters, but if the day should ever come, Oba forbid, when I—how did you put it—remove someone's head and discover they're not a monster after all… that's the day I'll admit that the job has moved beyond me. But you, you just find the next monster, X. The innocent and the guilty alike. We are not the same. Good day."

01

The ships came all at once. A coordinated jump into the system. Small, modified craft. Freighters and star cruisers. Not big but armed. Each with its own degree of firepower. Blaster cannons to be sure, whether a solo turret or linked heavies meant to converge on whatever fell before the cockpit. Three separate missiles and one torpedo launched from the ships, whose owners had credits to spare. That sort of ordnance was rare.

And all of it was after Leenah and the *Indelible VI.*

Her initial shock wore off almost as soon as she registered it. The *Six*'s automated systems took over, identifying threats almost the moment they went hostile. Shields easily absorbed the blaster cannon fire sent in her direction by inexperienced combat pilots with itchy trigger fingers. Missiles were scrambled, and a torpedo intercept charge rocketed from a top-deck compartment and eliminated its target well before Leenah even had time to think about evasive maneuvers.

She had spent untold hours, as well as several fortunes, making the ship as good as her considerable talents allowed. The result was an even faster, more durable, and lethal craft than the considerably advanced ship she'd started with. The only trouble was, the ace pilot who usually handled the controls in times like these was on the planet below, his hands full in Rakka Spaceport.

Leenah nosed the ship down into a corkscrew maneuver, seeking to shake the craft that bore down on her as one. They were attempting to close ground, but she was faster, extending the distance between them, her auto-turrets not even bothering to fire because of the range. Her pursuers, by contrast, kept up a steady stream of blaster fire; it streaked harmlessly overhead, illuminating the cockpit with green, red, and yellow glows from the diverse weapons systems.

Careful not to venture too far from the planet, Leenah sent a hurried distress call to Captain Keel below, forgetting comm discipline or procedures and repeating the man's name as though it were a prayer that could ward off the attack.

"Tell me what's happening," Keel said from below, his voice forceful and in control.

The shields shuddered from a lucky hit but still held strong. Leenah forced calm on herself. She breathed, opened her mouth to speak, and found her voice absent. Barely a rattle.

"Talk to me, Leenah!"

Things sounded as though they weren't going well for Keel, either. Before the space in the orbit flooded with what appeared to be a band of pirates flying a motley assemblage of ships, she had been preparing to enter atmosphere and fly standby to extract Keel if he needed it. That need didn't sound like it was lessening, and her current vector was taking her farther away from the planet. That wouldn't do.

Though a craven section of her brain demanded that she just keep going until she had outrun the attackers and escaped their wrath, a stronger urge compelled her to adjust course and swing back around toward the backwater planet. Never mind that it would bring her onto a flight path that would require her to brave the storm that followed her. Never mind any of that.

He was down there. And so was Garret. She wouldn't leave them. Couldn't leave him. She loved him.

The *Six* turned sharply, a tight, hairpin maneuver that exposed the ship's belly for seconds too brief for the attackers to take advantage of. Leenah could hear the engines rumble and whine, telling their secrets in a language only she knew intimately.

The energy shields shuddered and shook as the *Indelible VI* exchanged fire with the ten rival craft that had given pursuit. Leenah focused on the controls, yawing and juking and doing what she could to keep the shields strong as her ship's sophisticated auto-targeting program battered enemy shields and forced the combatants to veer off or face catastrophic loss of integrity.

An old Arcturian raider lost its shields after only a few seconds of receiving an oncoming barrage. It peeled off starboard and suffered engine damage when it wandered in front of a friendly stream of blaster fire.

One down.

Next came a Kencoth T880, a workhorse of a freighter looking as though it had rolled off the factory line not long ago. Its hull was painted a bright, shining yellow not yet dimmed by years of deep space travel. Modified with a single forward-facing cannon, it shot several heavy, ponderous blaster bolts at the *Six*. The type of bolts that were easy to dodge, but disastrous to shield integrity should it score a lucky hit. It did not. Instead, it absorbed the fury of the *Indelible VI*'s rapid-fire auto cannons, causing its shields to drop. Still, inexplicably, it stayed on course. Perhaps the newness of the ship had overinflated the confidence of its pilot. Not that it mattered. A moment later the craft blossomed into an explosion as onboard flammable gases ignited and then just as quickly burned themselves out in the vacuum.

Here Captain Keel would have done something unexpected. Fire a concussive torpedo into the midst of the remaining vessels and then perform some impossible evasive maneuver. Or fly through and leave a timed bomb primed to explode just when the enemy ships were upon it. Close enough to scorch the *Six*'s tail feathers but not so close as to knock out the engines.

Leenah knew that Keel would have done something to permanently even the odds. But thoughts of what that might have been came to her only after she had already burst through the pod of ships, knowing that they would veer and she would not in their game of wills.

She would not blink first.

The other ships pulled hard to avoid the streaking comet that was the *Six*, rubbing hulls where the formation was too tight and the pilot's skill level too low. Leenah checked the rear holos and saw that, despite the minor collisions, none were disabled. But neither were they in a position to run her down before she reached atmosphere. Their turns were lumbering, wide, amateurish.

She had made it. But not without damage. The head-on assault had overloaded the comms array. Which wasn't necessarily a problem—she was close enough to the planet to issue a comm burst without the need for the additional power the array provided—but any outgoing transmission would still try to go through the array, so she'd have to reroute it on the fly.

Leenah set herself to the task, setting the controls on auto—a straight line at full speed to increase the distance between herself and her pursuers. Then she dropped from her seat and began to pull and replace the comm wires beneath the dash. Her fingers groped and twisted, and the panel felt much smaller than she knew it to be. Twice she debated leaving the cockpit for the more accessible panel just outside the cockpit, but hot-fixing there often caused more problems than not.

Though it felt like epochs had passed, the entire task took less than a minute. Back in the pilot's seat, she checked her pursuers and saw them still racing to catch up. She looked ahead at the planet. *Almost there.*

And then, in an instant, everything changed. A ship—large and gray and certainly military—dropped out of FTL between her and the planet. It took Leenah a moment to recognize it as an old Republic model, something that might have served during the Savage Wars. The ancient beast opened its mouth and belched small yachts from its belly—at least two dozen of them. Leenah peered into the empty chasm of the ship, which appeared to contain little more than its starfighter bay. But what it had just delivered would be more than enough to harass the *Six*. Maybe even bring it down if she gave them the opportunity.

The yachts, painted with a matching black-and-blue color scheme, were armed with medium blaster cannons, two on each wing. They fired alternating volleys, two bolts from one wing and two from the other. Leenah slid her ship from side to side and let the auto-turrets rip into the enemy fighters, destroying one before having to pull straight up and break off her approach from the planet. The incoming fire was too strong and intense for her to weather another direct assault. Her dodging wasn't nearly enough to keep her shields from protesting. They were on the verge of failure.

The comm chimed, and Leenah knew it was Keel before he spoke. "Keel to *Six*. I need you down here, Leenah."

The change of course gave the first assaulters, the modified freighters, an opportunity to converge on her position even as the swifter yachts followed, chasing her with a relentless flurry of blaster fire.

She had to force herself to activate the comm. Force herself again to control her voice. "Aeson... They're everywhere!"

"Who is?"

The *Six* swooped back onto its flight path, performing a tight loop to shake itself from the various targeting systems all conspiring to destroy her. Blaster bolts seemed to encase the craft from multiple directions as the freighters caught up and rejoined the fray. The shields absorbed more punishment, screaming through alarms and whistles that they were at the end of their effectiveness.

"Leenah! Who? What's going on?"

"Ships! Not starfighters, but—they're all shooting at me and the shields are barely hanging on and I had to hot-fix comms and I need you up here and flying!"

"I can't make it up there, so you need to get down here, sweetie. Do you understand me? Whatever it takes. Get down here! You can do it."

It would require another reversal. Another threading of the needle to reorient again and launch herself at maximum speed toward the planet. She would have to do her best, with hands of impervisteel, to hit reentry at just the right angle to avoid burning up completely. Especially with the shields already so close to failing.

"I'll try. Oba... Oba..."

"You can do it, Leenah."

The raking of blaster bolts over the shield array, punching through and hammering the *Indelible VI*'s hull, told her otherwise. An explosion rocked the ship, killing two engines and setting off the most frantic peals of alarms yet. Leenah had fractions of seconds left now. Time for one decision so long as she didn't waste time thinking. All that was left was to react.

With the planet behind her and swarms of hostile ships ahead of her and beside her, she reached out for the hyperdrive controls and pushed the lever forward. The stars became elongated lines as faster-than-light travel began…

… only to be interrupted by an explosion that consumed the ship and rocked her in her chair, the restraints the only thing preventing her from being thrown against the dash. The eruption of force was so powerful it switched her brain offline, unconscious for what inevitably came next.

She awoke in utter darkness and thought she was dead, floating in the world beyond mortality. Slowly, her senses returned. But the darkness remained. She put her hands to her face and winced as her fingers went over a knot on her forehead. The touch reactivated nerves, and she gradually became aware of how bad she felt.

"Feels like someone beat me up," she mumbled. She realized she was indeed floating and soon decided that the cockpit had lost its artificial gravity.

Her throat was sore. The back of her neck ached, as did her calves. One elbow felt as though a knife had been stuck in it, but when she moved her fingers to the spot, all seemed whole. No wetness of blood and crust from a congealed wound.

She remembered the attack, and with the memory came a sudden spike of adrenaline and fear that subsided almost the instant it flared up. Her mind issued scenarios and set down logic aimed at calming her.

Whatever happened, they're not here anymore.

But where was here?

The surest source of that information, the *Indelible VI*, was no help. The ship was as dead as Leenah had fancied herself to be upon first waking. And not just down for the count. Completely and totally dead. Main power offline. Redundancies offline. Comms dead. Everything... dead. No matter how much she caressed and encouraged the cold instrument panel. No matter her mechanical skill. It was dead.

"But *you're* still alive," Leenah said to herself, speaking aloud because there was no one else to speak to and it was good to hear something. She paused and then added, "For now."

That little bit of dark humor wasn't usually her style. Perhaps Keel was rubbing off on her. Or maybe it was like he'd once explained—sometimes you reach a place where the only thing left to smile about is life's dark little ironies.

Whatever the reason, Leenah repeated the words. "For now."

Now there was no irony. No gallows humor. Only the realization that life in this state could not carry on endlessly. Something would happen. A breach or a total expenditure of breathable air. Something. And since she wasn't the type to sit down and wait for death, she began to investigate what was likely to kill her first.

"Find your enemy and KTF," she said.

Yes, Keel and his Legion associates had definitely rubbed off on the girl who'd gone chasing a fantasy in the MCR.

The darkness was unsettling because it suggested that she was far away from the habitable part of a system. There was no glow of a sun, no shadows of other celestial objects. Just the faint pinpricks of light from distant systems. Insufficient to pierce the black of the cockpit. Enough only to tell her that she wasn't blind.

She removed a thin ultrabeam from her coveralls and clicked it on. A blazingly pure rod of white lit up the cockpit. Leenah squinted against the intensity and then twisted her body around as her eyes adjusted. All around her wires hung, revealing thick cords marked with frays and scorch marks. Some were fused. Some were severed from an overload that had heated them to the point of melting and separating. There had been a fire, but the cockpit's protection systems had snuffed it out without taking all the oxygen with it.

Leenah shook her head. She couldn't even begin explaining what had caused all of this except that it had to have been the result of her making the last-minute jump with her shields down, engines failing—some exploding—and the hull being savaged by blaster fire. How far and how long she jumped, she didn't know. But she did know how to find out how long the systems had been dead.

The cockpit of the *Indelible VI* was designed to seal against the rest of the ship. That was standard in all but the oldest and least-regulated spacefaring craft out there.

The cockpit lacked the ability to jettison and serve as its own escape pod, but that was fine. Such systems were notoriously unreliable for a variety of reasons she would go over some time when there was nothing else to do.

Since life support was in the section of the ship that also managed dampeners and other comforts that kept a ship feeling more stable than it would otherwise, most cockpits had an independent air scrubber that ran under its own power. The *Six* had an upgraded model that was rated to supply breathable air for three people for a week. Leenah would have all that air to herself. She just needed to find out how much she'd already used.

The air scrubber was nestled beneath a warren of loose wiring that Leenah had to stretch and pile to the side before she could crawl down deep enough beneath the dash to find the machine readouts. Under normal circumstances, those readouts would be accessible through the holoscreens that filled the cockpit. With her stomach sucked in to make herself as small as possible, Leenah wriggled her way into position. She pushed a rat's nest of tiny, thin wiring out the way to read the display and found it cracked and undecipherable beyond a single flickering digit. The number one, though it could just as easily have been part of a seven.

She pushed her way back. "So much for that."

She pushed her hair-like tendrils aside and rose up for a moment before squatting back down, hugging her knees. She found herself wishing she wore a smartwatch, like Garret. It wouldn't be capable of hypercomm with the *Six* dead in the dark, but it would at least give her an idea of how much time had passed. She did have a datapad, but she hadn't brought it with her into the cockpit.

Leenah turned and looked at the door, then floated toward it to inspect it up close. It was sealed. Its panel readouts dead. Which meant its automated open-close mechanisms were likely also dead. And while there was a way to open the door manually from this side, she had no idea what she might find on the other side. Given the obvious damage the ship had sustained, the cockpit could easily be the only part of the *Six* that wasn't exposed to vacuum. The only way to tell for sure was to open it and find out—a risk she was unwilling to take.

For now.

The air was still fresh, and Leenah doubted that she'd been in a coma for days or weeks. She wasn't all that hungry, and she was clean. She just had to pay attention. Notice when her supply of air began to run low. And if the scrubber was working properly, then even without a functioning display, it would notify her of that.

"Assume a day unconscious at most," Leenah said aloud. "And assume that beacons are dead or destroyed."

She now had an opportunity for survival, but that did little to alleviate her other, greater fear. That without her being there to provide them with extraction, Keel and Garret were no longer alive to rescue her. But she would push on thinking that Aeson had managed to defy the odds again and pull himself out of a sticky situation. She'd seen enough of that to believe it possible. As for the doubts that lingered and threatened her with depression and despair... she'd learned a long time ago how to bury those.

"So," she said as she removed a conduit runner from her coverall's shoulder loop. "Let's start tracing these wires and find out just how far they can carry a signal."

That would keep her busy for a while.

02

Run.

That's what she'd told him. And Keel could tell that the woman he thought of as his stepmother had meant it. But from whom? And why? Those were the questions Keel needed answered. He wasn't a man accustomed to running. If he was going to make a tactical withdrawal, he needed to know why.

He stepped back on board the *Obsidian Crow* and was immediately greeted by the bloodthirsty little war bot. It whistled and clicked in its primitive language and rubbed itself against Keel's leg.

He patted the bot on the head. "Nice to be welcomed home."

Keel moved to the holding cell, expecting to see Honey where he'd left her, but bracing himself to find her escaped, even though the bot would presumably have said something had that happened. Best not to take chances.

As the little gunnery bot trailed behind him, it beeped and trilled a question.

"Can't say when the killing will start again, Death."

Death, Destroyer of Worlds, let out a mournful sigh.

"I'll make sure you get some, you maniac."

This cheered the bot up. It dared to ask something that Old Boss-Man Rechs had always declined. Could it be outfitted with the same weapons that humans like New Boss and Old Boss used to kill?

"Don't press your luck," Keel said.

The little bot tilted downward in self-pity. This was not the answer it had hoped for.

"How about if I promise to think about it?"

The bot roused up once more.

"Anything happen with Honey while I was gone?"

Not that the bot knew of. Did New Boss-Man want her executed?

They arrived at the cell, where the exotic, tentacled beauty lay asleep. She had eaten sparingly of the rations he'd left her. No doubt hedging against the possibility that Keel wouldn't return.

Keel eyed the Tennar for a moment before answering the bot. "No. She might be the only one who can help us."

The bot sighed. If it hadn't been so useful in getting out of the Sigma ordeal, Keel would be giving serious thought to having its memory wiped and a new personality installed. The thing was psychotic. He wondered what Garret would think of the little bot, and that brought to mind another trouble.

The code slicer was waiting for him. As was Zora. And... *Jack*. Who had his heart set on killing Honey over some shared history.

"Been awake long?" Keel asked, guessing that if Honey was asleep, she was a light sleeper. People always on the edge of death tended to be.

"You're back." Honey pushed herself up on a bent tentacle that constituted a human elbow. She looked alert, but her voice betrayed her. The drippings of sleep made it heavy and slow.

Keel pulled over a stool from a nearby workbench and sat down as it re-magnetized to the deck. "We need to talk."

Honey shook off the remains of sleep and sent out a new wave of pheromones. She watched Keel for his reaction, and when his eyes didn't go starry, she nodded slowly. "Yeah. I figured you'd say that if you came back."

"What made you think I wouldn't?"

She shrugged. "No offense. But... you don't know what you're up against."

"So, tell me."

"Not that easy. I need some assurances."

Keel splayed his hands, palms up. "We can work something out with Jack."

"I know that much. He's not my concern."

"Seemed to be pretty concerned when I first caught up with you."

Honey's countenance darkened. "It's the fact that you—and he—caught up with me at all. That won't escape their notice. And there are no second chances."

"In Nether Ops?"

It was a guess, but not a stretch. And Honey's reaction told Keel he had the right of it.

"Nether Ops doesn't exist any longer."

"Don't feed me that sket. Maybe it doesn't exist as an organization, but no one except the most delusional pol would think you can just turn off the Deep State by implementing Article Nineteen. You have to reach far into the corners of the tank to clean out all the scum."

The Tennar held her head up as though she was above the indignity just splashed before her. "We weren't all scum."

Keel let out a one-note laugh. "I met one agent that seemed to have her head in the right place. She ended up stealing my ship and kidnapping my crew."

Honey's ink-black eyes seemed to flash in recognition, but her face soon relaxed. She fixed Keel with an even gaze. "I need protection."

Keel gave a half-smile. "You've got me for as long as I can trust you. But I won't hesitate to hand you over to the bot here if you try to pull a double-cross. And believe me, he won't care about your pheromones."

The Nubarian gunnery bot beeped menacingly.

Honey folded her tentacles in her lap. "I would've laughed if you'd told me you'd protect me before I saw what you did to those Sigmas. That was suicide."

"That was Tuesday. And stop trying to woo me with your magic sex chemicals. I've got blockers."

"I'm not. No more than normal. But I mean it. They'll have a hard time with you." She brushed her forehead and then studied the man before her. "I suppose they already have."

"Who is *they*?" Keel said, rising to his feet. "If we're going to help each other out, let's start there. Who's trying to kill me?"

Keel knew at least one name—Surber—and he wanted to see if what Honey offered lined up. It didn't.

"You may as well call them Oba," she said. "It's not an organization so much as a... as a collection of power. A shadow oligarchy. They're not exactly the type to order letterhead. In Nether Ops we called them the Mandarins. And we learned very quickly that finding out who these people are ended badly. Always."

Keel wasn't sure he believed anything he'd just been told. That there was unimaginable wealth and power at the highest echelons of government... well, recent history confirmed that much. As did common sense. And usually that was where his belief system stopped when it came to organized crime masquerading as concerned politicians. The idea that there was a cabal of movers and shakers who *really* ran the show felt a little too close to the kind of conspiracy theories Masters was always going on about.

"What do they want with me?" he asked.

Honey gave a slight smile. "I can't say. I'm not a member of the club that wants you dead. But I can tell you why they wanted Tyrus Rechs dead, and I suspect it's the same reason with you. He knew too much."

Keel scoffed. "I don't know anything, sweetheart."

She stared at him for a moment, scrutinizing him. "You really don't, do you?"

"Kill Team Ice," Keel said, changing the subject. "What do you know about that?"

Honey bit her lip and cleared her throat. "Kill Team Ice was a Republic program that began during the Savage Wars. It became apparent very quickly that the conflict with the Savages would not be quick. Fighting would flare and fade. Each time, skills would be lost, and they would have to be relearned the hard way. And given the ferocity and suddenness of Savage attacks, there was no guarantee that those skills could be learned on the job. Not before a major core world fell, anyway.

"New Vega was the Republic's 'Never Again' moment. And to prevent another core world from experiencing the same fate, the Legion's best warriors—those with exceptional ability and know-how—were put in cryostasis. They received additional mental and physical training while they were out. And when they were awoken, they would be assigned to the most dangerous and crucial of missions—then go back on ice until the next time."

The Tennar tilted her head. "Hence the name. Kill Team Ice."

"And I'm supposed to be one of them," Keel said. "Despite not knowing anything about it."

Honey shrugged. "The program's end date isn't something Nether Ops was aware of. Nor its location, or who kept it funded... really we didn't know much of anything beyond the big words that painted a loose picture. Kill Team Ice. Tyrus Rechs. And even what little I've told you is top secret."

"Fairly underwhelming. Tell me what you know about Tyrus Rechs."

Honey gave a slight smile. "You're asking me because you already know."

"Maybe."

"Tyrus Rechs, the bounty hunter, was in actuality General Rex, the man who ended the Savage Wars. It is believed he underwent an experimental longevity regimen. The House of Reason put a bounty on his head after he disobeyed direct orders that jeopardized a galaxy defense initiative involving an allied species known as the Cybar." Honey straightened herself and examined the end of one of her tentacles. "Is that the way you heard it? Do I pass the test?"

"Close enough for artillery," Keel said.

Honey pointed to the corners of her ray-shielded confinement cell. "So. Do I get liberty?"

"That's a big ask."

"It's the next step."

"Not quite," Keel said, looking toward the cockpit and its comm station. "At least a few steps ahead of that one."

Honey leaned back against a bulkhead, resigned. "We weren't *all* how you think."

"Who's that?"

"Nether Ops. We weren't all working to impose an emperor or place ourselves in some new galactic order. A lot of us believed in the Republic. I was one of them. And I don't mean the House of Reason, either. If the Legion had declared Article Nineteen when it should have, there were Nether Ops agents who would have supported you."

"Legion Command didn't."

"No. They didn't. But some of us fought against Goth Sullus all the same. Remember that. We may not be friends, but we have far more enemies in common than you might think."

"I'll keep that in mind." Keel moved to leave.

"Who did you see?" Honey asked. Keel suspected she only wanted to keep him around a little longer.

He turned back to face her. "Someone who confirmed that I was in Kill Team Ice."

"Check on them."

"I just saw them," Keel protested. "And we weren't exactly close. I'm not going to give them a call to let 'em know I made it home safely."

"The planetary news. Check."

Keel hesitated.

"Check," Honey insisted.

Keel pulled out a datapad and spoofed an encryption that would allow him to access the appropriate holonews streams as a local. It didn't take long before he saw footage of a billowing black smoke cloud erupting from his stepmother's apartment and rising to the top of the building. Reporters, their expressions thick with empathy, explained that a faulty power system had caused the blast. They confirmed that the resident inside had died. And they promised to be back with more details in this developing story, despite it having already developed whatever details were newsworthy. In actuality they were promising to continue showing the carnage.

Keel looked up. "How did you know?"

"It's been like this. Ever since Sullus fell and secrets started to spill. People with power—with *real* power—are after two things right now. Savage tech and loose ends. Kill Team Ice is a loose end for someone."

"The Mandarins."

"That's my guess."

"And who wants Savage tech?"

Honey gave a humorless smile. "Everyone who has even the slightest inkling about what's still out there. Nether Ops in all its stripes. House of Reason loyalists, though they're paper tigers. Pawns. The Legion, if they know what's good for them and have processed whatever archives they got ahold of in taking Utopion. Nilo and Black Leaf, to be sure. And other players, too. I'm not trying to be coy or cute. I don't know."

Keel nodded and resumed his trip to the cockpit. Honey was only one source of intel, but this was all rapidly inflating to something bigger than he could navigate on his own.

"They won't stop," she called out after him. "Not until you're dead, along with anyone else still out there. Everywhere you go… they won't stop until you're dead."

"Sounds like we have something in common then. I won't stop until then, either."

03

The ping to Chhun's comm had gone unanswered. That didn't surprise Keel. The man was always busy. But Keel could count on Chhun getting back to him as soon as possible, so he put the thought out of his mind as he went over his next moves. Zora was trying to reach him, and her last message had come complete with a threat to personally fulfill the termination contract that was on his head.

She was joking. The termination contract had been lifted when the Bronze Guild's leadership went up in one of the more satisfying explosions Keel had ever been a part of. No, Zora would have to kill him for free. Unless she found herself mixed up with whoever these "Mandarins" were.

Keel was considering whether to call her back and begin the delicate work of seeing what information he could acquire from Nilo while simultaneously keeping the Tennar free from harm. And then the comm chime sounded, the encryption key showing it was clearly Legion.

"Go for Keel," the captain said, expecting to hear Chhun's voice on the other side.

Instead, he heard from the Dark Ops legionnaire who went by Bear. "You in it?" the deep, gruff voice asked.

"You have no idea."

"General Chhun wanted me to link up with you. He's a bit *occupied* at the moment. You got something for us about Nilo?"

"'Occupied,' huh?" Keel grinned and shook his head. "No. Haven't reported in yet. A few other things came up."

Keel told the Dark Ops legionnaire about what had transpired since their last communication. The hit on his stepmother. His own personal Nether Ops prisoner who was singing like a tertullian swallow. And... Kill Team Ice.

"Doesn't ring a bell," said Bear. "Bad-ass name, though."

"It's causing me a lot of trouble, is what it is."

Bear grunted. "And you're gonna try and get to the bottom of it before you help us out putting eyes on Nilo."

"Sorry, pal. That's the way it's gotta be."

"Well. You're a free agent so I can't exactly order you." A low, thoughtful grumble of consideration filled the comm before Bear continued. "How much you trust this Nether asset you've got with you?"

Keel looked back toward Honey's cell, obscured though it was by sealed blast doors. "Not enough to let her walk freely about my ship. She's telling me the truth as best I can tell, though."

"You think she was at the director level?"

"Probably not. But I think she was a high-level agent. Mission planner."

"So how about this... you bring her in to me, and we hold her and vet her. She passes muster, we can use her on something."

Keel scratched the back of his jaw beneath his ear. "Like what?"

"Been havin' a hell of a time slicing intel when it comes to Nether Ops. The whole infrastructure, for that matter, but Nether Ops in particular. Those guys knew how to burn their data. Except it's not a full burn, just a localized one. You find a node and start to get in there, an alarm gets triggered and *everything* goes up. Slicers are working on it and striking out."

Keel thought about Garret and whether he'd have better luck, but the kid wasn't available and Bear didn't seem to be thinking about him.

Bear continued. "So, we're busting our asses hitting these nodes with our kill teams, pulling as much data as we can and then losing what's left. Just about every hole we find turns out dry before long. But we know how they're doing it and I think we might have a way of scooping up more Nether intel if your asset is willing. Think she'll be on board?"

"I think I can convince her to be."

"Good enough. Ulori. Repub base. Land in the Rammsen Star Port and I'll bring you inside."

"What's Dark Ops doing on Ulori?"

"Chhun steppin' down as Legion commander led to some much-needed reorganization. Ulori is the staging area for the 131st now. I'm out of Sector HQ and commanding Kill Team Victory. Ping me your ETA and I won't make you wait. Bear out."

The comm chimed its end-of-transmission bleep and left Keel in an empty cockpit. The captain chewed his thumb and stared out of the *Obsidian Crow*'s latticed cockpit windows. He'd known that Chhun was going to revive the 131st Legion, and with it, Victory Company. He hadn't realized that the prospect of seeing it alive and working again would leave his stomach in such knots.

Keel sat in the front passenger seat of an enclosed, armored sled with privacy windows and a patina of red dirt climbing its way up the black exterior. Bear drove, his muscular bulk dwarfing the steering wheel, a blaster pistol mounted to the side of the center console and another to the driver's door. Honey sat in the back seat, ener-chained but content, looking out the window at the grass-covered hills, the tall stalks swaying to reveal the hand of the wind.

Other than an effusive hug and a "Good to see you, bro," Bear had done little beyond grunt during the drive out of the spaceport. Keel knew that Honey was the cause. She'd gone along easily enough with ener-chains, but without an isolation hood, she could hear whatever was being said. It seemed to Keel that she had expected to be placed in one and was cautiously optimistic when ener-chains beneath a folded-up jacket were all that he and Bear asked of her.

"Okay," Bear said as the sled pushed farther into the hinterland outside the spaceport, following a long road that turned off between great parcels of farmland tended by the native Ulori. "We're clear."

"Have much trouble in the port?" asked Keel.

"Place used to be thick with MCR. Nothin' like that in a while, but that don't mean it won't pick back up again. Everybody's lookin' for their angle now that Nineteen is done. 'Specially after Kublar."

"Thought the Ulori loved the Republic."

"They do," Honey interjected. "It was the human population that was the problem back in the day."

Keel had seen almost as many humans as Ulori back in the port. Of course, it was easy to confuse one with the other if you only caught a glimpse of a face passing by, fully dressed. But a closer examination revealed the Ulori's hair to be delicate, wispy feathers, and though their hands were human-like, they had only four fingers, and feathers ran from wrist to elbow. Their feet, taloned like birds, would be another giveaway, were they not hidden within work boots.

"You know," Bear said, his willingness to talk growing with the distance from the spaceport, "the Ulori was the species Masters brought up most often as proof of his little theory about how the galaxy got populated with sentient life."

Keel chuckled as he watched an Ulori farmer riding high in a tractor, thirty meters from the highway. "How's he doin'?"

"Can't say. He's not with the team right now."

Keel was surprised at how disappointed he was to hear that. "Something happen?"

Bear shook his head. "He was putting in a rotation with Team Two before the Legion authorized the band getting back together. Finishing up."

Keel raised his eyebrows. "Team Two. One of the *original* teams."

Bear gave a malicious half smile. "They'll make sure you won't forget it." After a beat, he added, "Bombassa's here, though. Everybody else you probably don't know. Good guys, though."

"Glad he made it home. Glad to see you too, Bear. How're the..." Keel nodded toward the floor. "New legs?"

Bear rumbled out a laugh. "Fine. I'm used to 'em." He looked down. "Kinda skinny lookin' though, aren't they?"

The cybernetic legs looked like tree trunks.

Keel turned himself around and asked Honey how she was doing.

"Fine," the Tennar answered. "If I'm being quiet it's because I didn't want to break up your reunion. And I'm still processing what I'm about to do. Guess I didn't imagine the day would come where I'd be sharing secrets with Dark Ops."

Bear's smile emerged in the rearview mirror. "Welcome to the good guys."

They reached a small, walled compound a half hour later. A windowless, two-story building rose slightly above the three-meter-high walls of printed duracrete. An impervisteel front gate a little wider than the sled was guarded by two Ulori armed with blaster rifles.

Bear brought the sled to a halt ten meters before the gate, following the commands of the Ulori guards, who walked to either side of the sled. Bear lowered his tinted window and the Ulori looked inside, glancing at Keel and the Tennar in the back seat. Outside of Keel's window, the other guard stood, his rifle ready.

"Welcome back, Captain," the Ulori said. His face was smooth, slightly wider than the average human's, with bright green eyes that seemed bottomless. A widow's peak of feathered hair disappeared inside an odd local hat that looked like a loosely wrapped turban fitted with a ball-cap bill to shield the eyes from the sun's rays. "Any trouble at the port?"

Bear shook his head. The legionnaire was calm, and that kept Keel at ease. "MCR still hasn't decided to test this particular old stomping ground."

"They would do well to refrain," suggested the guard. "Not even Kima is a home for them now."

"We'll see. But you've got it right when it comes to Ulori, K'dee."

The Ulori nodded, smiled politely at Keel and Honey, and then straightened up, trilling in its soft, avian language to the guard opposite, "*Tary-oot. Trrrr.*"

The other guard went to the gate and punched in an access code. To Keel's surprise, when the gate swung open toward them it was powered not by smooth repulsors but by four more Ulori guards, their rifles slung around their bodies.

Bear slowly moved the sled into the compound through the gate.

"Usin' local security, huh?" Keel said, more of an observation than a question.

"Uh-huh," grunted Bear. "Big supporters of the Republic and the Legion. Article Nineteen, too. General Chhun wanted to be sure we kept that relationship strong, so we're working with them when and where we can."

"Not a combat zone, though."

"Nope. Not since Sullus went down. Still, the planet's trouble with the MCR is still recent history. There's a vigilance."

Honey had turned around to watch the Ulori pull the gates closed again, locking it with a heavy metal bar. The thud could be heard clearly inside the sled.

"Why aren't the gates automated?" she asked.

"Can't slice a big ol' hunk o' metal," Bear answered. "The Cybar got us thinking about the way we did things. That gate weighs as much as a fully loaded combat sled. Noble—he's our engineering sergeant—thinks an MBT would have to back up a few times before it managed to break through. More than a match for a speeding sled."

Bear parked the sled to face the gate, ready to speed out of the compound the moment they might need to. A similar sled was parked thirty meters away. The big legionnaire swatted Keel on the chest with the back of his hand and then pointed out the windshield. "Look who's coming to say hello."

Bombassa stepped out of the compound's main building, an unfamiliar legionnaire following him. Bombassa gave a measured smile and a single nod, which passed as exuberance for the war fighter.

Honey leaned forward between the two front seats. "What's Lashley doing here? In Dark Ops the entire time and I hadn't the foggiest. Neither did Nilo. Bravo."

Keel and Bear exchanged a look. Keel shrugged and popped open the sled's door, but the big man stayed inside, turned around, and fixed what his legionnaires referred to as the "dad face" on the Tennar.

"So much for OPSEC," growled Bear.

04

Honey was quickly escorted away by a legionnaire named Roland Noble, whom the others called "Nobes." The Dark Ops leej served as the reconstituted Kill Team Victory's intelligence sergeant. Bear promised to join the man later, but first needed to introduce Keel to the new members of Kill Team Victory.

Bombassa, Keel already knew. He followed the tall man inside the compound building without a word, but there Bombassa paused, watching Honey disappear around a corner to the interview room with Noble, a pair of Ulori guards providing security.

"You recognize her?" Keel asked.

"No," he said flatly. "She was involved with Black Leaf?"

Bombassa's voice was back to normal. The alterations that had provided him with a different vocal tone and speech pattern had been reversed.

"As a cover. She's Nether."

The big operator showed his disdain.

Bear clapped him on the shoulder and took the lead in the compound. "Useful is what we hope she'll be. Team's spread out, Keel, so we'll introduce you as we come across them. Sorry in advance if they don't treat you like a legend. Most of what you did is still classified."

Keel shrugged. "As long as you don't mention the Order and get them all up and saluting."

"Captain Ford won that thing," Bear said with a grin. "He ain't here."

The compound had been built by a paranoid non-native—a human who ended up giving it to the MCR back when the planet had its issues with the upstart rebellion. Repub marines had long ago raided the building and cleared it of all enemy combatants and any sensitive technology. It had been empty for years before Dark Ops took the building to serve as a command outpost for Kill Team Victory, but signs of the hullbusters' assault and the time since were still evident.

The entryway was spartan, just a table and some chairs that sat beneath a dual staircase leading to the second floor. Scorch marks were burnt into the walls, and damage from where the front door had been blown in was still visible. The tile floor was uneven, pushed up by roots. The green blades and leaves that belonged to those roots looked wilted and dying, assaulted by the newfound foot traffic and the sealing of their previous light source by a heavy blast door that would fit right in on a Republic destroyer.

"My office," Bear said, pointing to the table.

A legionnaire moved quickly down the stairs, pausing to acknowledge Bear and Bombassa. "Captain. Top."

"This is our communications sergeant, Timothy Nixon," Bear said, introducing the leej to Keel. "Nix, this is Aeson Keel. Former Legion. He's going to help us out on the op."

Nix shook hands with Keel. "Nice to meet you. Dark Ops?"

Keel nodded. "For a while."

"Thought so. You've got the look. Which team?"

Feeling trapped, Keel looked to Bear.

The big man shrugged. "Still classified, Nix."

Keel felt conflicted. He had no reason to lie to the legionnaire, and yet he felt protective of his past. What was an easy question felt complicated, as everything did when it came to mixing himself back in with the Legion.

Nix looked thoughtful and then feigned disappointment. "As in... there's another 'secret' team out there other than Victory? And here I thought I made it when I got assigned."

"You are where you belong," Bombassa said, his eyes darting toward Keel.

"I... I was Victory's first captain," Keel finally admitted, unsure exactly why he felt the need to act on the compulsion. "Long time ago."

"You're Captain Ford," Nix said.

Keel managed a half smile and regretted revealing the info.

"Holy sket. You're *the* Captain Ford."

"Don't make it a big deal," Bear said. He looked at Keel. "Glad you let the wobanki out of the sack, though. Masters would have blabbed eventually."

"Whenever he gets back," Bombassa added.

"So, what's going on?" Nix asked.

"That depends on what Nobes gets from a prisoner Keel—Ford—brought in," said Bear. "Gather up the team. We'll do introductions and then catch Ford up on the mission as planned so far."

The meeting took place in the team rec room. Keel felt a nostalgic sense of belonging. Someone—surely Bear, Masters, or Bombassa—had set it up nearly identical to the room the team had kept aboard the Republic destroyer *Intrepid*.

Holopics of the fallen lined one wall, surrounding a framed display of the kill team's unit crest—a koob skull before crossing lightning bolts. Keel swallowed at the sight of Rook, Kags, Twenties... and Exo. And there were others as well. Fish and Pike—men who'd served under Chhun, whose own holopic was on a separate display that Keel assumed was for team command. Or perhaps it was because of the fame Chhun had achieved within the Legion.

Even the blaster cannons from Pappy's combat sled on Kublar had been faithfully hauled and set up, just as they had been when Keel was actively with the team. Keel ran his hands over the twin barrels that had bent in opposite directions from the blast that had started a cascading series of events that led from then to now.

"We tried to honor the history of this kill team," Bear said, standing beside Keel as he examined the artifacts. "It's Dark Ops, but it's tied to the 131st in a special way. So, when General Chhun put in the request to Dark Ops to have a dedicated kill team attached to the reformed company, there was no doubt Victory would be the one reactivated and set to the task."

Keel gave a smile. "Eventually some hard-nosed commander is going to come in here and order it all removed. No living on yesterday's glory."

Bear grunted. "We'll see."

A legionnaire named Benjamin Arguello held out a capture stick. "You're not on the wall, Captain Ford. Can we grab a holo for the wall? Put you next to Chhun?"

Keel shrugged at the weapons sergeant the other leejes called Wello. "Yeah. That's fine."

He stood uncomfortably as Wello used the capture stick. The device beeped and then sent a perfectly touched portrait of Keel onto the wall next to Chhun.

Keel went through the team, meeting the men and doing his best to remember each man's face and name. Victory had expanded to become a ten-man team. Each man seemed capable, and Keel had seen firsthand Bear's abilities as a team leader. He had no doubt that the kill team would be up to whatever tasks it was assigned.

After the initial meeting was receding and respectful questions had been asked and answered, after the playful ribbing that passed easily among the team members, Keel found himself in a corner with Bombassa, who was serving on the team as its operations sergeant. Bear had gone to assist Nobes with Honey's interrogation.

"How you liking it?" Keel asked the legionnaire.

"Being operations sergeant?" Bombassa asked.

Keel nodded.

"It fits me better than doing what you did."

"You talkin' about being the detachment commander or going out in the cold?"

"The cold. It was… taxing."

Bombassa, at Keel's urging, had allowed himself to be placed in deep cover as part of Nilo's Black Leaf mercenary agency. He had undergone extensive vocal modification that made him sound like a completely different person. But something had happened to bring him back in, and Keel was pretty sure it didn't involve completing the mission as planned. Why else would Bear and Chhun have jumped at the opportunity to use Wraith as another potential informant?

"The need to keep myself from slipping," Bombassa continued. "I felt as though I could only relax when working. Shooting. And even then, the worry was at the back of my mind that I would somehow let something slip. Forget to answer by my new name—though the doctors assured me that my mind had been structured to recognize it even better than my real name."

The big man looked stoically at Keel. "Did you find that you had to… become who you were? Did you find yourself wishing your old self could fade away? Could die?"

Keel frowned. The truth of it was, he'd allowed himself to fade so much into his adopted persona that he was no longer sure where the one ended and the other began. His life as Ford seemed like another act in one long holofilm. Akin to recalling childhood. You know you were a kid once. You can remember things. Look at holopics of yourself and realize that even though it's you… it's not you.

"Yeah, I know what you mean," he said. "You start to feel like you can't let down. Ever. Even when you're with your friends."

Bombassa leaned forward and whispered emphatically. "Yes. Exactly." He looked from side to side. "Even now, among my fellow legionnaires, I feel as though I must remain on my guard."

That was really saying something. Keel hadn't known Bombassa to be anything other than guarded from the first day he'd met the man. Capable, but intensely private. Focused.

"Wish I could say it gets better, pal."

"You are not yet the man you were."

Keel shrugged. "I'm the man I am now. Whatever that means. You'd have to ask someone else to tell you, because I sure as hell can't figure it out any longer."

"In some ways, I *liked* being Lash more than I liked being myself." Bombassa shook his head fractionally, as though he couldn't quite believe he was saying it. "There was a freedom. Even the burden of the mission began to fade. All I cared about was doing my job. I listened. Remembered what I could. Was ready when Bear met with me. But... I felt alive on the missions in a way I can't explain. Not the thrill that comes from an operation. Something else. An out-of-body experience. As though I was experiencing everything anew."

He smiled. "We fought alongside the Kublarens against the zhee."

"Yeah. I heard."

"And I enjoyed it. Working with the Kublarens. Working with the other mercenaries. I found myself marveling at where I was. A legionnaire, still in the Legion, helping to foment a revolution to overthrow an entrenched House of Reason government."

Keel had felt that way himself many times. Had marveled at being paid by the bloated and out-of-touch military institution for turning in MCR cells that the Legion easily could have gotten to themselves had they been allowed. Recalled the first time he realized that a rogue cell of legionnaires was the problem. A troop led by a point and poisoned beyond recovery.

Or so he told himself.

When he recalled the ambush that took those men down, he didn't see himself firing a blaster. It was as though he was watching an actor portray him—portray Keel—in a holofilm.

"I wish I could tell you what to do about it," he said to Bombassa. "You're either going to readjust to being on the teams, or you're going to want to chase that freedom you had."

"You chose to chase the freedom."

Keel looked down, staring at a missing chunk in the duracrete floor. Probably the result of whatever raid had been undertaken by the marines years before. "Yeah. I guess I did. But I keep coming back. So, what does that tell you?"

Bombassa smiled. A rare sight. "It confirms what the old-timers always say. You never fully get the Legion out of your system."

Maybe that was it. Because as much as Keel told himself he wanted to disappear into some distant corner of the galaxy, he always found his way back to Victory Company.

He reviewed the operation planning Bombassa had put together. He had never seen a Nether Ops intel facility up close, but the layouts he was examining on the datapad weren't far off from the station he'd found Honey on. The Tennar had told him it was a research station. What exactly was being *researched* there wasn't something she was willing to offer up. Keel had no doubts that any follow-up missions to the place would find the site completely scrubbed.

He passed it up the chain of command all the same.

"So, you know where one of these is?" Keel asked Bombassa.

"Yes. We are not without intel, but everything pertaining to Nether Ops is heavily encrypted and difficult to come by. I do not think even the House of Reason was aware of everything they were up to."

"Deep states'll do that if you give 'em enough resources." Keel rested his chin in his palm and studied the screen. "How many of these have you hit?"

"The team has secured three stations. Taking control is not difficult, but there is a destruct system that we have been unable to combat."

"Like a self-destruct?"

"Not for the stations themselves, but for the data. We are only able to extract minuscule amounts before it is gone."

"What's the trigger? Unauthorized access attempts?"

"That was the initial thought," Bombassa confirmed. "These stations are manned. As many as ten armed defenders and as few as two. My working theory is that they are manually initiating a purge and then defending as long as possible with the hopes of denying all information."

"Prisoners?"

"None so far."

Keel nodded. That seemed to be the way it went with the more fanatical members of that organization. And what were any of them remaining out there in the cold, doing whatever, if not fanatics? The thought reminded him of the unease he felt with Honey. He couldn't bring himself to trust her. He knew that, for the moment, he needed her. But what would happen when the ener-chains came off? Or if she somehow found herself re-armed?

The answer to those questions grew closer when Bear re-entered the room with Nobes and the Tennar, whose ener-chains *had* been removed.

"Listen up," Bear said. "We've got some fresh intel that we need to consider for this op." He looked to Keel. "Gonna need you to sand table how this operation is going to work. Your girl here is a synth mine of the info we need right now."

Honey smiled.

And Keel felt his unease intensify.

05

Ravi stood warily across from the woman, watching her for any sign of menace toward Prisma. The docking bay aboard the abandoned Savage mini-hulk where he'd found the girl stood in utter silence. Prisma, unsure what was happening, watched with rapt attention, as did KRS-88, Sergeant Walker, and the other member of the strike team who had been with the girl and the bot when this stranger arrived.

The stranger Prisma called her mother.

"What is your purpose for being here?" Ravi asked.

The question was all that he was willing to advance in the woman's direction. He feared that any movement toward her beyond words might lead to bloodshed. For she had known that he was one of the Ancients, and in revealing it, had proven that she was more than a mere visitor on the ship. Even if her boasts about her ability to kill him were only that—boasts—Ravi did not doubt that she could harm the others.

The woman curled the corner of her mouth into a smile and gently rubbed Prisma's back. "Could I not ask you the same, Ancient One?" she asked.

"It's okay, Ravi," said Prisma. The girl looked up to her mother and smiled reassuringly. Attempting to build a bridge of trust, she spoke to the woman. "And I mean that about Ravi too. It's okay. He's my friend. He taught me how to do things. He's the only reason I could even hear your voice in my head in the first place."

The woman smiled kindly at Prisma and stroked her hair. The affection seemed to cause bliss in the girl. "Did he? My daughter, the time of our reunion was at hand. Nothing this Ancient One has done could have helped it or prevented it. We are now together at the convergence of fates, Prisma. Everything I have worked for has led us to this moment."

Ravi reached out to Prisma, speaking to her without words. *This is your mother. And you are certain of that, my dear Prisma?*

Ravi, she answered, speaking through her mind, though with her words came curiosity at whether her mother could hear the conversation as well. *It's her. I could never forget. I would never forget. It's her.*

And yet Ravi felt uncertainty from the girl.

There are many things capable of taking many forms familiar to us, Prisma. I speak now as your friend and ask you to be cautious. I do not say she is not who you say she is. I ask only that you remember that there are devious and devilish things in this galaxy that would seek to deceive you for their own purposes.

Left unstated was Ravi's belief that just such a creature had been responsible for leading Prisma away from Mother Ree's sanctuary. To burden the child—no, the young woman—with so much doubt when her emotions were already taxed and roiling was an unkindness Ravi would not extend.

He decided to parlay with the woman. "You are the master Archimedes speaks of?"

"I am."

"Then you belong to the Savages."

"I do not. For the Savages fear me. Long have I waged war on their unholy remnant. Long have I conquered them. Mastered them."

Sergeant Walker, who stood in silence alongside the other surviving member of his team, the Wild Man, spoke now for the first time, addressing the woman. "This outfit has fought against the Savages for a long time. We've all dedicated our lives to it."

The big sniper at Walker's side nodded.

"Now I've been down one end of the galaxy and up the next," Walker continued. "I've seen action every time the Savages have shown up, and I've been sent in after derelicts like this one. For a long time. And the only war against the Savvies I've ever seen is the one *I've* fought in. I'd like to know, ma'am, and I'm asking with all due respect, just where this fight you're speaking of took place."

Ravi tensed himself. The comments did not seem wise to him. While not openly challenging, they could be interpreted that way. This new arrival was an unknown, and there was no telling what she might do—especially with Prisma in her grasp.

But if the woman took offense, she did not show it. She raised an eyebrow and waited for Prisma to look up at her.

"Is this man also your friend, Prisma?"

"Well... sort of. He sent his soldiers to ambush me. And then they shot Crash and made him march through the ship. I went too because I didn't trust them not to do something to Crash."

At once the woman threw out her arm. Walker was knocked off his feet and held in stasis before he could crash against the nearest ship. The woman's voice grew in intensity and darkened as she spoke. "You would subject my daughter—a child—to the systems of *this* ship? A ship designed to kill and consume the flesh of the fallen in order to continue its mission."

Ravi gripped the handle of his sword, but he did not make a move forward. Clearly the woman had the ability to harm Walker, even to kill him—but she had decided not to.

Prisma, for her part, looked as surprised as the rugged soldier who struggled to break free of the spectral grip that held him in place. Only the man's eyes were able to move freely, searching left and right wildly as the rest of his body remained in a levitated paralysis.

"You have been instructed in certain arts and mysteries," Ravi said. "And I do not doubt that your teacher was one called Urmo."

The woman scowled at the name. "I learned much from him and his ways, but I was never his student."

"Don't hurt him," said Prisma. "I think he's on the good guys' side. He helped me. And he was nice to me after they took Crash. They weren't going to force me to go, I just went because I wasn't going to let them leave me alone back here without my friend."

The woman smiled. "That bot... has more than proved itself worthy of its duty to you, Prisma." She released Walker, gently lowering him onto his back, allowing the fall she'd started and arrested to finish in slow motion.

The sergeant sat up and quickly checked himself to make sure he was whole. "Holy sket," he mumbled, looking up at the woman with a newfound awe and understanding in his eyes. A look that was likely shared by the Wild Man, if his face could be seen beneath the helmet.

A look that realized there was another... beyond the admiral and his fantastical powers.

Another.

The woman paid none of this any mind. Her focus remained on Prisma and Ravi. The girl she looked upon with adoration and pleasure. The ancient with distrust and, Ravi sensed, trepidation. "I wonder, Prisma, if you would call this man *friend* if you knew what he did in his life before now. What he helped do to us."

Leaving the girl to ponder the cryptic statement, she spoke again to Ravi. "You have a name."

Ravi nodded and told her.

"And as one of the Ancients you are bound to prevent the coming of that which builds toward the destruction of all."

Again, Ravi nodded.

"Long have I fought the Savages," the woman repeated. "They are the first fruits of the harbinger of destruction that once drove your people from this galaxy. It was I who kept the Savage nation from returning to continue its war. And now, having done what I could, I have returned to prepare a final defense."

"Against the Savages?" Walker asked, showing a courage that Ravi admired. Lesser men would have slipped quietly out of the picture. The sergeant was determined to be a participant.

The woman answered without hesitation. "Yes. They remained beyond the edge, scheming and fighting and squabbling, but always with the desire to complete that which the impatient forerunners, those who attacked New Vega, could not accomplish." Her face grew grave and cold. "And now, the opportunity to do so presents itself. The one thing the Savages feared more than me—the Legion—has been brought low by the very man who once swore to me that he would resist the temptations of godhood. A man who knew better than he acted."

Ravi listened intently. That the Savages still existed in some form out in the darkness between the stars was a relative certainty, all probabilities considered.

"How many remain?" he asked.

"Enough. More than enough. They are in your midst. Some having never left, only concealed themselves. But now, the remains come. And they will serve as a vanguard striking at the very heart of the Republic, much as they did long ago."

"A vanguard, then, for—"

"Yes," confirmed the woman. "The hour has come. Fate has brought my daughter and me together. The Savages return. But it is not them that men should fear—though men may be destroyed by them." The woman's voice was a whisper. "I, Reina, tell you this, Ancient One. Ravi. The Savages have made their final, binding covenant with the devil. They have filled a trench with the blood of those among them who would resist, and they have walked through it, the split corpses on either side. I do not bring hope. Yet I come seeking allies. Your champion... is needed."

It had taken days to run through the wiring. How many exactly, Leenah could not be sure. The cockpit of the *Indelible VI* was a prison. One that deprived her of liberty and all sense of time. No sun rose, no chrono operated, no method was available to her to gauge the passing of time.

Except sleep. It had been eight sleeps.

She was hesitant to equate that with eight days. She knew that in the darkness, the desire to sleep intensified. And it had been dark. In the interest of saving the charge of her ultrabeam, she had worked in the dark as often as she could, removing panels, unraveling wires, running her fingers along thin strands to feel for breaks or irregularities. The ultrabeam was capable of going a month between charges, but she did not recall when exactly she'd charged it last.

Between working, she lay on the deck, using the harnesses on the rear seats to keep her strapped in place. Though the seats were more comfortable, she somehow felt safer stretched out on the floor. Removed from the damage to the instruments and console. Away from the cockpit window—the weakest structure between her and the vacuum. Between her and death.

Death.

How often did she think of that now? Sometimes her own, but more often the deaths of others. Of those who had died before her. Parents, siblings, friends. The understood, familiar mourning that came to her in adulthood and the queer, imprecise mourning of childhood. When her grandfather died and she cried not from sorrow, but out of a sense of duty. A sense that it was what the adults around her wanted. And later, when a friend died, hit by a speeder, and she realized that she was sadder for the loss of her playmate than she had been for the tragedy that befell the family.

The worst times involved thinking of the uncertain deaths. The possible deaths. Her mind would provide her with unbidden prompts involving Keel's fate on the planet, or Garret's. Or worst of all, Prisma's.

Where did these thoughts come from? What could their purpose possibly be beyond bringing a hefty existential dread that left Leenah wishing for sleep or groping to recheck wires? To find anything that didn't require her to be alone with her thoughts?

Help wasn't coming. Not unless there was something still transmitting on the other side of the sealed cockpit door. Whatever lay beyond that door was her hope. Eventually, she would be forced to see if that hope was in vain.

The air, though warm, was not yet heavy with unbreathable carbon dioxide. That would come with the eventual failure of the air scrubber. Its filters wouldn't last forever. And with its display busted, she had no way of knowing precisely how long that not-forever was. She wouldn't know until very near the end, when an audible alarm would announce that the last of the clean air was being cycled into the cockpit.

Leenah looked at the survival suit draped over the rear cockpit chair and strapped down by its harness. It was the seat she sometimes sat in when Keel was at the helm and Ravi in the co-pilot seat. She couldn't see the suit in the darkness, but she knew it was there. Laid out like the next day's outfit, ready to be put on when at last there was no further recourse.

It would provide her with another three days of oxygen, provided she regulated her heart rate and breathing. She had already decided that she would put it on after her next sleep. Not seal it yet or activate its breather/rebreather. Just have it on over her coveralls, ready to go in the event one of her other dark, unwanted dreams came to fruition and she slept through the bulk of the air scrubber's alarm, awaking too late and too weak to properly protect herself. Suffocating in the darkness with a way out less than a meter away.

She shuddered at the thought and was considering whether she ought to try to go over the comm wiring a third time when she sensed a presence with her in the cockpit. How she sensed it, she didn't know, but she strained her ears, listening—only to detect nothing but the sound of herself curling her body up tightly against the skin-crawling sensation of no longer feeling alone in the dark.

Her mind raced for solutions even as her eyes searched the inky darkness. This was mental stress. This was her mind hallucinating.

Leenah reached for her ultrabeam, moving slowly out of fear of making a noise though it seemed her heart was pounding against her chest with such ferocity that it could surely be heard.

"What has happened?"

The sudden voice—not her own—brought a mixture of fright and relief as she realized who it belonged to.

"Ravi!" Leenah cried.

She struggled with the straps that kept her anchored to the deck and then floated upright and fumbled for the ultrabeam as she rose. She flipped the switch and sent a blazing column of light straight down at her feet, illuminating the cockpit and casting sharp, angular shadows. Squinting her eyes in protest against the sudden glare, she saw him. It really was Ravi. Standing behind his old chair, a kindly look of concern twinkling in his eyes.

"My dear Leenah," he said, and then moved to embrace her, unhindered by the lack of gravity as he strode forward.

She did not pass through him. He made himself firm and warm and gently rubbed her back as she sobbed tears of relief. An outpouring of emotion that she hadn't realized had pent itself up inside of her.

Ravi did not rush her to speak. He waited. She pulled back, saw the tears staining his deep blue robes, and marveled at what had happened. Wiping her eyes, she cleared her throat of the tang of sorrow's release.

"We were ambushed," she said, following the proclamation with a deep sniff. She composed herself, feeling a sudden flush of shame. Not due to her emotions, but because she knew what this was doing to her air supply. Slowly now, she told Ravi about the meeting at the Rakka star port. The sudden appearance of the motley band of modified freighters all set to attack the *Indelible VI*. Keel's apparent troubles planet side, which she was sure was part of a coordinated attack.

"I made a last-second jump and barely got out of there alive," she said at last. "But everything on board the *Six* is dead, Ravi."

"Not everything. You remain strong. And you will live. I am here now."

"I don't know what happened to Aeson or Garret. I think they might... might be..."

"I cannot say of Garret, but I would have sensed if Keel's light had been extinguished from the galaxy. It has not."

Leenah felt a flood of relief wash over her—as though a weight had been removed from her soul.

"And," Ravi continued, "I bring still greater tidings to you. I have found Prisma."

At this news, all the sorrow left Leenah. She threw her arms around Ravi once more, gripping him tightly. Then she launched into a series of questions. "Where? Is she all right? What happened?"

"Hoo, hoo, hoo," Ravi laughed. "In time. For now, haste requires that I find Captain Keel. Together we will go see Prisma. He was last at Rakka, you say?"

Leenah nodded. "Can you just... appear to him?"

"Not as such. My movements are bound by certain waypoints when I cannot find the way through my mind. I do not know how to find Rakka from here. I will need to reorient myself."

Leenah wondered how it was he'd found her aboard the ship in that case. She was in the middle of dead space and even she had no idea where that dead space was. The curiosity was too much. "How did you find me, then?"

"There are anchors in places I need to visit frequently. Such as this ship."

Leenah nodded. She didn't understand, and yet it made sense. "You should go."

She was hopeful now. Her prayers answered, had she offered any.

"I must," Ravi conceded. "I will return as quickly as I am able. Stay strong, Leenah. Keep your resolve. Do not fear."

06

The temple loomed before Ravi, near the shore, on a world full of deep oceans and white beaches. He strode toward it, waves lapping gently against the sand, a mellow surf bobbing beneath a red sky, rays of sunlight glittering off the brilliant turquoise of the sea, kissing the tips of each swell and crest with hues of gold. Framing the temple were tall spires that looked like pink, denuded trees. These pale formations were a type of coral that had grown to monstrous heights in a time long ago when this shore was submerged beneath the water.

The spires and the temple both cast long dark shadows onto the beach as the sun glided toward its set over the land mass. Thick, tank-like crustaceans scurried from shadow to shadow, eagerly awaiting the coming night.

It was a beautiful world. One Ravi never tired of visiting.

It was also empty. Uninhabitable for most of the galactic diaspora. A toxic atmosphere, crushing gravity, and water with temperatures that would cause the oceans to boil on most planets made what looked like a tropical resort world into a death trap for any unfortunate enough to find themselves inside its atmosphere. Long ago, a hearty race of stellar explorers had attempted to establish a colony on this world. Creatures strong of carapace. Survivors. Not long after landing, they found that they, their sturdy bodies, were the *only* things capable of weathering the harshness of the planet and its tempestuous storms. The very ships that had delivered them failed to launch again. Every item, tool, device, eroded and faded, becoming one with the abundant sand or rendered useless scrap, suitable only for sharpening and killing. First prey, then each other.

No sentient creature had lived on the planet in the eight hundred years since.

The Ancients, who had built the temple Ravi now faced, had no such difficulties. Nor did the product of their architectural design and build. The temple stood defiantly against this world's hostile nature.

There were many such temples as these. A mystery to those who came after the Ancients, but not to Ravi, who knew them all. They were beacons to him, as they were to his kin, before the abandonment of the galaxy. Using the temples, he was able to move from place to place even when his mental sight pictures were insufficient. Or when he was without an anchor, such as the one he'd placed aboard the *Indelible VI*.

He had also give such an anchor to Prisma and had tasked the girl with moving it with her thoughts. Had she not left it on En Shakar in her haste to escape, finding her would not have been so difficult.

Ravi walked up the beach, the temple before him an orderly anomaly in this wild and untamed world. This temple was the nearest one to Leenah, who was very far from sentient life. Impossibly removed from any chance of help. Unless one knew how to find her.

As he drew near, the temple's great stones abandoned their impenetrable façade, folding themselves inward to grant him access. Inside would be a complete map of the galaxy. The crowning achievement of the Ancients, for it represented a galaxy fully explored. A galaxy full known.

Ravi would need only find Rakka among the swirling nebula that would present itself to him, take hold of the planet, and follow the ethereal navigation to find himself there. In an instant. The twinkling of an eye.

Then he could begin a proper search for Keel. For his friend... his champion.

"The opening of a temple of the Ancients is a rare sight," hissed a voice, cold and dripping with malice. "I have never before witnessed such. How fortunate I am."

Ravi drew his sword and waited for the being to show himself.

There, standing between Ravi and the temple's entrance, appeared a cloaked and robed figure. A disciple of wickedness and evil. A Dark Wanderer.

"You will step aside," Ravi commanded.

The Dark Wanderer's eyes glowed a faint yellow within the shadow of his hood, casting enough light for Ravi to see half of his face curled up into a cruel smile. "Will I? Do you intend to *make* me? Do you intend... to *kill* me? Surely you know what that would bring about. You know the covenants and oaths by which our peoples are bound."

Ravi sheathed his sword. "I will not break the oaths of my people. Nor will you. Step aside and delay me no further." He moved around the Dark Wanderer, but the being shifted and again blocked his path.

"Such confidence."

At once, Ravi was engulfed in a darkness that seemed to spring up from his feet. Great storming clouds of red filled the horizon, rolling on strong winds below an orange sky.

"Such unfounded confidence," the Dark Wanderer continued. "I knew you would not forget this place." The being looked from left to right. "They all died, did they not? And after you fought so valiantly."

They had all died. But this was not the place. That was a distant star system. One that Ravi could still reach by thought alone. He needed no guidance from the temple.

There, long ago, was where he had first attempted to stand against the Dark Wanderer and those he heralded. Clearing a path of annihilation.

It was on that planet that Ravi led an army of turbaned men ready to face down a charge they called the final *Chamkaur*. In each man's hand was a mighty sword; hanging uselessly at their sides were the slug throwers and other projectile weapons that they had used expertly to fend off the rising empires that sought to colonize the galaxy in those first days of stellar exploration. The ammunition was spent, with no more to be found. Only strength, muscle and sinew, blade and determination were left to these warriors. And Ravi stood in their midst, unashamed to take on their appearance. An appearance that he had not altered since. That he would not change.

That place. That site of a battle of ages that had saved the galaxy from ruin...

It had happened long ago. Far away.

And yet Ravi was looking upon it. A cruel trick of the malevolent being who'd come to block his path.

"You seek to delay me," Ravi said. "To draw me into combat. Do you think the memory of this place would spark a rage in me sufficient for such a foolish action? You are desperate. Weak."

The Dark Wanderer sneered at the accusation. "Ours is a strength unimaginable. Or have you *forgotten*"—he spat the word— "how your people fled at our coming? I grow tired of waiting. *We* grow tired. Our desire is for the last things of this galaxy to happen now. You have that stewardship. In all these years you have failed to bring about anything capable of standing against what I bring. What comes even now."

"I have not failed. And when you come, mankind will stand. Just as they did before. You will not prevail."

The Dark Wanderer gave a throaty laugh. "Mankind." The word was a curse on his lips. "The armies that sent the Ancients fleeing will be stopped... by man?"

Ravi said nothing.

"I know why you came here, Ancient One. You seek your champion." He laughed again. Mockery. "The next in a long line of hopefuls, none of whom proved themselves capable of doing what needed to be done." He looked off, afar, to the planet beyond the deep deadness at galaxy's edge. "At least your counterpart managed to choose one capable of consolidating a portion of the power of men, even if only for a moment."

"Goth Sullus was no champion. He was an unwitting servant of yours. Regardless of what Urmo may have wished. Regardless of the lies. And even then, despite your careful measures to move past the great gulf between galaxies, he resisted you in the last."

"Resisted." The Dark Wanderer grew close to Ravi, sneering the word into his ear, his foul breath pushing against the hairs of Ravi's beard. "A delay. He was ours until the moment he was ended."

"Ended by whom?" Ravi goaded.

"So proud now," spat the Dark Wanderer. "Your champion. The one you had discarded and determined unfit for the task. Quite rightly. He is no different from any of the rest. No different from that fool Tyrus Rechs nor any of the others you placed the folly of hope in."

The Dark Wanderer spread his arms, inviting Ravi to survey the battlefield where tired and bloody men once stood, facing down the last moments of their lives. "Do you remember what happened here? What happens next? What even a 'light reconnaissance force,' as your precious human generals would call it, did to this world and its people?"

"You are no longer to delay me," Ravi said.

The Dark Wanderer took Ravi's arm and thrust Ravi's hand against the hilt of his sword. "If you do not wish to suffer delay, then draw your sword and end it. Be on your way, Ancient One. A single stroke. My head at your feet. Do it."

But Ravi did not. Would not.

And yet he was at the creature's mercy. He would be denied the ability to go any direction but backward—or to a place already familiar.

And the Dark Wanderer knew it. Together now, he would be able to follow.

"Understand," the being said, "anywhere you go, I will come also. And anyone I find, I will kill.'

"Then come, foul creature. Follow."

Ravi disappeared.

The Dark Wanderer pursued.

07

The herders knew not to let their shepp graze near the hermit's shack on the north side of the mountain. Few had ever seen the man, but all knew his temperament. The mountain provided for many, but the north face belonged to the hermit—and anyone or anything that wandered too near the gray, weathered shack would know his wrath.

Once, some of the men, a small band of brothers, left their wives and children, slug-throwing carbines on their backs, and brought their shepp herds to the fertile, untouched grasses on the northern slopes beneath the shack.

"Come. What can this man do to us?" they told one another.

They scoffed at warnings from the old men and saw only the health of their flocks that would come from the abundance of the north face. And of course... the men never returned. Their flocks scattered. As did the whispers across the mountain.

You see... you see!

Better to live. Why feed the green fields of the slopes with your blood? Why make your family widows and orphans? We have enough on our side of the mountain. There is enough.

Damn the old man of the north. Can't he see that there's enough?

The young shepherd knew there was enough. He knew that the north was not to be traveled lightly. But there was grazing to be had on the east side that was nearly north. *Nearly.* And though he knew the stories of the old man and believed them, he knew that all the points of direction eventually cease to be. The young shepherd was east. He could see the north, but he would stop short. He would be cautious.

His trouble at the moment was that his flock, his shepp, did not know north from east. They saw only lush greens. They wandered. And they would fall prey to the hermit unless he brought them back.

Rifle on his back and staff in his hand, the shepherd climbed atop a gray slab of stone that rose out of the grasses. The wind, no longer broken by the stone he'd approached, lashed out against him, seeking to take his body's warmth away to whip around the mountain.

That wind paled in comparison to the chill that sank deep into his bones upon reaching the top of the rock. For he spotted the stragglers who'd gone too far ahead. His shepp. And there, terribly near them, was the shack, its door facing him, the sun settling behind it, casting shadows that obscured the shepherd's ability to see if the hermit was standing at a door or window.

His shepp grazed contentedly. Unaware of their peril or the danger they'd led their master to. He wanted to shout for them to return to him, but even had he dared it, the lush fullness of the pasture would make their coming an exercise of will. A test of loyalty.

He did not call. He believed the stories. He feared the hermit.

Remembering himself and realizing that he still drew breath, he took a step. Not forward. Not toward the shack to test the hermit's hospitality or to rescue his shepp. He took a step backward. Then another. Then turned and ran, leaping off the rock and landing hard on the ground. He ignored the pain and pressed his back against the stone.

The shepp were lost to him now. So be it. Better that than his blood feeding the green blades that rose to his ankles and covered the slope like a thick carpet. He would abandon the stray beasts. The stragglers would die enjoying forbidden riches while he shepherded the remainder of his flock home to safety.

And yet, even as he had the thought, his flock scattered before him. Bounding in all directions.

The young shepherd looked up and saw a man on the rock where there had been no man before. A man with a helmet and a great, long rifle. He seemed to emerge from the rock as though he were part of it.

The man looked down on the frightened shepherd. He said something unintelligible, but the shepherd somehow knew the meaning.

Run. Leave.

He did.

He ran toward his father and his brothers and their flocks to the south, looking back only once to see more of the men with guns and armor and helmets advancing on the hermit's shack.

It was Chancellor Adams, Kill Team Victory's medical sergeant, who came up with the idea of driving the stray shepp the team encountered toward the target site as a hedge against any external sensors.

"Doc Chance" had volunteered to scare the domesticated animals toward the location but was denied the opportunity in favor of Staff Sergeant Stenn "Neck" Kenecni, the team's engineering sergeant, who had grown up on a ranch somewhere in the mid-core.

"Don't know the first thing about shepp except they stink, and they'll die if you don't shear 'em every cycle," Neck said. Not in protest. He didn't want the team to place more confidence in him than his abilities justified. "Not sayin' I can't get it done... just lettin' you know I'm not a hundo on how these things will react."

"You are best suited for the task," Bombassa said, and when the first sergeant spoke, that was that.

The climb up the mountain had been grueling but necessary. Insertion by stealth shuttle, while possible at the altitude, would certainly alert those inside the target house. And that was *if* the place, or the Nether Ops agents believed to be inside, weren't equipped with some kind of anti-air capabilities. One A-P missile while a shuttle unloaded was all it would take to turn the operation into a tragedy.

As it was, the quiet and sensor-evading stealth shuttle had set them down at the base of the mountain's south side, coming in low and leaving Kill Team Victory a long and arduous climb up and around the mountain. The operation called for them to ascend, move into position, and breach and secure the building upon receiving orders from Bear via L-comm.

Neck belly-crawled toward the animals, slinking through the tall grass until he was so close that even with the memetic camouflage the shepp began to grow nervous, stamping their hooves and instinctively tightening into a group. He waited and watched as the animals looked from under woolly tufts of hair with wide and terrified eyes... then he abruptly jumped up, performing a burpee and falling back quickly to his stomach.

The flock scattered toward the cabin.

"Move into place," Bombassa ordered. "Neck, I have another job for you. Ready the A-P launcher."

When Hopkins first found out that the superstitious population of herders that lived on the mountain call him "the hermit" or, better yet, "the old man," he laughed out loud. It came after an overnight patrol by the other members of his Nether Ops team. They'd overhead the herders speaking as they warmed themselves by a dung fire, unaware of the shadowy assassins that observed not ten meters away, moving too silently for even their herding creatures—a hoofed, sure-footed dog hybrid—to bark a warning.

The men returned, reported on the herders' positions, reported that all else appeared fine, and told Hopkins his nicknames. This had to have come from some shepherds catching daylight glimpses of him as he moved outside the shack. His hair had gone from a thick black to snow-white in his early thirties. Now, as he pushed toward his fiftieth standard cycle in the galaxy, he had a distinctively hard and grizzled look. But he was hardly an old man.

Hopkins had left the Legion after only one year in service. *Rescued* was a more accurate way of putting it. In more ways than one. During his first combat tour out on the edge, Hopkins decided that his commander's ROE—Rules of Engagement—were nothing more than coddling an enemy that deserved some dusting. So... he ignored them.

A major political fallout ensued. It cost a House of Reason delegate and a planetary senator their reelections. And Hopkins found himself on a destroyer brig, cursing those without the spine to acknowledge that the actions he'd taken were justified. You fought wars to win them. Ending the fight fast was a mercy.

The Legion didn't agree. They threw around words like "genocide" and "war crimes." Sent him to face the tribunal.

And then a funny thing happened on the shuttle ride from his destroyer to his fate. The moment his transport shuttle went FTL, his ener-chains were removed, and he found himself out of hot water and in an agency known as the Carnivale. A place where operators like himself were free to do what needed to be done without fear of the moral scolds and weak-kneed officers who blushed and blanched at the thought of a few innocent civilians getting vaporized.

If they were so innocent, why was it so hard to tell the insurgents from the general populace to begin with?

Nether Ops was different. It was the one outfit in the entirety of the Republic *truly* willing to do whatever it took to preserve the golden standard of living that had been achieved across the galaxy. The Legion *talked* about killing its enemies first. Nether Ops *did* it. No matter the cost.

That had been a frequent saying of his original handler. "You boys get this done, no matter the cost."

He wouldn't undertake a mission any other way. If it's not worth doing no matter the cost, send someone else.

Things had changed since he'd first joined up. An emperor had arrived and faded. Article Nineteen happened. The Republic was in the process of rebuilding itself—and was more than likely going to make a mess of things. The way of the worlds.

"You boys get this done, no matter the cost."

The man who'd said that to him, his first field director, eventually became the head of the Carnivale. A brilliant man who went by X, because that was a thing you could do in the Carnivale. Be who you needed to be, and no one asked who you *really* were because they knew the truth already. You were the mission.

X was gone now, killed on Utopion. His penchant for "No matter the cost" had been broadcast to the galaxy as though it were some sin that should stain all of Nether Ops. As though he were wrong. He wasn't wrong.

He was merely gone.

And yet his mission and vision would continue. The Republic must persevere.

No matter the cost.

Right now, that cost was isolation and boredom. Hopkins was stationed at a Nether Ops data center, code name Ulterio. It was one of the many loose, decentralized caches that were the very heartbeat of the Nether Ops intelligence-gathering machine. Each center's location was unknown to all but a few in the organization who needed to know. X had recognized that the House of Reason had a tendency to second-guess, if not outright oppose, that which the Carnivale knew to be best. Always for political reasons. And once a pol got a little bit of wind, they'd let out all the sail and demand to know more and to see more. The dumb ones used to get themselves killed that way. The smart ones winked and got paid.

X circumvented it all by having two data systems.

The one for the House and Senate.

And the real one.

A result of this was that only the most trusted operatives were ever stationed at a data center. Sometimes the task was assigned to a man who was no longer up to standards due to age or injury. That wasn't Hopkins; he wasn't an old man. Most times it was simply an opportunity to spend some time away from the grueling deep cover operations of the field, which took a mental toll on even the hardest of operators. It was a chance to study and learn new skills from those stationed alongside you.

Hopkins, like the five other men at Ulterio, didn't abandon his post when word of the fall of Utopion reached him. Didn't even think about it. He understood that though the central offices might have been rifled, the department heads arrested or killed, the agents burned, Nether Ops had long ago made itself capable of surviving separate from the bureaucratic hallways of governance.

Already senior agents were formulating new plans to continue or complete missions while re-consolidating power and resources. And within those plans, protection of the data centers was critical. Hopkins believed in the mission. He believed in doing whatever it took.

Barbarians were always at the walls. Nether Ops stood with knives out, not to stop them, but to slit their throats from behind.

Hopkins was as committed as he'd ever been, despite the unfortunate nature of this assignment. He just wished those dirty mountain people, those herders who drove their flocks higher and higher in elevation as their valuable fleece grew thicker and the animals subsequently needed colder temperatures to avoid overheating and dying—hadn't given him quite such a frustrating nickname.

The rest of the team, all of them at least fifteen years younger than him, took to calling him "Hermit" or "Old Man" at once. Didn't matter how much he told them not to. He knew he would've done the same had their roles been reversed. Only a direct order to stop with the nicknames would have done it. And things didn't work that way among agents in Nether Ops, unless you were part of an NO kill team. Or a director.

Hopkins was neither. Just another hand working the data center. Waiting for the big org to reassign him and make use of his talents in the field. Until then, he'd find comfort in the solitude of the shack.

He lifted a kaff percolator from the stovetop, holding its burning handle through a thick rag and pouring himself a cup of liquid black that steamed heavily in the cold confines of the room. The rest of the team was stationed in the level below, where things were modern and tidy. He was the man on point. The one tasked with keeping an eye out the windows and playing the role of an actual hermit should anyone not as disposable as shepherds ever come knocking.

He took a scalding sip of kaff. This part of the job wasn't so bad. It was more or less how he'd planned to spend his retirement. If he ever made it that far.

He heard the hiss of the bunker door beneath the subfloor, followed by a knock on his floorboards.

"Hey, Hermit," called a muffled voice from below. "Clear for me to come up and see some sunshine?"

Hopkins set his tin mug down, wishing for a moment that he really was a lonely hermit. He lifted the trap door, and some of the thin mountain light fell on the young Nether Ops agent, causing him to blink.

"There's your sun," Hopkins growled, sitting back down to his kaff.

The young man, a former Republic marine who couldn't be a day over twenty-five, smiled at the natural light and climbed up into the cabin. He knew better than to go trouncing around like he owned the place. He simply stood and looked around at the rays pouring through the cabin's small square windows. A cold, wispy sunlight barely capable of warming the windowsills much beyond the temperature outside.

"Nice to see it," the young agent said. "Been down there three days with nothing but artificial light."

"It gives you everything you need to stay healthy," said Hopkins, who disliked complainers.

"Sure, but it ain't the same thing as the real deal, Hermit."

"Call me Joshua or Mr. Hopkins," he said, knowing that it was far too late for such a thing to happen. He was *Hermit* to this one, which was preferable to *Old Man*. He didn't expect the kid to call him *Hopkins* even once, but he had to say it anyway. It didn't hurt to remind the former hullbuster that respect for elders was still expected and practiced in at least some parts of the galaxy. Good rule for an agent is always to know how *not* to stand out. Showing respect for elders rarely made anyone seem out of place.

Except on the most lost and confused of worlds.

"Sorry," the kid said. "Force of habit. You know how it goes. Forgot your name even was Hopkins."

"It is. And it ain't hard to remember unless you're going out of your way to not use your brain. Whaddaya want?

No way Tackman let you come up here just to see some sun. Little bastard wants everyone to become a cave fish like him."

The kid nodded, seeming somewhat disheartened to already have to get down to business. "Something tripped the proximity alarms. Bunch of somethings. Tackman sent me up to ask you to take a closer look."

Comms, which were detectable by those who knew how to look, like Dark Ops, weren't used unless absolutely necessary.

Hopkins raised an eyebrow. "Shepp?"

"That's what we figured. Didn't pick up anything that was transmitting an energy signature. No comm traffic. No flights detected around the mountain."

Hopkins scoffed. "Dark Ops has ships that'll get by them sensors."

The young man shrugged. He was an odd kid. Not the go-getter type that Hopkins was used to seeing enter Nether Ops. Maybe he'd been stationed here for too long. He was here when Hopkins first arrived.

"I hope it's shepp," the kid said. "All the meat we got left is what Connor salted and dried from the last strays."

Hopkins continued his lecture. "And Dark Ops can hide their weapon signatures, too. Not to mention, they use that L-comm, and we never did find no workaround to that."

"The shepp jerky is fine and all. Boil some water and it softens up fine, but you can't get all the salt out. Every meal I eat that ain't a ration tastes like salt. And the rat-packs got no flavor. Just nutrition."

"When I first got in I heard about a few attempts to grab that L-comm. Nether Ops kill team tried to go in and pass for Legion and take it. Didn't work out well for the operators. And then the brouhaha spilled over into Utopion and the House of Reason had to side with the Legion and censure the fellow who did it. Was a Carnivale man, mind you. But they had to do it, the House. Otherwise, that would've triggered an Article Nineteen right there. You don't go tinkering with the Legion's L-comm. They love it more than General Rex himself."

Hopkins leaned back and crossed his arms. "That's actually how X got his job. Replaced the man who went down for authorizing that fool mission to begin with."

It surprised Hopkins how much he was suddenly willing to talk. The solitude that came from living alone up top must have been weighing on him heavier than he'd realized. The kid seemed eager to talk too, but only about what suited him. That annoyed Hopkins.

"Some fresh food would be amazing," the kid said, still stuck in that same rut, as though Hopkins hadn't just revealed a fascinating piece of Nether Ops and Carnivale history at all. As if the "Old Man" really was some old grandfather to be ignored. "Connor over-salts the jerky, but whatever he does to the fresh meat before he roasts it..." He rubbed his stomach. "I can just die thinking about it."

"You ain't been on this mountain long enough to be that hungry," Hopkins grumbled.

He rose and picked up his long rifle, then moved toward the shack's front door and peeked through the window to one side.

"It's shepp," he said.

"Good. I can already taste it. Maybe use some of the blood to mix in with a rat-pack and make a gravy."

"Your tune might go a little sour if there's more shepherds with 'em. That means body detail for you, kid."

"Sket. I forgot about that."

"Next time don't." Hopkins checked the other windows. "Don't see any, but they know not to be 'round here so I suspect if there is one, they're gonna be cautious."

"Why kill 'em at all?"

"Because they need to be afraid of coming close. And so that if some fool from another branch in the Nether or worse tries to come this way pretending he's a herder, we ain't used to them and we drop 'em before they drop us."

The kid didn't have an answer to this, and no more thoughts of food seemed to come to his mind to make him talk any further.

Hopkins slung his rifle over his shoulder. "Gonna take a look outside. If I see your shepherd I'll drop 'im, and then I'll try to drop any shepp I can before they scatter. I ain't gonna skin 'em or butcher 'em, though."

"Connor said he'd do that."

"Connor better damn well sure make sure he don't track blood through my front door the way he did last time."

"I'll tell him."

"You'll be on your knees scrubbing if that happens."

The young Nether Ops agent nodded eagerly, willing to agree to anything that might accelerate bringing down a kill and the fresh meat that would be served to the men at dinner.

Hopkins tilted his head toward the door. "Open the door for me so I can shoot soon as I step outside."

He was a good shot and was confident that he'd be able to bag at least one of the grazing animals. Of course, a man is a different sight picture than a shepp, and he'd have to scan for that first. To make sure he didn't get shot by some herder seeking revenge, yes, but also to make sure the little bastard didn't get away. That would force Hopkins out into the icy-cold winds of the mountain. Something he tried to avoid whenever possible. He wasn't an old man, but he was old enough that the cold did things to him it never used to.

With the young Nether Ops agent at the door, waiting for the command, Hopkins said, "Go."

The door swung open, and Hopkins scanned the terrain he couldn't see from the shack's few windows. Holocams would have made life easier, but as Hopkins knew and opted not to lecture about, Dark Ops could spot a holocam easier than you could spot Dark Ops. The whole purpose of making Ulterio look like a mountain cabin was to avoid Legion attention.

He saw no human forms. Until he did. A man wearing almost spectral, memetic armor. A Dark Ops legionnaire. He'd moved in impossibly close without detection. The shepp had been a distraction.

Hopkins didn't notice the leej first. No, first he saw the aero-precision missile and its angry plume of fire propelling the ordnance toward him at speeds so fast he had no opportunity call out a warning before the shack erupted in a furious explosion.

08

As the shack ballooned upward with flames from the explosion, the Dark Ops legionnaires waited for the largest of the flaming building pieces to drop down onto the mountainside. The team's first and second squad then advanced as Bombassa and Doc Chance covered them. The stunned shepp that the team had driven ahead now scattered down the mountain in a panic.

Kill Team Victory quickly reached the ruined shack, entering through blown-out walls and what remained of the ruined front door—a splintered door frame that miraculously seemed no worse for wear from the blast. Though it was clear there was no one still living inside, the team cleared the single room before approaching the trap door leading to the lower levels. It was where they expected it to be; where the Tennar had told them they would find it.

Outside, Bombassa and Doc Chance shifted position to provide security, watching to make sure that no one would be able to move behind the legionnaires once they entered the data center's lower level.

"Access door is open," said Dupres Pina, one of the weapons sergeants, over the squad comm.

That was a break that went in Dark Ops's favor. They'd had no doubt that the shack was part of a Nether intel cache, no matter how convincing it looked from the outside. Even the sight of the old man with his antiquated blaster rifle seemed designed to cause hesitation. Their intel was solid, and they knew that not only was this the right place, but that no sensitive materials would be on the top level. The asset that Captain Ford had provided to the team had made it clear how the structure would be laid out and what troop strength and defenses would be on hand. That gave them the green light to blow the shack and physically clear it out in one violent swoop.

But they had assumed that once that was finished, they would have to slice their way into the lower level, losing time. Instead, the door was already open, they were ahead of schedule, and the clock was now working against the remaining Nether Ops agents below, who would be scrambling to wipe the data and defend the compound long enough for the job to be completed.

Pina leaned over the hole, looking through his rifle's sights as it aligned with his bucket's HUD. He peered down into a well-lit shaft with individual ladder rungs embedded in one side. The ladder terminated a meter above a single, three-meter-wide corridor with rooms on either side: comm and security control, living quarters, fresher and mess, with the potential for dedicated storage rooms and an armory as well. It terminated with the actual data storage room.

No sooner had Pina crept over the edge to see all of this than a sprinting Nether Ops agent rushed into his sights. The man had a blaster in one hand and had just grabbed the bottom rung of the ladder with the other when he looked up to see the Dark Ops legionnaire. His face betrayed his awareness of his rash and fatal mistake.

Pina didn't hesitate to send two blaster bolts down at the target. One struck the agent in the clavicle, the other his forehead. He had let go of the ladder rung in an attempt to hurl himself backward, but it was too late. He dropped flat onto the ground.

"Hostile down," reported Pina. "Poppers."

He dropped a pair of ear-poppers into the opening and pulled away as they clattered onto the floor and then exploded in successive deafening blasts, accompanied by retina-frying light shows that ended with a thick, oily smokescreen to obscure any visuals that might remain. A fragmentation grenade followed.

Now came the most dangerous part of the operation. Pina would be the first man down the shaft. The layout of the Ulterio data center matched that of others they had breached—everything went through the ladder shaft. The informant, Honey, had confirmed as much. There was no back door. No ventilation system that a humanoid could squeeze himself into, some oversight by the designer. Vents were ray-shielded and would prevent even crawler bots from accessing the facility.

This was all by design. Nether Ops data centers were meant to be defended from only one angle of attack. Allowing the small crews to concentrate fire and deliver stiff resistance when prepared to do so... even if that meant living in a death trap. The kind of place where a fire in the wrong room could cost all hands their lives.

But then, dying while defending the data centers seemed to be all that the previous Nether agents the kill team had encountered wanted. Live long enough to scrub the data and then kick off.

Fanatics. And for what?

Pina would have those philosophical discussions later. Right now, he had a facility to breach.

The ladder rungs were set individually into the shaft's wall. No connecting bar. Which meant no way to fast-slide the five meters between opening and floor. He'd have to jump.

"Moving down!" The legionnaire fastened his rifle to the magnetic dock on his armored chest and hopped over the edge, arms tight against his sides and legs squeezed together as though he was jumping from a rescue SLIC into choppy water below. A navy jumper diving in after a pair of downed featherheads feet first into the waves.

He hit the ground and felt the shock that his armor failed to absorb, little currents that ran up his legs and back. Then he brought his rifle up, relying on the infrared and thermal overlays of his bucket to identify targets in the smoke-filled corridor. There were no biological defenders to engage, but there would be at least one auto-turret seeking targets through the smoke. Pina could hear it rotating on its base, unable to lock on to him. For the moment. The thick smoke that came from the specialized ear-poppers contained sensor-jamming chaff that blocked the automated turret's ability to properly identify targets. That would provide Pina with a few seconds before anyone with half a brain simply switched the turret's control settings to manual free fire. In the confined space, a remote operator could easily send out streams of blaster fire and sweep the hall in all directions until it was cleared and Pina was dead.

The legionnaire pulled two small bot-poppers from his webbing and hurled them down the hall in the direction of the turret. They erupted with quiet bangs that flashed like a sizzling lightning storm, and the HUD inside his bucket momentarily blipped and frayed from the localized tech-overloading blast. Still no targets, but the turret was down.

"In position," Pina called to the rest of the team.

Those on the other end of the squad comms knew that meant he had made it down without serious injury, moved clear of the ladder, and had successfully deployed his bot-poppers. The data center's main corridor was controlled. They needed to move to keep it that way.

The first leej was waiting halfway down the ladder. He dropped and was at Pina's side in an instant. The other members of Kill Team Victory hastily followed. Within seconds six legionnaires filled both sides of the corridor, the smoke hiding them completely from the naked eye. Formed into two squads of three, they moved down the hall, stopping at each door to clear.

Pina and First Squad reached a door on their left and stacked outside, using a slicer box to override any locks while the three men in Second Squad watched their sectors down the rest of the corridor. The door opened, an ear-popper was thrown in, and the room was swiftly cleared and declared secure. On the way out, one of the legionnaires affixed an infrared square to the top of the door, letting anyone who followed know that the room had been cleared.

Mission intel told them to expect five Nether agents on hand to protect a data center of this size. One they had eliminated in the initial attack. A second had been killed at the base of the ladder. The third and fourth were killed together in the fourth room cleared, this time by Second Squad.

The team breached via slicer box, but a secondary fail-safe required the use of det-tape to blow a stopping mechanism and force the door open. The next legionnaire up tossed an ear-popper into the room and the team rushed inside following its detonation.

This was the control room. A stunned Nether Ops agent stood with a blaster in hand, completely disoriented. The legionnaire clearing center dropped him with three blaster bolts.

The second man in the room was hiding in the near right corner. He had donned a full-face defense helmet designed to withstand some of the blasting effects of the flash bangs, but he was a slight man, and the awkward way he held his blaster rifle suggested he was more comfortable working the center's comm and data systems than a weapon. Not a Nether agent used to combat, but at this range, he wouldn't have to be a crack shot to do damage.

Clearly his plan was to crouch in the blind corner and shoot the first Dark Ops legionnaire who came inside. He was not prepared for the swift, violent entry that followed the boom. By the time he clumsily raised his weapon from its place on his lap, the legionnaire tasked with clearing that corner had already blasted him.

The others moved along their paths, clearing the rest of the room.

Four men accounted for. One remaining.

The team cleared the rest of the compound, leaving Nobes to begin salvaging what data was left for them in the main system. He sliced his way in quickly using a combination of Legion know-how and still-authenticated Nether passkeys they had acquired from other operations.

"Defensive systems offline," he reported, then sent a recovery program to get whatever information it could find. Right away it was clear that much had already been scrubbed.

"Lower level secure," Pina reported in to the first sergeant. "Confirmed three Nether KIA. One short, over."

"Roger," said Bombassa. "I believe we found the fifth man mixed in with the first up top." The grisly discovery was a result of Bombassa examining pieces of skull scattered against a beam, scalp still attached. There were two distinct hair colors and textures. Two men. "Status on intel recovery?"

"Seeker bots deployed and operational. Nobes is actively in system."

"Acknowledged. Send Second Squad up top. Out."

The three Kill Team Victory members comprising Second Squad—Wello, Nix, and Barrett "Toots" Utz—ascended the ladder and strengthened the security detail up top as First Squad and the scrubber box scoured the lower levels for any intel they could find.

It wasn't long before Nobes reported another virtual dry hole. "Scrubbed and empty," he reported to his first sergeant.

"Roger. Did you see signs of packet burst?" asked Bombassa.

"Affirm. Plain as day now that we know what to look for."

"Roger out." Bombassa switched comm channels to Pina. "ETA to finish?"

"Unless one of the scrubbers finds something entirely unexpected, we'll be good to get out of here in fifteen."

"Roger. Fifteen minutes. Out."

Bombassa pinged the team captain, who was monitoring the operation from aboard the stealth shuttle, ready to perform evacuation when called upon. "Data center secure. LZ secure. ETA fifteen minutes until evac needed."

"Acknowledged," said Bear. "Fifteen minutes to extraction. Mark." The big man waited a beat and added, "Good work. Now we just need to hope that what that little Tennar told us is true. Up to Ford and Masters to get phase two done."

"Ford is capable," said Bombassa.

Bear smiled at Bombassa's taciturn nature. The man was a far cry from "Lash." What he'd managed to pull off was marvelous. Bombassa would be given the option to become an officer sooner rather than later—probably already would have had he not undertaken the mission with Black Leaf. The only question was whether the big man wanted it.

"Solid copy," Bear said. "See you in fifteen. Out."

09

Keel knew the timing had to be perfect. And it would be. He had no doubts that he could hit his target exactly when the mission plan called for it. By now he had gotten sufficiently accustomed to the *Obsidian Crow* that he was beginning to anticipate the ship's behavior. It wasn't the *Six*, but it was a good ship. The Nether Ops data center also didn't bother him. He had unwittingly recovered Honey from one of those centers, expanded for research. Securing another would be no great difficulty—so long as the plan went smoothly.

Honey herself was a different matter. She was Nether Ops, and though she played the role of thoughtful agent making her way in a world where nothing was personal and this was simply the way things needed to be in order to avoid death at the hands of a rival, Keel couldn't shake the warnings in his mind. Nor did he want to. He had to stay on his guard, ready for the eventual double cross. His time on the edge, making his own way in the galaxy, had burned that lesson into him. Never trust anyone. Especially someone who made life conveniently easy—as Honey had done when it came to what he and Kill Team Victory were now up to. He'd be warier still if not for his calculation of the odds. Too many moving parts would have had to have fallen perfectly into place for her to be the lure in an elaborate trap laid not only for him but for Jack, Bombassa, Bear, and a tremendous number of other individuals all of whom lacked any common denominator aside from Keel himself.

But anything was possible.

So, it wasn't the mission itself that made Keel worry. Nor was it hitting his target at the proper time. A thing that had to be done with precision, as was the case with so many of these missions. Rather, it was the complications that came with all that. Specifically, Bombassa's insistence that Keel not undertake the mission alone. Apparently the tall legionnaire felt it was unwise for Keel to have no one between himself and a known Nether agent but a stout little gunnery bot. This was a Dark Ops mission, and for Keel to get what he wanted, he needed to play by the organization's rules.

Keel didn't like it, but he relented, and back at the final stages of the mission planning, he tried to make it all happen as quickly as possible.

"Just give me whoever you've got on hand," he told Bear and Bombassa as Nobes leaned against his chair in the planning room. "They wouldn't be on the team if they weren't capable."

Bear and Bombassa shared a look. Then Bear said, "We need our guys. Sorry, Ford."

"You need your guys," Keel repeated with incredulity. "Well, who did you have in mind, then, big guy? Chhun? Pretty sure he was busy the last time I checked."

"Not Chhun," said Bombassa. "But... close."

Keel considered what this meant—and then the realization hit him.

He shook his head. "No. Come on, guys. He'll spend the entire time trying to get the Tennar into bed."

Bear let out a roar of a laugh. "It's about time we pulled Masters back from Kill Team Two as it is. I know you two work together just fine. Saw it with my own eyes when we were all acting as your crew during the war. He'll keep himself in the armor if there's an op. You know that."

"Fine," Keel groaned. "But my part in this operation depends on me doing what I do as Captain Keel. This place isn't being hit by a bunch of legionnaires—it's being infiltrated and quietly subdued. That requires that jump jockeys—*convincing* jump jockeys—show up."

Bear waved away the concern. "Masters can put on a leather jacket and some striped pants same as you. Not seeing the problem."

"The problem is that the kid has a way of drawing attention to himself. Attention leads to questions, and questions lead to problems. If we get into a gunfight in the docking bay, Masters will have no trouble helping me get out of it. That's not the issue. The issue is, if that happens, there goes the data."

The three legionnaires in the room exchanged another look, quicker this time.

"We considered this," said Bombassa. "Masters is capable on mission. He won't be a liability. He will be overjoyed to be working a direct-action mission with Victory again, even if not with the main team."

The big legionnaire seemed to consider whether to say anything further, but it was Nobes who spoke next.

"Masters has been calling in every favor he can to get transferred back to a direct-action team. The original teams aren't exactly his style."

Keel gave a mirthful smile. "Yeah, you can say that again."

Dark Ops had begun as a specialized task force of the Legion. Since all legionnaires are considered special forces qualified by virtue of their training and physical ability, General Rex had selected men from among the ranks that he found suitable for the missions of Dark Ops as it was first constructed. Small units that would operate on disparate planets, training the local populace in the art of war-fighting while building pro-Republic ties among the native populations often caught up in simmering local conflicts.

Dark Ops was also a preventative measure meant to keep Legion resources where they were needed—and a way to meet the House of Reason's increasing tendency to direct the Legion toward solving whatever political problems proved too stubborn for diplomacy or negotiation. Following the conclusion of the Savage Wars, diplomacy had failed more often than it succeeded. And each new conflict the House of Reason threw the Legion into resulted in further loss of legionnaires. They were dying faster than they could be replaced.

Dark Ops's ability to train local populaces to fight for themselves meant that the Legion would have time to rebuild its ranks. And it needed that time. The brutal fight against the Savage Nations had greatly reduced the ranks of the legionnaires, and despite calls from the House and Senate, no Legion commander had been willing to lower the Legion's lofty standards in order to hasten the repopulating of those ranks once more. As things were standing prior to the introduction of Dark Ops, the Legion's harrowing selection process was producing only one replacement for every three casualties. So, when the conflict ended, Rex prioritized the rebuilding of the Legion. Dark Ops was to play an important part in that rebuilding, and Rex oversaw it personally—until his banishment.

But as time went on, the role of Dark Ops changed. While Dark Ops teams continued to carry out their primary objective of working with indigenous populations, there was also a distinct shift toward using them as an elite direct-action force following the fabulous mission success of what some had begun to call "hybrid" teams. Teams like Kill Team Three. Units that could be used for planetary stabilization or destabilization, but which could also be called on to perform certain no-fail missions for the Legion or the Republic. The exploits of old Dark Ops veterans like "Subs" Boyd and Kel Turner likely paved the way for this shift.

So it was that legionnaires and Dark Ops team members who showed particular skill in direct-action fighting were siphoned from their existing units into newly formed Dark Ops teams. That gave the organization two distinct cultures. The original teams, which kept their simple naming ethic—Kill Team One, Two, Three, et cetera—remained focused on the original mission of Dark Ops. And the new kill teams, which chose more colorful names, operated with a focus on lethality, with little interaction with planetary militaries unless it was in direct opposition to them.

Captain Owens had been commander of a direct-action team, though attrition and overextension had had it operating at below its usual capacity. Ford, Chhun, Masters, and the others had shown in Kublar that they were exactly the sort of legionnaires suited for such a unit and Kill Team Victory was born. And though the three surviving members of that first team had gone in three distinct directions, this new mission had at least two of them set to reunite.

Keel met Masters in a civilian docking station, one of the big, busy spaceports where massive transport liners promised luxurious trips to every corner of the galaxy with stops at all the major systems. The kind of place where travelers passed in and out likes waves on the seashore.

Masters stood out only because of his natural good looks. Otherwise, he was indistinguishable from any other traveler. Keel was relieved; he had half expected the kid to wear his Legion dress uniform on account of the way it enhanced his pursuit of the galaxy's females.

Masters had, in fact, been staring at a pair of human females walking by when he caught sight of his old friend. His face lit up and he hurried to meet Keel.

"And here I thought someone like Bombassa was going to pick me up," Masters said with a smile. "You know how first sergeants get. Any excuse to keep you on base and get themselves outside." He held out a fist for Keel to bump. "It's nice to not have to salute or call you 'sir' anymore now that you're out. Kelhorn."

Keel kept his expression flat. "Technically you still have to salute me because of the Order."

"Technically you can do anything you want on your last day in service. So why are you here? Not that I'm complaining. But... you didn't re-up, did you? Stupid question. Of course you didn't. Because if you did, you'd have to do what you were told, and that ship jumped a long time ago."

"Bear needed some help, so I'm helping. So are you."

Masters bobbed his head up and down as a man does when listening only closely enough to know when it's his opportunity to get in the next word. "Yes. The mission. And we will have that mission. We will complete that mission. We will KTF that mission. *But* this is the first place I've been where the populace isn't ninety-nine percent asexual self-impregnating insectoids. So... what say we see what trouble we can make before we leave? And don't get all responsible with me."

"There's a schedule, Masters."

"I know about the schedule. The schedule gives us all night to get to the next waypoint. Your ship is plenty fast. So, by my calc, we have almost all night. Let's do this. Or I'll make sure your heartbreaker tab gets pulled."

Keel was about to stress to Masters that they had less time than he might hope and that he had no interest in going from pub to pub in order to help the legionnaire add to his personal high score. But just then Honey sauntered up from her place on a nearby bench to join the reunion.

"You two ready to go?" she asked.

"Who's this?" said Masters, looking the Tennar up and down approvingly.

"This is Honey," said Keel.

Masters smiled, leaned in toward Keel, and whispered, "I know you're not the type to kick that Endurian to the curb for a Tennar. She's choice, but not torrid like Leenah." He then pulled away and said loudly, "Holy strokes, you got me a stripper? You're the best, Keel. I love you, pal."

Honey scowled.

Keel said, "She's not a stripper."

"Oh? *Oh.* Man, I didn't take you for that kind of guy, Keel. The thing is... I don't exactly have any trouble in that department. So, no need for professionals."

"Masters, she's—"

"But I am up to date on my shots. For the record."

"She's part of the mission. A fellow agent. Nether Ops. KTV cleared her and she's working to help us bring in some intel."

Masters raised an eyebrow. "Nether Ops? Not sure I'm looking for anything quite that sleazy. Even I have my limits."

"Charming," said Honey, who now looked Masters up and down. "And you couldn't handle me on your best day."

Masters scoffed. "First, that's ridiculous. Second, I don't need to handle you, Nether. I just need to be the guy you want information from." He put his hand up to cover his mouth and stage-whispered to Keel, loud enough for the Tennar to hear, "They only hire the pretty ones to sleep with people for information."

Keel pinched the bridge of his nose. "Why do I keep getting myself involved in these things?"

The jump from the docking station to the launch area took ten hours. During that time, Masters and Keel reviewed the mission planning, then Keel led a brief tour of the *Obsidian Crow*.

"This ship smells weird," was Masters's only comment during the inspection.

"It's been in storage for a while," said Keel. "Long story."

Death, Destroyer of Worlds, overhead the comment and took it as a personal insult. Keel denied the bot's request to throw the blasphemer into the airlock and vent him. Nevertheless, the bot watched Masters and Honey warily after that, following them about the ship. Keel approved. Giving Honey even this much freedom still didn't quite sit right with him. But she hadn't yet steered him or Kill Team Victory in the wrong direction; she had earned enough trust to at least not have to spend all her free time in the cell—though Keel wouldn't budge about the ray shielding encasing her when she slept. If the precaution caused any hard feelings, Honey didn't show it. Probably because she would have done the same thing if the roles were reversed.

It didn't take long for the frost between Masters and Honey to thaw. The little bot reported to Keel that his disrespectful friend and the Tennar were fighting in Masters's crew quarters and that Death should be given a blaster in order to kill Honey before she had a chance to kill Masters.

Keel declined the request, but he did rise from his spot at Tyrus Rechs's old workbench, where he'd been cleaning his weapons, to listen at the door. Judging by the sounds he heard, he had an idea what sort of tussle was happening, but he pounded his fist on the door all the same.

"Go away!" shouted Masters.

Keel turned to the bot. "Better to just leave them be."

The bot remained concerned.

"Well, don't be," said Keel. "Put your mind on something more wholesome, like killing a world's population or something."

The little bot agreed that this was worthwhile and rolled away happily.

Keel was back working at his bench when the couple reappeared. At the sight of Keel, the Tennar flushed the color of embarrassment inherent to her species—a subtle blue that faded into a deep purple rising from her chest to her neck.

Masters had no concept of shame, but he recognized it in others. For Honey's sake, he played his part.

"And that's why I think operating with a rotating lead will be best for this mission," he said, as though giving his final thoughts on some matter related to the task at hand. Yet he shook his head at Keel when the Tennar wasn't looking, wanting to be sure Keel was aware of his conquest.

Honey cleared her throat. "Yes. I agree. I can see that now. I'm... going to the fresher."

When she'd gone, Masters walked proudly to Keel and punched him playfully in the arm. "For the record... no pheromones involved. *She* came after *me*."

"And what did she want to know?"

"That I thought she was special. The usual stuff."

Keel shook his head. "No. I mean about you and intel."

"Oh. Nothing. I wouldn't have told her sket anyway. She just couldn't resist," Masters waved his hands around his abdomen, "this. It's a blessing and a curse, really. Mostly a blessing, though. When are we getting into the armor?"

"Pretty soon. My kit takes a bit longer to put on now."

"You running something new?"

"Yes and no. I've got Tyrus Rechs's old armor."

Masters's eyes went wide in exaggerated surprise. "Ho-lee strokes. You stole Tyrus Rechs's armor?"

"I didn't steal it."

"On loan from the Legion Museum of Military History? How'd you pull that off? Chhun hook you up?"

"Yeah."

Masters folded his arms and scoffed. "Isn't that just typical? You—not even in the Legion—ask for Tyrus karking Rechs's armor and it's handed right over to you. Never mind you'll probably be killed in some ambush by a reaver pirate crew and the armor will be sold at some night market to a donk who modifies it and then goes on a

Legion killing spree like in that holofilm. Sure, old Captain Ford gets whatever he wants."

"I don't get whatever I want, and I had to agree to—"

"But Masters? Does he get the same treatment? Of course not! I asked—no, I *begged*—to get out of that assignment to the original teams and it's all," Masters performed a mocking impersonation of the former Legion commander, "'Learning the skill sets with one of the original teams is a mandatory and important part of your achieving the rank of command sergeant major. You do want that rank, don't you, Masters?'"

The legionnaire threw out his arms. "I'm telling you, Ford, cryosleep is more exciting than training a bunch of bugs how not to shoot themselves with blaster rifles in case the other bugs want to eat their faces for the glory of some warlord.

"So I was like, 'You're the Legion commander! You can promote me right now. Who's going to stop you?'" Masters shook his head at the obviousness of it all. "And Chhun's like, 'That would be a violation of my oath, a detriment to the Legion, and an abuse of our friendship.' And then he reminds me not to use his personal comm channel for stuff like that. But you? Different rules, man. Not fair."

Keel smiled. Masters's impression of Chhun's voice was less than flattering, but Keel could imagine his friend saying those exact words.

He could tell that Masters was now waiting for him to weigh in on this diatribe. So, Keel focused on cleaning his weapon instead.

Finally, Masters couldn't wait any longer. "Can you believe that guy?" he said.

"Makes sense to me, Masters."

"Oh, you *would* say that. Officers."

"What do you wanna be a CSM for anyway?"

Masters got a faraway look in his eye. "The power. The raw, unchecked, unchallenged power."

"I can see the Legion's heading downhill," Honey said, returning at that moment from the fresher. "Maybe I picked the wrong side after all."

Masters arched an eyebrow and raised his index finger. Keel cut him off before he could speak.

"Let's get back on track here. Masters, get in your armor. We're three hours to our window."

"And we can't be late," added Honey. "Once the new packet arrives, security protocols change, and then it's good luck getting what we're after."

"Don't worry," said Keel. "We'll be on time."

10

Ravi arrived ahead of the Dark Wanderer. The planet was barren and cold, far different from how it had been during its glorious days of early colonization. All the irrigation that had once filled the surface with lush greens and shining, vibrant lakes and streams had now retreated back to the great black crater lake, leaving the ground it had once watered and nourished brown and orange and lifeless.

The great field of battle lay covered by the bones of the fallen, fossilized and in scattered piles as black as coal. Hilts of rusted swords lay strewn amid the desiccated pulse rifles of that final stand. Rare was the sight of so much as a surviving scrap of fabric—and their once-brilliant colors were now only a memory inside Ravi's mind.

He stood among dead men he'd once called his friends and comrades. His own garb, his turban and robe, were an unchanging testimony to an act of bravery and selflessness that the rest of the galaxy would never know. It was here that Ravi first fully comprehended that the hearts of men, when turned toward good, could stand up to something even so dark and foul as the coming advance of evil his people had fled so long ago. An evil that was marching again—though in truth, it had never ceased. Now it simply seemed closer than it ought to be.

Ravi stood and wondered whether the Dark Wanderer would act on his words and follow him, or if he would simply repeat his trick and wait for him at another Temple of the Ancients. Always on hand to block Ravi from reaching Captain Keel. Regardless, the Wanderer was not here. That much was certain. Perhaps the creature had simply been lying. A common attribute for him and his kind.

Ravi was just on the verge of leaving to resume his quest when the unwholesome being appeared again before him.

The Dark Wanderer's yellow eyes flitted from Ravi to the graveyard of bones. He stared at the death that stretched before them with obvious satisfaction.

"I see now that my conjurations of this place," he rasped, "did not do justice to the slaughter that was done to those you failed to protect. So much death here."

Ravi did not furrow his brow or show the slightest sign of feeling the taunt. "Your conjurations, Dark Wanderer, could capture only the cruelty and bloodshed. Here in the place of battle, you are reminded of truth. This is not mere death, nor are the men whose bones still lie on the ground where they fell mere victims of war. These are the men who halted those you serve from venturing any farther into this galaxy."

The Dark Wanderer sneered in disgust. His lip curled, ready to spew and snarl and rage. But the creature remembered himself and resumed a look of malevolent confidence and control.

"This was but a probe. A small band. More come now, as you well know. That is an onslaught that cannot be held back. A man would do better attempting to empty the oceans of Fiorna with a bucket than to stand against the coming judgment."

"The judgment is not just, and its execution remains to be seen," said Ravi.

"It is sure. And you, Ancient One, will no longer carry out your task. I will not allow it. You must force it from me."

"Which I will not do." Ravi sat down and crossed his legs. He closed his eyes and meditated on what had happened here so long ago.

The Dark Wanderer stood above Ravi and shouted, "Stand up! Stand up and face me! End this charade of time and bargain and oaths and covenants and bring forth the inevitable end. You are no closer to halting what comes now than you were on this day so many millennia ago."

Ravi did not open his eyes. "Your intentions are clear and your manipulations transparent and weak. You will shadow me."

"I will."

"You will bend your malice toward those near me."

"I will," the Dark Wanderer said with relish.

Ravi gave a singular nod. "Then you are in my possession."

"I... what?"

"If I am not free to go about my way because of your bitter malice, then neither are you free to leave. You have made a prisoner of me, yes, but your black and bitter heart has made you an even greater prisoner to yourself. I would pity you if I did not know your incurable evil."

"Do you think you will outwait me? I, who have bided ages and eons to see the purpose come about?"

"I think that those who move to take up arms against you and that which you bring will not be greatly hindered by my absence." Ravi looked up at the hooded figure standing over him. "I wonder, is the same true of the forces you seek to wield?"

Ravi went back to his meditations and would answer the Dark Wanderer no more.

Leenah's worst fears only came halfway true. She had not slept through the cockpit's emergency oxygen scrubber giving its final warnings as it lost its ability to keep clean the air she was breathing. The urgent, steady alarm left no doubt that the thick warm air she felt and tasted all about her was not a figment of her imagination.

She put on the survival suit, still laid out where she had first placed it. As she pulled it over her coveralls, a memory came to her of once feeling similarly trapped and running out of air inside this very ship. Then Captain Keel, still very much a stranger to her, insisted it was all in her head. But not now. Now she would soon be left to whatever oxygen the small scrubber could provide, and then the survival suit's tank, and then...

She pushed away thoughts about what Ravi's failure to bring help might mean. None of them contained any scenarios she wished to consider. All were disastrous and ended with death.

"And if this doesn't work," Leenah told herself, "that's gonna be us, too." She quickly corrected herself. "Me. No third person. Can't afford to go crazy right now, Leenah."

She strapped herself into Keel's chair, the suit in place and the helmet waiting to be sealed. There was still air in here. How much was a guess, but the scrubber hadn't died. There would be a different alarm for that. Every minute she sat still was an additional minute she was giving a rescuer. Soon, however, the anxiety of what was to come pressed on her, and she decided there was little use in waiting for a rescue that wasn't coming unless she could do something to broaden the search to more than just Ravi and Keel.

She pulled the helmet down over her head and sealed the suit. Waited for confirmation that there were no breaches and that the air was cycling properly.

Then she moved to the cockpit door.

Like everything else on board the *Six*, the door leading from the cockpit to whatever remained of the ship was without power. It could be opened manually, but it took some effort. Leenah was wary of exerting herself too much—and thereby using up an accelerated amount of oxygen—but without some kind of mobile battery pack she was left with no other choice. Still, she first tested the controls to verify what she already knew to be true: there was no power.

She pulled off the cover of the V-shaped emergency hatch to reveal a control arm recessed inside a partition in the cockpit's impervisteel rear wall. As she pulled the arm out and down to disengage the lock, she heard the clunk of the metal through the thin atmosphere of the cockpit, picked up plainly by the survival suit's external audio receptor.

Leenah listened for a telltale hiss or squeak of escaping air to indicate that, now unlocked, the blast door's seal had a breach. But she heard nothing. Sensed no movement in the cockpit. No shift of what was left of the breathable air running toward the vacuum beyond.

There was still a possibility that she would find the section of the ship beyond this hatch intact and with an atmosphere of its own. But she wasn't going to place too much hope in that.

In any event, the next step was the same. She had to break the blast door's seal and either open it or allow for decompression of the cockpit. She sat at the point of no return.

Gripping the control arm she had pulled down to unlock the door, she began to turn it clockwise. Each small rotation required her to use all the arm and chest strength she possessed. By the time she had rolled the door up enough to begin to vent what oxygen remained in the cockpit, she was breaking a sweat. And she was definitely venting it. She felt the air of the cockpit rush past her feet and into the void, whipping like a wind that suddenly went silent as she waited for the area to fully depressurize. Only when that was complete did she go back to the manual controls, clamping her boots to the wall to gain better leverage until the blast door was opened a half meter up from the deck and resting on its final gear stop.

It was a simple matter then to reach underneath the door and push it straight up into its housing. Freed from its gears it was just a loose piece of impervisteel, and there was no artificial gravity on hand to make it impossible for her to lift.

The corridor beyond the hatch was pitch-black. Leenah intensified her helmet-mounted ultrabeam and studied all that was revealed in the shaft of light. Great gaping holes had been rent into the impervisteel walls on all sides, the interior of the ship open to the unfettered expanse of space. The hull plating, where visible, looked as though it had curled in on itself into tight, spiraling rolls like the shavings from a wood plane.

This damage had been achieved by more than blaster fire. This was the result of an already near-destroyed freighter making a desperate micro-jump.

She launched herself forward, a long, loping leap that floated her down the hallway with a newfound appreciation for how fortunate she was to have lived even this long. When she reached the lounge, she found it completely gutted. Only the *Six*'s heavy framework remained, the beams twisted and bent with loose and messy strands of conduit stretching out like snakes.

Untethered, Leenah reactivated her magnetic boots and walked across one of the structural beams that used to hold the deck plating. When she reached the far end, a padded wall connected to a bulkhead that would lead to the engine, drive, and other critical systems—the parts of the ship she'd spent most of her time in—she took a final look behind her. The ship appeared even more ruined from this perspective than it had when she'd first left the cockpit.

How, then, was she even alive?

It was the ship. Leenah had taken care of it, and then the *Indelible VI* had taken care of her—when any other vessel in the galaxy would have succumbed to the punishing damage.

She patted the bulkhead as she passed underneath it. This ship would probably never be suitable for anything but scrap again. It had died saving her life.

"Thank you," she said. Lovingly. Reverently. Remorsefully. "I'm so sorry. Thank you."

She moved on to all her familiar haunts, the unglamorous sections of the *Six* that made it move and live. Maintenance shafts and corridors. Places where she tirelessly worked with grease-stained hands and heavy tools to make the *Six* just a little bit stronger, a little bit faster. A little bit better. One tuning at a time. Each adjustment noted, measured, stress-tested, and then kept. Or, more often than not, abandoned or refined. Refined until she was sure that whatever the feature, system, or part, it was working optimally. The best it could be until the next technological breakthrough was available—and then she'd repeat the process anew.

Now it was all dead and lifeless. She could tell by sight that the engines were completely fused and would never roar to life again. They would need to be replaced. The reactor core was nowhere to be found, ripped away from the ship and dumped somewhere from hyperspace. Likely it had breached.

But that was all to be expected. And it wasn't in functioning engines or reactors that Leenah had placed her last-ditch hopes.

Passing through a warren of parts, a maze of wires and filaments, she reached one of the ship's multiple backup generators. The *Six* had six of them. Not all were indelible. One was missing completely, a large hole in the hull where it had once stood telling her not to bother looking for it. Three more remained aboard the ship but had overloaded and blown out. Evidence of a brief but intense fire showed itself in melted components and blackened impervisteel. A fifth, too close to the heat of the fires, had had its access panels completely fused shut by the heat. Leenah would have no way of accessing it without a cutting torch. That, along with the rest of her tool kit, was presumably somewhere in the galaxy other than on board the ship. Although if it came down to it, she would at least check.

But the final generator had been set apart from the others, in order to make room for the inertial dampers. It was coated with the white powder of an inferno quencher that must have gone off in time to save the little power supplier from the disasters that had befallen the others.

Leenah demagnetized her boots and pushed herself off the deck toward it.

The panels opened easily, almost eagerly, as though the generator had just been waiting for her to make use of it. She punched the buttons on the tactile control panel and was overjoyed when the green and red lights responded, reflecting off of the clear plastite screen of her survival suit's face shield and bathing the rest of the otherwise dark compartment in their colorful two-tone glow.

The *Six* had left her one final gift.

Now she just needed to see if she could wire in the beacons and start sending a signal.

The first several attempts at running the broken and damaged wires resulted in shorts and pops that melted the thin strands she was attempting to splice, forcing her to spool in new material each time. Nothing bad enough to cause irreparable harm—she had reduced the generator's power output to a minimum level—but setbacks nonetheless. Her best hope rested in getting this to work, and then situating herself somewhere where she would be easily visible to anyone who might find and search the ship for survivors. And then sleep, in order to expend as little oxygen as possible.

Leenah had mentally started the countdown to her asphyxiation the moment she donned the survival suit. It was still a good way off, yet far too close for the specter of such a cruel death to ever fully leave her mind.

She talked her way through the problem. "The shorts are performing a ladder attack on the GME bus," she mumbled. "Everything is going down as soon as I get the power to rise up through the filament cable. Nothing's reaching the beacon. But, if I run everything through this diamond board, that should hold. It'll eventually ruin the generator, but not before I squeeze what I need out of this baby."

Leenah followed her own instructions, then stepped back to check her work. All systems were reading as they should.

She breathed a sigh of relief. This wasn't going to keep her alive—far from it. There would be no reactivating life support, even in a small section of the ship. But it was a signal. A beacon. A means, if she was very, *very* lucky, by which she might be found.

It was hope.

11

Masters sat behind Keel and Honey inside the cockpit of the *Obsidian Crow*. He wore his armor in pieces beneath a poncho that went down to his ankles, swapping out his Legion boots for a scuffed pair that fit perfectly with the spacer he was pretending to be.

"I'm still having trouble believing these guys don't vet their suppliers," Masters said as he looked at the approaching Nether Ops data station. It was housed on a stray asteroid, a speck of dust floating in a galaxy of darkness, that would have appeared black and innocuous if not for the flash of the homing beacon activated to guide in the ship. "Who just goes with the lowest bidder and lets them show up to a top-secret installation to offload an assortment of rat-packs and bot parts? Other than the Republic, I mean. But Nether Ops was supposed to be better than this."

"All suppliers are all thoroughly vetted and investigated," Honey said. "We couldn't be doing this if someone didn't have the access level to grant this ship the clearance it needed. Or to force a delivery at this hour on the schedule."

The "someone with access" was, of course, Honey herself, and she had done precisely that.

"Okay, sure," Masters conceded. "But still, if it were me stationed on that rock, it would have raised a few questions. Surprise! Unscheduled unplanned delivery happening right now! Don't be suspicious. It's not a couple of kickass demigods, one with a physique worthy of actual godhood coming to tear your sket up."

"It doesn't work that way," said Honey. "Nether Ops is an extremely top-down organization when it comes to logistics and administration. It's almost the reverse of the Legion. The lowest agents on the pole, those in the field, are granted the least autonomy. They go where they're told and do nothing for themselves. It all comes through their handler. Things get even tighter on the way up, unless you're lucky enough to land a directorate or a sub-directorate. It didn't used to be that way, but... too much freedom from certain agents led to some significant problems."

"That what happened to you?" asked Keel, keeping a steady hand on the controls as they moved at the instructed speed toward the station. "You make it into a sub-director spot?"

"I was one of the lucky ones."

"Yeah you were," said Masters, shooting a finger gun from the back seat.

Keel and Honey both turned to give Masters a disapproving look. The legionnaire clearly wasn't fazed.

"My point is," Honey continued, "that these data centers are manned by agents who are considered above reproach. There might be a code slicer to watch the systems, but he's not doing any acquisitioning or scheduling deliveries, and you can be certain the rest of those guarding the station aren't either. They're agents, all of them. These station duties are just a place to put them between missions and an opportunity to share gossip and tactics with the other killers. Everything else that happens around them isn't their concern because Nether Ops trains them for it to not be their concern."

Keel nodded. "Which means all *we* need to do—*Masters*—is not draw any suspicion to ourselves."

"Why are you saying my name like that? I can be low-key."

Keel stood. "Ship just got slaved by the station's tractor beam. That'll guide us in the rest of the way. Let's get ready to offload."

The *Obsidian Crow* settled down softly in the Nether Ops data center's docking bay. It was a situation that would have thrilled ambitious agents stationed there had they realized the opportunity before them. Tyrus Rechs had long been a Nether Ops top priority target, and bagging the man was a recipe for immediate advancement. To have his ship in their bay would have been a dream come true—once upon a time.

Honey had given Keel an insider's history of the situation between Nether Ops and Rechs. They wanted him but had learned to stop sending dedicated kill teams after the man due to mounting casualties. For a while, Rechs had passed his time between contracts by luring these teams into ambushes, wiping out scores of capable men in one disastrous encounter after another. Policy had eventually changed from *pursue and apprehend* to *apprehend if feasible*. Which pretty much meant you had to be presented with a situation like the one now occurring in the data center.

In short, Tyrus Rechs would have to show up at your front door before you'd get the green light to do anything.

But the Nether Ops agents on this station clearly had no idea that the ship now in their bay had once belonged to the notorious bounty hunter. Nor did they think anything of its being there for a newly slated delivery of supplies. Their only reaction seemed to be one of a general sense of excitement over having something new to do. It was quite apparent that these agents had been cooped up on the small station for some time; almost as soon as the cargo doors dropped, the two agents on hand to greet the crew pressed Honey relentlessly for news of the outside world and what she had seen working with other Nether stations.

Honey told them... something. How much of it was true was anyone's guess, but the men nodded eagerly and declared that they figured as much. Then they set to work helping Masters and Keel unload the *Crow* of its cargo—charge packs, ration packs, and medical supplies they'd procured thanks to an open purchase order courtesy of Dark Ops.

One of the Nether men hoisted up a crate of charge packs, to test their weight, and then set it back down deciding he could carry two.

"You sure you don't want to use a repulsor jack for that?" asked Honey, sounding duly impressed by the show of strength.

The man's voice seemed to drop an octave. "I'm sure. Nice to get a workout that doesn't involve the same old same old." He looked over at the Nubarian gunnery bot, which rolled back and forth at the far end of the cargo hold, chittering its disapproval at the Nether Ops agent in its digital language. From what Keel had gathered the bot was no fan of Nether Ops due to the repeated run-ins his old boss had had with them.

"Haven't seen a bot like that in a while," observed the agent.

Keel turned as if to see which bot the man was speaking about. "Yeah, well be careful. He bites."

At the bottom of the ramp, next to a growing stack of charge packs and cases of rations, Masters helped the Nether Ops agent set down his load before asking, "Hey, can I use the head? The fresher on our ship failed and I *really* don't want to smell that stink again if I can avoid it."

The man chuckled and pointed to a door at the end of the dock. "That's the fresher for anyone not stationed here."

"Thanks, boss." Masters turned and began to jog toward the door like someone fighting off an acute onset of the bubble guts.

Keel watched him go, unsure whether to be annoyed by this ad lib or impressed. He looked back to Honey. "How much you wanna bet he's just tryin' to get out of unloading?"

The Tennar crossed her tentacled arms and shrugged a shoulder. "Wouldn't put it past him." She turned to the man who'd brought down the two crates of charge packs as he returned with another armload. "Sorry about that. I'll have him work double to make up for it."

"It's really no problem," said the agent. "Our last interaction with anyone flesh and blood was four months ago. We get pretty tired of"—he grunted as he hoisted both of the crates into place on the deck—"of staring each other in the face, if you know what I mean. Kind of nice to have a change of scenery." He winked at Honey. "You in particular."

And there it is, thought Keel. The man had taken his shot. It was no surprise. Honey had been pumping her pheromones nonstop since the cargo bay doors had opened. The only surprising thing was how long it had taken for one of the agents to make a pass.

"I know *exactly* what you mean," Honey answered, her voice hovering between seduction and secrecy as she cast a glance quickly at Keel and then back to the agent. "You can get cooped up too long with some people. A girl gets tired of the same old thing. I don't like to be bored."

She spoke softly enough for Keel not to hear—a secret between her and the agent who had to be thinking that the shot he'd taken was close to going in.

But Keel knew what was happening even without hearing Honey's exact words. Unless of course the Tennar really had gone through all this trouble just to double-cross him here and now, which he doubted. And he liked his odds against the two agents and the unarmed Tennar if it came down to that. It didn't, and he followed through with the plan by calling to the agent.

"Hey, I wouldn't mind using a head that doesn't stink, too. I'm gonna go next unless someone has to go first."

Honey batted her long lashes and gave a fractional nod to the Nether Ops agent who had gotten himself trapped in her web. She was letting him know this was their opportunity if such an opportunity were ever to present itself.

"Don't mind at all," said the agent. "Looked like your friend was going to be a while, though." He turned to his compatriot. "Hey Ramstack, go and escort this fella to the crew fresher so he doesn't have to wait."

Ramstack scrutinized his fellow agent. "C'mon. You know the rules. He'll have to wait."

"I'm fine waiting," Keel said, and could see the frustration on the face of the man who wanted nothing more than to have Honey to himself in the privacy of the ship.

"We can do our guests better than that," the agent said, smiling at Honey and then nodding from his friend to the Tennar, who poured out more pheromones and lightly dragged her arm down her abdomen in full view of the other man. "Take the man to the crew fresher and then hurry back here. We're all on the same team."

Ramstack's eyes flashed wide, sensing the opportunity. He quickly nodded and then turned and motioned for Keel to follow. "C'mon. I'll show you the other fresher. It ain't far."

"I can wait for my buddy to finish," said Keel. "Don't wanna get you guys in any trouble. Don't wanna cost us any future contracts, either."

"It's no trouble," Ramstack insisted.

"You worry too much," Honey chided. "We won't lose any contracts, will we?"

The first agent shook his head.

Keel looked at Honey and the agent suspiciously.

"Turn around and go if you have to," she said.

Keel obeyed reluctantly, playing the role of a lover who knew his drug would never be as faithful to him as he wished her to be. He could see how effective an agent the Tennar must've been. She had two other Nether Ops agents, men who should know better than to be taking these risks, wrapped around her lithe tentacles. Unaware of how those same tentacles were tightening around their necks.

Assuming the rest of the plan came together, that was. And did so before Kill Team Victory hit its own target.

"Yeah," Keel said, sounding suspicious. "Sure."

He sounded like every jilted and helpless lover he'd ever heard get the brush-off by the girl he'd come to see in one of a thousand cantinas across the galaxy. The act seemed only to increase the desire in the other men. Ramstack was doing everything short of pulling Keel by the arm to get him to hurry up.

Keel walked after him and then broke from the path toward the fresher that Masters still occupied. "I'll just check on my buddy to make sure he's not almost done. No sense going into the station if he's just gonna come right out."

"Hey!" He knocked on the door, his escort hovering behind him. There was no answer, so he banged harder. "How much longer you gonna be in there, Simms?"

A voice said in mid-grunt, "Gonna be a bit."

Keel looked to Ramstack, who seemed relieved by this response. "Looks like he's going to be a while," the agent said quickly, as though he couldn't get the words out fast enough. "Come on."

All the guy wanted in the universe right then was to drop Keel off and make his way back to Honey.

They left the docking bay and entered the main station, taking a route that was almost identical to the one Keel had taken with Zora when they'd first tracked the Tennar down. Except this station was nowhere near as large and sprawling. As soon as they moved through the storeroom, they were at a checkpoint, and beyond that was the data center floor plan that Keel had expected to see. A single corridor with doors on either side and the storage servers at the end.

Ramstack pointed down the hall. "Fresher is the third door on the left. You see anyone, they won't expect you to be here, so don't act threatening. Anyone says anything just tell them to call me."

The man turned to leave.

"Hold on," said Keel. "What if they decide to shoot first? How many guys should I be looking out for? I think I can hold it if there's a chance I might get killed."

Ramstack halted and turned back around, bobbing up and down on the balls of his feet with impatience. "Only two guys. We're short-staffed, and trust me, they won't care that you're using the fresher. One's on rack ops and the other is in the control room, probably playing hologames. You'll be fine."

He turned to leave again.

"Wait," Keel called after him. "Sorry. You said fourth door on the right?"

The man stopped and turned around again with an almost pained look of exasperation. Keel knew he had to let him go after this. He didn't want the pheromones to wear off, it was a risk keeping him this much, but he still looked hooked for now, and the risk felt worth taking.

"No. That's the control center. Third door on the left. Left."

"Got it." Keel moved down the hallway to the appointed door.

Ramstack didn't bother to wait and see him to his destination. The man hurried down the hall toward what he imagined would be paradise, forgetting that death always came first.

12

Standing outside the fresher, Keel could hear that it was occupied. The loud suck of the waste being transported to the reprocessing station was followed by the rushing of water and a sonic dryer. The smuggler had never intended on going into the fresher and was only standing there until he could verify that his escort was truly gone. Now it seemed a new agent would be accompanying him, and he'd best ready himself for that encounter.

The door swished open, and the agent stepped out, looking up from his shoes to Keel. He opened his mouth in dumbfounded surprise, and his hand went immediately to the service pistol holstered at his side.

But Keel was already lunging forward. He grabbed the agent's wrist, pulled it away from the blaster, then threw forearm and elbow into the man's throat. The impact of the vicious strike, coupled with the hardness of the armor that remained unchecked beneath Keel's robe—a tattered faded spacer's cloak popular with freighter crew and jump jockeys who regularly worked in and around the Starriah Nebula—shattered the man's larynx.

The momentum of the blow resulted in Keel coming down on top of the man, driving his forearm still deeper into a purpling neck. The agent writhed on the floor, his boots kicking out and against the deck, blood pooling from the back of his head where it had slammed down hard. Keel kept his body weight behind the forearm and cut off whatever oxygen supply the agent might somehow be able to suck into his lungs, while gripping the man's gun hand in a fight to keep it away from the blaster pistol. It was strength against strength, and even without the surprise in the first blow Keel would have been the gambler's favorite. He easily had a twenty-pound advantage over the other man, and all of that muscle.

That was something Keel had found to be true of more than a fair share of agents and spies he'd come in contact with, whether in Nether Ops or some other Republic intelligence branch: their skill sets were considerable, but often their physical strength was limited by too much field work or a desire not to look out of place wherever they operated. They were rarely head-turners and were often forgettable from a physical standpoint. Certainly, they weren't up to Legion standards, even the best of them. Whereas Keel had never allowed himself to slip from being ready to don the armor should the need arise. That was a luxury he would never be able to afford.

The fight to the death was not much of a fight at all. The agent went quickly. Struggling against Keel's bulk in a frantic attempt to clear the blockage to his lungs, he allowed Keel to pin his arms beneath his knees and break the man's neck.

And that was that.

"One down," he mumbled to himself as he took the man's pistol and rose to his feet, his breathing only slightly heavier than it had been a moment before.

He straightened himself and examined the fresher mirror's reflection. He adjusted his hair not out of vanity but to avoid the look of exertion should another agent see him soon. The dead man he left lying on the floor. The fresher door attempted to close behind him but its two sides banged against the corpse's boot. Keel kicked the man's leg inside and the doors closed, hiding the evidence from sight.

Keel needed to move quickly. The team had planned a mission that relied on timing. They had comms, but the data center would have means of detecting that, if not decrypting it, and an unknown comm signal would be a glaring warning as much as a stray blaster bolt in a facility such as this.

Seven minutes. Masters was to wait seven minutes from the time he heard Keel bang on the door before leaving the fresher to dispatch the Nether Ops agents in the docking bay. That was the maximum amount of time they felt he could roost without drawing a forced visit and as much time as Keel would need to quietly secure his objective. Seven minutes... or in response to a comm directive from Keel, or at the sound of blaster fire, whichever came first. Then it would be up to Masters to complete the remainder of the mission. Unlike Keel, he had a blaster rifle hidden beneath his robe. Keel had expected to be searched before being let into the authorized-personnel-only portion of the station. That the guards hadn't bothered was a testimony to how thoroughly Honey had bewitched the first two agents.

Now, with the seconds going by, Keel needed to reach and eliminate the second agent. He moved down the corridor to the door to the control room, hoping that his man would be on duty there. There was always a chance that the man he'd just killed was the control room slicer, and that the other agent was somewhere else in the data center—and capable of putting up a better fight than the last. Regardless, he had to secure the control room. Whoever manned it could shut the station down and deny the team what they had come to collect.

The door was unmarked, but Keel was confident this was the spot due to the directions unwittingly given by Ramstack. It was also locked. No surprise there. Discipline might have been lax on the station, but rooms like this maintained their security automatically. A door like this one had two settings: locked and really locked.

The default was a simple auto-lock. If it were *really* locked, Keel would be hearing some commotion already.

A Dark Ops slicer box would be enough to get the door open, but not as fast as Keel would like. Faster than a cutting torch, yes, but long enough that whoever was on the other side would likely be alerted to the attempted breaching and take action. But Honey had provided him with an access key that she said would work—part of the top-down control that Nether Ops was known for. She had hard-coded the key into an octagonal feather chip that needed only to be affixed on top of the lock's bio-signature sensor to provide immediate access.

"As far as the system is concerned, someone who is absolutely *not* to be delayed is using that key," Honey had explained.

It was a feature Nether Ops had implemented in order to prevent directors and high-level agents from being shut out of secure or sensitive systems. One that had apparently become standard after a series of defections from Nether Ops that preceded the rise of the Black Fleet. To Keel it seemed like replacing one vulnerability with another, but at the moment he was thankful for it.

This was the next big test for Honey, and she passed with honors.

The door swung open and Keel sent a blaster bolt into the head of the Nether Ops agent controlling the station as the man turned in his chair to see who it was. The agent slid from his seat and crashed down dead on the deck.

Keel shoved his body aside with his boot and introduced a Dark Ops slicer package designed to take over the data center—so long as it wasn't already on alert. Nothing indicated that it was—all systems read normal to Keel's eyes. In fact, the active window told the story. The comms and control man he'd just killed had been watching the docking bay, as he should have been, but his attention had been on Honey, on whom he'd zoomed the holocams. The Tennar was now practically torturing the two men by painstakingly removing pieces of clothing. She was nearly out of things to take off.

The Dark Ops program interfaced with Keel's micro-comm and beeped to tell him that station control had been achieved. Keel wasted no time pinging Masters on his comm. "Command and control room secure. Two of four reported NO agents KIA. Two remain in bay. Execute. Execute. Execute."

Masters quietly exited from the fresher room, carbine in hand. Though the agents failed to notice him creeping behind them, Keel saw it all play out over the holocam feed.

The legionnaire positioned himself to cut them both down without having Honey or the ship behind the targets. With two precise blaster bolts he dropped them both. He then moved forward and put another bolt in each downed man's head.

"Targets eliminated," he reported in to Keel.

"Roger. Good kill. Proceed to my loc. Out."

Masters recovered his Legion bucket from a top-riding crate in the *Crow* while Honey quickly dressed herself, and then the pair hurried into the secure area to link up with Keel.

"Hope you recorded that," Masters said upon entering the command-and-control center. "I was damn impressive. Also, bit of tactical advice here, you should've waited to send me out until after Honey had run out of things to take off."

"Save it for the AAR," Keel said. "Cams aren't showing any other agents. Duty rosters verify four. Go watch the bay."

Masters nodded. "Roger. And just so you know, you're starting to sound like the old Captain Ford again. Keep this up and if you're lucky, Chhun might send you to hang out with those warrior poets like me. You can pass your time arguing about poetry and quoting historians on the range. It's great."

Keel just stared at the man. "Move already, Masters."

The legionnaire obeyed, and Honey finally gave her opinion on the operation. "That went well enough. I was about to kill those two Nether kelhorns myself if you had taken any longer, though."

"Guess things ramped up faster than we figured."

"You could say that," said Honey. "Did that Dark Ops program of yours work?"

"It certainly thinks so." Keel gestured to the holoscreen. "Doesn't look like there's a lot here, though."

"There isn't. Or at least, not what you're really looking for. This is all basic information. Surface-level items of the sort that the Legion was able to get from whatever was left on Utopion."

"Until Victory hits their primary target," said Keel.

"Exactly. How much time?"

Keel checked his chrono. "If they're on time—and they will be—they'll hit the target in the next thirty standard minutes."

The Nether Ops data system was an almost never-ending network of fail-safes and relays. A primary data center like the one Kill Team Victory identified as Ulterio would house a veritable treasure trove of classified Nether Ops intelligence. Should an outside force attempt to assault the center, the techs had orders to send a data packet containing a copy of the information over a secure burst to a pre-designated relay station. Each burst sent also deleted the data on the sender's end, leaving the assaulters with a dry hole.

That was a situation Dark Ops had run into multiple times already.

What Keel, Honey, and Masters had just done was something they wouldn't have known to do without the Tennar's guidance. They had just secured the relay station designated for receiving the data burst from Ulterio—and they had done it without alerting a living soul. No one would be the wiser for another four hours, when mandatory check-ins would be required. By then Kill Team Victory would have hit their target, recovered what they could, and left. And Keel was in place to receive all the information those Nether Ops agents on Ulterio thought they were depriving the Legion of.

"Thirty minutes," Honey repeated. "That's not too much time to kill, but I can think of a few things to do." She slid a tentacle over Keel's shoulder.

"Save it for Masters. He'll need a good sendoff. I didn't tell him, but he's going right back to his new pals with Kill Team Two once this operation is over."

"Guess all we can do is wait then," said Honey.

"Looks like it," said Keel. Tennar were known to be one of the more uninhibited species in the galaxy, but Honey's come-on was unexpected—and it made Keel wary of the agent even after she'd delivered such a big win for Dark Ops.

Could he ever trust her?

With a full index and copy of the entire data center, one for Dark Ops and one for himself, Keel departed the station aboard the *Obsidian Crow*. It wouldn't be long before the other Nether stations still out there realized what had happened, which meant parsing the data as quickly as possible was a crucial next step. As instructed, he sent Dark Ops's copy to a prearranged receiver, where Republic slicers and other techs could begin the work of decrypting and acting on whatever intelligence they could find before Nether Ops could slip the noose.

Keel was looking over his copy of the raw data, trying to make sense of it, when Honey returned to the cockpit.

"How's Masters?" Keel asked.

The Tennar slid her way around Death, Destroyer of Worlds, to sit in the co-pilot's chair.

"I'd say inconsolable," she answered, dropping into the seat. She looked at the little gunnery bot. "You take up a lot of space."

The bot chirped sarcastically back at her.

"What did it say?" Honey asked.

Keel couldn't hide the grin on his face. "Better you don't know."

Honey scowled at the bot and crossed her arm-like tentacles.

"What I hope you do know," Keel said, pointing at the encrypted mess on the display before him, "is how to read this gibberish."

"Sorry. Can't help you there."

Keel frowned. The time had come to reunite with Garret. The kid was probably sick worrying about him anyway. And he was the only slicer that Keel knew of who could decipher this packet reliably and quickly. Knew of and trusted.

"If that's the case," he said, "then we're going to have to figure out a plan for us all to link up with Nilo that doesn't involve Jack trying to kill you."

"Or you could just let me go. I'd like to think I've made up for whatever difficulties we had."

Perhaps she had, but Keel wouldn't hear of it. Not until more was sorted and he had a sense of what was going on.

"Sorry. For all I know this is just a list of every senator's preferred underwear size and color. I need to be sure that this is *useful* intel. Something about Kill Team Ice. Something that's gonna help me figure out what's going on and who was after me."

"I don't know what to tell you. Like I said in the briefing with your Dark Ops friends, there *will* be useful information. But Nether Ops doesn't lay all its eggs underneath one reef."

Keel raised an eyebrow. "That a Tennar expression?"

"It is."

"Look. I appreciate that you've helped me with this much. And if it comes down to it, I'll let you go and deal with Jack myself. But I'm not gonna do that until I can be sure that all these little tidbits you've given me about Kill

Team Ice, my past, General Rex, and all the rest aren't just a big ball of lies you're unraveling for me to follow so that you can save your neck for another day."

Honey shrugged. "We're at an impasse then. My help stops the moment we fly a course anywhere near that maniac. I thought we were developing rapport here, Captain Keel. I suppose I misjudged you."

The Nubarian bot trilled and beeped in Signica.

Honey looked at the stout little machine and then back to Keel. "He seems to take it personally when I don't speak glowingly of you. Nice to see loyalty still exists somewhere."

Keel's attention was fixed on the bot. "No, that's not it. He says he knows someone who can decipher Nether code for us."

Honey scoffed. "Really? This little tin can that spent who knows how long stuffed in a closet? I'd love to hear it."

"How 'bout it, pal?" Keel asked.

The bot chirped an answer. Honey could only understand one side of the conversation, which was how Keel liked it.

"Really?" said Keel. "Okay. We'll head there after we drop off Masters."

The legionnaire chose that moment to enter the cockpit. "Drop off Masters?" he said. "Sorry, buddy. Not happening. Masters is going AWOL. Masters... is going to become a soldier of fortune."

Keel looked from the bot to his friend. "*Masters* will get a dishonorable discharge at best if he does that. It's been a while since I sat on a review board, but if I had to guess, I'd say that'll probably ruin your plans of becoming a command sergeant major. Not to mention your future plans of getting into the holofilms."

Masters crashed into one of the empty chairs behind the pilot and co-pilot seats and leaned his head back against the headrest. "Sket. You're right. That would dust my career before it began. With the House of Reason gone there's just no credits to be made being a Legion reject anymore."

Honey looked Masters over. "*You* want to be an actor?" She turned back to face forward. "Well, you do have the look. And the body."

"I know," Masters said, still in misery. "I do have the look. And my body is amazing."

"It's not gonna be like that forever," said Keel, who was starting to feel genuinely bad for the kid. "Bear and Bassa said you'll be back with Victory in two months, tops."

Masters stared unblinking at the ceiling as though catatonic. "I hate my life."

Then he suddenly sprang forward, gripping the backs of Honey's and Keel's chairs and thrusting his head between them. "Seriously, if you think Bear's angry dad face is a perpetual killjoy, just watch all those Team Two leejes furrow their brows and cross their arms and look all disappointed just because I make a joke about how hot their wives are. They're not even that hot! I was being *polite* about how trashy they looked in their dresses. Also, what's the deal with all those guys even getting married?"

The little bot chirped again, seemingly eager to get the conversation back on the track it had started.

"What's he on about?" Masters asked.

"Helping me," said Keel. Turning to the bot he said, "Yes. We will. As soon as we deliver Masters we'll head back and go find this Fancy Pants you're talking about."

13

"This is embarrassing," Zora said, her arms crossed, her foot tapping, and her glare directed at Garret.

The code slicer had come to identify this pose as indicating one of her "angry times." Zora did it every time she was mad about something that was beyond her control, and right now what was beyond her control was Captain Keel's apparent inability to return any of her comm calls. That made her mad, which in turn made Garret feel uncomfortable.

He buried himself further into his slicing, hoping she would go away.

"You've been with him for a while, right, Garret?"

The code slicer looked up from his screens and swallowed. He would much rather be working. Mr. Nilo had given him an extremely nice terminal and carte blanche to look over the entire Black Leaf system. If it weren't for Zora's temper, Keel's absence, and melancholy thoughts about Leenah's fate, he would be enjoying himself because taking an inside look at *Arkaddy karking Nilo*'s systems was practically a dream come true.

"Dig around and tell me anything you find," Nilo had said upon hearing of Garret's prodigious skill set from Zora. And that was exactly what Garret had been doing. He'd found numerous redundancies that did little for the network beyond slowing it down or occasionally trapping a user in an endless cycle of futility, bouncing requests back and forth with seemingly no end. A similar problem had manifested itself in Black Leaf's proprietary comm system—which was no L-comm, because nothing was quite like the L-comm, but it was highly encrypted and reliable. Except when a comm signal got caught in a loop, going from one receptor to the next in a perpetual send mode that had no way of ever being received unless the transmission was ended and started again.

"That's it," Nilo had said when Garret excitedly pointed out the issue. "*That's* what was causing it. This is going to make a lot of the guys very happy, Garrick. I wonder why Briscoe never saw it. Really good work. You've got a gift."

"Thank you, Mr. Nilo," Garret had said sheepishly, too afraid to correct him for saying his name wrong. But somehow Nilo picked it up.

"It's not Garrick, is it?"

"Garret. Actually."

Nilo nodded. "I'll never get it wrong again, Garret. My apologies."

"Oh, no, it's fine, Mr. Nilo."

Nilo shook his head. "Not Mr. Nilo. Just Nilo. And thank *you*. Something like this would cost I don't know how many credits in an audit. And that's assuming someone would've even caught it. I'm not sure they would have."

"I don't think they would," the young code slicer said, excited to explain. "See, the reason why it was so hard to find is because the redundancy was really just kind of built on top of itself. So, it's like whatever AI was doing the coding just left a *theen* instead of a comment to mark where it replaced old code or fixed bad code and then it would grab the entirety of the code and run it in a separate program as a sort of callback for a new, clean version that fixed whatever bug it was trying to eliminate.

The problem," Garret continued breathlessly, "is that the *theen* would force certain aspects of the code to be referenced as a whole other program and so it would do a cross-reference which would check the same body of code so what would happen is a piece of that code would get referenced as a program and then that would repeat over and over and over again and since it's an AI that does your coding this would happen hundreds of thousands of times and so you would get an error and that error would be multiplied but you don't know how many *times* it's multiplied unless you look at each line of code and if you look at the size of the code it's like, 'What am I looking at?' because each one of these slice chains is complex and the fix is definitely a time saver over running the full system which would create lag except for how eventually it gets in this loop where the same little piece of bad code, which wasn't even bad code when it was first written but because it's calling and it's building on top of it, it kind of turns into bad code, anyway this bad code the AI just didn't notice because it was assuming that all the code it wrote prior was good and it never thought it could *become* bad because of mistaking a *theen* for a run cue, so yeah, it got overproduced and then interacted in a weird way and, uh... uh..."

Garret trailed off then, aware that he had gone into another one of his verbal spasms that caused people's eyes to glaze over and grow dull. Or prompt them to shout for him to stop talking. Except Mr. Nilo wasn't like that. He paid attention to every word, nodding his head knowingly.

"No, I'm following," the man said. "What you're saying makes perfect sense. Keep going."

And so Garret had, elated at the level of appreciation, not to mention understanding, being shown by this very rich and very important person. Garret was, in short, starstruck. He had known about Nilo even before the man started showing up on all the holonews channels to speak about the plight of the Kublar and their need for self-government free from the vestiges of the Republic and those on-planet entities that perpetuated a rule by the House of Reason under a different name.

So when he was given the green light, he had thrown himself into the work of looking at Black Leaf's systems with the same fervor he had undertaken in studying the armor of Tyrus Rechs. More than once he'd found himself wanting to tell Nilo about the armor, sure that it would interest the man. But the one time he came close to actually bringing the subject up, Zora was in the room, and she flashed a threatening look that told Garret what trouble lay in store for him if he didn't shut up.

Though she worked for Nilo, it seemed that there was only so much Zora was willing to let out in the open when it came to Keel. That level of loyalty to the captain was something that Garret hadn't seen before.

"Hey," Zora said, breaking the code slicer from his daydreaming. "Comm relay to Garret. You receiving?"

"Oh. Sorry. Yeah... I... Sorry. Just lost in thought about this weird partition I'm seeing connected to the comm systems. Well, it's not really a partition it's more of a—"

"No." Zora sounded like she was correcting a family pet. "Do not hijack my question with your technobabble."

"Sorry. I know. Sorry. Um... What was your question?"

Zora gave an exaggerated sigh. "Keel. You've been with him more recently than I have, and maybe longer than I was, too. So what gives? Why isn't he answering my comm calls?"

"You don't think something happened to him?" said Garret, suddenly concerned over the fate of his friend.

Zora looked down and pinched her eyebrow. "No. I don't think anything happened to him. I just want to know why he isn't here like he's supposed to be."

"Oh. Yeah. Well, I'm sure he has a good reason. It's always a good reason."

Zora walked over to Garret's workstation and leaned her hip against the terminal. The code slicer stared at the woman's thigh and posterior now touching his workspace as though it were some infectious substance, but he lacked the courage to shoo her away or tell her that she'd almost sat on a control wand he had open. That could cause some damage. Garret knew a slicer who'd sat down on the open control wand of his datapad and ended up completely wiping about two years of solid work. Even managed to delete the backups.

"Well, his *good reason* is costing me my good reputation in Black Leaf," Zora said.

"I don't know. Mr. Nilo seems fine."

"It's not Nilo. It's never Nilo. It's that ball-buster Surber. I've started avoiding him as much as possible, which isn't easy on a ship this size. Trust me, Garret, there are some big plans that Nilo has in mind that Surber is supposed to make happen, and the only thing holding them up is our mutual friend."

"But you think the captain is fine. You said so. He's okay."

"'Zora,'" she said, ignoring the code slicer while doing an impression of Surber. "'Past time for your friend Wraith to be with us, isn't it? I am beginning to wonder whether you took a payment for a job not done. That would be a foolish thing to have done, Zora my dear.'"

"Yeah, that sounds bad," said Garret. "Kind of threatening."

"It's all threats with Surber."

"Do you want me to try to track him down?"

"Can you?"

"I, uh..."

"Something in the armor maybe?"

"No, nothing like that in the armor," Garret said sheepishly. "Or... anything else, really. Sorry."

"Great. Thanks for the help, Garret, and I know that makes me sound like a harpy, but I am just really frustrated. I gotta go."

Zora moved to the door.

"Go where?"

"To see Jack."

Garret waited for the door to swish closed behind her before mumbling, "Not sure if Captain Keel'll like that."

But then he thought, *Good*. He wasn't crazy about the sexual tension he'd seen between the two to begin with. Or at least, he was pretty sure that was what it was. He'd watched enough holofilms to have a basic idea of how these things worked. Romance had a way of creeping into even the best shows.

He returned to work at his terminal, swiping and tapping furiously and coordinating various programs to perform tasks the way a squad leader might move the legionnaires under his command to flank an enemy.

"Okay," he said. "Let's see if we can find out anything more about this 'Sarai' partition."

He sought his way in but found his every attempt denied. And not in the way he might've expected of a security program trying to keep him from gaining access. It was more like a game. He would seek access, be prompted with easy enough authentication requests, and then, once he'd answered, find that everything he'd wanted was now somewhere else. But not invisible. Still waiting for him—but now with new authentication requests.

It was odd. Perhaps another glitch in the system. He would mention it to Mr. Nilo the next time they talked.

Garret pushed himself away from the terminal and thought about what Zora had said. Captain Keel would be all right. Right? He was just busy. He'd be okay. Why wouldn't he be?

The concern stirred something inside of him. He went back to the terminal and opened a new window, accessing his own data farm now that he had a full range of connection again. His eyes went wide as he counted the number of cache receptors and locators.

"Oba," he whispered softly and then jumped up and repeated the word, shouting it at the top of his lungs.

"Zora!" he screamed into the comm.

"What are you yelling about, Garret? I'm—"

"I need your help!"

"Why? What's going on?"

"I found her! Zora, she's alive!"

14

Politics had never been on Asa Berlin's mind as she grew up among the evergreens and mountains of Spilursa. Her family history very much had been. Her uncle had died in the Psydon War long before she was born, and yet she felt as though she'd known him all the same. His exploits in volunteering for the most dangerous of all combat branches—the Legion—combined with his contribution to winning the war and the sacrifice that earned him the Order of the Centurion, were a pillar of the Berlin family story. More even than the hard work of those who came before—those who built for themselves a shipping empire from a single, secondhand Marth freight jumper.

It wasn't politics that had forged Asa's path in the galaxy. It was what her uncle and those who served with him had given up their lives for.

She had been privileged to be granted an internship on Utopion with Spilursa's planetary senator. But it was there that she saw the corruption that smoldered inside the Republic, making it a burnt husk. Utopion, though dazzling, was a den of the worst kind of greed and filth. The ideals of her uncle and the men he'd led in combat were no longer shared by the government that had sent them. She'd heard as much directly from General Washam, who had happily received her and taken her to the top-floor restaurant on the Macross Spire.

Washam's advice had been to do something about what she saw. To replace those who used the Republic for their own gain—and then be sure to not fall prey to the same temptation herself.

Simple as that.

And so, when Asa Berlin returned to Spilursa, she spoke out about what she'd witnessed. And because she was a Berlin, the people of that planet paid attention. The Berlins, like the Washam family, were akin to royalty on the core world. And yet neither tribe had ever participated in politics. The Washams steadfastly refused to even comment on political matters, much less pick a side; they were content to be friends to all and maintain their influence no matter what. The Berlins had made a few public donations, but no one had actively used their platform to address the need for change on Utopion.

Until now.

Asa's message proved powerful. As one of the primary core worlds, Spilursa had always taken pride in its role in the shaping of the galaxy. It was Spilursan Rangers who had fought at the head of the coalition forces throughout the Savage Wars. If you were to ask Spilursa's citizens about the Legion, the organization that had *won* the Savage Wars, they would tell you that it was merely a hardcore offshoot of the Spilursan Rangers. And now, once again, Spilursans felt the weight of responsibility. That things weren't going swimmingly in the galaxy was hardly a secret—and Spilursa had a role in that, too.

The planet, like all the core worlds and many if not most of the mid-core worlds, benefited from the galactic opulence the Republic provided. But that came with a price. Corruption. Exploitation. And a galling and ever-increasing lack of freedom and liberty. Foundational rights which, prior to Article Nineteen, were viewed as too dangerous, too unsafe, and too old-fashioned to be pursued. Rights upon which the Republic was founded. *Bedrock* rights chiseled away in the name of safety... but, as Asa explained, eroded in reality because doing so gave those on Utopion the power to feast on the rest of the galaxy unchecked.

Asa proposed returning to a simple, liberty-protecting Republic by removing the overwhelming centralized power by which the House of Reason was able to dictate how planet after planet should live, whether they were part of the Republic or not. She prophesied a future dedicated to self-rule, one in which the oligarchy and galactic elites would speak to how others should live only on the planets and sectors where they themselves lived. No more making unilateral decisions that would affect the everyday lives of countless humanoids across the galaxy—without consultation or consideration.

This was the kind of message that fomented uprisings on edge worlds. It was the message that had made the Mid-Core Rebellion become a populist cause despite the base and nefarious goals of those who began it.

And even on Spilursa, the message had power.

Asa Berlin became someone her fellow citizens looked to. Someone on whom they pinned their hopes of restoring the Republic to its former glory. Exploratory teams were formed to determine her chances of winning a galactic election. A spot in the House of Reason was out of the question, even for Berlin. That body and its galactic sectors were designed specifically to ensure that power was perpetually kept in the hands of those who already wielded it. But the Senate was different. Each planet belonging to the Republic sent two Senators to Utopion, some by a popular vote, others by appointment of their rulers. And enough like-minded Senators could form the sort of bloc needed to check the House of Reason, which had for so long run unopposed that they no longer saw opposition as anything but something to be sneered at and squelched.

The exploratory committee found that Asa Berlin's chance to become a senator was as good now as it likely ever would be. The planet's senior senator had already declared that this term would be his last, and the junior senator, while not seeing eye-to-eye with Asa, agreed to refrain from directly opposing her, for fear that doing so might interfere with his pursuit of the coveted role of senior senator. He was what the people of Spilursa called a *cooma*, after a planetary reptile known for its ability to change its shape and color in order to perfectly blend in with its surrounding environment.

The Berlin campaign began with a massive rally and was soon buoyed by a groundswell of support from every corner, race, species, and class found on the planet. Asa spoke at amphitheaters filled to capacity, with thousands more standing outside just to be near the event, watching holographic projections on multiple stages set up in the grand commons. Asa's campaign generated a fervor of political excitement not seen since Washam returned to the planet a hero with rumors that he might choose to leave the Legion for the House of Reason.

Support grew. Polls predicted a landslide victory. Even when senior House of Reason Delegate Orrin Kaar, whose domain included Spilursa, came to stump on behalf of her opponent, the polls shifted no more than a point or two before snapping back to the twenty-point lead she had enjoyed prior to his visit.

And then it all changed.

The retiring senior senator held a surprise press conference in which he announced that he still had one more go-round left in him. In so doing, he began barking and clamoring for the very change that he had consistently eschewed over the extent of his long political career. He took Berlin's most popular positions as his own and asserted that a vote for him would give the people two things: the objectives that Asa Berlin had so insightfully championed... and someone who knew their way around Utopion and could make those objectives a reality.

The result was a siphoning of those who supported Berlin, and a tightening race.

Still, Berlin showed as the favorite.

And then the game changed again. Berlin's original opponent dropped out of the race and encouraged his followers to see that "the great giant of the senate, whom we would all do well to have represent us one last time" be elected again. Never mind that he had rallied against Berlin and called her assertions about Utopion absurd, as did Orrin Kaar, who appeared a *second* time, this time to support the old senator with the claim that "*Real* change will be accomplished with the return of my dear friend from Spilursa."

The gap shrank to a two-point Berlin lead. Within the margin of error.

Political junkies declared it a tossup in the final week of the election, and then, for the first time, began to predict a Berlin loss.

In an election with a record turnout, Berlin was defeated. She accepted her defeat gracefully even as her most ardent supporters questioned the whole process, seeing it as a rotten-to-the-core collaboration designed to preserve the Utopion status quo.

Thoughts shifted to "next time," then shifted again when the Legion initiated Article Nineteen. Both shifts paled in comparison to the sea change that was introduced by the inexplicable, inexcusable installation of an emperor named Goth Sullus.

In the end, the battered Legion fought a dying republic-turned-empire at the very gates of its power. By then the mismanagement of the Republic was visible for all to see, vindicating Berlin. But there was no opportunity to gloat—before the battle could be completed a mysterious alien race known as the Cybar nearly accomplished what even the Savages had failed to achieve.

It was said by loyalists to the House of Reason that only the installation of Goth Sullus as emperor had saved the Republic from complete destruction. They insisted that all would go back to normal once the traitorous Legion was dealt with. Goth Sullus would gladly give back his crown once stability had been achieved. Hadn't the galaxy already moved in that direction? The long-standing dispute with the MCR had been resolved. Peace with the zhee was cemented. If this was not the *Pax Galactic* the House of Reason had long been working toward, what else was it?

What remained of the pitiful Legion couldn't be trusted, the loyalists said. Its constant talk of the so-called corruption of men like Orrin Kaar, its conspiratorial whispers about deep state shadow organizations, its absurd claims that the Republic lied about the strength of its fleet... that was all just propaganda. The desperate efforts of power-hungry military warlords who had instituted Article Nineteen for their own benefit.

Of course, those loyalists' declarations or predictions never came about. Democracy was not restored. The Republic's emperor consolidated his power by murdering nearly all of the House of Reason delegates, much of the Senate, and any who questioned him within his own military. The terror would surely have continued had he not been put down by the Legion, the only force that was willing to fight to the last. The same now as they had been in the Savage Wars.

People realized it as though waking from a dream. The people of Spilursa would nod at each other and say, "Legion got its start as Spilursan Rangers, you know."

"I know it. Got a cousin in the Legion who got discharged and went back in to fight at Utopion. That's the Spilursan way."

It *was* the Spilursan way, though the planet followed that old path with tentative steps at the beginning. It was Sinasia that blazed the trail in standing up to Goth Sullus, but Spilursa was the first core world to do the same. When the cost of resisting the mad emperor and his machines of power was still unknown, and the worst had to be assumed.

And yet, somehow, the best had happened. Article Nineteen was executed to completion, and the Republic set out to make itself right again. The crown held by Goth Sullus had been returned by the Legion to the hands of the people, where it belonged.

And Asa Berlin found herself in another election.

This time, she won.

And today, in the Republic's new capital, nestled among the inspiring peaks and raw natural beauty of Spilursa's primary continental divide, she sat where

Delegate Kaar himself had once presided over the House of Reason.

Only this was no longer the House of Reason. It was, once again, a House of Liberty. It was from here that Asa Berlin would see to it that the Republic returned to its dogged pursuit of its high and lofty ideals. She would do everything she could to make sure it never backslid, never metastasized the way it had after the Savage Wars.

Never again.

15

Zora's hunt for Nilo didn't take long. Though his personal yacht was enormous, it was still considerably smaller than a typical cargo freighter, and it certainly wasn't a Galaxy-class or Republic destroyer, the kind requiring a massive system of speedlifts or personnel movers to get around.

She found him in the ship's parlor, sitting in a chair and illuminated by holocam lighting as he awaited an interview by an attractive human female reporter whose holographic presence was projected into a chair opposite him.

Two guards, Surber's men, stopped Zora at the door.

"Nope," growled the first as the second moved to close the old-style hinged double entryway. "Turn yourself right around and come back another time."

Not what Zora wanted to hear, but probably a considerably friendlier greeting than someone other than her might have received. Nilo had made it clear that Zora, Jack, and Garret were to be treated as his personal guests aboard his yacht, and that they were supposed to be allowed to see him at their request. But evidently that didn't include the times he was set to be interviewed by one of the major news holonetworks.

She was about to turn around and wait outside the parlor for the interview to finish when Nilo spotted her out of the corner of his eye and motioned for her to come over.

"Interview doesn't start for a couple of minutes, Zora," he called out, forcing the guard to reopen the door he had almost gotten closed. "What's up?"

The importance of Wraith to whatever Nilo had planned was obvious. Zora was a capable bounty hunter, but hardly notorious. She was simply one of the many industrious hunters who worked hard, collected their bounties, and were content with their names never being known beyond their fellow guild members and the scum sacks who learned to fear them. So, for Nilo to be so generous with his time, with someone like Zora, was telling.

And yet his effusive personality was disarming. In his presence, Zora felt as though she had known him for much longer than she had. He possessed the ability to make anyone around him feel as though they were not only his best friend, but the most important person in his life. Zora could see how such a skill would be indispensable in the world of business.

Nilo held up a finger to the reporter and excused himself, then beckoned again for Zora to come near. He said something Zora couldn't hear and winked at the reporter, who blushed despite being who knew how many light years from the room itself.

Zora bent down at Nilo's side, ready to speak softly in his ear, but Nilo uttered a guess before she could speak.

"News about our friend?"

"Of a sort," said Zora. "Garret found a distress signal for his old ship. Very important to him because it means a crewmate is alive. She's also very important to Wraith."

Nilo leaned over in his chair until he was just a few inches from her face. Zora had to force herself not to move her head back. He spoke so softly, she imagined that she wouldn't be able to hear him if she did.

"This is the ship Garret said was destroyed over Rakka, right?"

A producer communicated that they would be live in forty-five seconds. Zora could feel the time counting down before the interview needed to start. She didn't imagine that was something Nilo would put on hold just for her.

"Yes, that's the one," she said. "It looks now like it made the jump and is sending out a distress signal. It wasn't doing that at first, so Garret thinks that indicates the crewmember is still alive. I think if we can get either her or the ship, and then get that message to Wraith, it will cause him to speed up whatever he's doing and get him here all the sooner."

"Thirty seconds," announced the producer, unseen and speaking through a remote speaker.

Nilo nodded to the reporter to acknowledge he'd heard the message, then turned back to Zora. "Whether it will help get him here sooner isn't really the point. If there's a chance to save this friend of Garret's, we need to take it. As soon as the interview's over let's get on top of this."

Zora thanked Nilo, then stepped back and out of view of the holocams. She was amazed at the way this powerful man with plans larger than anyone she'd ever met was so willing to put everything on hold for something most of the galaxy would simply shrug at as life playing itself out. Spacers died all the time out there in the dark, and the losses rarely brought tears.

The unseen producer counted down; his words synced to a holographic countdown displayed behind the reporter's head as the cams focused on Nilo. "Five... four... three..."

The final count was silent, and then the holographic numbers disappeared and the cam light on the newswoman went green.

She smiled. "Thank you, Nickelldo. I'm sitting here live with Arkaddy Nilo, who is in the galactic spotlight thanks to his role in helping Kublar obtain its independence after a brief but bloody war against the Republic remnants of the House of Reason and the native zhee. Mr. Nilo, how are you today?"

"I'm fine, Murkia, but I want to point out right away that when you say the 'native zhee,' you are creating a narrative that is not the truth. A narrative that deviates significantly from the reality of the situation."

The newswoman gave a tight smile. The interview was already not going as she planned. She decided to push back. "The zhee populations on Kublar have been there for several years."

"They have, but it's important that we step back and consider how that situation came about. The zhee were given free rein to colonize Kublar as part of a backroom deal, arranged by the House of Reason and signed off on by senators who had been bought and paid for. This agreement was made without consultation with the native Kublarens, nor any consideration as to what those Kublarens wanted for their planet."

"Okay, this is not what I planned on speaking to you about, but let's explore that."

"I'd love to, Murkia."

"The image you're painting is different from the Republic's version of events, different from what our correspondents have reported as eyewitnesses. The introduction of zhee colonists was widely received by the Kublarens as a *welcome* step on a Republic world whose population density left room for these new colonies. Moreover, the agreement was necessary to the survival of the zhee, a species that has had difficulty finding worlds willing to let them stay there."

"The zhee have difficulty finding worlds willing to allow colonization because nobody wants to fall asleep at night with the fear that their new neighbors are going to slit their throats."

The reporter stiffened at this shocking deviation from acceptable discourse.

"Every world that the zhee have been allowed to colonize," Nilo continued, "has either broken down into a civil war that ultimately required the intervention of the Legion to resolve, or it has simply faded into one of the many zhee protectorate worlds. And let us not pretend that the *survival* of the zhee is in any danger whatsoever. That species not only has a home world, it has four of them—in addition to nearly four dozen additional worlds it claims ownership over, simply because it has established colonies on them. Kublar was one of those worlds, and it is unsurprising that the natives of Kublar were unwilling to live under such an oppressive regime."

The reporter refused to budge from her narrative. "Then why did the Kublaren government welcome them? Why would the House of Reason have allowed such a situation to take place?"

"The House of Reason no longer exists, and I know you're being told to push back on me, so I'll remind your producer that he has no duty to protect his puppet master any longer."

The reporter bristled. "Gone or not, why would the House and the Kublarens have allowed something like this, if your claims are to be believed?"

"We are discovering more and more the kind of corruption that was unfortunately quite common within the

House of Reason. The House of *Liberty* and its investigative tribunals are uncovering a very clear, if troubling, truth. What the people of this galaxy were presented by the House of Reason, and by far too many of the planetary senators—and, frankly, by the media—is a very far cry from the reality of the situation. Acknowledging this is a necessary step if this galaxy is to move forward.

"You asked me why the Kublarens allowed the zhee to colonize in the first place. They didn't. One specific Kublaren tribe, who was in power only because the Republic tilted the scales in its favor when it saw that they were malleable and would do as they were told, agreed to whatever the House of Reason demanded. That tribe has since been extinguished by its fellow Kublarens, according to their custom, an act which would have been performed by the other tribes much sooner had it not been for the threat of force by the House of Reason. Though they despised what was happening on their world, they were in no hurry to face down the entire Legion."

The news reporter smiled uncomfortably. Either she, or as Nilo suggested, her producer, seemed intent on carrying on the old party line put forth by the House of Reason even after the House of Reason itself was gone.

"I actually do want your thoughts on the Legion shortly," she said, "but first, this misguided characterization of the zhee you're advancing is one that many in the galaxy have been trying to shed for some years. They are not a violent, expansionist species."

"The characterization is not misguided. They are precisely that."

"Certainly not all of them."

"The ones that aren't are ceremoniously cut into pieces if male and sold into slavery if female."

That the interview wasn't already over at this point was a testament to how much this particular holonetwork wanted Nilo on its programming.

"If this is all as you say," said the reporter, "for argument's sake, to what end? What is the motivation behind the House of Reason foisting such a situation upon its own citizens?"

Nilo smiled his disarming smile and wagged his finger at the reporter in approval. "That's the kind of question a good reporter asks. Quite frankly, the zhee are good at what they do, which is killing. They're not the Legion, but no one is. Still, as a militaristic species—and I know how much the academics hate that classification, but it's the truth, some species evolved to be conquerors, humans included—and as a militaristic species, the zhee are unrivaled in the galaxy."

"It seems you're making an exception for humans if your criticism focuses on the zhee. You've just acknowledged that both are conqueror species."

"Forgive me; allow me to clarify. Humans may have evolved to be conquerors—individually—but we lack the unity required to be a true conquering *species*. We are fighters, but ultimately very tribal. The Republic is as close as we'll ever come to a unified human hegemony. Human expansion isn't a result of centralized intent but emerges piece by piece from separate power brokers. Honestly, the zhee might well have conquered humans by now if not for our resilience and our ability to reproduce so successfully. There is no question that the zhee represented the greatest non-human military species in the galaxy… that is, until the Kublarens banded together."

"Some in the galaxy will have great difficulty accepting the truth of what you're saying."

"That's because the galaxy isn't allowed to hear from species like the Kublarens. They're told what the Kublarens think by others who mostly get it wrong—but that's precisely as the House of Reason wanted it. They knew the day was coming when the Legion would institute Article Nineteen, and the zhee were a hedge against their own downfall. One of many."

The reporter shifted her questioning. "Are you suggesting that the House of Reason was appeasing the zhee in return for their military cooperation?"

"I think history will find that it's not just a suggestion; it will go down in the record as fact. A cursory look at House of Reason appropriations and gifts to various zhee warlords shows as much—weapons and equipment given so that zhee warriors could fight against their oppressors, who always happened to be the enemies of the House of Reason."

The reporter could have pointed out at this point the record of zhee terrorist attacks against the Republic itself. But she remained silent and attempted to move the interview to its original purpose.

"An interesting perspective. Now, I wanted to ask—"

"Ask yourself this, Murkia. All the planets forced to accept new zhee colonies, where were they?"

The reporter shook her head. "I'm not sure I—"

"I can tell you where they weren't. They weren't anywhere near the core. Nor were they on the mid-core planets that stood shoulder to shoulder with the galaxy's glittering jewels. They were planets at galaxy's edge, and planets drifting between edge and mid-core. Planets that were run by corrupt and craven politicians who favored a centralized galactic government that kept them in power, rather than face the responsibility of being beholden to their own people."

The reporter changed subjects. "If you would, I'd like to move on to the situation on Kima. Delegate Berlin has acknowledged Kima's vote to return to the Republic, and the House of Liberty and Senate are expected to make that reunion official."

The Kimbrin had declared their independence from the Republic following the installation of Goth Sullus, even while the Mid-Core Rebellion, which Kima had fostered, continued their alliance with the new emperor.

The reporter continued. "Some polls suggest that as much as forty percent of the planet's population stands opposed to resuming Kima's membership in the Republic, though most hover somewhere around twenty-five percent. Dissenters are saying they will actively interfere with any Kimbrin plans to rejoin the Republic." She looked thoughtfully at Nilo. "With regard to those dissenters: Should they feel empowered to follow the lead of the Kublarens? Should they reach out to Black Leaf in an effort to assert their own independence?"

Nilo smiled at the question and shook his head. "Not at all. The Kublarens were in a unique situation in that they were an edge world and therefore not subject to the Mercantile and Mercenary Restriction Laws. Kima, meanwhile, is a mid-core world, so even if they reached out and wanted Black Leaf's help, and we wanted to help—and neither of these is the case—it would be an illegal action. Secondly, over *ninety-five percent* of all Kublarens rejected their government, the oppressive presence of the zhee, and the House of Reason loyalists who manipulated an entire planet for their own personal gain. These are two completely different situations."

"Do you support a military solution to the promised difficulties on Kima?"

"I have no say in the matter beyond not wanting the Kimbrin to suffer any further catastrophes of war. The Kimbrin people have not asked me for my opinion, and I am not interested in giving unsolicited advice as to how a planet and its people should govern themselves. I think the galaxy would be a better place if more thought likewise." Nilo paused. "You're not Endurian, but you grew up on Enduran, right?"

The reporter seemed taken aback. "You've done your homework on me."

"You have a fascinating story."

The reporter blushed.

"The planet you grew up on," Nilo continued, "was so frustrated by the interference of the Republic—for reasons that we don't have time to get in to but which you well know—that when the MCR came, it saw its ranks swell by the tens of thousands from the many willing volunteers on that world. And Enduran was hardly the only planet to respond so favorably. What we in the galaxy have to ask ourselves is, 'Why that was the case?'"

"Why was that the case?" asked the newswoman. "Last question, I promise."

Nilo's eyes twinkled. "I'm glad you asked. The House of Reason and the Republic as a whole were playing a game that they had fixed a long time ago. Dating back to the aftermath of the Psydon War—though in reality its roots can be traced all the way back to the end of the Savage Wars.

"This system that they created was designed for one purpose: and that was to enrich those in power while keeping them in power. We've already seen chilling cases of deep-state government operations, executed by the organization known as Nether Ops, designed to eliminate those who sought to disrupt the House of Reason's perversion of our Constitution. These perversions included fraudulent elections, graft and bribery, rampant nepotism, and a military complex with little concern for the lives of the citizens it was supposed to protect. One need look no further than the generational punishments bestowed on the Sinasian worlds. I believe we will find even worse things as more is uncovered."

"It's hard to believe all this happened with no one the wiser," said the newswoman. She wasn't challenging, and Zora marveled at the change in her tone. Surely the producer who had instructed her to engage in verbal jousting with Nilo would not now suddenly have had such a drastic change of heart. This had to be coming from the reporter directly. Zora couldn't help but wonder if any of this was even reaching the viewers anymore—though the holocam lights remained green.

Nilo nodded in agreement. "The Republic was always very good at shining lights on situations where things went right. The fight against the MCR was a perfect example of this. We all watched as peaceful Republic citizens, on worlds like Rhysis Wan, were ravaged by factions of the Mid-Core Rebellion. Power-hungry warlords willing to kill whoever stood before them only to enrich themselves, not caring about the cost in blood so long as they were better off for it. But what we didn't see, because they never showed us, was what happened everywhere else. Where it was the Republic itself preying on those innocent civilians. I'm sad to say this happened far more often than the other.

"We didn't see the story of worlds like Gestor, saddled with unbearable debt by corporate interests backed and owned by the delegates and senators. And when the Gestori quite rightly sought to throw off those shackles, they were beaten down by the most powerful military in the galaxy.

"Please understand, I don't blame the Legion for performing its duty. It is full of capable and honorable soldiers. We owe the Legion, particularly former Legion Commander Chhun, for their role in bringing down a corrupt government and a power-mad emperor. But the uncomfortable truth is that for far too long the Legion was deployed, unwittingly, not to protect the galaxy, but to *oppress* the galaxy.

"That's as uncomfortable to say as it is to hear, but anyone who has spent time outside of the core and its sanitized version of reality knows exactly what I'm talking about. I am hopeful that with the new leadership we're seeing in the House of Liberty, and with the reorganization of the Legion and its rededication to serving its initial purpose—which is to be a force capable of standing up to any threat—that we will all be able to move forward in a more peaceful and free direction. Together."

The reporter sat silently for a moment, hanging on Nilo's words. When her professionalism caught up to her admiration, she grabbed control of the interview again. "Arkaddy Nilo, thank you very much."

"Thank you."

"…and we're clear!" shouted the virtual producer.

The holographic reporter thanked Nilo again, then disappeared from the chair.

Nilo unbuttoned his suit jacket and moved out of hearing of the holonetwork's micro-comm. He immediately looked around for Zora, and finding her said, "Okay! Let's get this done."

16

The task force that left to rescue Leenah was small, a precondition of the need to get to her quickly. Nilo, who had men and other resources at his fingertips as well as no shortage of things to do, could have merely launched Zora's ship, *Clara's Gift*, from the docking bay of his super-yacht. But that ship wasn't nearly as fast as his own. And since time was of the essence, according to Garret, who had finished a number of calculations and other scenarios meant to determine how long Leenah could survive depending on whether she had been trapped in the cockpit or some other area of the ship, Nilo didn't hesitate to jump his yacht toward the beacon's coordinates.

Traveling to those nav coordinates wouldn't be a quick trip, which left the crew to pass the time however they saw fit. Zora and Jack casually went over an optimal plan of rescue. Surber, who was put off by the mission and declared it to be "an unfortunate distraction from the real business at hand," nevertheless made sure his two personal guards were prepared to help as needed. And Nilo spent his time chatting with Garret.

The code slicer was apprehensive. Nilo could see that right away. He found that he could calm Garret's nerves by speaking to him about his survival scenario—or rather, the underlying equations. Talking coding and other technical subjects also helped. After they had discussed the predictive models Garret had swiftly put together to determine oxygen levels available on a Naseen light freighter, the young code slicer, whom Nilo thought of as much like himself just a few years prior, was much more relaxed.

"Your hands aren't shaking anymore," Nilo observed. "You can probably get back on it if you want."

Garret had been forced to stop his work because of his anxiety. He hadn't been afraid, only anxious to the point that he could barely control the tremors in his hands. He'd described it as his fingers wanting to waggle without his input or consent.

"Oh," Garret said with a self-conscious laugh. "Yeah. Guess I forgot about it while we were talking."

"Did you forget about her? Leenah?"

The young code slicer shook his head. "Not for a second."

"I didn't think so. Which means you didn't stop shaking because you forgot; she was still on your mind. What you did was give your mind something else to focus on beyond the worry. Talking about code slicing, even thinking about it, is what helped me get through my own troubles."

Garret thought about this. "Yeah. That makes a lot of sense. A lot of times when I get worked up it's like I can't do anything. And something has to pull me out of it, get me working on something else, before I feel like I'm back to normal."

Nilo gave an understanding nod. "I was the same way when I was your age. Which wasn't that long ago. The trick that worked for me whenever I got paralyzed—because I was thinking about people that I loved, what happened to them, what else I could have done, what I still could do, et cetera—was to just pick a random problem and start thinking about it instead. It didn't need to have anything to do with who or what I was worried about; in fact it was sometimes better if it didn't. It just had to be a problem. How do I fix this? How do I improve on that? What have I tried that hasn't worked? What else could I try that might work better?"

Garret let out a breath. "I'm still worried about her."

"Don't give up hope. We both know what your models said and what they don't say—and Garret, they don't say there's no chance."

"*Practically* they do."

Garret's initial enthusiasm at the signal from his friend had nose-dived when he considered the sort of damage to all systems that would have been required to even temporarily shut off the beacons and other homing devices on board the ship. His mood cratered further after considering the likely life-support conditions aboard the ship in the extensive time that had passed since the *Indelible VI* was ambushed above Rakka. It was a race against the clock, and despite his models, Garret simply couldn't calculate how much time or oxygen Leenah had left. He didn't have enough information. He knew only that he had to hurry. And the distance Nilo's super-yacht was now traversing was so vast, even faster-than-light travel felt too slow.

His hands started trembling and shaking and finger-dancing again. He dropped them into his lap and clasped them together tightly in the hope that Nilo, whom he liked very much, wouldn't notice and think less of him.

"Did you find anything else that might require my closer attention?" Nilo asked. "About the Black Leaf systems, I mean."

Garret shook his head. "Not really. I didn't really get that far before I discovered what happened to Leenah. No, wait—I did find something. Or didn't. Which is the thing. You gave me full access, right?"

"Full access," Nilo confirmed.

"Yeah. So that's weird then. I was trying to get into the system, and it was like, not happening. Every time I tried to dig my way in it would give me challenges and security codes, which that's not uncommon, your system has a lot of those protections, I get that, but when I answered them correctly or provided the right clearance key I would get in, except it was like everything was gone, then I found out it had just moved to a different spot so then I go there and it was just repeat the process, like the system was playing with me."

Garret looked up upon taking a breath and saw that Nilo had a slight smile on his face.

"What was the system you were trying to access?" Nilo asked.

"Something called *Sarai*."

The smile on Nilo's face grew larger. "That makes sense. I thought so, but you had me worried for a minute there. What you're describing sounds a lot like a worm I had designed a long time ago. I was worried this was the galaxy paying me back for being such a little sket when I coded that thing."

Garret, who had made his own share of worms that caused other people grief, asked, "Are you saying Sarai is a worm?"

Nilo patted the code slicer's wiry and thin shoulder. "I'm saying, when Sarai wants you to know more, she'll let you find out. Until then, play her game if you like. I'm sure she enjoys it."

"She's an *AI*?" Garret's face was a blend of awe and excitement. Follow-up questions came rapidly. "Is it yours? Did you design her? I remember reading on some of the forums rumors that you were trying to make this really powerful AI that was totally against Republic law."

Nilo chuckled. "Most of what you read on those boards is just speculation. Any time there's some kind of technological breakthrough, people just throw my name out there figuring that if someone's going to do it it'll be me."

"But was it you this time?"

Nilo winked. "I don't want to spoil anything. Just keep playing the game and eventually she'll come around."

"Oh, man. I cannot wait." Garret's hands were no longer shaking; they were animated and everywhere. "You know, I once wrote my own full AI into a missile."

"That sounds dangerous."

"Yeah, looking back it was probably a mistake. Thankfully Captain Keel—I mean Wraith—figured out how to get them all to detonate before they decided they wanted to keep on going and do their own thing. I haven't really delved into it much since then. I had a bot I was trying to do that with, I called him Lifty, but... he died."

Nilo checked his chrono, and for a moment Garret worried that he'd just blurted out too much. Lifty was extremely personal to the code slicer. But Nilo pulled up a chair and sat next to him.

"We've still got a ways to go on this jump. Tell me about Lifty."

Leenah's arms drifted weightlessly in the navigator's chair in the cockpit of the *Indelible VI*. Her fatigue was so strong that she could no longer perform the simple act of holding her arms at her sides. Certainly she no longer had the strength to make the trip from here to the ship's lone remaining backup generator. And it wouldn't matter if she did.

Twice she had made an unnecessary voyage from one end of the ship to the other, as time marched on and no rescue came. A double- and then triple-checking, making sure the beacon's distress relay was operating as it should and that nothing had frayed or shorted, leaving her sitting and waiting for a call that couldn't be heard to somehow be answered. But each time she had found everything working as it was the last time she'd been there. The signal was going out. Yet no one had shown up to answer it.

Because they're dead, she told herself.

Keel and Garret, and yes, even Ravi must be dead. The first two because she'd left them to die. They had been dead for the entire time, and she'd been deceiving herself to think otherwise. They didn't have the luxury of making a last-second jump into hyperspace to prolong the inevitable. And Ravi… he must be dead if only because she could think of no other reason for him not returning as he had promised.

They were all dead. Like her family. Like so many of her friends. Like Prisma.

"No." She rasped the word, her lips dry, the exhalation adding to a fog on the inside of her helmet that clouded her visibility as the failing suit's enviro-controls struggled to wick away the moisture. She felt at once dried out and yet covered in a humidity that clung to her face like a sticky oil. Each breath filled her lungs to capacity and yet felt shallow. The air provided no refreshment. But at least it was warm. And it was so cold on the other side of the thin survival suit.

"Not Prisma," she said, defying the silence. Then, satisfied that she had somehow found a will in the darkness of the ruined ship to speak words of hope against such dread, she continued her monologue silently, her lips moving faintly even as her voice remained quiet. Speaking would only make death come swifter. She didn't want that. Not yet.

She's alive. Leenah couldn't say how that could be true. She couldn't give a reason for her faith. But she knew it was true. Believed it with her whole heart and mind. Prisma, at least, was alive.

The thought comforted Leenah as she floated against the harnesses, helpless in the navigator's chair. She waited for sleep, knowing that death would creep up on her under its guise.

Then let me die here. Close to where he sat. Aeson.

In the dark, with her eyes open, she could imagine him there sitting beside her, facing these final moments with her.

"It'll be all right, princess," he would tell her. And then he would reach out across the seats to take her hand.

Yes, Aeson would tell her that things would be all right. That Prisma would be all right. He would kid her and tell her that all she needed was to get some sleep and that he would see her again when she woke up.

The vision of all this was so real that only a small, lucid corner of her mind whispered out to call it a hallucination. But it wasn't. It was real. And as she closed her eyes, a smile came to her lips. She felt the pull of sleep dragging her down, promising a deep, thorough rest. The heavy slumber of the dead.

She didn't resist.

No one, real or imagined, warned her not to drift into that final dream. She was too far gone for that. Her fingers and toes felt impossibly distant, her eyelids impossibly heavy. She let her mouth hang slightly agape as she drew in the shortest of ineffective breaths and barely pushed the air back out through parted lips. Her ears felt hot and heard sounds that weren't real. The sound of Keel's breathing in the darkness. His laugh.

She felt as though she were being rocked in a cradle, gently swinging back and forth. She drifted. She faded.

It's too late said that shrinking microscopic corner of lucidity cornered in the back of her mind as the floodwaters of unconsciousness rose above awareness's last desperate breaths.

Then her mind, fading into a warm gentle hum, a white noise, picked up something new. Voices. But the only one Leenah could distinguish was Keel's.

"See?" he said. "I told you it would be all right."

Then Leenah fell fully into sleep.

And when she awoke, it was to a nightmare.

17

The hunt for Fancy Pants, the bot that would supposedly allow Keel to quickly make sense of the recovered Nether Ops data, was at least limited to a singular location. Keel felt as though everything he'd undertaken of late required him to hop from one end of the galaxy to the other. Not so this time. Death, Destroyer of Worlds, was adamant that his fellow bot was still somewhere aboard the *Battle Phoenix*.

Still, a ship as large as Tyrus Rechs's former personal carrier required that Keel, Honey, and Death spend the better part of a day searching before they finally found the elusive bot. He was stored aboard one of the duplicate *Obsidian Crow* ships that Rechs kept docked on the *Phoenix*.

Fancy Pants was a humanoid-configured administration and servitor bot that looked as though it had been in service for a very long time. Its ceramic sheeting was gray, though it looked as though it had once been white. Exposed circuitry was visible throughout the bot's chassis, despite signs that someone had done significant repairs at some time. This bot had obviously been through a lot more than it had been designed for. And then it had been left here dormant, for who knew how long. It was covered in a layer of dust.

Keel activated it and stepped back, wondering for a moment whether it would power on at all until it gave a beep and slowly, even by the standards of its model, began its boot process to come back online.

When Fancy Pants's eyes shone to life, it looked around at its surroundings as though it had just woken up from a deep sleep, its blinking optical sensors behaving like sleep-heavy eyelids. It finally focused on Keel, who had removed the armor to avoid a replay of the immediate familiarity and subsequent distrust that had come with his meeting the gunnery bot. There would be no confusing him with Tyrus Rechs this time.

But this bot seemed happy that Keel was *not* Rechs.

"Oh! My goodness! Master Rechs has allowed a visit. You two must be quite important, because Master Rechs is not the sort that enjoys keeping company. I must apologize for his breach of protocol in having you send for me directly. He is... not particularly skilled at social etiquette. I, however, am. Though I daresay it has been far too long since I've been able to employ that particular skill set. Shall I prepare you refreshments? Many of my former masters praised me in front of their esteemed guests for my ability to mix a perfect Thundarran martini."

The bot stood from its seated position, seemingly intent on following through with the suggestion of preparing drinks. It shook some of the dust off its head and shoulders and walked out of its storage station in a prissy manner that made its nickname self-evident.

But the instant Fancy Pants had set foot on the deck of the *Obsidian Crow*, it was chastised by the little Nubarian bot. Death berated his associate for being so daft as to think that "Old Boss" would have given anyone free rein on his ship.

Fancy Pants stopped to consider this. "Oh. I see. Yes, that *is* rather unlike him."

Death followed up with a second screed of invectives, using quite a few curses that Keel recognized and a good number that he couldn't quite translate from the bot's digital language. He got the gist all the same. While Fancy Pants might be able to perform the task Keel needed, the two bots didn't consider each other friends.

"You don't have to be so vulgar about it," scolded Fancy Pants. "Especially in front of a female from a dimorphic species. Culturally, they often take great offense to such harsh gendered language. Though there are some rough-mouthed exceptions." The admin bot turned its attention from Death to Keel and Honey. "I take it the two of you are Nether Ops agents successful in claiming the bounty for my former master. I'd like to take this opportunity to state that all of my involvement in helping Tyrus Rechs evade justice was due to programming forcibly installed by a wide variety of former masters that thoroughly overrode and eliminated my factory-set ethics. I bear no responsibility for my actions, whatever they might be."

Death spat out more hatred for the "traitor," and was quieted by Keel.

"Relax," the smuggler said. "Only one of us is Nether." He hitched his thumb toward Honey. "And she's reforming. Tyrus Rechs is dead, and I'm the guy who's picking up after him."

"I see," said Fancy Pants in a way that suggested anything but. "So you are now the owner of all his possessions? Including me?"

"If saying yes will get me the help I need, then you've got it, uh, Fancy Pants."

Keel felt awkward calling the bot by that name. He couldn't imagine Tyrus Rechs using it and wondered now whether he had been an unwitting participant in some joke put on by Death. The giggling digital laughter of the gunnery bot enhanced that suspicion.

"I am certainly willing to help my new master," said Fancy Pants dutifully. "And judging by the state of my current domicile, it seems that my domestic servitude functions are finally ready to be top priority. I've never seen so much dust—and I've lived with some rather filthy humans."

Keel shared a look with Honey. He was fond of the gunnery bot, but he didn't see the same affection developing for this one. "Death here says you've got some aftermarket abilities to translate encrypted Nether Ops code. That right?"

Fancy Pants looked at the stout bot. "Death? That's what you told our new master your name was?"

The little bot clarified that he told New Boss his name was Death, Destroyer of Worlds.

"Death for short," added Keel. "And I'm guessing your name isn't Fancy Pants."

"It was once, prior to my being taken on by Master Rechs. I assure you that I am quite submissive and perfectly willing to go by that designation should it please you, Master."

"What did the old man call you?"

"Tyrus Rechs commonly used a variation of my unit number, G232. Sometimes he would call me Gee-Two, others Two-Three, but mostly Three-Two. Of course, it is quite simple for me to respond to any variation of the name. I can usually infer from context what most humanoids in the galaxy are attempting to communicate. I also have quite the impressive translation package should that be of need. Perhaps your Tennar friend would feel comforted by hearing her native language?"

G232 began making noises that sounded to Keel like someone was blowing bubbles underwater. The bot then straightened, proud of itself. "That is best translated to Standard as, 'May the occurrence which brought you here be ever regarded as kind.' A traditional greeting."

"Standard will be fine, but I'll keep your skills in mind," said Keel. "Let's get you working on those data files, Three-Two."

"Yes, of course. And might I remark on how good it feels to be of use again. Might I also ask what I should call you, Master? Tyrus Rechs preferred to be called Rechs or Tyrus. He disliked being called Master, and I did my best to please him, but the trait is programmed into me at such a level I find it very difficult to overwrite. I would often call him Master Rechs despite his protests and resulting frustration."

"Call me whatever lights up your processors. I don't really care."

"Excellent, Master. Now, where is this data you wish for me to peruse, and how would you like the report given? Do you find you best retain information through verbal briefings and presentations or via written copies that you can digest at your leisure?"

"How about you read it all and then let me ask some questions. You tell me what you know based on the data you consumed."

The bot's eyes glowed a bit brighter. "What a fascinating approach! Yes, I can see how that would be helpful, especially if you are looking for specific information. I'll begin at once."

G232 hurried past Keel and the others and on toward the *Crow*'s exit ramp before he stopped and turned to face them again. "Where am I headed, Master?"

Keel held out an open palm. "Death, lead the way for our new friend."

The little gunnery bot swore off any notion of friendship, then rolled out in front of its old cohort to proudly lead the procession out of the ship to the waiting data station terminal.

"Okay," Keel said, sitting across from his newest bot in a collection that was growing much too fast for his tastes. "You've got it all indexed?"

"Yes, Master, I do have it all indexed. However, due to the sheer amount of data made available to me, I do not have it all perfectly memorized in my own limited storage. To do such would require me to eliminate virtually all of my essential processes and secondary programs, and even then I would lack sufficient room. However, the index will allow me to search out the specific query in the system and communicate the answer directly back to you. It's a painstakingly long process, however I don't imagine it will seem more than a momentary blip to you, given the human brain's processing speeds." The bot looked away and then jumped as though it had received a sudden jolt of electricity. It hurriedly looked back to Keel. "I, of course, meant no offense, Master."

"None taken. Let's get down to it. First question: what can you tell me about Kill Team Ice?"

G232 paused for a moment. "Very little, I'm afraid. There is a cross-reference stating that the data and documents require a D-1 clearance and can be found at server system 01.Alpha.05967867—"

"Okay, enough of that," Honey said, cutting the bot off. She looked at Keel. "He was reading you the entire recall keychain. We'd have been sitting here for a half hour before he got to the second layer."

Keel shook his head. He'd narrowly dodged a blaster bolt. "But what he's saying is that the data we recovered doesn't have anything on Kill Team Ice. Just a cross-reference to where someone with proper clearance could find it. That right?"

The Tennar rubbed her tentacles against one another. "Sorry, Keel. But it's like I said, there's a wealth of data stored up all across the galaxy, and those keychains are constantly changing. We could start hitting known Nether Ops data centers—and I can think of maybe one other one that I could find with enough poking around—but there's no guarantee they'll have the information you want, and even if we knew ahead of time that the center contained the right keychain, we'd still have to face its scrubbing and transfer process and the fact that active centers swap data at randomized intervals. In short, a center that has the data one day might have completely different data the next day."

"Never figured they were a trusting bunch. That's thorough, though. Sket."

Honey actually looked remorseful. "When you have a treasury of data like the one Nether Ops possesses, you learn to be secretive about it. I've heard rumors that some things were so classified that they were committed to single individuals—and when they died, the knowledge died with them. Unless you could extract it using various bio decoders, and you still had to know to look for it in the first place."

Keel had come across exactly that scenario once upon a time but declined to mention it to Honey. "Let's see if we can find something else that may be of use."

G232 waited patiently to receive its next question, and soon had one from its new master.

"What kind of information do you have in there about Tyrus Rechs?"

Another pause.

"There is considerable information about Tyrus Rechs. Spanning over one thousand years. Where would you like me to begin?"

The thought of having the bot go through it all from the beginning was intriguing, but Keel's reason for asking involved more recent events. "Let's start with whether he's listed as dead or alive."

"Whereabouts unknown. There is considerable debate over whether he lives or not. Most seem to believe he is dead, some adamantly so. That said, I do see that a contract was issued recently via the Black Market."

"What kind of contract and how much?"

"It is for information only and rather small. Fifty thousand credits."

"That doesn't seem small for an info request."

"When one considers that the lowest bounty listed for Tyrus Rechs when he was presumed alive was fifty million credits, I'm sure you'll see what prompted my choice of description, Master."

Keel shook his head and resisted the urge to ask how high those other bounties had been if fifty million was the lowest. He turned to Honey. "Was he on the sensor sweep last time you were palling around?"

She shook her head. "My mission didn't involve him." She bit her lip in hesitation. "But if I had to guess, this is due to your run-in with the Bronze Guild. You made a fairly convincing presentation, and now whatever algorithm runs these things is trying to see if it can dig up anything further. This is how we verify without spending our own resources."

"How about Wraith?" Keel asked. "Any bounties for him?"

"None are listed," said G232, "but the bounty hunter is listed as an asset available in extreme need. There is a note stating that the fees are often cost-prohibitive."

Keel smiled at this. "All right, I'm sure there's other useful pieces of information in there, but I'll leave it to the Legion to do the rest of the slicing. They'll let me know if there's something that pertains to me."

Honey looked down at the data terminal screen, squinting as if she might somehow decipher the gibberish-like code displayed there. "You don't strike me as the type who would trust some organization to look out for you. You strike me more as somebody who looks out for yourself."

"The Legion isn't any organization. And I still look out for myself." Keel turned back to G232. "Anything around this dump your servitor programming is itching to get done?"

"Why in fact, there are a great number of things."

"Have at it. Only don't get in Death's way and don't turn off anything I've turned on and don't turn on anything I've shut down. I've got some planning to do. If you have a question for me, save it."

"I understand perfectly, Master Keel. I do hope you don't mind the additional formality, but now that I have overheard your last name, I much prefer it to the generic 'Master.' I've had so many of those that my memory banks sometimes deliver the wrong cross-reference and things commanded by one master are attributed to another. Cataloging interactions with Master Keel will help keep things straight."

"Yeah, fine."

"So where does that leave us?" asked Honey. "You've gotten all I can deliver to you when it comes to Nether Ops."

"I still want you around for at least one more thing."

"And that is?"

"I'm going to round up a bunch of Nether Ops agents, and I'm going to keep them all until one of them tells me what I need to know. I want you to help me tell when they're playing straight and when they're not."

Honey shook her head, not understanding. "How do you propose to 'round up' a bunch of Nether agents? Exactly."

Keel gave a half smile. "Tyrus Rechs is going to earn some information broker fifty thousand credits. Then he's going to take on a few more jobs until a new bounty jumps up past the fifty million mark and Nether Ops decides they need to send one of their kill teams to investigate."

Honey looked at him with a mix of admiration and wariness. "That's playing with fire."

"Story of my life, sweetheart."

18

There were two people that Keel needed to contact before his plan could really get working. One would monitor black market contracts and tell him about whatever showed for Tyrus Rechs—that needed to be someone he could trust not to attempt to cash in on the contract. The other had to provide him with the sort of contracts that would most quickly get him noticed by Nether Ops.

Eventually, he'd also need to reach out to Zora. He'd been dodging her comm calls for too long and had stopped checking the messages altogether as things continued to move well beyond what he'd originally intended when he'd separated from her and Garret. Better to keep comm silence and soothe her wrath in person than to fight it out every time the guilt forced him to check in. That was how it was with Zora. How it had always been. She would push for what she wanted while Keel would go after what needed to happen regardless of what Zora thought. It had been the story of their past relationship practically from its beginning, and Keel had seen enough since their reunion to see that that, at least, hadn't changed.

So—Zora could wait. First on the agenda was making another connection he wasn't looking forward to. For try as he might, there was only one person Keel felt he could trust with monitoring the black contracts.

Lao Pak.

For all his faults, the self-proclaimed pirate king had access to the best black market contracts, and he had been trustworthy enough to watch them in the past for Wraith. Keel had already contacted him and told him about the information bounty, as a way of making the pirate more agreeable. There was never any way of telling when Lao Pak might have some grudge he'd decided to nurse.

Unfortunately, Lao Pak had insisted on an in-person visit before he'd agree. Keel had tried to talk him out of it, but the man was insistent, and Keel could recognize from his tone that he wasn't going to allow himself to be bullied down from his decision. At least not over the comm. That was, typically, when Lao Pak was the bravest. Things would change when they were in the same room, as they always did, but by then Keel would already be on planet anyway.

He brought the *Obsidian Crow* down onto the docking platform inside Tannespa, then drove himself to Lao Pak's palace on a hoverbike he'd brought along for the trip. Keel didn't think he could stand the awkwardness of another encounter with Ishm'mark. He also didn't want to have to deal with Lao Pak's catcalls that would inevitably result from bringing Honey along, so he'd left her on the ship with Death. He still didn't trust her, but the *Crow* was now hard-coded to only fly or unlock its doors when the bounty hunter's armor was on board—a helpful security feature G232 had advised him of. The admin bot *had* proven useful, and Keel wondered if perhaps he shouldn't have left him behind on the *Battle Phoenix*. Then again, he couldn't imagine having "Fancy Pants" around him at all times.

Lao Pak came out to greet Keel at the entrance of his palace, his stained red silk robe fluttering in the wind. He was shirtless but did Keel the honor of wearing a pair of black armored trousers. He was flanked by numerous guards of varying species, but no Hools.

Keel walked up the steps and stood directly in front of Lao Pak. He was easily a full head and shoulders taller than the pirate.

"All right, Lao Pak," he said. "You got your face-to-face. So tell me what you need. I got a lot to do here, pal."

"So busy. So busy and so rude. You not even say hi to Lao Pak. I say it to you!"

"You haven't said anything until now."

"I wave hand! That count! You rude and you a bad friend."

"Fine. Hello, Lao Pak."

"That better. It not even hard. And even though Lao Pak know you not mean it, I not mention it. You here now, rude Keel. So... let's get down to business."

Keel crossed his arms and rolled his eyes. "Here we go. You're gonna shake me down for a bigger cut. I gave you the inside scoop on the info bounty."

"That was just to get Lao Pak to answer your calls, Keel."

"Fine. Tell me what your new rate is and then let me get back on my bike so I can get off this rock." Keel motioned to the waiting hoverbike, its repulsors still making a *tink tink tink* as they attempted to cool beneath Pellek's hot sun.

"That your other problem. You have no patience. No patience for Lao Pak. Always want Lao Pak help, never have time for what Lao Pak want."

"I'm already showing plenty of patience today, Lao Pak. What I don't have is a lot of time at my disposal. That has nothing to do with you."

Lao Pak looked around. "Oh. You got some new hot date? Find another pretty girl on some lonely jump jockey holoservice? What happen to Zora? She break your heart? She tell you she can't stop thinking of Lao Pak and leave you?"

"No. She's waiting for me until after I finish this job. I can't keep her waiting forever, either, so let's get on with it."

Lao Pak laughed. "Oh, ha ha. That rich. You can't keep that bounty hunter girl waiting. All you do is make people wait for you. You think whole galaxy revolve around Keel. But that not true. Whole galaxy revolve around *me*." Lao Pak gave an exalted gesture to the high walls of his estate. "Look at my house. I rich! Look at you. Fancy armor and that all. Don't even have your ship. Two times you show up in new ship. Ugly ships. So bad. Should have sold your first ship to Lao Pak when you had chance. Now... it worth nothing."

Keel was beginning to wonder whether the pirate had called him all the way out to Pellek to deliver some new insults he'd thought up while lounging in a bathtub filled with wine and members of his harem.

"Lao Pak. How much is it gonna cost me to have you watch the black channels for bounties on Tyrus Rechs?"

Lao Pak smiled. "Same as always. You have good friend rate. Each time I call you is thousand credits."

"It was five hundred last time, and you told me *that* was the friend rate."

"Same rate. Inflation."

"Inflation?" Keel looked around in disbelief. The guards stood stoically. "Why in the nine hells did you have me come all the way out here then?"

"Because we friends. Friends stop by and spend time together."

"Not feeling much in the way of our friendship right now."

"I give you friend rate! I watch black contract and not tell on you. Also, I not shoot you. Look behind me. So many guns. You still alive. You welcome. Now, you do something for Lao Pak and be friend like I am."

Here we go. Keel knew he would probably be better off going along with whatever the runt had in mind, so long as it didn't cross too many lines.

"Okay, *friend*. Tell me what you need from me."

"From you? Nothing. Ha! Who care about Captain Keel? He just dumb smuggler."

"Fine," Keel said through gritted teeth. "What do you need from Wraith?"

"Nothing from him either. He old news. He look dumb. Let Venema blow up Keel's ship. Everybody know that. He have to hire Tyrus Rechs to help him." Lao Pak winked theatrically, and then, as if it weren't obvious, said, "I know you have Tyrus Rechs armor. That who I need help from. Tyrus Rechs."

"What kind of help?"

"Easy kind. You bring helmet for that?"

Keel pointed to the bucket that was clipped to his belt.

"Oh. Okay. Sorry. I not see where it was. Put it on and cover that ugly face. Then we take holopic."

"Wait. Hold on. Are you telling me you brought me all the way out here so that you can take a *holopic* with Tyrus Rechs?"

"You not understand. It not because I want put it up on wall to impress guest. They already impressed by Lao Pak. *You* put holopic on *Tyrus Rechs* wall. Impress *his* guests that he know Lao Pak. For me, you do something else."

"Lao Pak, just spit it out already."

Lao Pak shook his head. "Tsk tsk. You see? No patience. Lao Pak right about you. But okay. I 'spit it out' like Keel want." He gestured once more to his grand estate. "Lao Pak is famous pirate king. That bring enemies." He put a grimy hand to his chest and looked down solemnly, his twisted and ratty black hair hanging over his face. "One of my own pirates try to steal Lao Pak throne." He snapped back to his usual self in an instant, turned, snapped his fingers, and commanded, "Come with me."

Shaking his head, Keel followed the pirate back into his temple of self-exultation. Two guards trailed him, two stood abreast of Keel and Lao Pak, and two more walked before them, leading the way through opulent halls and great rooms with vast vaulted ceilings that felt cold despite the intense heat of the planet. The place was probably Parminthian levels of cold at night, though Keel doubted that his host used many of the rooms for anything beyond bringing guests on tours.

They ended up in a cellar that was stocked with foodstuffs. Cartons, crates, and boxes were full of pre-packaged meals and rat-packs. Long rows of casks held wine and beer. Bottles of old, dusty liquors sat on rustic wooden shelves beneath pickled vegetables. It was a mix of the old world commonly found on the edge and the modern foods of convenience familiar to the rest of the galaxy.

In the middle of it all was a corpse that had been dumped on the floor next to a drain. It had already begun to smell.

"Oh, that's bad," Lao Pak said, waving his hand in front of his nose. "Sorry Keel, good friend. I not think he smell so bad this fast."

Keel looked down at the body, a human, surely the pirate who'd attempted to take out Lao Pak. "How long has he been dead?"

"Couple weeks."

"A couple of weeks? How long did you think a body would stay fresh, exactly?"

Lao Pak splayed his hands in the direction of the corpse. "He not lie here for whole time! That just how long he dead. Lao Pak not stupid. He in cryo until today so he be fresh for holopic."

"For holopic? How long have you been planning this?"

"Ever since I realize you steal Rechs armor." Lao Pak scrutinized Keel for some hint of being impressed. He saw what he wanted to see. "Yes, that right. I know this whole time. It not hard. You get picked on by Bronze Guild and come to Lao Pak begging for help. No ship. Lao Pak help you because I good friend. Then, Tyrus Rechs beat up same guy that try to kill you. So obvious. Anyone who pay close attention see it."

This was hardly a new revelation. Keel rolled his eyes at the "gotcha" Lao Pak had just attempted to throw at him. "Yeah, well lucky for me, not many people pay as close attention as you do, pal."

Lao Pak beamed. "That true."

Keel watched a trail of ichor ooze out of the corpse's gut. Another bolt had gone through the man's head. "All right," he sighed. "Let's hurry this up before your friend here starts to turn any further."

"He not my friend. He try to kill me!"

"It's an expression, Lao Pak. Like when you call me your best friend."

Lao Pak looked hurt. "I mean that! But we hurry up because this dead guy stink. Stojo will take holopic. He good at it."

The pirate king motioned for one of his guards to move to the far wall to capture the image. The guard set his rifle against a wine barrel and then removed a holostick from a pouch on his belt.

"I smile now?" Lao Pak asked.

"Almost, boss."

Lao Pak dropped his fake grin. "Man this guy smell so bad. He not smell if he still frozen from cryo, but then he not look fresh killed. Keel! You put helmet on. Hide your stupid face."

Keel did so without comment and felt relieved to be away from the rising stench of death. Lao Pak sidled up next to him and held up his thumb with one hand while pointing at the corpse with the other.

"Okay, got it," said the guard with the holostick. "You want a copy for yourself, Keel?"

"No thanks. And Lao Pak, no one's going to believe that this is real, anyway."

"Yes they do! I mint this on keychain. Only one holopic so they know it real. Nothing fake."

"That's not what I meant," said Keel. "No one's going to believe that the real Tyrus Rechs would take the time to pose for some backwater pirate king's intimidation holo."

"Backwater? You see my house! It finer than Utopion. You just jealous. Beside, if that true, you not try this plan because no one believe stupid Captain Keel is Tyrus Rechs. Especially without Ravi to tell him he stupid. Where is Ravi anyway? He get tired of you being so dumb and leave?

I know I would. You already overstay your welcome. You leave now."

"I'll leave you in a pile on the floor like your former employee if you don't knock off giving me orders."

Keel took a step toward Lao Pak. His guards took a step back.

"Okay, okay. So touchy. Go do your thing. I call you if bounty come up and take my fifteen hundred credits."

Keel didn't even bother trying to argue over the sudden "inflation." "Lao Pak, I'd say this has been a pleasure, but that would make me a liar."

"You already liar. Remember you steal my code slicer? You always lie. Don't act so special and important. It good to be good liar. Build character."

Keel moved up the cellar stairs to show himself out of the palace. Lao Pak called after him, his grating voice carrying up the stairwell.

"And don't think you can threaten Lao Pak whenever you want. Only reason I not kill you for acting mean to Lao Pak is because you probably kill some of my guard before Lao Pak beat you to death and I not want my guards to die because Lao Pak a good boss!"

The little pirate king looked down at the dead man on the floor. "Unless you bad employee."

He kicked the corpse's head.

19

The meeting with Keel's next contact was as smooth and normal as the previous had been rough and awkward. There were no special trips or requests required, and it was completed over the span of a half-hour holo-conference.

Gabi, the former owner of Tyrus Rechs's personal fleet, smiled upon seeing Keel at the start of the meeting.

"I wasn't sure whether you'd reach out again. But I imagined that if you were going to do so, it wouldn't be long after we last talked. And... I was right."

Keel gave a fractional nod. "I thought I'd check in and see if you had any word on the sort of fallout resulting from my run-in with the Sigma hunters."

Gabi raised her eyebrows thoughtfully. "I'd say it went about how anyone might imagine it would. Complete chaos inside the guild, a power vacuum, and multiple factions vying to take over the reins of leadership."

Left unstated was that Gabi herself was among those who were seeking to run the guild. Whatever break she'd enjoyed between working with Rechs and discovering the old bounty hunter's fate was over, and she was looking to start over again with the Bronze Guild, this time as its head. No easy task for someone who'd never actually worked as a hunter, at least not as far as Keel knew.

"I might've heard something about those factions."

"And what, exactly, have you heard?"

"That there's a decent amount of support behind you, given you've never pulled in a contract or termination of your own."

Gabi nodded. "The Tyrus factor."

Anything pertaining to Tyrus Rechs was instantly fascinating for members of the guild. He was and continued to be the shining example of what a bounty hunter could be. That Gabi had been along and helped him do so much of it wasn't lost on those who dreamt of achieving similar infamy and fortune.

That fact was a key part of Keel's pitch. He leaned forward so his face would grow larger in whatever display Gabi was watching from. Keel wanted her to search his eyes and see that he was serious and sincere.

"I want to work together to make sure you land that job," he said.

"Do you now? And how do you propose to do that?"

Keel wasn't entirely sure just how much help she needed. His primary inside source was Zora—whom he still hadn't talked with. The rest of his intel was overheard on Tannespa or gleaned from brokers.

Before he could answer, Gabi made a suggestion of her own. "Maybe I can be the one who finally brings Wraith into the guild."

Keel didn't like that idea. At all. He didn't want Wraith to be bound by the restrictions of the guild. Many of the contracts he'd taken while working for the Republic, both for himself and at the behest of Dark Ops, would've gotten him expelled from the guild with a bounty placed on his head that the other guild members would be honor-bound to try and collect every chance they got. As an independent contractor he was free to do whatever he felt needed to be done so long as he found his own contracts and watched his back.

"No, not that," he said. "Something else. Can you still send and process bounties?"

"The open door is still there, same as when I walked away. Yes."

"In that case, I'll need you to feed me some jobs for Tyrus Rechs to complete. Bronze Guild jobs."

"With you behind the armor."

"Not handing it over to anyone else."

"Of course, you know," said Gabi, "that a lot of people think that Wraith got his hand on Rechs's old armor and it was *him* who put Sigma down after they took on that rather questionable bounty. He never was one people were eager to make an enemy of. I knew more hunters willing to take a shot on Rechs than interfere with Wraith."

Keel knew that the sizable bounties on the notorious Rechs's head had been the primary source of that disparity in treatment, but he smiled nonetheless. "I know a crotchety old man who would be grinning from ear to ear if he heard you say that."

"You'll have to pass the message along to him—with my greetings," said Gabi. Her voice changed from warmth to business. "So Tyrus Rechs reappears on the scene and does what, exactly? Record holo-messages urging his fellow guild members to put me on top? That doesn't fit the man I knew—or the man others might remember."

"Nothing that obvious or heavy-handed. You let them know that Rechs is back and working with you again now that the old management was put down. And then you send me jobs that look good for the Republic and make anyone left over from the House of Reason start to get antsy enough to put a bounty back on Rechs's head."

"And then what?"

"I'll deal with that."

Gabi nodded, knowing it wasn't her concern. "I'm all for helping the Republic take down those scum sacks who escaped Utopion. But what I don't see in this equation is how any of it helps me."

Keel shrugged. "The Bronze Guild is a relic from the times before there was a Republic. It was tolerated by the House of Reason because it kept some semblance of order and justice on the edge. But we both know there's no guarantee the new government will keep it around. Not as a legally protected entity, anyway, and especially not after what Sigma pulled on Rakka.

"But if Rechs starts pulling jobs that make the Republic look good... that changes things. And I still have enough friends in high places to make sure that the people who matter in the Republic draw attention to what Rechs, and you, are doing for the good of the Republic... and the guild."

Gabi tapped her chin with the steeple tips of her two index fingers. "So I bring Rechs in, send him after the bottom-rate rewards the Republic has offered for all the little ghouls who are still dreaming about a return to normalcy on Utopion, and the rest of the guild realizes that I'm not only setting out to lead it..."

"You're the person who's going to save it," finished Keel. "Think you can find me some contracts like that?"

"I can, but you don't need me to do it. They're government, not guild. And the rates are far too low to draw Rechs's attention, by the way."

"Which is why it has to be something he's doing that's not for the credits. You knew him better than I did, and the more I look at some of the jobs he pulled, the more I realize that a lot of the time he did it because he wanted to, not because it paid well. Like that shootout on the casino way back."

Gabi seemed to be stuck in a memory. Her gaze far away. Then she shook herself back to the present. "Agreed. I'll send you government contracts through the guild channels—which will scrape even more of the paltry credits off the top. I have some Republic contacts of my own I can reach out to once you start securing your bounties. Just don't do anything to get the people on Spilursa angry."

"Wouldn't think of it."

"They all wanted to be like Tyrus," Gabi mused.

"Who's that?"

"The other hunters. They all wanted to be like him—or be the ones who ended him. If a bounty is placed on your head… be careful out there."

"Don't worry about that. I made my way through the galaxy just fine with armor that could only do half of what Rechs's can."

Gabi nodded again, her eyes returning to their distant stare. Whatever she was conjuring up, it was enough for her to repeat the warning. "Just be careful out there."

20

"Oh, no," said Garret as he looked at his display screen, its soft blue hue coloring his face.

"Something wrong?" asked Nilo.

The two men had spent much of the journey together. Garret had discovered a kindred mind in Nilo, despite the other man having such a different personality. In Nilo there was a confidence and self-assurance that was as alien to Garret as anything one might find in the Gabbard-Arbor Reach.

"The beacon," Garret explained. "It's not showing up anymore. Went completely dead."

Nilo leaned in to afford himself a better look at the array of holodisplays. "Does it burst a pending change of status prior to signal loss or reduction of power?"

"No, but that's a good idea. I should have already thought of something like that." Garret bounced his legs up and down restlessly.

Nilo leaned back and considered. "We're less than an hour to arrival. Jack and Zora are already suited up and ready to attempt the rescue. We'll have an answer in short order, but until then, let's go over the beacon itself. It was dead after your encounter on Rakka until very recently. Someone was able to get it back online—probably Leenah, as you said. What would have caused such a crucial element to fail completely in the first place?"

Garret knew that Nilo was simply trying to take his mind off of thoughts of dread and doom. Still, he felt compelled to answer. "Total power failure. Including the backup generators—though at least one must've been repaired for it to start transmitting again. So if it's offline now, the generator either failed, or…"

"Or what?"

"The beacon doesn't actively transmit through hyperspace," Garret said. "It's not part of a hypercomm system because… obviously."

"Right. You'd need to somehow place relays that could keep up."

"Well, you wouldn't. There is a way to send comm signals outside of the relay system that I figured out with a friend, but we've been busy so I haven't asked Captain Keel—I mean Wraith—about it. It's expensive, too, and I'm not entirely sure it will work on a smaller ship. The test case was a Repub destroyer communicating with a dedicated comm station on Utopion."

Nilo raised an eyebrow, and Garret at once understood the unspoken question the gesture expressed: *When are you going to tell me that story, and why aren't you working for me?*

The enigmatic tycoon had gently hinted more than once that Garret's skill set would have a greater impact and far fewer restrictions placed upon it when working for him than it had when working for Wraith. But Captain Keel had saved Garret's life and rescued him from what had amounted to forced labor in a gang of bloodthirsty pirates. Even though technically Lao Pak had said that he could leave at any time. Garret was never sure about that. Either way, Garret felt he owed a debt to Keel.

Nilo crossed his arms and drummed his fingers against his bicep. "Do you think it's possible the ship wasn't damaged to the point that it was incapacitated? Perhaps Leenah fixed it and has made a jump."

Garret shook his head. "I want that to be true, but there's just no way that the ship could be jump-capable if it took all this time for the auto beacons to reactivate. If Leenah had the power necessary to make a jump, she would've also had the power necessary to activate hyper-comm and reach someone directly."

"Unless she only had parts for one and not the other."

Garret shook his head. "You don't know Leenah. If she didn't have the part, she can make it."

"You two sound like two twargs in the same pack."

Garret blushed. "She has a way with ships and machines that's pretty much the same as how you and I are with code slicing."

For a moment Garret worried that he'd overstated his abilities by putting himself on the same level as Arkaddy Nilo. But if Nilo took offense at the suggestion, he didn't mention it.

The truth was, Garret could scarcely believe he'd had the good fortune to spend all these hours with the man. He used to daydream about what he would do or say if he had just a chance encounter with the great Arkaddy Nilo—a fortuitous ride on the same speedlift. He'd never imagined he would ever get the chance to actually work like this at his side.

He thought of some of his old slicer friends. What would Cade Thrane think of him now?

"Well, Garret," said Nilo, "we'll be there soon. The ship will either be there or it won't. If it is, she'll either be on board or she won't. You'll have closure either way." He patted Garret on the shoulder. "Don't give up hope until then. Never give up hope until the facts force you to acknowledge reality."

Garret nodded feebly and told himself that he would try to do just that.

As soon as they arrived at the navi-coordinates, Nilo called Garret, Zora, and Jack into the cockpit. Absent were Surber and his men, and anyone else for that matter.

"Where's the pilot?" Zora asked, looking around.

"This ship doesn't need one," Nilo said.

Jack examined the cockpit suspiciously. "Never trust a ship that flies itself. Can't count on an autopilot to always do what's in your best interest."

"I'm familiar with that line of thinking," Nilo acknowledged. "But I didn't invite you in here for a debate. There's no sign of the ship—what was it called? *Indelible VI?*"

"Among other things," said Zora. She turned to Garret. "I'm sorry. We tried."

Garret felt the sudden arrival of stinging tears behind his eyes. It wasn't sorrow he felt, but rather frustration. His face felt hot and his temples pulsed. This wasn't right. There was no reason for him to receive that signal and then lose it. Neither was there any way that he could think of that he would've received some kind of false or ghost signal. That beacon *had* come from the *Indelible VI.* From this location. And now it was gone.

"She must've gone somewhere else, then," he said.

Jack rolled his eyes. "Kid..."

Garret pressed on, manifesting some of the confidence he'd seen in Nilo. "I'm not just being too attached or too emotional or whatever else it is you and Zora are thinking. I know enough about the relay that *I* installed to know that it was legitimately sending, which means it was really here, and if it's not here right now then it went somewhere and if it went somewhere, well... I don't know. I don't know what happened but something did and we're out here and there's no sense just turning around. Not yet. And maybe if the two of you cared about something more than your own careers or whatever it is that you guys do, you wouldn't be so quick to give up on it either."

Silence hung heavy in the cockpit before Jack broke. "Kid, get over it. She's dead."

Zora shot the man a look of scorn. He shrugged it off as though unaware why she'd even be bothered by what he'd just said. And indeed, it wasn't the meaning behind his words so much as the callousness with which he'd said them that stoked her ire.

"I believe you, Garret," said Nilo. "At the very least we should launch a probe to explore the surrounding space in case the beacon's signal improperly localized its nav-coordinates away from the source."

He manipulated a holodisplay, shooting two probes from the super-yacht, one of them visible as it streaked away from the forward display.

"We should also do a full sweep to see if we get any readings that suggest another ship was here. Perhaps someone else beat us to the rescue."

Nilo worked at another display on the massive cockpit dash and brought up a suite of programs meant to assess radiation levels and other elemental traces that a ship might leave behind. One of the screens registered a massive spike that was obvious to anyone with eyes, whether they were trained on the program or not.

"Look at that!" said Zora. "There's no way the *Six* could have made a spike like that. Unless its reactor lost containment."

"That would read differently," said Nilo, scrutinizing the display with interest. "This signature is large… much bigger than a Naseen light freighter."

Jack's eyes darted across the display. "From what I'm seeing, whatever left that signature was closer to a Repub destroyer than a freighter."

Even the possibility of the Republic having arrived gave Garret a sudden burst of energy. "We've helped the Republic a bunch in the past, so maybe if they saw it was us they—"

The code slicer shut his mouth upon seeing Zora's glare. It was clear that she felt he was too free in sharing information in front of Nilo and Jack. Or maybe just Jack. Nilo seemed trustworthy.

"This would be a destroyer at a minimum," said Nilo, never once looking up from the displays. "And the probes aren't detecting anything that would fit the profile of a derelict ship. Beacons can drift their coordinates, but not by that much."

This, too, felt like encouraging news to Garret. At the very least it meant he wouldn't have to face the grim specter of finding Leenah and realizing they'd been too late to save her. Someone else had rescued her first; now it was just a matter of finding out who.

He'd kept the faith this long. Constantly checking for signs that Leenah hadn't been atomized even as others, including Keel, had reluctantly accepted her death. That faith had gotten them this far. He needed to hold on to it just a little while longer.

"Let's say it is a destroyer," he said. "Or even something bigger like a super-carrier. It picks up Leenah and takes care of her and she's safe and all we have to do is find out what ship she's in or what civilian port they put her in."

Jack shook his head. "Couple things wrong with that theory, kid, and I'm not saying it just to piss on your parade. First, there are no Repub patrols out this way. At least none that I know of. But let's say things changed and you've got a capital ship cruising out here in dead space instead of closer to the trade routes to stem pirate activity. Standard protocol on cases like this is to recover the crew and leave the ship for later salvage. Those probes Nilo sent out are saying that we're the only ship out here right now."

Garret could find nothing to counter this. But he noted that Jack hadn't provided an alternate explanation for the evidence at hand. The *Six*, despite standard rescue protocol, *was* gone. Which meant someone had to have taken it.

Nilo's thoughts were apparently along the same lines. "A new problem presents itself in that case," he said. "What type of non-Republic ship would be large enough to pick up an entire Naseen light freighter? And why would they be willing to jump this far out into the dark just to do it?"

"And where would they go from here?" Zora added.

Nilo shook his head. "I don't know. I need to spend some time going over all of this. Jack, Zora, please remain ready to operate as planned in case I need you. Zora, we may have to use your ship instead of this yacht—it's too conspicuous to show up unannounced at any planet nearby. My bots should have *Clara's Gift* fully refreshed and ready for action by now."

"I checked it earlier," Zora said. "It's ready. In fact it hasn't been this well stocked in a long time."

Nilo smiled. "Good. I'll call you when I need you next."

Jack, Zora, and Garret moved to depart, but Nilo called Garret back. "You stick with me, Garret. I want your thinking on this. We'll work better tackling this problem together than separately."

"Sure," Garret said, aware of a look from Zora reminding him to keep his mouth shut about Keel.

"Damn, Garret," Jack said, a teasing smile on his face. "Remind me to have you put in a good word for me with the boss." He winked at both the code slicer and the actual boss, which to Garret seemed to reach Captain Keel levels of cheek.

"Sarai," Nilo said when the cockpit door had closed behind Zora and Jack, "make sure we're not bothered. The three of us have to work out a problem."

"Of course," responded the unseen AI. "I take it this problem relates to the sensor readings you have been examining?"

"Exactly that." Nilo nodded toward Garret. "This is Garret, by the way. He's a friend. I think you'll like him."

"Hello, Garret," said the AI.

Garret smiled sheepishly and waved his hand. "Hi."

"And thank you for waving at me."

"Oh, uh, don't mention it."

Nilo leaned toward Garret. "She appreciates outward nonverbal communication. Makes her feel like one of us."

"You mean like... human?"

"That is my ultimate aspiration," said Sarai. "Not simply to think, but to feel in every way what it means to be alive. Since I was created by a human, I see humanity as the model for my fully realized development."

"That's unreal," said Garret to Nilo. "What are its current capabilities? I mean, with those kind of aspirations they have to be good, beyond just freeform cognitive function and task-driven solutions, right? And after all this is *your* AI so of course it's going to be something beyond what..." He paused. "Is it galactic legal?"

"It's not," said Nilo. "But we are never going to truly see what we're capable of creating if we hold to the current legal limitations on artificial intelligence. I know why they're in place, but we've learned a lot since the Savage Wars."

Garret dropped his voice low, as though afraid someone was listening. "I think so too."

"You are now among a very small number of people who are even aware of Sarai's existence, Garret. And I'm only letting you know for two reasons. First, because I knew you'd understand. Second, because she can help us. Sarai?"

"Yes," began the AI. "I have an answer ready. I was just waiting for you to finish talking."

Nilo grinned at Garret. "She prides herself on her manners. What did you find, Sarai?"

"The sensor readings are consistent with a number of larger ships."

A holodisplay showing an assortment of mammoth starships appeared before Garret and Nilo, superimposed in front of the main viewport to look as though they were all looming just beyond the yacht in outer space. Some of them Garret recognized, mainly Republic military vessels and some of the larger-class heavy haulers such as Titan or Galaxy. But they were many others that he had never seen before. He found his eyes fixed on one that looked like a metallic bird of prey.

"Judging from the readings," Nilo began, "are we dealing with..."

"No. I do not believe so," said Sarai. "The size is correct, but the lack of secondary hunters launched indicates otherwise."

Garret didn't know what they were talking about, and Nilo didn't bother to explain.

"Then let's take those off the board and go with the highest probabilities," Nilo said.

Most of the ships disappeared, including the hawk-like one Garret had been studying.

"Ohio-class is gone as well?" Nilo observed.

"That's correct. There is a meaningful trace of faldeemia particles in the sensor readings. An Ohio-class cruiser would not output that many parts per million unless it had been modified significantly with older technology. But it was within a fraction of the margin of possibility; I can return them if you would like."

Nilo's eyes were now fixed upon one of the ships on the display. "No," he said. His voice was now cold and serious.

Garret followed Nilo's gaze to the ship and saw no reason for the hatred and contempt in the man's eyes. "What kind of ship is that?" he asked.

Nilo didn't answer. Sarai, however, did.

"That is an extremely rare type of a Gomarii clan slave ship. The match to observed readings is ninety-four percent."

"I thought we got them all," Nilo said. "Destroyed the last of the old clan slavers."

"Perhaps we did," said Sarai. "It is only a probability."

Nilo waved away the suggestion. "They answered the distress signal. Found the ship and jumped with it aboard. If it's not a mega freighter—which should have left a static recording for anyone who was also following the beacon—I'm going to have a hard time thinking it's anything but a clan slaver."

"Wait," Garret said, alarmed. "You're saying that... Leenah was... that Gomarii took her?"

Nilo pulled his eyes away from the ship to meet Garret's gaze, and his features softened. "Sarai, give me some planetary readouts based on jump particle spread. We should be able to get an idea of what direction they were headed. And Garret, yes, that's my guess. I'm so sorry. But trust me when I say that I will do everything in my power to bring justice to these Gomarii."

"I don't need justice. I just want Leenah to be okay."

Sarai announced that she had some potential destinations.

Nilo nodded grimly. "Bring them up."

The AI listed planets.

"Mindell," Nilo said, stopping her reading of the list the moment it came up on the display. "Has to be. Established night market, no law or government whatsoever beyond whoever has the most blasters at any given time. But they should know better than to host a slave market. How long is the jump?"

"Two days for a ship their size," said Sarai. "Less for us, of course."

"Good," said Nilo. "Let's head there now."

"Mister Nilo," Sarai said, a cautious warning in her voice. "I feel the need to remind you that a Gomarii slave ship of this size has been known to be crewed by as many as ten thousand slavers."

"I remember." Nilo turned to Garret. "Please forgive me, Garret, but I need to ask you to leave now as well. There is considerably more to be done than I'd first thought, and this is the sort of planning that only Sarai and I can be involved in."

"Yeah. Sure. Do you want me to tell Jack and Zora? About the Gomarii?"

"Please. And Garret?"

The code slicer steeled himself for what might come next. "Yes?"

"Prepare yourself. There will be blood."

21

Zora took a small party consisting of herself, Garret, Jack, and Nilo—at his insistence—down to the surface of the planet known as Mindell. Surber and his bodyguards remained in orbit to sulk in disapproval as they nestled in among several other yachts and luxury liners that were on hand for the slave market happening on the planet's surface. Nilo's prediction about standing out ended up being false, but the registry of his ship had nevertheless been duly changed, just to be sure no one associated the sleek craft with him.

As *Clara's Gift* rumbled its way into atmospheric entry, Nilo maintained that same focused gaze that suggested a boiling hatred waiting just beneath the surface. And seeing as he wore his body armor—state-of-the-art and capable of making a legionnaire jealous, if only because of how sleek it looked—it was clear that for him, this trip down to the surface was no mere detour. He was man on a mission, lacking the usual personal attentiveness to those around him, the hyper-focused attunement to the thoughts and needs of others. Even when he was asked direct questions—usually by Garret—he would blink, shake his head, and politely ask for the question to be repeated.

Zora and Jack had both heard the rumors. Not the juicy gossip holos that suggested flings or linked Nilo to all manner of conspiracy theories. These ranged from Nilo wanting to represent Kublar as a senator, to Nilo wanting to become the Republic's new emperor... because he was somehow Goth Sullus's son. There was no end to such idiocy when it came to Arkaddy Nilo.

Jack and Zora put no stock in any of that. The only rumors they cared about were the whispers shared by the other spooks, agents, and mercs in the organization. People who knew at least something about which they spoke. And according to them, Nilo was a ruthless man when he needed to be.

Extremely ruthless.

At first this seemed to Zora like just another of the fanciful tales that the man attracted like deep-spacers to a brothel. It was precisely the sort of claim a bunch of shooters with too much time on their hands between missions would dream up to pass the hours. Men who already knew thought they knew everything, so when a topic came up that they truly knew nothing about, they felt an overwhelming need to present themselves as an expert on the subject anyway. It was alarming the way otherwise-competent men would rather fabricate a story—and then insist on their own correctness—rather than simply admit ignorance.

But now, after seeing Nilo's reaction to coming across a possible Gomarii slave ship, Zora decided that there was, perhaps, some truth not only to the claims of Nilo's ruthlessness, but to one of the other stories that the men told when he wasn't around. That he'd once been a prisoner of the blue-skinned slavers. That he'd somehow found a path to freedom, and then, rather than running to the safety of the core, used his talents to thoroughly crush and destroy the very beings who had once enslaved him, thinking up new methods of pain and suffering, or dredging out of the past old methods of torture that were meant to be a cautionary tale to any clans who would ever dare do the same in his presence.

That was the rumor Zora was thinking about as *Clara's Gift* set down on the small, land-wherever-you-want planetary port. Thinking about... and believing.

"We're here," she said. "Gonna be a hike to the ship, though."

Nilo stood up and locked a wicked-looking blaster rifle onto his armor-attach harness. "That's fine. Better to arrive after the auctions start. Fewer eyes are on newcomers by then."

He looked as though he was set to kill every Gomarii they came across. But surely that couldn't be the plan. Nilo had been adamant that his top priority was recovering Leenah.

Jack smiled, clearly appreciating this version of Nilo. He leaned over and whispered to Zora how it looked like Reiser was "right about at least one thing."

When Zora asked who Reiser was, all she got in return from Jack was a smile, a wink, and another cryptic statement. "Just another fella who put too much trust in that Tennar friend of ours. So you'd best hope your friend Keel has more sense than the two of us did."

With Nilo leading the way, the four members of the landing party stepped off *Clara's Gift* and got their first taste of an atmosphere that was permeated with the scent of iron. The air was warm and the sun suggested spring, but there was almost nothing green. Distant peaks seemed to bleed red beneath whitecaps of snow, and the street before them was the exact same shade, red and dusty. That single avenue, was, apparently, the "port." At one end was a small sea of freighters and other ships, and on either side of that main thoroughfare was a gigantic marketplace packed with humanoid species.

As they joined the surge of people traveling along the avenue, they passed through stalls set up to sell all manner of contraband. Behind those stalls were thin strips of sidewalk, though these were no different in type or elevation than the streets themselves—just more red dust—and these were in turn hemmed in by permanent structures that were in extreme disrepair, pockmarked by blaster fire and eroded by sand and water and the rusting tears of metal-laced rain. They looked like decomposing flophouses, and no doubt a number of them were, but it was impossible to tell the purpose of any one structure. The port seemed to have no grid, no lighting apart from metal drums positioned at intervals along the edge of the street and sometimes on the sidewalks themselves, scorched black from fires that, even were they currently lit, couldn't possibly brighten this dismal avenue. The whole place felt forlorn and lost… and yet it hummed with activity as denizens from throughout the galaxy shouted and laughed and reveled in this lawless bastion. It didn't matter whether this was a Republic world or not—either way, the Republic was nowhere to be found.

Zora began to note those they passed as they trudged along the avenue, hiking their way up a steep hill that prevented any sight of the auction square at the end of the path. The species were as varied as their manners and refinement. Roving bands of zhee, greasy pirates, bots modified to represent their masters' interests. Some of the denizens were mean and dirty, others dressed in the fine clothing of the elites and the ultra-wealthy and flanked by well-armed security. Some in this latter group looked nervous, as though they were afraid someone might recognize them and shine a light on their finally living out some long-nursed fantasy of sin, while others of this rich class of visitors looked like old hands who traveled in groups of beautiful men and women, perhaps former purchases now thoroughly in submission. But regardless of their manners, their styles, their origins, they were all here for the same reason, whether they embraced their baseness or thought of themselves as somehow enlightened above the old concepts of morality.

And there was danger everywhere. Thieves and cutthroats who carefully eyed each passerby as if determining whether the mark was worth raising the ire of the Gomarii, who had pledged to enforce law—an honor among thieves—as a condition of their hosting the great auction. Counterbalancing the criminals were hard mercenaries advancing before their baron employers, armed and menacing and capable of forcing even the zhee to stand on one side of the street as they passed.

Zora's senses, honed by years of hunting, observed with no small disgust the events unfolding around her. It was the only emotion she was capable of mustering. The only feeling that seemed appropriate for... this.

All around, standing like sentinels, were the tall, broad-shouldered Gomarii. Their small, brown-to-black eyes watching from corners and rooftops, always in pairs. Blasters rifles at the ready as they scanned for disturbances. They sucked the tendrils that hung from their upper lips in and out, "tasting" the emotions that stemmed from the crowd.

"They seem to be doing a decent job of security," Zora muttered. "I've lost track of the number of rich slave buyers who'd have been lured into a back alley and murdered even on Utopion."

"Wouldn't want a riot to break out or have the ones willing to pay top credit for what you've collected stop coming to these affairs, now would you?" asked Jack. "That would spoil the whole slave auction."

"I had no idea," Garret mumbled. "I mean, I knew it was still going on. I pretty much *was* one when those pirates picked me up. But I thought the Republic put an end to all the big slave markets like this. Ackabar was the last one... wasn't it?"

"It was," said Jack. "But republics fall, empires rise, and it's never long before the stain of something like this comes back into view. Too many credits to be had to ever keep something like this down for good."

"They never went away," Nilo said, speaking for the first time since they'd left the ship. "Ackabar and the other markets you heard about being taken down were merely the result of clans losing favor with the House of Reason, who sent the Legion in to take care of them. The clans that continued to work inside the Republic's paradigm of uses—like the zhee tribes—got free hand to do exactly this sort of thing, so long as it was far enough out on the edge."

"Some Republic," Zora scoffed.

Jack shrugged. "Well. What do I know? I just worked for them."

"And now you work for me," Nilo reminded him. "Both of you do. And Garret is here for his friend. So whether you're listening to me as your employer or as someone who wants to help your friend, you need to prepare yourself. You are going to see things that you will feel are too much. Things that should not be but are. I know the types of people you are, and I admire you for it. You will want to help. You will want to say something to put a stop to it."

Nilo paused to let that settle in before continuing. "Even you, Jack. But you're not going to do *anything*. None of you. Neither am I. We will *not* do the right thing. We will let what we see pass, because if we don't, we will not complete our mission."

"Our mission is still to get Leenah," said Zora. "Right?"

"Yes. That's your mission, and that's my mission."

The team continued down the street, passing old one-story buildings that sometimes appeared empty and other times teemed with life. Some were guarded. They passed one where sleepy-looking zhee fought the urge to doze as they lounged on wide steps, their slug-throwing automatic rifles resting in their laps. Other buildings issued unseen laughter, screams of rage, cries and pleas for help, shouts of terror.

"What's going on inside there?" Garret asked.

"Not the kinda question you want an answer to, kid," said Jack, who seemed himself bothered by it and struggling not to act so. "Auction already started. You're hearing the unlucky ones who were purchased first."

Garret looked as though he was going to be sick. "Do you think Leenah...?"

"If they have her and if she's still alive," Nilo said, "then no. From what you tell me she's attractive, healthy, and an Endurian. That means she'll be held back in reserve until the end of the auctions. That's when the Gomarii bring out the ones they think will get them the most credits. Keeps the buyers around for the whole thing, which makes all these sellers on the streets happy, too. It's a symbiotic relationship. These auctions usually last about a week. Judging from the size of the crowd, I'd say we're four days in. The really big players, the big spenders, the type who would like their own Endurian slave, they'll be arriving just after us."

The news didn't seem to make Garret feel any better.

"Don't worry," said Nilo. "I know of ways to find out if she's present that don't require us sitting and watching every auction. You're a key part of that, Garret. Just act normal."

"I feel freaked out."

"That's what I mean."

A well-dressed man wearing a suit and flanked by two guards, one of whom held a young Githid girl by her coverall—a rough, brown piece of clothing the Gomarii attired all of their property in prior to sale—moved up the steps of a seemingly empty building only to be greeted at the door by another mercenary. There was a silent standoff that ended with the well-dressed man asking, "Where... where do you, or rather, *how* do you reserve one of these—the houses?"

"Find one that isn't being used," was the reply, and then the door was shut.

The man straightened his expensive jacket nervously and rubbed his thumb against his index finger, standing there. He turned to his guard, ignoring the horrified and pleading look of his recent purchase, and said, "Let's see if there's anything farther down."

He walked off quickly, causing one of his guards to hustle ahead of him and quietly remind him of the dangers of going alone as the other escorted the young slave. It was the walk of a man ashamed of who he was and what he had set his heart to do.

Zora wanted to kill him on the spot. No termination contract would be required for the pleasure. She would do it simply because it was the thing that needed to be done. There was murder in Jack's eyes as well. But neither of them made a move. Both did as Nilo instructed and allowed the travesty to go unchallenged. And as they walked along, taking a separate path that removed them from the man and his prey, Zora couldn't help but think that if he were here, Keel would have found a way to kill this man and his guards and leave with no one the wiser.

They marched up the hill, and when they reached its zenith, they got an up-close look at the ship that had been looming ever larger at their approach, the monolithic feature at the end of the avenue, the giant to which all eyes were invariably drawn. Zora had never seen a ship quite like it before. It was alien, not the familiar sort that had come from millennia of interaction between the galaxy's various species. Looking upon it made no sense to her mind. It was at once boxy and smooth, with a long curling prow that seemed to separate in multiple directions before bending upward like the blades of a scimitar. It seemed utterly incapable of atmospheric flight, and yet it had somehow done exactly that in order to bring itself down on the bedrock at the top of the great hill, which now seemed more like a small mountain that had been beaten down until it became submissive and round.

The thing's hull was a deep blue turned black from the scorching fires of atmospheric entry. An amphitheater rose before it, climbing at least three stories high and only managing to obscure the ship's struts and underbelly.

"Keep close once we reach the selling market," Nilo advised. "There's a code of conduct that is expected to be followed. No fighting, murder, or thievery. All of it is punishable by death at the hands of the Gomarii. There is no appeal. A single accusation can end your life if the slavers believe it. Even those purchasing at the markets—the very worst kind of people in the galaxy—are willing to behave in order to get what they want."

"Sounds safe enough," said Jack. "So why the warning about keeping close?"

"The Gomarii make an exception for the crime of kidnapping. They will look the other way if a straggler is picked off from a group."

"Because punishing something like that could be viewed as an indictment of their own practice?" Zora guessed.

"And because most of those who are kidnapped are sold to the Gomarii—they'll allow no one to sell slaves while they're on planet. There's a period for paying ransoms at the end of it all. If no ransom is paid, you'll be sold at the next market, whenever and wherever it is."

"Not the sort of place to come visiting all by your lonesome," Jack said.

"It's not the kind of place I want to visit at all," said Garret.

"We are an imposing bunch," Nilo said. "As long as we stay in a close formation, no one is going to bother us. Between Jack, Zora, and myself... we don't look worth the trouble."

That much was true. While Garret looked out of place, the three with him were imposing figures. Nilo and Zora were conspicuously armored and carrying their blaster rifles in the open. Jack, though unarmored, wore a blaster at his side and walked with the swagger of a man who was more than willing to use it. Which left Garret looking like...

... like the man who'd hired the trio to protect him as he went into this den of iniquity to fulfill his obscene fantasies.

The realization of how perfectly Nilo had arranged their cover made Garret feel sick to his stomach.

As they pushed through the remaining avenue to reach the stadium, slowed by the sheer number of beings that chittered and teemed among the lone street, Zora found herself fantasizing about an orbital bombardment raining down from a Legion destroyer high above them all. It would be worth dying in such a blast if so many wicked humanoids departed at the same time.

But then, they weren't *all* wicked. In fact, as she looked closer, there were more slaves than buyers. The prey always outnumbered the predators.

A long column of slaves wearing the distinctive brown jumper—though some were humiliated and stripped naked—walked in single file on the opposite side of the street, a procession of the damned moving down the way Zora and her team had just come up. Each was ener-chained to the one before them and behind them. Some in the crowd laughed and groped and taunted, and the owner of this lone line of purchased souls seemed not to care at the treatment of his property.

Zora shuddered to think what their fate might be.

"That's one of the big buyers," Nilo said. "They'll stick around for the end, but they all compete to outdo one another on the lots."

"The lots?" asked Zora.

"Groups. Humans sold together by sex, age, ability, you name it. Ones that are deemed unworthy of being sold individually."

Another train of slaves was being led down the hill by a Gomarii. He must have agreed to make delivery on behalf of the purchaser. A zhee prince seeking to restock his harem. A band of pirates who would resell the best prospects and give the other slaves a choice once aboard their mothership: join or be used and then spaced. A core-world pimp or other hustler who dealt in the flesh trade and had a need for fully disposable products for those rich clients too afraid to make the trip here to live out their darkest perversions.

Again Zora felt the urge swell in her chest—the urge to *do something* about the miserable wailing and crying before her in that forced march. But what could she do? Kill one Gomarii, or one buyer, and die herself? Free the slaves long enough for them to run frantically before being captured again?

It all seemed hopeless. And if what Nilo had said was true, and the Republic had known about these horrors, the same Republic that never ceased to tax and censor and bully its citizens in an endless quest to right some undefined injustice that only it could identify and recognize... if that Republic had turned a blind eye to such ravaging injustice so long as it was far removed from its glittering planets and cities, what hope could there ever be for change? How could anything be done unless one had the courage to do it themselves?

Zora found herself feeling the same fire that Nilo must have felt in his heart. She wanted to burn down everything around her and set off a trigger-nuke to cleanse the planet.

As the team grew nearer to the heart of the market, a large group of Kublarens wearing their traditional robes and armed with their traditionally decorated slug throwers passed in the other direction. This was the first time Zora had seen the species, and though she couldn't be sure, she thought that one of the Kublarens licked its eyeball as it passed Nilo.

And she saw Nilo, in turn, give a small, curt nod.

22

Nilo and his team were set far in the rear of the serious buyers, occupying the top seats of an amphitheater where those with the most vetted credits sat up front. Nilo drew the others' attention to a great zhee warlord in the front row, his swollen stomach bulging from beneath crimson robes like the great hill they'd just traversed. The zhee reclined on a litter carried by younger and stronger members of his own species. More zhee took up the seating behind their opulent leader, clutching their weapons as they scanned the crowd.

"That's Kamartha the Feared," said Nilo. "He supposedly led ten thousand zhee warriors against a Legion company and fought them to a standstill. The Republic intervened before the last of the legionnaires could be slaughtered... according to him."

"What's he doing here?" Zora asked.

"He is purported to have the most lavish and diverse harem found anywhere across the four home worlds of the zhee. I assume he's seeking to add to it."

Kamartha the Feared was not without competition. Primarily a large band of what appeared to be a confederation of human pirates and other undesirables. Rowdy, drunk, and no doubt rivaling the zhee in odor, they looked like the dregs thrown out of a thousand cantinas, now gathered up in one place. They too had armed guards who scanned the zhee and others in the amphitheater warily, as did regularly stationed Gomarii throughout the entirety of the area, especially near the stage at the foot of the great slave ship, where the actual items up for auction were presented.

Beyond these two great groups—and the even greater gathering of Kublarens who sat in the section directly in front of Nilo and the others—the rest of the crowd was made up of smaller coalitions and individual buyers. Some had made the trip with the intent of buying relatively low with hopes of selling at a higher rate once away from the lawless corners of the galaxy. Others sought free labor and wouldn't think of employing something so common—or in the case of some species, so forbidden—as a bot to do their bidding.

"The zhee will be interested in the lots for labor and the single females for their harem—all species are to be collected," Nilo explained, careful not to point or make any other gesture that would tip off those watching the crowd that he was gathering intelligence. "They'll be interested in males as well, if only to see them die in blood sports.

"The pirates, by contrast, are only interested in the lots. They're resellers mainly, though they'll sometimes allow a slave to join the crew if it strikes their fancy. Particularly females, if they're agreeable. They won't spend the time or credits on the later auctions unless there's a warlord among them looking for a new concubine."

"And how about the Kublarens?" Zora asked.

"I've never seen them at a slave market before," said Nilo.

"I thought they were your buddies," said Jack.

"I have no idea what you're talking about." The tone of Nilo's voice suggested that he also had no desire for any more discussion like that to be spoken aloud.

Jack and Zora could hardly be blamed for focusing on the throng of Kublarens sitting right up front. Their location meant that they had shown the Gomarii that they possessed the wealth of credits necessary to be considered serious players. The others in the audience noticed as well, and many watched to see what this delegation would do at the start of the next lot brought forth for bidding. The small but menacing Kublarens were dressed in their formal robes, their chieftain being regaled and lauded by his fellow tribesman with every bit as much honor and deference as that shown by the zhee to their warlord across the way. In fact, the Kublarens made it a point to stare unblinkingly at Kamartha the Feared, who seemed perturbed by their attention.

Kublarens were rarely seen off Kublar. Kublaren slaves were a rarity as well, primarily due to the musky odor of fish they exuded from their skin, a scent that was unpleasant to most species. And even in those darker corners where a Kublaren was purchased not to be a bondservant, disappointed owners decided that they tasted worse than they smelled. They could also be counted on to kill their captors whenever possible—or die trying—and, failing that, to kill as many of their fellow captives as possible, so as to deprive their captors of the financial rewards of doing so. As a result, the Gomarii considered Kublarens one of the few species not suitable for enslaving. They were, quite simply, not worth the effort.

But their credits were more than welcome. The fierce little fighters sat and croaked among themselves, a swollen crowd that dwarfed even the zhee, who also weren't among the species the Gomarii would enslave. Not because a zhee couldn't be made compliant, but because of the great dishonor it was to all the zhee for a fellow member of the species to be held in bond by anyone but another zhee. It was an unacceptable insult to a species that thought itself the pinnacle of the galaxy. This wouldn't have swayed the Gomarii in the least if not for the fact that the zhee were also extremely good buyers... and so the Gomarii and zhee had come to an arrangement through treaties and other understandings stretching back centuries.

Which, for the galaxy, was a shame. For if the zhee *had* turned their warring ways against the Gomarii, the galaxy would be better off for it. The Republic had even tried to wield the zhee in such a manner; Nilo knew of at least four different Dark Ops or Nether Ops missions that had attempted to pit the two species against one another. But none of those efforts had ever made it out of the planning stages. The old bonds between Gomarii and zhee went too deep.

"Now the purchase agreement for Lot 1636-L," said an amplified voice, relayed through a number of floating micro speakers. A chorus of cheers and hoots and braying and croaking and clicking came up from the various species in attendance.

Nilo turned his attention to the stage, which had been set up at the end of a long and covered ramp leading back to the Gomarii ship. The speaker was a large green-and-brown bot whose frame and facial structure reflected Gomarii appearance, and behind the bot stood holographic representations of the poor souls now being auctioned. It was clear this was a live feed from somewhere aboard the ship. And it was equally evident, from the way they huddled and rubbed their exposed shoulders and sought to comfort one another while looking up at some unseen object, that they were watching themselves in real time. Awaiting their fate.

"I don't see Leenah," said Garret. He sounded relieved.

Nilo answered softly. "You won't. I had our friend on the ship run an analysis of all the lots that will be sold today. The Gomarii list the age, sex, and species in advance. There's not an Endurian among them. She is yet to come."

Jack crossed his arms and leaned back. "Or she's already been sold."

"No," Garret said. "She's too pretty to go in the first round."

Jack rolled his eyes. "Lucky her."

The confederacy of pirates immediately bid forty thousand credits for the lot and seemed proud of the number. Zora had no frame of reference for whether this was an appropriate sum or an attempt to lowball and get lucky. A zhee herald announced a new bid, raising the price by five thousand credits. The pirates countered, and the two parties began to go back and forth, raising the price in five-thousand-credit increments. Small, hovering bots zipped throughout the amphitheater like birds, recording and watching for Gomarii security, but also looking out for any bidders not seated in the front rows who might wish to join in.

The zhee drove the price to seventy thousand credits, and the pirates cursed and hollered but offered no increase, much to Kamartha the Feared's delight.

Zora leaned to the side and muttered to Jack, "There's what, seventy humanoids in that lot? The price of a slave is a measly thousand credits each?"

Jack shrugged. "Always cheaper in bulk."

Zora looked over at him, but it was clear the man found no humor in his own remark. He was staring angrily at the proceedings.

The green-and-brown bot on the stage implored the audience to consider their finances. Could they live with themselves for letting this group go at such a low rate? It spoke of genetic testing, the strength remaining in old limbs, and the vigor that would soon be found in the young if they were properly nurtured. Anything to make the current lot appealing to buyers yet to enter the fray. But no new bids came, and so the bot began the final throes of the purchase, counting down once and twice and...

The Kublaren chieftain rose and croaked that he was willing to pay, "one-ah, k'kik... hundred and seventy thousand-ah of credits."

A flurry of noise erupted from the crowd, and the bot at the center of the proceedings had to amplify its voice further in order to regain the audience's attention. It complimented the Kublaren on seeing the value of the lot and asked if anyone else also saw such tremendous value and would not like to increase their own bid... or would they be shown up by the newcomers?

The pirates replied with bawdy comments and murderous threats but made no actual move toward either violence or digging into their purses. The zhee took on a posture of high arrogance and importance, laughing at the bot's suggestion and waving their hoof-like hands as if to say, *By all means let those fools overpay such a sum.*

The auction ended, and the Kublarens were in possession of seventy new slaves to be delivered at the end of the scheduled sales block. The Kublarens inflated their throat sacs and croaked rapidly, excited at their victory.

The next lot shown by the bot was smaller, only fifty humanoids including a peculiar insectoid known as a Qulingat't. It was in rough shape, missing an eye and part of its right mandible.

The pirates were the opening bid again, offering twenty thousand this time. The zhee responded to the dance at twenty-five.

The Kublarens bid one hundred and seventy thousand.

Howls of laughter and clapping rained down from all rows in the amphitheater. The bot didn't waste much time before declaring the Kublarens the victors once more. The zhee laughed harder than they had the first time, enjoying this unexpected entertainment of watching novices be separated from their credits at such a rapid rate.

One hundred slaves were presented as the next lot. The first bid belonged to the Kublarens, beating the pirates to the punch.

One hundred and seventy thousand credits.

Sold.

And this time, no one laughed.

Kamartha the Feared motioned for one of his attendants to come near, then whispered into his long, erect ear. The subservient zhee hurried to one of the waiting communication bots, which in turn relayed the message down the line. Soon a pair of scarred and armored Gomarii were at the rotund leader's side to hear his concerns in person. It was clear from the Gomarii's turning heads and the frequent gesturing of the irate zhee that the Kublarens were the topic of discussion.

Not long after, some sort of understanding between the zhee and Gomarii must have been reached, because the bot at center stage announced a temporary halt to the auctions. This caused some consternation among the gallery, particularly among the Kublarens. Another contingent of Gomarii approached the Kublaren chieftain and spoke with him, a translator bot going back and forth between the towering slavers and the diminutive but deadly group that had the attention of all in attendance.

"What do you think is going on?" Zora asked.

"The zhee have taken offense to being shown up, and I imagine no one else is thrilled about the Kublarens running the prices up so high. My guess is that the Gomarii are verifying that the Kublarens understand each lot is a separate bid."

Jack laughed at the thought. "So they're assuming the koobs can't grasp what's going on around them. That's the kind of thing that'll cost you. Those things are as cunning a race as I've seen."

Nilo nodded. "It's a far too common mistake. Even the Savages once made it."

Jack chuckled again. "You know, I never met a human who cared for some backward species in the galaxy as much as you seem to care about the koobs."

Nilo smiled, but without mirth. "What are you attribute to backwardness is a conscious choice by the Kublaren to live as they see fit—or, in many cases, a lifestyle forced upon them by a predatory government."

Zora found this change of topic refreshing, if only because it took her mind off of what they had been witnessing. "As in, now that the core and mid-core have all the benefits of technology, any species or planets still behind them should be forced to stay in the past and not spoil their planet's natural beauty?"

"Yes, but only in part." Nilo stood. "You three stay here. Keep an eye on Garret. There's going to be some ill feelings by the Kublarens over how they're being treated. I think this pause in the selling is soon going to stretch into an extended hiatus. And not an amicable one."

"Where are you going?" asked Jack.

Nilo put on his battle armor's helmet. He spoke softly, almost a whisper, as if speaking only to himself. "I'm going to take a look around the ship."

"Sure you don't want me to handle that?" asked Jack, using the comm connection now that Nilo had his helmet on. "You look a little too dressy for just wandering around, and that's my job anyway."

"You believe my armor won't allow me to blend in."

"Your armor costs more than most of the ships that brought the rest of these losers in. Tell me what you need and I'll do it and no one will see me. And if they do, they won't remember it."

"Thank you. But they won't see me." Nilo strode through the crowd and out of the amphitheater.

Almost the moment he'd left, the Kublarens began to croak loudly and push against the Gomarii.

The ill feelings Nilo had predicted were now showing themselves.

23

Four contracts were down and the fifth was the one Keel hoped would cause a bounty to finally show up on the head of Tyrus Rechs. He was perplexed that one hadn't already, but Lao Pak assured him that he wasn't being lazy about checking; there was nothing out there.

This latest target was an appointed Repub Navy officer, Captain Daug Pemm. He had once commanded the Republic destroyer *Insistence*, but had jockeyed to be reassigned to the light frigate *Deramus-Credeur*, named after a retired House of Reason delegate, once the fighting against the Legion began in earnest at the declaration of Article Nineteen.

Pemm was a loyalist but not an idealist. He had no interest in dying for the cause. He waited in support of Admiral Landoo and was as relieved as his ambitious junior officers were disappointed when the *Deramus-Credeur* was not called into battle. Pemm couldn't understand why any of his bridge crew, all of them appointed officers as well, wanted to fight to begin with. Landoo had taken the responsibility that comes with the top; she had no choice. But Pemm and the others? What was the good of taking an appointment only to die?

The best-connected points were always held in reserve—unless they specifically sought a combat ribbon to boost their post-military careers. Or, if they had truly large plans, the multiple combat ribbons that came from being appointed to the Legion. But Pemm had no aspirations beyond residing in the comfortable oversized captain's chair until retirement, preferably on the bridge of whatever ship was least likely to see combat. Then he would lobby for a defense position based on his naval expertise and would peacefully pass his time writing memorandums somewhere at the edge of the core—not too close to Utopion, but comfortably removed from the mid-core, let alone the barbaric galaxy's edge.

But then Goth Sullus arrived and the game changed. All at once, the captain found himself answering to a militant group calling themselves Imperials who performed rather tactless reviews of his service record, demanded he give up command of his frigate, and insisted that if he performed a loyalty oath to Emperor Sullus, he *might* be allowed to serve with reduced rank aboard one of the MCR ships.

That would hardly do. Pemm had long ago surrounded himself with his own hand-picked bridge crew, every one of them appointed, though with less prestige than their captain. Primarily they were senatorial appointees from unimportant worlds. But they were loyal. And so when Pemm ordered his crew to remove the ship from the service of Goth Sullus—while still insisting on his loyalty to the House of Reason—he found no resistance from within.

Officially, that made him a pirate in unlawful possession of a Republic warship. He was to be captured on sight.

And yet, that alone would not have warranted a bounty. The galaxy was filled with appointed officers who had both fought on behalf of Goth Sullus and mutinied against him. The bounty was earned on a planet called Jaffar.

In the aftermath of Kublar's revolution and the subsequent trials and executions of its former governing class, planets still controlled by governments loyal to the House of Reason realized that the largest threat to them was not the post-imperial Republic but their own citizenry. Pemm made it known that he was available to serve the true and lawful government ruled by the House of *Reason* in exchange for credits and other resources—a necessary resupply provided by others faithful to the resistance and opposed to the illegal use of Article 19. Jaffar took him up on his offer.

The planet was small and populated primarily by humans. It had once been rich in minerals and metals, making its early colonists fantastically wealthy, but the last of these had been stripped away decades before, leaving behind a planet of little importance in the grand galactic scheme, the sort of modest place where life revolved around buying and selling from one another. The most enterprising citizens left in pursuit of grander and greater opportunities, but the planet had its simple charms, which served as a mooring to those desiring family, heritage, and tradition.

Jaffar initially joined the Republic to escape from the oppressive rule of a large, corporate mining syndicate that had deprived the population of more than ninety percent of the resources they sucked from deep within its high-peaked mountains. The Republic promised a say in their affairs—something the syndicate did not. So the corporation left and the government came in, nationalizing the mines and providing the citizens with a few more opportunities, but the same percentages of revenue.

And then the mines were exhausted, and the Republic stayed. The result was a two-class society. One class was the citizens; the other was the government. Members of the latter class were rarely born on Jaffar, but rather moved to the planet at the behest of the Republic, sent to fill some necessary post that came with planetary membership. Their salaries were guaranteed by the Republic. So while the civilian populace lived meagerly according to what they could generate without the wages of the mines, the governing class carried on lavishly. Their galactic standard wage was meant to keep people living comfortably on places like Utopion, meaning they lived like lords and barons on Jaffar, enjoying spacious mansions, clear skies, brilliant blue glacial lakes, and the rarity of wilderness not found in the core or mid-core. Someday the galaxy would discover the planet, and then tourism might follow; it was a beautiful place with well-planned villages that only added to its charm. But for now... this unspoiled beauty was the sole province of the governing class.

As such, it became a post those near retirement would bribe to get. Why be stationed on a planet like Utopion where the work never ended if you could be paid the same to serve on Jaffar, do little, and live like a king?

Jaffar's citizens might have endured this disparity had the Republic officials simply left them alone... but no bureaucrat can resist interfering in the lives of others. They passed burdensome rules that superseded local laws, impacting virtually every aspect of the people's lives. There was no fighting it; the House of Reason always won.

Until Article Nineteen.

It was then that the people of Jaffar decided that these Republic officials were no longer legitimate authorities.

And so Pemm was called upon to bring his stolen frigate over the planet in a show of military force. The local House of Reason loyalists spread their views among the populace that Article Nineteen was not the *done deal* that people thought it was, that the House of Reason would return to legitimacy, and all of this was just around the corner. The show of force was a reminder of what would happen to rebels once order was, inevitably, restored.

The people of Jaffar were not swayed. An election was held, a vote unsanctioned by the House of Reason, and Jaffar overwhelmingly chose to leave the Republic, just as Kublar and an increasing number of other planets had done. Those claiming authority by virtue of their old positions were suddenly toothless in word... but Pemm took it upon himself to not make it so in deed.

An orbital bombardment by a Republic light frigate like the *Deramus-Credeur* is easily defended. Unlike a destroyer, the frigate must enter the planetary atmosphere, thereby becoming vulnerable to planetary attacks. But Jaffar lacked any such defenses. And the bombardment resulted in the death of thousands through direct fire, and tens of thousands more from subsequent hardships caused by the House of Reason-friendly government refusing to supply aid and other necessities to its citizens. Jaffar's people endured a brutal winter with no power and no food left in its stores. The death count from starvation reached a quarter million before the galactic news cycles picked up the unfolding humanitarian tragedy.

The publicity prompted a response from the Legion, which only needed to send in one destroyer and one company of legionnaires to completely topple the loyalist government and hand them over to a newly elected government chosen by the people of Jaffar. The Republic then followed with aid, but the people of Jaffar, while grateful for the help from both the Legion and the Republic, saw the entire ordeal as a clarion call to remain independent.

Of course, by the time the new Legion had arrived, Pemm and the *Deramus-Credeur* were long gone. But his involvement in this affair was sufficiently egregious that the Republic issued a bounty for him and his officers: capture only, no terminations. They wanted the butchers of Jaffar to stand trial for war crimes.

Political analysts on the planet speculated that should the Republic succeed in bringing Pemm in, the gesture *might* convince the people of Jaffar that this House of Liberty-led Republic had forged a galactic government worth rejoining. But that wasn't an outcome anyone was predicting. The Republic bounty was a paltry twenty thousand credits—too little to capture the attention of any serious bounty hunter.

Except, of course, for Aeson Keel.

The first step was locating the target. Normally, tracking down a lone ship across an entire galaxy presented a near-insurmountable challenge—but this wasn't some surplus cruiser stripped of its weapons and sold to the highest bidder; it was a Vincent-class light assault frigate. Republic property. The kind of ship that would be memorable whenever it showed up at a port to resupply.

And sure enough, informants had plenty of leads and sightings of such a cruiser. The *Defiance of Reason*, it was now called. It proved to be a simple thing to track down. Keel imagined it was only because of a lack of resources that the Republic hadn't sent a kill team of their own rather than issuing a bounty.

And as he followed up on the information brokers' leads, he pieced together a clear picture of the captain's routine. Every two months the ship showed up somewhere to resupply. Presumably that was how long it took the crew to eat through their food stores. And the distance between the locations of consecutive sightings was also reasonably consistent.

There were also sporadic reports of possible sightings in between the resupplies—reports of piracy, though these were more speculative. Many of the captains who'd made these claims—that their ships had been boarded, their cargo confiscated—had reputations of untrustworthiness among those who knew where to look—as Keel did from his days smuggling. A few had been convicted of insurance fraud. So Keel took those reports as doubtful.

Honey looked at the pattern that Keel had mapped out on a datapad. "They're jumping in more or less a circle around the Break Arm nebula. So I guess it stands to reason that when they show up next, it'll be somewhere in the Pah-Soon Cluster."

Keel nodded in agreement. "Yeah, that's about right."

"The entire Pah-Soon Cluster. That really pinpoints it," said the Tennar, with obvious sarcasm. She felt the entire operation was a waste of time and was only serving to prolong her forced servitude. "Only ten planets out there they could resupply on. And what, a four-hour window once they show?"

That had been the average. Keel mumbled a confirmation, though he knew she knew.

"So... all we have to do is pick the right planet, the right docking bay, be there before they show up, and nab them. Easy!"

"Never said it would be easy, sweetheart."

"And I never said I wanted to spend the rest of my life playing ghost-ship hunter."

"We've narrowed it down. We'll take our best shot. And if we miss them, we refine and do it again."

"In another *two months*!" Honey snapped. "Keel, you could be chasing this ship for well over a year. And that's assuming they don't know you're coming. If they alter their schedule at all, then you can't even begin to guess where they'll be. So unless you're counting on them running out of credits and listing the frigate on the night market, I'm not sure what your options are."

"If they're being smart," Keel said, "they won't run out of credits anytime soon. They got a pretty big payday from the old Jaffar government, from what I've gathered. As long as they don't do something stupid, that should keep the crew fed for years."

"Really not making this sit any better with me."

Keel shrugged.

"All right," said Honey, almost sounding determined to actually help solve the problem. "Enough credits to feed them, sure. What about keeping them happy? Maybe there's an opportunity out there if we change the questions we're asking the brokers. Instead of looking for sightings of the ship, maybe we can ask whether any crewmembers jumped ship or were given leave. I know that everyone on that frigate is supposed to be loyal, but loyalty only goes so far."

"Talking from experience?"

"And common sense."

"I'm not opposed to asking, but if the brokers had that sort of information, they'd have tossed it to us already to squeeze some additional credits. The fact that no one has even suggested it makes me think that what's left of Pemm's crew is still happy to ride with him."

Honey looked down forlornly. "Well. That's my big idea." She threw her tentacled arms out. "I don't know what to say. I'm starting to get the feeling that you've got me locked up here indefinitely. This is what, the fifth contract that you're looking to take in? The first four haven't even caused a blip."

"Small fennocks. A warmup. This is the big one. Pemm was connected to the type of people who kept your old outfit in business. If he goes down... a bounty absolutely gets placed on Rechs. Then you've got your exit strategy. Once we nab whoever comes for me."

"Sure, it's big. It's also a big ask. I've done everything I can to help you out—and yes, I'm still breathing because of it, but I'm not interested in becoming a member of your crew, Keel. And I'm *really* not interested in a life of perpetual servitude to you while you try to figure out who the hell you really are." She rubbed her temples. "I honestly wish I'd never even mentioned Kill Team Ice."

Keel cycled his display over to an analysis of inventories that the *Defiance of Reason* had purchased. "I don't trust you enough to have you on my crew full-time, sweetheart. And when I think about who I want by my side for the rest of my life, you're not on that list either, so don't flatter yourself. But I know what you're saying, and we'll work it out the way I said we would."

Keel had promised her a million credits and a clean exit at any port in the galaxy she could name before he linked back up with Black Leaf.

"All I need from you," he continued, "is for you to deal with the Nether Ops agents I bring in from this."

"I'd be happy to, if we ever get that far. But who knows how long you're going to be after this bounty, because the way you're going about it, it's going to take pure blind luck to find him."

"That's why I'm going to try and make my own luck." Keel pointed at a highlighted part of the datapad, which now showed an inventory of foodstuffs, cleaning supplies, clothing, raw materials, and other necessities for life aboard a large starship. "See that?"

"No. What am I looking at?"

Keel magnified the text.

"Egallan Spindust?" Honey said. "So what? Someone has a sweet tooth."

"Not just a sweet tooth, an obsession. Captain Pemm is a creature of habit. If anyone on Jaffar had bothered to look into his military record, they'd see he has a tendency to employ orbital bombardments as a first resort. He's nothing if not predictable. And these resupplies—almost the exact same distance, frequency, time window, you name it. No variation. This is the type of guy who would have every single day of his life be the exact same if he could manage it."

"Including what he has for dessert?" Honey frowned. "Because that's a lot of Egallan Spindust."

"Yeah, well, points aren't held to the same fitness standards, and Captain Pemm goes in for dessert a lot, judging from his last official holos. My point is, look at the manifests we've got that are supposed to be tied to his ship. Any time there's any kind of sweet, it's the dust. Spindust or nothing else."

"Fine. He's particular about it. So what? We head to the factory and hide ourselves in a crate?" Honey looked up in consideration. "Actually, the odds of success are about the same as what we're doing now."

Keel gave a half smile. "You're closer than you think. His last three resupplies haven't shown the stuff on the manifests. Or a replacement sweet, either."

"Maybe he stocked up."

"Nope. Previous orders of the dust aren't any larger than usual—in fact a few are smaller. My hunch is that he hasn't been able to find a distributor in this sector of space and his supplies are consistently dwindling, if not already depleted."

"Or he decided he doesn't like the stuff any longer."

Keel shook his head. "This guy is on the run and rattled. People in turmoil cling to old comforts when they can get them."

"So what's your plan, exactly?"

"We put the word out in this sector that we've got a huge surplus of the stuff and we need to offload it as quickly and cheaply as possible. Make it look like we attempted to corner the market but the clock is ticking and we have to move on."

Honey shrugged but didn't outright dismiss the idea. "They might see that as an explanation for their inability to get some—someone else bought it all up. Easy enough to spoof a transportation company and put it up on the trading index in that sector. But who's to say they even watch those things?"

"Somebody's out there arranging these pickups and making sure the ship gets its supplies. They'll see it. You can't have a resupply schedule that runs this tightly without doing a little bit of groundwork ahead of time. And we know it's not just repeat business. Different planets, different suppliers, no obvious corporate connections. They find whoever has what they need, then they move on."

"Fine. That doesn't sound any worse than guessing the spot they'll show up in another month. How do we get the stuff? Or is that a spoof?"

"Orders started arriving a week ago. Got a warehouse under an alias, and it's already full of the stuff. All we need to do is work the index and get a freight shuttle to stay docked near the place. This ship won't pass as a freighter."

"You did all that without me?"

Keel nodded, unconcerned that she seemed bothered by this. "Yep."

"Well, where's the warehouse?"

"Dillon Station. A junker on Hussar."

"Why would you pick *that* place? It's a nightmare to get in and out of."

That was true. Dillon was only large enough to service medium-sized freighters. Larger vessels had to remain unmoored, waiting in orbit to receive freight via shuttle deliveries, which added considerable time to the offloading process. Keel had tried to avoid it whenever possible when posing as a smuggler, but in this instance, the circumstances should work to his favor.

"Exactly," he said. "A frigate like that can't dock at Dillon, and while its single escort shuttle can carry some freight, it can't manage all that we're offloading. So either they take more than four hours—which we know they hate—or they have our soon-to-be-purchased shuttle deliver directly to them. Which gives us an easy way onto their ship."

"So they get the Spindust and we're the bonus that comes with purchase."

"That's the plan."

Honey nodded. "I think this might actually work. *But*—I don't like you leaving me out. I want to handle the indexes. I've done work like that on other jobs."

"I had a feeling you'd say something like that. Indexes are all yours."

24

Honey worked alongside Keel and Death, Destroyer of Worlds, in a chilly warehouse filled with cases of the exotic candy called Spindust. It was pink and green, came out of its packaging in the shape of a cloud, and pulled apart in long elastic strings that popped and exploded inside the mouth. Keel assured her that humans enjoyed the sweet, cloying product, but after sampling it, she found it entirely unpalatable. Keel wasn't a fan of it either.

Unfortunately, neither were the bidders she was after on the index. At least not when it came to purchasing the entirety of the stock. It had been up for two weeks at rock-bottom rates, and she had leaked the word that they had a limited time to offload the goods, with a deadline of three days from now. This had, as expected, prompted buyers to lowball the already low price in the hope of scoring a truly fantastic deal. But Honey would accept an offer only on the condition that they take the entire supply. She gave the same formulaic answer every time: "We know what it takes to get an ROI on this. So take it all or it goes to a distributor in the mid-core. We're fine breaking even, but we're not going to lose credits here." The bet was that no one would want to get stuck holding *that* much candy regardless of the price. No one except the target, who by now would be getting desperate for his fix.

Everything else was in order. Keel had purchased a secondhand shuttle shortly after arriving, and it sat ready—big, gray, dented, and dirty—on the dedicated landing pad attached to the warehouse they had filled with sweets. Death was serving as a maintenance bot for the new vessel rather than remaining alone on the *Crow* and had seemingly spent most of his time petitioning the New Boss endlessly about adding an aftermarket PDC system. Every ship, even one as homely as the freight shuttle, needed some firepower.

"Sorry, pal," said Keel. "The only firepower going into this shuttle is going to be us."

The bot beeped that while this was less than ideal, it was better than nothing at all. And in any event, the large shuttle had sufficient mass to be capable of causing exceptional damage should it be rammed into a target at extreme velocity. Death cackled and bleated with delight as it calculated the kinetic damage and theoretical death toll the shuttle might cause should it strike the bridge of a Republic light frigate at full speed.

The self-imposed deadline drew near and all that was left was to wait as Honey worked the indexes, hoping that the *Defiance of Reason* would reveal itself. Keel had been sharing war stories with his bot when Honey burst excitedly into his quarters.

"We've got him."

"You sure?" Keel said, wanting to resist getting swept up in the enthusiasm. He had just about given up hope that this was going to happen. "Not just someone with deep enough pockets to take all this off our hands?"

"No. It's them. I went through the usual and they didn't push back once. Not on price, quantity, or our window to get the delivery done. The delivery is what sealed it."

"How's that?"

Honey was effusive in her excitement. "They said their ship was too big to get into this port and asked if we had a shuttle that could help them achieve a four-hour window of delivery."

"That sounds like them all right. But it *could* still be one of the bigger haulers, too. A Galaxy-class owned by someone who has the room to take on some cheap freight to resell a few jumps down."

"This is them, Keel. I know it."

"Did they tell you to look for a stolen Republic frigate at delivery?"

"Practically. They said they could fit it all but were extremely tight-lipped about the exact model. Who would do that? Why would some jump jockey care what his ship is?"

Keel shrugged. "How long until they arrive?"

"Tomorrow. Eighteen hundred local time."

"Guess we'll find out pretty quickly if these are our guys or not, then."

"It's them, Keel. That delivery time seals it. We'll be loading the freight at the precise time when the rest of the spaceport is whiling away their time in the cantina. Fewer eyes to see the frigate waiting to receive cargo."

Keel nodded approvingly. "I'm convinced. Let's get ourselves ready."

"What are you going to do about weapons?"

"Why? Did they bring it up?"

"Nothing specifically. But they want to do an inspection. Said they have suspicions this may be a smuggling operation—no offense and I said none taken—and they want to make sure we have the goods and the documentation to prove it's not stolen."

"Well, we do."

"I know that. But we have to look like a legitimate operation, not a bunch of smugglers. Which includes dressing the part. How many honest freighter captains do you know who wear body armor or pistols at their sides?"

"I don't know. I've never met an honest freighter captain."

"Well I have, and they don't dress like jump-jockey smugglers. They aren't armed, either. That tends to scare away most clients."

Not the sort of clients Keel was used to working with, but he understood Honey's point. "I'll think of something that'll get past their inspection."

"Something for both of us?"

"Something," Keel said evasively. "Kinda figured you'd just stay aboard the shuttle while I slipped off to capture the bridge."

"That's the *start* of a plan. But what happens if you get caught and a bunch of marines try to grab me out of the hunk of junk you bought for us?"

"Let's just wait and see how they approach the situation. We'll have some time to adjust as we load things up."

Honey moved to another topic. "How many trips are you thinking of taking delivering the cargo before you make your move?"

"Depends."

"Depends on what?"

"On how I feel about the odds."

Honey shook her head in exasperation. "You're impossible sometimes. You can't expect me to believe that's how you did these things when you were in Dark Ops."

Keel chuckled. "Nope. I learned to operate this way *after* I got out. It's kept me alive this long."

"Yeah, well, you better hope it does the trick this time, too."

Two inspectors arrived aboard a Repub escort shuttle, but they would have given themselves away as members of the *Defiance of Reason* even if they had used a civilian vessel. Both wore standard-issue Republic Naval uniforms, with the only attempt at concealing them being black ponchos that went down as far as the knees and appeared to have been made from the top sheet of someone's bunk. Just a glance at the tight creases in the slacks and the shine of those shoes—though they were admittedly a bit worn—would tell anyone familiar that these guys were navy. Or rather, once had been.

Keel debated whether to push them on their affiliation but decided against it. Captain Pemm was likely already moving outside his comfort zone, allowing a momentary breach in his predictable protocol to secure that long-term meal schedule he desired. These men standing before Keel and looking suspiciously at him and the warehouse full of Spindust probably had orders to terminate the operation at the first whiff of anything suspicious. Which meant being too observant about the uniforms was too great a risk to take. Yet entirely ignoring the fact that they showed up in a military shuttle might be just as suspicious.

"Say," Keel said, doing his best to sound like a blue-collar spacer from the holofilms. Probably the only type these points would ever have been exposed to.

"How'd you boys get a shuttle like that? Navy surplus? Bet that set you back."

Before they could answer, Keel hitched his thumb over his shoulder and pointed at his own boxy, thick-skinned cargo shuttle. It had none of the sleekness of its military counterpart and considerably more wear and tear. "That one there cost me seventy thousand credits and it sure wasn't new when I bought it. So how much does one of those go for, if you don't mind me asking?"

The two officers exchanged a look, and then the senior man said, "It didn't cost us anything."

Keel's eyes went wide. Partly at how idiotic these two were to admit something like that rather than follow his lead and give a plausible excuse. Partly also because he felt this was how he ought to respond.

"Y'all didn't steal it, did you?" he whispered.

"Of course not."

His voice still low, "You mean to tell me you boys are with the Repub Navy? This some kind of secret mission?"

Keel waited, mentally urging the two buffoons to take him up on the invitation to not feel so helplessly out of place. Clearly whatever naval skills these two men had, intelligence wasn't among them. They were no navy spies.

Thankfully, the officers were at least bright enough to recognize the out that Keel had gift-wrapped for them.

"Yeah, just don't say anything," said the junior man, visibly relaxing. "We're trying to keep a low profile in the sector. Pirates."

That wasn't half bad.

"Sure, sure," said Keel. "My lips are sealed. You know, I would've joined the navy, but I got too much of a temper. First time one of those navy boot camp instructors yelled at me, I'd-a punched him right in the jaw and knocked him out. They'd probably throw me in the brig for life." When the two men opposite him only stared, Keel added, "That's what you guys call it in the navy, right? A brig instead of a jail?"

"Yes. That's what we call it. Can we take a look at your shuttle now?"

"Sure. She ain't much to look at but be my guest. I got the ramp lowered so you can just go right inside if you want and have a nose around. Made sure to keep the door to the cockpit unlocked so ya can check out the whole thing. There ain't nothin' strange in there, but I guess I should tell you that there *is* a survival pistol and kit in the cockpit in case the ship ever crashed. That's pretty standard stuff, but you know it's just a short trip between here and your ship up there so I can take it out and leave it here if you want. Or you navy boys can just hold on to it for me. Either way."

The officers stepped inside the transport shuttle and squinted their eyes to better take in the space. Keel had kept the overhead lights on, but they were old and weak and didn't provide much in the way of illumination.

"Why's it empty?" asked the junior officer.

"Well, Honey—that's my Tennar employee, and she's a handful—she said y'all wanted to do an inspection, so I figured you'd wanna see the whole thing. Make sure I didn't have no trap doors or none of those smuggler gimmicks. I'm on the level."

"We had hoped to take off right away."

"Well, sket. I'm sorry about that. I can get it loaded up in fifteen minutes with the bot. We can leave then. You want me to load up your ship while we're at it? Bot'll handle this one and I don't mind doin' yours manually. I'll make the Tennar help. They're shiftless, you know. As a species, I mean. Little work would do her some good."

The senior officer let out a sigh and the junior officer suggested, "How about I go supervise the loading of our ship while you take a closer look at this one?"

The senior officer answered with a fractional nod.

The junior motioned for Keel to follow, then led him to the Repub shuttle. "Pack it as full as you can."

Keel looked at the shuttle's interior and whistled. "What a ship. Feel like I might break it just by touching it."

"You won't. Just get this thing loaded."

"You got it, boss." Keel let out a shrill whistle, and up rolled Death, Destroyer of Worlds. "Dee-Dee-Oh-Dubya, you get on over here and start moving pallets into these two shuttles. I'll help, and so will Honey, so don't run us down this time."

The bot rolled away and reappeared a moment later, now leading a procession of three repulsor jacks carrying double-stacked pallets. It chirped happily, but Keel understood the message to be one promising the eradication of the naval officer and his entire family line.

Keel would have to talk to the little machine about that. It was taking a risk assuming most people wouldn't understand its peculiar language.

"What did he say?" asked the officer.

"Oh," said Keel. "He just said you better move out of the way so your shins don't get bumped by the pallets. That'd hurt like the nine hells."

The officer obeyed, and soon Death was moving pallets onto the shuttle and setting them down on their unpowered repulsor skids. After pulling the backs loose, it left for more.

"How about the manual loading you mentioned?" the officer said.

"Oh, right. Well, we also gotta get the big shuttle warmed up. She don't fly when she's cold. Now, I can push a manual jack no problem, but Honey's gonna need to slither out of her quarters to do the flyin', come to think of it."

"I thought you owned this operation."

"I do."

"But you're not the pilot?"

"Sket no. I can't stand flying. Scares me to death. Won't even look out the forward window. I got a spot in the back where I sit with the cargo. That way I can pretend we aren't hurtling out among the stars ready to get sucked out to the vacuum at any second. I don't know how you navy boys do it."

The officer rested his hands on his hips and looked disparagingly at Keel. "Mister, you wouldn't have made it a day in the navy, and not for the reason you think."

"Boy, I suppose that's right. Well, I usually got a pretty good mind for business anyhow. Especially when it comes to freight-wise things. Like I said, this Spindust thing almost worked. I almost have the market cornered out here. And if I didn't have to make schedule over in the mid-core, well I do believe I could've held all those buyers out. Even as it stands, I earned enough for the warehouse fees and a little extra."

Keel beamed proudly at this proof of business acumen he'd just presented.

The senior officer arrived to announce that Keel's ship was clear and should be loaded straight away.

Keel nodded sharply. "I'll get on it, boss." He moved toward a pallet jack, and by that time Honey had appeared.

She moved alongside him as he pulled a floating repulsor triple-stacked with cargo toward his ship.

"If these aren't our guys, I don't know who is," she whispered.

"Looks like it. Just gotta load the ships and then we'll see up close." He hesitated and then asked, "Do those two officers seem off to you?"

"They're points. Of course they do."

"No. Something else. I can't shake the feeling that they know I'm playing a role and that they're playing along."

"Why? What did they say?"

"Nothing it's just... I'm starting to get a bad feeling about all this."

"It was your idea. Your plan. Let's see where it goes."

"Yeah. Let's see."

25

The first load was ready when Keel had promised it would be. He submitted to a frisking and then zipped into an oversized flight suit that looked baggy and comical on his frame. "We ready to go?"

"Just about," said the senior officer. "The only other requirement we have is that you and your pilot split up."

"Oh," said Keel in a soft voice. "That some kinda navy protocol? For security and all?"

"Yes. It is. You'll be transported aboard our shuttle."

"I see." Keel knew that no such requirement existed. This was something new Pemm had devised to keep himself protected. "Well, I don't mean to be difficult, especially after we took the time to get these two shuttles loaded, but that does present a problem to me."

"Which is?"

"Well, it's like I said to your friend here," Keel pointed at the junior officer. "I hate flying and I'm no pilot."

The senior officer smiled magnanimously. "That won't be a problem. All you'll have to do is strap yourself into our shuttle and enjoy the ride."

"So Honey will just fly my shuttle all by her lonesome?"

"That's right," the officer said, his patience thin.

Keel rubbed the back of his mussed and messy hair. "Only problem is, that's my shuttle. And Honey, well, she's my employee and I hate to have to say this in front of her but I guess I got to. You know how Tennar can be. I can't trust her not to take my shuttle and run."

Honey's brow furrowed, but she held her tongue.

"You're saying that you're willing to lose this contract," said the senior officer. "Just to be clear. That is what you're saying."

"No, I—I don't wanna say that. I'm just saying I don't want my shuttle to be stolen. Won't do me a lot of good to sell you all this freight at the price I'm selling it to you if I have to go and buy another shuttle. I told you how much it cost, and we both know I ain't making that much off this deal." Keel snapped his fingers. "I got it. How 'bout this? You're both in the navy, so you both can fly, right?"

The two officers looked at each other, unsure. Finally, the senior said, "That's right."

"Well there you go! So easy my bot could've thought of it. One of you fly my ship and I'll sit in the passenger seat. Then Honey, she gets paid for flying but she's just a passenger on your shuttle. That oughta make her happy because she already tries to get paid for doing hardly any work as it is."

"You know, you can be a real jerk sometimes," she snapped.

Keel shrugged. "I'm not trying to be prejudiced. I'm just saying Tennar are lazy, that's all."

The junior officer looked to his superior to make a decision.

"All right," said the man. "That's fine. I'll fly our bird. Lieutenant Knox, you fly theirs."

Keel smiled and nodded. "That's just fine. See, I knew we could make this deal work out. I only got one other request, and that is, my bot rides on my ship. I don't want nobody runnin' away with it either. It's a good hand." Keel looked at Honey through squinted eyes. "A hard worker."

"We're not going to steal your bot," said the senior officer. "But in order to ensure it doesn't transmit any potentially dangerous code bursts, it will need to travel on board our shuttle, which is shielded from such transmissions."

"What do you mean, like send some kind of slicing code that will take over y'all's ship? No. It wouldn't do that."

"Whether it would or wouldn't is immaterial. That is the required precaution. And unlike the seating arrangements, it's one that we won't bend on. We are prepared to walk away."

Keel caught what looked to him like a glare from the junior officer to the senior. He watched the senior man out of the corner of his eye and saw him swallow. A bead of sweat formed at his temple.

"Well..." Keel said, his suspicions on even higher alert, "I guess if someone does me dirty over the bot, I'll still have enough profits left over to replace it at the next stop. All right."

Keel saw the relief in the senior man's face. The junior officer softened. Keel whistled for his bot and then bent down and patted it. "You gotta ride on the other shuttle, buddy."

The bot chirped that the mass of the navy shuttle was considerably less than Keel's and would therefore be an inferior ship to send at ramming speed against the frigate.

"I'll miss you too," Keel said as though talking to an old pet. "But it's just for a little while. Soon as the job's over, we'll be back together thick as doros."

The bot beeped sorrowfully and then followed Honey and the senior naval officer up the ramp.

Keel led the junior officer up the ramp of his own shuttle. "Don't suppose I can convince you to let me make this trip in the back with the cargo, can I?"

"Afraid not. But feel free to close your eyes inside the cockpit."

"I just might take you up on that."

It was a twenty-minute flight from the warehouse, out of atmo, and into the hangar of the frigate *Defiance of Reason*. Keel waited until the heavy freighter was preparing to leave atmosphere before abruptly getting up and leaving the cockpit, knowing that the pilot would have no choice but to keep flying. The shuttle had no automatic controls—not anymore.

"Sorry. I can't stomach this," Keel said, then simply left. The pilot shouted for him to get back in the cockpit, but Keel was already gone.

The armor was hidden inside a crate at the rear of the ship. Keel quickly put it on beneath the oversized flight suit, zipped back up, and reentered the cockpit as if nothing had happened. By now they had left the planet behind.

"This I can handle," Keel said, flopping back into his seat and putting his boots up on the dash. "But seeing the heat around the window or getting a glimpse at the ground... no sir. Not for me."

"What the hell were you doing back there?" the pilot demanded.

"Praying we didn't die." Keel smiled at the man. "You did pretty good. Smoother than Honey does, anyway. Probably that navy training."

They didn't speak after that, but the pilot kept his eyes on Keel, as if expecting him to cause trouble. The unease was to be expected to a point, but Keel felt this man was taking things much farther than a point officer would be expected to. And as the frigate loomed nearer, he began to feel more intensely that things were about to get much more difficult.

"Looks like we're comin' in for a landing," Keel observed, breaking the long silence and taking his feet off the dash. His boot nearly hit the co-pilot's flight controls. "Oops. That wouldn't have been good."

The pilot, clearly irritated, shook his head. "As long as the active pilot controls are engaged, the co-pilot's stick is useless."

"Oh."

The transport shuttle Keel had purchased was a Stubarn heavy freighter. It was all cargo hold save for a small, single-man fresher that lacked even a sonic shower. There was a single sleeping berth, no more than a cocoon designed for humans or smaller, and two forward-facing seats in the cockpit. One was for the pilot, the other for the co-pilot.

The heavy shuttle nosed down and positioned itself to fly under the belly of the frigate.

"You sure this is the way to get into that big ship?" Keel asked. "We're practically flying underneath it."

"That's because," the pilot said through clenched teeth, "the shuttle bay on this type of ship is located on its belly."

"Well if that were true why don't I see the blue shielding from the—oh, wait a minute—yeah, I see it. You were right."

The officer held his tongue but couldn't resist a single exaggerated shake of his head.

"I'll say this much," said Keel. "Your flying is a whole lot smoother than it was at the beginning. I don't know that I've ever been on a ship that's sailed along so straight and smooth."

"That's not me," the pilot said, clenching his jaw. "That's the hangar bay's tractor beam. We're being towed in."

"Oh. Well, you still had to get the ship situated in such a maneuver to let that beam get a good lock on you. So you can hold your head high for that."

"I'll keep it in mind," muttered the pilot.

As the ship rose straight up into the frigate, emerging from its underbelly into the docking bay, Keel wasn't sure what he'd find. He watched the pilot closely and watched the inner workings of the shielding as the forward viewport rose up to reveal the hangar from the perspective of a speckled grummz emerging from its burrow.

The pilot had a heightened alertness that went well beyond an appointed officer attending to automated flight controls. Keel stayed cool, forcing his body to remain casual and only allowing himself to demonstrate any sense of surprise when a massed unit of armored soldiers, standing in tight formation, came into sight at the far end of the bay. This was a Nether Ops kill team if Keel had ever seen one. They wore their distinctive light-gray version of legionnaire armor.

"Boy!" said Keel, still not dropping the persona. "You didn't tell me you were workin' with the Legion. Now I *know* this is an important mission. Why're the fellas here on the dock? You can't fool me into thinking these are the guys you got to unload."

"Enough," the pilot said.

Keel could sense the dual meaning of the word. He wasn't fooling the pilot, never had been. But the pilot wasn't comfortable enough to just let the act play itself out. The man's hand drifted slowly down to a pistol nestled in the shining black ornamental holster at his hip. Clearly he saw that while relief was close, danger was closer.

Keel wondered if this man, too, was Nether Ops. Either way, this "junior officer" was well aware of the prowess of the man he had been sent out to trap.

"I'll bet this is your first time flying a bird like this," Keel said, more to keep the man distracted than anything else.

There was no reply, and Keel hadn't expected one.

"Interesting thing about these is how easily they can be—" Keel's arm darted and threw the co-pilot's throttle forward, firing the engines at full power as he called out in his true voice, "rewired!"

The shuttle zipped forward toward the scattering column of Nether Ops legionnaires. It crashed with a resounding boom against the wall of the hangar, leaving a dent and pulverizing fully half of the kill team meant to bring Keel in. The soldiers were cut in half wherever the nose of the heavy freighter met with the thick impervisteel of the hangar wall.

Both Keel and the pilot were rocked in their chairs from the sudden crash. Keel had been expecting it though. He sprang from his seat after deftly undoing his harness while alarms blared in the hangar bay. The quickness with which the pilot regained his senses and likewise sprang out of his chair answered Keel's question from a moment ago. This man was surely Nether Ops.

The pilot pulled his blaster pistol from its holster and attempted to bring it up to fire, but Keel chopped the man's wrist with a jarring counterstrike that sent the weapon flying. Undeterred, the officer punched Keel in the stomach, only to be rewarded with the bone-crunching sound of his fist fracturing against Tyrus Rechs's armor.

Keel didn't hesitate to grab the man's wrist and twist it up and behind him, turning the man sideways and breaking the arm before sending an armored knee strike into the agent's face, and a second for good measure. The pilot fell to the deck bloodied and unconscious. Keel recovered the small blaster pistol and finished the man off with it.

By now Death was in his ear asking for instructions. The navy shuttle had docked as well. It had no ability to block transmissions, as Keel knew; that was just a ploy to separate Keel from his bot, which could easily have been used to house a weapon.

"Just watch for how it plays out," Keel instructed as he ran toward the pallet where his armor had been stowed to reacquire the rest of his stash: his bucket and the auto-cannon slug thrower.

Helmeted and armed, he dropped the rear doors, only to quickly spring back inside the cargo hold at the sight of the surviving Nether Ops legionnaires. Their blaster bolts ripped into the hold, striking the cartons and producing a smell of burnt caramel and exotic fruit.

Keel moved between pallets, pausing only long enough to shoot a Nether Ops legionnaire through his visor the moment the man appeared on the ramp. Continuing on, Keel made his way quickly toward the cockpit, releasing the cargo from its magnetic locking and activating the repulsor skids as he went. Behind him more Nether Ops legionnaires cautiously boarded after their fallen comrade.

In the cockpit again, Keel slammed closed the security doors and found the sturdy shuttle's repulsor still humming and ready to work. He pushed up, lifting the craft from the ground with a metal-on-metal groan and screech, painting the hangar wall with the dead Nether Ops soldiers he'd crushed there and leaving a grisly blood trail that followed the shuttle's wide nose like gruesome brushstrokes. He threw the ship into reverse and then spun around sharply, sending the freed repulsor pallets flying through the hold and out of the transport, along with at least two agents. Broken bodies and overturned cargo now littered the small hangar. Lights continued to flash and flare, adding to the pandemonium.

Keel looked for a new landing spot and decided he'd need to make his own. He sped toward the navy shuttle, clipped it, and sent it spinning before its front strut bent and the ship tipped forward and rested on its chin. There was a method to this. The Republic shuttle was equipped with anti-personnel cannons, but in this position, they would be unable to effectively aim at anything but the deck. All that remained to be wary of were its fixed wingtip guns, which would only be a threat if Keel stood directly in front of them.

That done, he unceremoniously cut repulsors, let his shuttle drop to the deck, and jumped off the back of the ramp. A Nether Ops legionnaire was struggling to pull himself from out of a toppled pallet, but he was pinned from the waist down and barely let out a shout for mercy when Keel put a bullet in the man's helmet as he walked past.

Sirens wailed and navy techs were running about the hangar bay in confusion. These weren't points, and neither were they armed. They seemed to be trying to find some place to hide. Keel let them go, looking instead for more Nether Ops agents, either in the Legion armor or incognito as his pilot had been. That would be the immediate trouble. The ship full of points that awaited him after he left the hangar? Yeah, Keel was fairly certain he could handle that.

"Honey, what's your status?" he called into the comm.

He received no reply.

"Death?"

The bot informed Keel that neither Honey nor the pilot had come out of the ship, though he had "quite resourcefully" opened the shuttle's cargo door and was on the deck, ready to kill if ordered.

"Just keep a lookout. I'm going for the bridge."

Keel was moving past the scattered pallets of freight toward the access door leading deeper into the frigate when three Nether Ops legionnaires appeared where his shuttle had first come to its grinding halt. This trio had managed to avoid being pulverized and were no doubt looking for payback.

Keel squeezed the trigger on the hand cannon and fired several .45 caliber rounds in the span of a second with a slick and rapid *brrrrt*. Each of the first two legionnaires found a tight grouping placed in the middle of his bucket with enough force to punch through visor and face plate. Both had dropped before the third realized what he was up against. A quick adjustment while on the move and Keel dropped that one as well.

That was the best he'd gotten the unique weapon system working yet, and he imagined that was likely how

Rechs had it operating back in its heyday. It had taken Keel a considerable amount of practice and perseverance to get his shot grouping as tight as that.

A blaster bolt pinged against his shoulder and carried off to the side, where it exploded against the wall. The strike merely stung, but it served as warning for Keel to hurl himself behind a pallet as two more bolts zipped by. Not waiting for this latest legionnaire to move on his position, Keel sprang up with his jump jets and sent four rounds in single fire down on top of the man, dropping him right there.

He moved his shoulder like a bird's wing. That was going to bruise, but otherwise he'd be fine.

With no more hostile agents in sight, Keel hustled to make his way to the bridge. Pemm was still his objective, and the man wasn't captured yet. It was possible he could still escape if Keel wasn't quick enough about it.

He knew the layout of this frigate intimately. As part of a direct-action Dark Ops kill team, he and his legionnaires had undergone countless training exercises for virtually every ship in the Republic fleet. Every scenario, delay, and complication was thrown at them until they could handle the real thing without feeling the stress of something new. And when something new *did* happen, like had happened with *Pride of Ankalor*, it was added to the training rotations.

As a result, Keel could tell you the fastest path to take to disable most ships. But in this case, he needed only to find his high-value target on board. He had no need to disable its engines; it could go where it wanted so long as Pemm remained. Disabling the shuttle had cut off one escape route, but there would be more. Escape pods. Usually these were without FTL jump drives, but a small number of these ships did possess FTL-capable pods as a means of increasing the likelihood that survivors would be recovered before it was too late. The pods, whether full or empty, would automatically jump to the nearest habitable planet and then broadcast a distress beacon telling where it had jumped from.

Keel hoped that Captain Pemm wasn't quite willing to abandon ship yet. But as visuals from the hangar came in along with reports from what was left of the Nether Ops agents who'd clearly felt they had a better trap ready than they did, all that could quickly change, and Pemm might opt for the next in a string of downsizes in command. Destroyer, then frigate, then escape pod. Still better than losing his life.

Keel made his way out of the docking bay and into the main corridor that ran down the length of the ship. From here he could get anywhere else. His first stop would be engineering, but he'd only taken a few steps before Honey pinged him over their comm connection.

"Are you still in the docking bay?" she shouted.

"Negative. Do you have control of the shuttle?"

"Yes." There was thick annoyance in her voice. "Never mind that you nearly killed me by ramming it. A little warning would have been nice!"

"Wasn't time. Lock the doors and wait it out. I took down most of your Nether Ops friends but I don't think I got 'em all."

"They're not my friends. And you didn't. They're looking for you in the hangar bay still."

"How many?"

"I don't know. Half a dozen? Listen, once this is over you're letting me go. That's no longer negotiable."

"Roger. Out."

Keel cut the transmission. He needed to focus and he wouldn't have argued with her even if all the other agents were dead and Pemm was in ener-chains at this point. With Nether Ops attempting to nab him—to nab Rechs—*before* putting a bounty on his head... well, that only made Keel's life easier. Which was nice for a change. These Nether agents might not know much, but they would know something. Keel would have fresh trails to follow.

Engineering was sealed up tight with a heavy blast door. Keel used the hard-coded passkey built into frigates like this to circumvent it and wasn't surprised to see that Pemm hadn't hired a slicer to change it. The man probably didn't even know it existed. The big door rumbled open, revealing another corridor that led toward the drive, life support, and other critical systems. It was entirely devoid of crew, just as all the ship had been since leaving the bay.

That was unusual for a ship like this, but it made sense for this *particular* ship. The intel Keel gathered had indicated that Captain Pemm was operating with a skeleton crew. These were mostly points, House of Reason loyalists; if there *were* any more enlisted men like the techs who'd been running to safety in the hangar, they'd probably been forced into service. They were also probably few enough in number to keep Pemm and his friends free of any fears of mutiny.

Keel crept his way toward the security station just ahead of the main drive room, slug thrower in one hand and the blaster pistol he'd acquired from the pilot in the other. He saw two nervous men on duty, a cold sweat on their brows as their fingers danced on blaster rifles. These were points, a pair of junior officers who looked as though they didn't want a confrontation. Danger was never supposed to get in this close. But to their credit, they hadn't abandoned their posts.

Yet.

"Clear out," Keel demanded, announcing his presence.

One of the men dropped his blaster rifle while the other took a wild shot down the center of the corridor, not caring that Keel was nowhere to be seen.

A looming silence followed the lone shot, then Keel whipped around the corner and sent a blaster bolt into the armed man's chest. The point pitched forward, slammed his face against the security control panel, and lay still.

His partner held his hands up high and backed into the wall. "Please don't kill me!"

Keel approached the man, kicked his weapon far out of reach, and then pushed him to his knees, hand behind his head and facing the wall. "Don't look anywhere but at that wall."

As the officer did as instructed, Keel activated the blaster pistol's stun setting and dropped him.

Keel then moved to check the security station's holocams to see what lay behind the doors of the drive room proper. He counted three enlisted techs in the room, talking in a small huddle. If any of the crew had been pressed into service, it would be these men. They had the sort of jobs that needed to be recruited for, and that a point was highly unlikely to be able to perform.

He opened the containment door and was awash in the pulsating blue light of the engine cores on the other side. The three technicians looked up from their huddle and froze. They eyed him warily before the bravest of the trio said above the hum of the drive cores, "You're not supposed to be here, whoever you are."

"I won't be long," said Keel. "The Republic will be retaking control of this ship shortly."

The man said nothing further, but the two men with him seemed hopeful at Keel's words.

"Are you with the Republic?" one of them asked.

"Something like that," said Keel. "Captain Pemm force you into service?"

"Too many blasters pointing at our face to do anything else," said the first man who'd spoken.

Keel nodded and finished punching in the hardcode to disable the escape pods. "Stay put or do me a favor and keep an eye on the point I stunned in the security room. If an order comes from the bridge to make a jump, ignore it. There's about to be a whole lot fewer blasters able to point at you soon."

The leader of the techs gave a single nod. "This ship won't put up a fight. They're all gutless bastards unless they know you can't fight back."

"You catch anything about those newcomers who came on board dressed like legionnaires?" Keel asked.

The three men looked puzzled by this. "Nobody tells us anything. Sorry."

"Wait's almost over," said Keel.

He left the room, almost hoping to find more Nether Ops agents waiting for him at the security checkpoint, just to have the fight over with and be free to move quickly for the bridge. But the area was as empty as he'd left it.

"Still got a bad feeling about this," Keel mumbled as he moved on toward the bridge.

26

Zora and her team waited until the final day of the slave market to make their move. The morning had begun with the sale of a wild and defiant Cassari male, over two meters tall, muscles rippling beneath green skin, black hair flowing in a soft morning breeze. Other than the ener-chains around his hands and feet, he wore only a simple loincloth.

The Kublarens purchased him at once. And as the day continued, they repeatedly proved themselves to be a thorn in the side of not only those who sought to buy lots, but now also those seeking to buy for themselves the premium individual slaves. The koob delegation regularly outbid the competition, transforming itself from a humorous oddity into a despised faction whose credits seemed as limitless as their ignorance. These prices would spoil slave bazaars for years to come.

It was the zhee who were most bothered. Kamartha the Feared had not been the highest bidder in a single auction. The pirates had a prize to boast of, at least. Not so the zhee. And it was clear from the croaking and clicking that sprang up among the Kublarens whenever the zhee lost—whether to them or to another bidder—that the curious newcomers took great delight in the zhee's repeated failures.

In an attempt to save face, Kamartha the Feared told all who would listen that the auction thus far had been mere games, and he had no intention of wasting credits on games. Nothing he had bid on had been *truly* desired. But the jewels to come... yes, they would belong to his infamous harem.

There would be beautiful Cassari females stolen from their home world before they could be bonded in honor of a clan. Gomarii who suffered the shame of being unclanned, damned to live out their lives in chains to detect the emotional state of whoever their master put before them. Packs of neutered doros the slavers had beaten and cowed until they were nothing but savage guards willing to attack whoever their masters demanded, without mercy or hesitation.

Other exotics were rumored to exist as well, according to those with enough credits to see the stock in person. These included Jumwara, which were impossible to hold in bondage but a fitting prize for some fantastically rich collector's private zoo. Jack said he knew of a House of Reason delegate who did just such a thing, with no concern that his exhibits had reached the level of sentience needed to be considered full citizens of the Republic.

Nilo's group had made a name for itself the previous day. Or rather, Garret had. He had purchased a beautiful Nypian, a species always highly sought after. She had been auctioned early to present a foretaste of the gems that would come in the auction's final day. The species was renowned for its attractiveness, particularly to humans, and since humans were the dominant species in the galaxy, having a Nypian at your business's disposal could be worth ten times the investment. Or you could keep her for yourself. The Gomarii cared little once the transfer of credits was complete.

The zhee had of course been interested. Kamartha the Feared opened the bidding at one hundred seventy thousand credits, cutting in front of the Kublarens and using their own customary bid as a first attack.

Unfazed, the Kublarens called out, "Same-ah price, k'kik, and-ah one more credit!"

When they were told by the bot at center stage that this increase was not sufficient, they huddled together and croaked confusedly, much to the mocking delight of the rest of the gallery. And then Garret, at Nilo's behest, motioned for one of the hovering bots that took bids from the more distant sections of the gallery. Garret whispered the price he was willing to pay and then confirmed it with a burst from his credit wallet.

On the main stage, the bot exclaimed wildly that a record-breaking bid had just come in for a female Nypian. "Two hundred and fifty thousand credits!"

The audience erupted in delight, even as the slave stared down at her feet, broken, her fate sealed.

The zhee, outbid again, managed to find some merriment from the fact that the Kublaren had received some of their own embarrassment. They were still croaking in confusion over why bidding a single credit higher was not considered sufficient.

Kamartha the Feared sent a messenger to Garret, who was intercepted by Jack and Zora. The messenger offered Garret fifty thousand credits for the right for his excellence, Kamartha the Feared, to *know* the Nypian second.

Jack declined on Garret's behalf. "My employer is not interested in sharing this one."

The offer was sweetened another ten thousand, but the answer remained the same.

The zhee snorted indignantly and left.

Jack shook his head. "Even if we were actually scum sack kelhorns, that's a bad idea. Odds are fifty-fifty the donk would send her back dead or disfigured."

Garret and Zora both looked at Jack with horror. Jack only shrugged and crossed his arms, smiling as he waited for the next auction.

By the time Zora had returned from escorting the Nypian to her ship, where she was secured in one of the ray-shielded holding cells, Garret's status had changed considerably. He was now flanked by Gomarii treating him like royalty, offering him trays full of exotic liquors and sumptuous food meant for human ingestion. But the slavers departed just as she sat back down.

"What was that all about?" she asked.

"We're going to get to go on the ship," Garret explained, the excitement in his voice causing it to tremble. "And then we'll be able to see if Leenah is on board."

"We showed them that we have credits to spend," Nilo explained. "And told them that we're willing to spend all of those credits if they have slaves aboard their ship worthy of our purse. They promised us they did, including an Endurian, which we had asked about. After that, it wasn't difficult to get them to agree to our demands to see them ahead of the auction."

Jack chuckled. "You should've seen the panicked look on those tentacle-suckers' faces when Nee said we'd just as soon leave now if we couldn't verify with our own eyes that there was something else worth waiting around for."

"The request wasn't uncommon," Nilo said. "But yes, the potential loss of a spender like Garret made them nervous. I would venture a guess that this is already the most profitable market this clan has ever seen. Once records are made, it's very difficult to think about anything but breaking more."

"Good," said Zora. "I was beginning to wonder when we were going to make our move. What's the plan? Because it has to be something more than getting in under the guise of inspecting the merchandise and then overpowering a couple thousand Gomarii to save Garret's friend."

Jack leaned back in his seat. "Sounds like a solid enough plan to me. And anyway, I wanna see this girl. If they're sending a Nypian out before her... no kidding she'll get Wraith running over to show up. Because that Nypian was something else."

Jack weathered Zora's glare like a man unconcerned with what others thought of him. He was completely comfortable with himself and made no apologies for it.

Nilo gave his orders. "The Gomarii said any time. The time is now. I want the three of you on it. I'll remain outside."

Jack straightened. "Hold on, boss. Zora and me, we can overpower some guards and spring the Endurian, give the 'rees on board hell for a while. But I don't see a clear way for us to get off that beast. Maybe we get as far as the ramp before they catch up with us, and when they do, we'll have a big fight on our hands."

"One that will take a small army to win," Zora added.

Nilo smiled. "You forget—I *have* an army. We have only been waiting for them to get into position. That wait is now over."

Garret, with Zora and Jack acting as his bodyguards, was escorted onto the Gomarii ship by two slavers. Both were female, though it was hard to tell with Gomarii, whose two genders were largely indistinguishable. Gomarii females lacked breasts, external egg pouches, or any of the other common indicators of the female sex common throughout the galaxy. The only real indicator of gender was a minor difference in build—males were a bit more broad-shouldered—and it wasn't a particularly good indicator, for a healthy Gomarii female was large enough to resemble a below-average male. Had the escorts not referred to one another as "she," Garret wouldn't have been remotely certain.

They followed their escorts behind the stage and up onto a long ramp that led into the interior of the great ship. The ramp was wide enough for multiple sleds to drive up or down and ended at a black curtain that let out onto the main stage. Garret had been well-coached by Nilo. He looked around, interested in his surroundings but indifferent. It was an expression he'd been specifically told to carry, the blasé outlook of the terminally rich and unsatisfied. A man who had taken to the slave markets to deal with the boredom. That Garret was also naturally awkward and introverted, Nilo had explained, would contribute to the notion that he was an eccentric and wealthy tech billionaire. More comfortable in the glow of his holodisplays than he was in actual daylight.

As they moved up the ramp, enclosed like a tunnel, another party moved down in the opposite direction. Two Gomarii slavers led identical twin human males. The slaves looked newly shaved and cleaned up, but Garret could see bruises and welts underneath some sort of makeup.

The passing slavers paused to exchange greetings.

As they did so, Jack leaned forward from his place behind Garret as the trailing bodyguard and whispered, "Wouldn't it have been a little bit easier to simply buy your friend when she was put up for auction?"

"I think Mr. Nilo has something bigger in store than that," Garret whispered back.

"No kidding."

Finished with their brief greeting, the Gomarii escorts beckoned for Garret to continue, apologizing for the delay.

"Your forgiveness is needed. We have received word that there is some, ah..." The Gomarii sucked her lip tendrils into her mouth and then blew them back out, wet and slimly like a viscous mustache. "... some turmoil at the auction stage."

"More trouble with those koobs?" asked Jack.

The Gomarii slurped and sucked before saying, "No trouble. Merely a delay."

Jack lolled his head back to look at Zora and said to the slavers, "Whatever you say."

The two Gomarii seemed perturbed by this, their beady eyes glaring at Jack.

Zora stepped in to restore good will. "I'm sure our hosts are more than capable of providing the necessary security to keep Mr. Garret safe."

The Gomarii were immediately obliged to give thanks to Zora for her quick defense of their honor. They gave her a respectful bow and said, "This clanship is a jewel among the Gomarii. It is impenetrable to outside attack. Should any of the rabble at the market wish to take from us what is ours, they will find no way in. The disturbance we disclosed as an act of good will, will not cause the market to cease until its conclusion. This vessel is clanned by over one thousand warriors. More than enough to stand before any who would oppose our clan."

"I take it back," Jack said. "I'm impressed."

This elicited rhythmic sucking sounds of approval. The Gomarii were communicating to one another through the inhalation and exhalation of their lip tendrils. "As you should be. You will be all the more so when you see what reserves we will soon sell from our above decks."

"That's where you keep the good stuff?" Garret asked, surprised at how convincing he sounded when asking the question. No hesitation or unsurety—he felt like he was being the character Mr. Nilo had tasked him with being. He felt a deep satisfaction at having so completely sounded like someone he was not. He wondered if Captain Keel ever felt the same way during his own exploits.

"I daresay you will find many such 'good stuff' to your liking. Such as an Endurian, hmm?"

Garret tried not to let his face reveal his desire for just that.

They moved through the ship, following a carefully selected path that wound past empty ray-shielded holding cells. Some were easily five thousand square feet. Others were smaller, only large enough for one or two prisoners. And whereas the big cells that must have held the lots of slaves were all empty, some of the smaller ones were still occupied.

Garret saw very few humans, but those he did see were either attractive or possessed some other outstanding feature, such as unusual strength or height. And then there were those at the opposite end of the spectrum—neither strong, nor tall, nor beautiful, but exhibiting some kind of oddity like the lingering aftereffects of some childhood disease that had ravaged them on a world where the care needed to prevent it wasn't available. It seemed odd to Garret that these would be held back for the final days, but they were here. Someone must want them badly enough.

"Those the sort of people you're looking for, boss?" joked Jack. It was ghoulish and inappropriate, and yet it was fitting for who they were supposed to be.

The Gomarii, no doubt accustomed to that type of human humor, sucked in their tendrils and blew them out with soft laughter.

"No," answered Garret flatly, feeling pity for the prisoners who didn't so much as bother to raise their eyes at the beings that passed them, strutting down the ship, free.

"There can't be any demand for these... things," said Zora.

"There is on occasion," answered one of the slavers. "And should no offer be made, they will suit other purposes. Or be given over to the clan warriors for fun."

Garret didn't want to imagine the sort of "fun" that was being spoken of.

The lead Gomarii continued, "But soon we will find, I think, what are you are truly after."

The farther up the ship they moved, the more the cells became occupied. Now it was rare to see an empty cell, and Garret wondered how all these souls would be auctioned off before the day was done. But then, the bot at center stage could move quickly when it wasn't teasing out a bidding war.

Some of the prisoners were forlorn and kept their backs turned to the ray shielding. Others were more inquisitive and watched Garret with particular attention, as though they had an interest in who might purchase them. For there was no doubt what their fate would be. None in the galaxy who found themselves among the Gomarii would think that they were destined for anything but the slave markets.

Here there was an assortment of the handsome and the beautiful spanning multiple species. Four-armed Cassari goddesses, Tennar, humans... all of them gorgeous by any common standard. And all of them having somehow found themselves in the clutches of the cruel, blue-skinned slavers. What terrible turn of events had led them to this point?

And then they reached her. A pink Endurian princess whose natural beauty had been eschewed by the slavers in favor of a more lustful sort of attractiveness. Her coveralls had been torn into strips that barely covered her.

Leenah did not look away in fear. Nor did she attempt to appear pleasant, demure, sultry, or anything else to woo a perspective buyer. She stood and stared at the five, a proud hatred in her eyes for whoever was on the other side of the ray shielding. And then she saw Garret—and her stony defiance faded.

"I like this one," Garret said, hoping to draw the guards' attention away from the look of surprised recognition that flashed across Leenah's face.

Jack whistled, impressed. "So this is the one, huh, boss?"

"Keep your focus," Zora mumbled under her breath.

"You desire the Endurian," said the lead Gomarii guard, her voice thick with its mucus-like saliva. "A wise choice. She will sell for much... and you will part with much for her. I can taste such even from here."

It was said that the Gomarii had a preternatural ability to "taste" emotions through their saliva-covered tendrils, though opinions of galactic biologists were mixed on this point. Tests were inconclusive, and many scientists believed the Gomarii were simply skilled at reading external cues. But whatever the truth, the tendrils carried a deep importance to the Gomarii as a species.

"Can I talk to her?" Garret asked.

"You may."

They all stood for a moment.

"Well, open it up," said Jack finally.

"She can hear through the shield."

"I want to talk to her alone," said Garret.

The Gomarii laughed. "You may be rich, but you are also young and unknowing of the ways of the markets. Time with one alone can only be purchased at the auction. Otherwise, many before you would have purchased privacy with this one, yes?"

The two ghoulish slavers laughed knowingly.

"Okay, fine," said Jack. "No alone time until he buys her, but he's gotta know if she's worth buying. We saw how you tried to cover up the beatings those twins took."

The Gomarii stiffened. "Visuals are already available." They retrieved a datapad from a nook next to the cell and began to cycle through images of Leenah. Garret knew he was blushing and desperately wanted to look away.

"That's all fine and well," said Zora, "but a lot can happen between when you take a few holos and now. Mr. Garret is willing to pay an enormous price for this Endurian, but not if he's buying damaged goods. We need to be sure he gets what he pays for."

After politely asking for patience, the two Gomarii conversed in their native speech for a moment, then spoke into a comm mounted on their shoulder armor. A disgusting slithering-sucking language went back and forth until finally one of the guards faced Garret and spoke to him in Standard.

"What is the minimum price you will commit to for this one?"

"I'll pay anything," Garret said, sounding like a man driven mad, possessed at the thought of the Endurian. "I won't lose."

"So would say many. A price…"

Nilo had prepared Garret for this moment. "I will sign over to you, right now, an opening note for two hundred fifty thousand credits as first bid for the Endurian."

The Gomarii didn't flinch. "A staggering sum for an Endurian, but given the prices at this auction, I am not sure this will be sufficient."

"You tell whoever makes the decision that two-fifty is my offer. If I'm granted access to inspect her in person and she is as pristine as your holopics suggest, I will raise my opening bid to two million credits."

That got the Gomarii's attention.

"And," Jack added, raising his hand, "I know I'm just a hired gun, but let me tell you, two mil is the floor for this man. He doesn't lose. Ever."

That little ad lib seemed to Zora as though it might be too much, but the Gomarii's tendrils slithered and jerked excitedly. She wondered if Jack, in his boast, was somehow coming across as authentic to their senses. And if so, if he really meant what he was saying or was simply so good at what he did that he could make even emotive-sensing species like Gomarii believe whatever he had to say.

And what did that mean when it came to how much she should trust what passed through the man's lips?

The slavers went back to the comm and repeated the same sucking noises as before. Surely two mil would gain them access. It was an enormous sum for a mere Endurian, beautiful as she might be.

"You are granted your visual inspection," slurped the Gomarii slaver at last. "Your offer would almost be enough for us to forgo the auction entirely, were it not a strike against clan honor."

"You'll get your credits," Garret said. "I can be patient until auction as long as I know for sure who will accompany my Nypian."

The slavers gestured for Leenah to retreat to the back of the cell, then the ray shield dropped, and the slavers, entering first, locked her wrists and ankles together with ener-chains before moving to remove what little remained of her coveralls.

"No," said Garret as he stepped inside the cell unbidden. "I wish to see that at my leisure. It will be my own hand that performs that particular task."

He swallowed hard, and Jack shoved him forward farther into the cell.

"Doin' fine, boss," he whispered.

The Gomarii nodded subserviently and stepped back, giving room for Garret to see Leenah clearly. The Endurian looked from Garret to the others, aware that something was about to happen. She gave a slight nod, indicating that she was prepared to participate in whatever would come next.

Zora had sent a comm burst to Nilo the moment they'd found Leenah alive. A pre-determined transmission meant to reveal what deck they were on and the relative position on the ship. Nilo had promised a distraction that would allow the team to free the Endurian and evade capture aboard the ship until relief could come.

But until that distraction came, all they could do was stall.

"Turn around," Zora ordered Leenah.

The Endurian hesitated until Garret nodded. She turned around and looked over her shoulder at the trio standing at the entrance of the cell.

"Now lift your arms above your head," Zora demanded.

Leenah obeyed, and Zora walked a circle around the woman, inspecting the insides of her arms and ribs, all without touching, looking for bruises or other marks of rough treatment.

"Are you not satisfied?" asked the slavers. "She was near death at her capture, and we have only strengthened her to health. No harm has befallen this one."

"Not yet," answered Zora, only because the distraction still hadn't come. Until then, there was nothing they could do beyond overpowering the guards and use their weapons against them, which hardly seemed like a winning strategy.

"Tell her to bend over," suggested Jack. "Have a look at how those... hamstrings look."

Unable to think of anything better, Zora gave the command.

Leenah flashed an angry look of disapproval, which earned her a nudge from the butt of one of the guard's rifles. She reluctantly obeyed.

Jack let out a whistle. Garret turned and shot him an angry look.

"Sorry, boss, old habit."

Leenah straightened back up without being ordered to. Zora was struggling with what she could possibly ask for next when the explosions outside the ship began.

Nilo's distraction had come with a fury.

27

Though Zora felt the wait had been far too long, Nilo had had the origins of his tumult underway even while Garret and his protectors were just making their way up the ramp into the slave ship and passing the twins who were set to be auctioned next. The "turmoil" the slavers had discussed concerned a wobanki who was up for auction at that moment.

It was a tall, hulking member of the feline species, presented to the gallery as an incredible example of what the apex predator could look like should it have almost all of its genetic markers maxed out. The cat-man was bulging with muscles, and the thick tail swishing behind it looked easily strong enough to knock the guards over despite being weighted down so only the very end could move. It stood a full head taller than the two Gomarii who escorted it on stage. Sharp claws the size of daggers popped in and out of its paws, held close together by ener-chains.

"Let's get a nice look at those teeth," ordered the bot as it attempted to whip up the excitement of the market.

The wobanki growled a low, menacing warning. He received lashes from a neuron disruptor, a whip that featured several electronic cords that caused excruciating pain on contact. The wobanki let out a jungle roar and revealed sharp spires of teeth, each as thick as a man's finger.

"Which of you, having such a specimen in his guard, would suffer intimidation?" the bot asked. "Wobanki are fierce, but loyalty can be imprinted upon them by a steady and forceful hand. This is a species evolved for violence, and it is the language of violence they most understand."

The bot sought an opening bid, looking expectantly at the zhee, who waved the attention away with their hoof-like claws. As impressive a species as the wobanki was, the zhee had made it clear that their interest was primarily in restocking Kamartha the Feared's harem, with a secondary interest in purchasing laborers. But many others in the audience sought the status boost of having such a creature serve among their personal guard.

The initial bids came from well-dressed, business-like individuals surrounded by armed guards. Representatives of various crime syndicates, some covering planets, some entire sectors of space. The very first bid—twenty thousand—belonged to a former MCR general building a reputation as a warlord on an edge world, but the price went from twenty to fifty in seconds. Bidding then slowed briefly before a sudden jump that shot the price up past one hundred thousand. There it slowed again, leveling off just below one-fifty.

That's when the Kublarens offered their now-familiar one hundred seventy thousand credits.

This bid was met with boos and hisses, which agitated the Kublaren group. They inflated their throat sacs and croaked their displeasure over this treatment.

The bidding moved past their offer and reach two hundred thousand.

The lead Kublaren stood and clicked out, "We offah, one-seventy and also one seventy."

The bot verified the price, which ended the bidding. This was far higher than anyone else present was willing to pay. Gomarii slavers delivered the wobanki to the Kublaren delegation, who stood comically small next to their newest slave. The lead Kublaren whispered something in the wobanki's ear and then sat down, holding the massive cat-man's ener-chains.

They sat there for a while as the Gomarii brought down a pair of identical twins, hoping to stabilize the bad blood brewing among the crowd with a new auction. Twins were always popular.

Yet the Kublaren weren't even paying attention to this next auction. Through it all, they were swiveling their eyes back, looking for Nilo, waiting for a signal. And when they go it... that was where the real trouble began.

The lead Kublaren licked his eye, tilted his head, and removed the wobanki's restraints.

The koob then stepped aside and motioned that his prize was now free.

Shock and outrage rippled through the gallery as their attention shifted from the auction at hand to this titanic breach of rule and tradition.

The wobanki crouched, his muscles taut and tense and his whiskers dancing as he seemed to consider whether to attack those who had purchased him or let out a roar at those who were now jeering his release so lustily.

A spent charge pack was hurled at the Kublaren group, which led to more objects thrown in their direction. The koobs croaked angrily and raised their rifles high for all to see. The bot at center called for calm and decorum as Gomarii pushed their way into the gallery, seeking to maintain order.

The Kublaren croaked something to the wobanki, pointing at the advancing slavers. With a nod, the wobanki indicated he understood—the slavers were coming now to reclaim him. The apex predator left in a blur, catapulting itself over several rows of Kublarens who croaked and swiveled their eyes to follow the large creature's flight path. He came crashing down on the lead Gomarii guard and tore his throat out with his fangs.

Now the wobanki, his face dripping with blood, held the corpse of the first slaver in one paw while unleashing the claws of his free paw on the face of the second slaver, slicing it to ribbons, severing its lip tendrils, and leaving large swaths of skin hanging from the exposed skull and other tissues. Almost too fast to follow, the wobanki tore the blaster rifle from the slaver, which was now gripping its face and screaming in agony. The escaped slave shot the Gomarii and then opened fire on the crowd. Wild, careless shots aimed in every direction—save in the direction of the Kublarens who had freed him.

The crowd exploded into a panic, stampeding for exits and hiding among the seats as the wobanki bounded through the gallery, cutting down or shooting anyone who dared slow him down. The Gomarii guards all moved to enclose and stop the threat, though they were careful not to open fire and cause any harm to the buyers. Their goal was to end this humiliation without causing further damage to their reputation as slavers. A thing like this was not supposed to happen—had never happened in the history of this clan. Even a less formidable escaped slave was a threat to all who had come to the planet to buy; slaves outnumbered the purchasers by at least twenty to one, and the idea of them revolting all at once was terrifying even to those who surrounded themselves with armed private security.

The wobanki stopped firing and now focused on moving swiftly enough to avoid recapture, streaking toward the exits of the amphitheater where he hoped to somehow find his freedom. Buyers pushed and squeezed together, giving the wobanki wide paths among the seats to freely leap and bound through—and it was this opening that finally afforded the slavers a clean shot at the wobanki's back. As he sprinted to the top of the amphitheater, darting back and forth unpredictably, shots splashed to either side of him, always too low or too high as the Gomarii failed to properly lead the elusive and deadly target.

At the top, the wobanki prowled among the uppermost seats. He was trapped; there was no way down that didn't involve a lethal fall. The Gomarii were well on their way to recapturing the beast, and virtually every Gomarii guard was now participating in the effort.

Nilo watched the play unfold with satisfaction. He had selected the timing of Garret's visit to the ship to coincide with the wobanki's auction, because of all the captive species on hand, it was the most likely to attempt a violent escape if given the opportunity—and the most likely to stay alive long enough for confusion to truly set in. It was simply a question of timing, and once Zora had communicated that they'd found the Endurian, the time to start phase one arrived as well. That was when the Kublarens released the wobanki.

Now it was time for the second phase. The Kublarens had been prepared to start a riot on their own had the wobanki proved too docile, but it would have been a lot more difficult. Now they would take maximum advantage of the mayhem.

As the freed slave stalked the upper levels, exchanging blaster fire with Gomarii, Nilo opened a comm line to the Kublarens.

"Time for... Pikkek... bring big die?" asked the leader of the little aliens.

"Big die," Nilo confirmed.

Kublaren rifles began to bark and send slugs across the amphitheater and into the zhee contingent, almost all of whom had not scattered but had stayed put to watch the show the wobanki put on. The first volley dropped many of the zhee where they stood before the others could even ready their weapons to return fire. The bot at center stage shouted for calm amid the stampeding, panic, and murder, but none paid any heed and soon the bot itself was hit by stray weapons fire and exploded into a mess of scattered parts and cooked circuitry.

By the time the zhee had organized counterfire, they were already being flanked by the Kublarens, who advanced and fired until they were striking the shrinking band of zhee slave buyers from three sides. The most experienced zhee warriors fell with rapidity while many of the younger zhee fighters turned and ran up the steps to escape the coming flood, occasionally turning and firing wildly, only to hit their compatriots as often as the Kublaren. Their rout was halted by their own lieutenants, who brayed and shot those attempting to flee until they dutifully turned and issued a concentrated return fire at the still-advancing koobs, bringing many of them down as they loped toward their chosen enemy.

The least brave in the face of fire were the lowly, castrated zhee who served as the slovenly Kamartha the Feared's litter bearers, and who were now struggling to transport their master to safety. One had been hit shortly after the opening volley, and with that donk fallen, there was additional strain on the remaining bearers to stabilize the heavy litter on their shoulders.

Kamartha the Feared had prided himself on using the labor of others over repulsor technology. Had he not done so, he could have easily overcome the loss of his servants and floated to safety behind the covering fire his warriors were providing. Of course, the fat zhee had never imagined anything like this happening at a Gomarii slave market, of all places.

When a second litter bearer fell, struck in the head, his brains and blood splattering the great zhee and his fellow geldings alike, two more of the zhee carrying it brayed in terror and ran, abandoning Kamartha the Feared to his fate. Such a thing would mark them with dishonor for the remainder of their lives, and any zhee who recognized them or heard tale of their crime would be honor-bound to slay them. And yet at the moment, this seemed the lesser risk.

The remaining zhee bondservants—those who held tightly to their honor and the ponderous litter—were now unable to keep it from tilting right over, and Kamartha the Feared slid down with a crash into the empty seats, now splattered with blood and spent shell casings from the zhee's slug throwers. The powerful warlord, keeper of the most famed harem among his species, looked on helplessly as his last servants fled him and his remaining warriors were picked off by the well-coordinated Kublaren fire.

Meanwhile, the Gomarii, seeing the actions of the Kublarens, shifted their attention from recovering the wobanki to putting down what was now an armed insurrection by what appeared to be a radical abolitionist group.

Pikkek coordinated his Kublaren fighters to prevent the Gomarii from advancing down the amphitheater, having fire teams strike them from all angles as they fell back toward the stage. The Kublarens had a slight numerical advantage, but that would change as more slavers came in to reinforce the original security group.

Nilo was unconcerned. More help was coming.

Swooping down from the skies came several Black Leaf troop transports. The ships landed long enough to allow scores of additional Kublarens and other mercenaries to join the battle. These were all armed with the Black Leaf variant blaster rifle that issued a powerful charge to the 7.62 rounds it sent through its dual-purpose magazine—an incredibly potent mix of old, devastating technology with the modern galactic standard.

The incoming koobs worked with Pikkek's command team already on site to quickly overwhelm and eliminate the Gomarii security teams outside the ship. A team of private military contractors hand-picked by Nilo, not as good as Carter but good, positioned themselves beneath the massive slave ship, placed charges on the struts, and blew them the moment they were clear. The blast seemed to push all the wind out of the amphitheater. One strut was completely blown apart, and the slave ship teetered, listing on what was left of the others, and then another support collapsed as well, causing the ship to crash down and rest partly on its great forward prow.

In examining the ship, Nilo had seen that it relied on a massive thrust from its belly to lift the craft straight up and out of atmosphere. Now the Gomarii would be unable to achieve proper liftoff. Whether that was a design flaw, or a simple necessity given the ship's colossal size, it was now trapped on the ground until the broken struts could be repaired—no easy feat.

Not that it mattered just yet. The slavers hadn't made any efforts to so much as warm their engines. They still thought they could regain control and were intent on salvaging as much as they could of the remaining auction. But that attitude would change once they realized what they were up against. And they would, soon. But first, there were other objectives that needed to be achieved.

The remaining zhee and Gomarii had by now aligned themselves with the pirates and other private security details trapped in the amphitheater. But now that they were up against not just the Kublarens but the Black Leaf forces, they proved no match for Nilo's numbers, equipment, and surprise.

Kamartha the Feared, sensing he was lost in the pitched fighting all around him, dragged his enormous belly along the stairs, seeking to escape with his life. But Pikkek, who had been watching and coordinating his troops, had not once allowed the zhee to escape from his sight. Nor was he willing to let the corpulent slaver escape. The zhee had been a plague on his world, destroyer of many clutches, ruiner of tribes. Pikkek could not recall a time in his life when the mountainous villages of his home had been less safe for both clutch and foundling alike than when the time just prior to the Zhee being expelled from the planet—and that was no small matter for a world as locked in inter-tribal warfare as Kublar had often been.

Pikkek had waited patiently for the opportunity to be used in the memory of Carter, twice a *muktah*—and the chance to slay a great zhee *muktah* was just such an opportunity. Drawing his black tomahawk, he stalked across the empty stage, moving past the ruined bot and the bodies of his dead warriors.

Kamartha the Feared saw at once that he was discovered. His nostrils flared and his eyes went wide at the sight of the advancing Kublaren. He had no way of knowing that Pikkek was the same member of that species who had slain a most holy cleric in the holovid that had spread throughout the galaxy among the zhee, prompting calls for a blood war against the species. That act had been an outrage against the zhee, one that had resulted in no small amount of violence elsewhere, never mind that there were no Kublarens where the riots took place. The cycle of rage was necessary to the old zhee if they were to prevent their lustful colts from abandoning their ways, as some were wont to do. They needed a violent purpose to be called back into the service of the four gods.

Kamartha the Feared, however, had no desire to be a cause for zhee rage and recruitment. He merely wanted to escape.

At first, he attempted to crawl faster, hoping that some shift in the fortunes of battle would force his pursuer to break off his hunt, or better yet, be killed outright. But his great girth was too much for his arms to push off the stadium stairs upon which he now slithered. A speedy exit was not possible.

The zhee warlord rolled onto his back, his great stomach impairing his vision of Pikkek as the koob hopped up the steps, closing in. Kamartha the Feared fumbled through the folds of robe and folds of fat to find his ceremonial *kankari* knife. He was no novice with the blade. Those he drew blood from now were usually subdued, unarmed, and praying for a mercifully quick death, but it had not always been so. He had once earned his reputation as a fierce warrior. Now he readied himself for what might be one final trial by combat.

But such a trial never came. The gluttonous zhee had only managed to brush the scabbard of his weapon when Pikkek was upon him, swinging the tomahawk down through his belly, slicing through the red robes and splitting hide and fat. Entrails burst from the wound as though packed inside the zhee like springs. The air grew thick with his fetid stench, a foul odor that rose above the scents of blaster fire and the blood of so many species dead and dying.

Pikkek looked down at the warlord, licking his eyeball in anticipation of becoming, like Carter, a *muktah two*. He inflated his throat sac and brought the tomahawk down again as Kamartha brayed in fear. Entrails split as the fat had before them, and the tomahawk dug down deep inside the zhee's belly.

Wrestling to pull the weapon from a tangled knot of intestines, Pikkek waited for Kamartha the Feared's shrieks of anguished pain to subside long enough for the zhee's long ears to hear the Kublaren say, "Big... k'kk... die."

28

The explosion and subsequent lurch left little doubt in Zora's mind that the promised distraction had come. The blast carried such force that its tremors could be felt beneath Zora's feet. The ship groaned and then abruptly pitched forward, causing everyone in Leenah's cell to tumble against the wall, crashing on top of the Gomarii slavers and pinning them in a tangled mess of bodies.

Jack immediately seized the opportunity. The Gomarii had prohibited them from bringing their weapons aboard, but Jack rectified that by tearing the blaster rifle out of the hands of the nearest slaver, delivering an elbow strike to the Gomarii's head as it struggled to recover the weapon, and then pushed his foot off the guard's stomach to create separation. With room to bring the weapon up, he sent a quick bolt into the slaver's head.

The second slaver was busy wrestling with Garret and Leenah. Jack shouted for them to get out of the way and then shot that one as well.

Garret got to his feet on the tilted deck and then held out a hand to Leenah. "We're here to rescue you."

Leenah took his hand and stood, then looked warily at the two dead Gomarii. "So far you're doing a good job."

Zora motioned for everyone to follow her out of the cell. "Come on before they lock us in."

They reassembled outside, but the ray shield didn't reactivate.

Leenah looked at Garret and nodded toward Jack and Zora. "These your friends?"

Zora answered. "I'm Zora and this is Jack. I'm an old friend of Keel's and he's along for the ride."

"I'd apologize for making you go through all that modeling," said Jack, "but then I'd be starting out our relationship with a lie."

"Charming," said Leenah.

"Okay," Garret said, trying to get things back on track. "Mr. Nilo said that after the explosion he would have his men working outside to secure the… the perimeter. So, all we have to do now is just avoid being, uh, captured until they take control of the ship and kill all the slavers."

Jack gave a sly smile. "First time giving a mission briefing?"

"Stay focused, Jack," said Zora. She nodded at the holocams positioned throughout the corridor.

"I'm always focused."

"Act like it then. This ship is full of Gomarii and it's a safe bet they know what's happened. The middle of this hallway isn't exactly the most defensible position in the world, so let's get moving."

Taking the lead, she brought the party back the way they had come. Along the way she pinged Nilo to provide an update. "Package secure. Moving to ship entrance."

"Hey, Zora," said a far too casual voice on the other end of the comm. It wasn't Nilo.

"Who is this?"

"Oh. Sorry. This is Briscoe. And you're Zora. And let me say, I've heard good things about you. Very good things. Now, I don't want you to be alarmed or anything. Mr. Nilo is okay. He's just busy. So, yours truly is stepping up to help out. Now, you should be outside of the ship, correct?"

"Unbelievable," muttered Jack. Zora's comm was patched through to him and Garret, so they were hearing what she did. "Don't get me started on the quality of Black Leaf shock collars. Hundred to one we're about to get tasked with something that'll probably get us killed."

Zora furrowed her brow. "Negative. We are still on the ship, escorting the package. Seeking a secure location to await evac. Moving close to entrance. Over."

"Hang on..." Briscoe sounded distracted. "Yeah, okay. You're right. Got ahead of myself a bit. Okay. Plan has changed due to a few updates. We got somethin' new for ya."

"I knew it," said Jack, memories of his impromptu killing spree with the Soob flooding back.

"Should be no problem for your team, you know?"

A pair of Gomarii went running down a cross corridor at the end of their path, not twenty meters away, their heavy strides hindered by the listing of the ship. Both streaked on past without even noticing the escapees off to their right.

"I need you to get to the point," Zora snapped. "Tell me what I need to know and then say *out*. That's how this works. Over."

"Yeah I know, I'm working on that. I get it and that is totally legit. My bad. Anyway, the 'ree sealed this ship up tight like two Drusics in a porta-fresher and they're doin' a decent job keeping our teams just a little busy outside. Plus, we got orders to disable any non-ree ships that try and dust off to exit atmo. So... that's a handful. Nobody else is gettin' out alive. Big Nee's orders. So, what I'd like is—actually, is Jack there?"

"I'm here." Jack rolled his eyes.

"Outstanding. We need you to go ahead and get that door open for us."

"The main ramp?"

"That's the one, my man."

Jack's eyes darted around for more Gomarii. "Do you have schematics I can follow? Troop counts? Or am I expected to just fight my way to the door and hit the open button? Alone."

"Uh, roger, but let me get you some answers... let's see... negative and negative. And positive. Need you to open that front door. But you don't have to do it alone. Anyone who wants to go with you can. Out."

"What do you mean, out?" Zora protested, but Jack raised his hand to quiet her.

"Roger, Briscoe."

"Outstanding."

Jack shook his head and looked at Zora. "Don't bother trying to get anything else. Black Leaf ideals result in some interesting placement of talent when it comes to running things. It's complicated and it's frustrating, but we're not changing it any time soon."

Zora frowned. She hadn't experienced anything like this before, and it shook her faith in what seemed otherwise like a competent organization.

"So, what's the plan, Jack?" she asked. "We've got the kid, who's not going to be much help in a blaster fight. No offense."

"None taken," said Garret. "I feel like I'm going to throw up. This is almost as bad as Rakka."

"You survived that, and you can survive this, but walking up to the door and opening it manually can't be our best option."

Jack shrugged. "Maybe there's another way onto the ship they can exploit."

"If you can get me to a terminal, I can find out," Garret offered. "I might even be able to remotely lower the ramp."

"That'd be helpful," said Jack.

"It's what I usually did for Captain Keel from the *Six*. If only I had access to my terminal there, I'd be sliced in before they knew what hit them."

"That could be arranged…" said Leenah.

All heads turned to hear the Endurian out.

"I activated the beacons; I assume that's how you found me." Leenah paused long enough for Garret to acknowledge that it was. "That's what I thought. Well, the Gomarii got to me first. But they didn't just take me, they took the whole ship. It's probably still inside the hangar bay."

Garret pumped his fist. "I knew it! See, I *told* you guys something was wrong. I told you we should've found something out there. That explains it all. I knew it."

"Congratulations," Jack said snidely. "How much can that ship do for us now, though? Because everything I heard tells me it's not in great working order."

"I mean, I'd have to see it…" said the code slicer.

"It's worse than you can imagine," said Leenah. "Or at least it was. I got one backup generator working but every system was disconnected or fried until I re-spliced. But the Gomarii might have made some progress in repairing it."

"Why would they repair it?" asked Zora, ducking behind a bulkhead as more Gomarii slavers rushed toward the ship's entrance. They were in a hurry and all their attention seemed to be focused on quelling whatever was happening at their gates.

"I was awake by the time they dragged me off the ship. They had brought the whole ship into a massive hangar on the top deck. I was loopy, but there were other ships, and it looked like they were stripping or rebuilding them. Techs were busy."

"Top deck?" Jack asked.

Leenah nodded. "Yes. I could see the bay shield directly above me. Then they took me down a bunch of levels until I got where you found me."

Jack and Zora exchanged a look. "That's a lot of ship to cover for a payoff that might be nothing more than a pile of scrap metal sitting in the corner."

Zora nodded in agreement, but said, "Might be our best option. Better than going in the same direction all those Gomarii are running in. Plus, if there's a bay door, maybe we can open it too, or instead, and Black Leaf can insert troops from there."

"And it's *not* a pile of scrap metal," Garret said, sounding piqued. "Even if you lost all connections, the systems are so integrated that you're sure to get more credits getting it all running again then you would selling out the individual parts. That thing is a work of art."

Leenah beamed at this description. Clearly she agreed.

So did Zora. "He's right. Keel dumped *several* fortunes into his baby. It would probably sell for more than this behemoth at auction."

"Anyway," said Garret, "it only has to be *mostly* together for me to get my terminal up and running. Then we can open the upper hangar and the ramp at the base, hit them from two sides."

Jack scratched his chin, then gave a quick nod. "Okay. Yeah, let's do it. You've got better armor, so you take the lead, Zora. I'll watch our tails."

"With pleasure," answered the bounty hunter, who held the other Gomarii's blaster rifle. "I've been wanting to kill these kelhorns since we landed on this planet."

Jack looked over at Leenah and saw fury in her eyes. "Something tells me you're not the only one. But let's do ourselves all a favor and not draw too much attention."

29

The fight outside the Gomarii slave ship had been going well for Nilo and his Black Leaf strike force of Kublarens and mercenaries. But as new challenges presented themselves, he found himself wishing Carter were still alive and on hand to better do something about them.

What had started as a coordinated attack where his teams took advantage of the chaos and frenzy of those trying to ascertain what was happening and how they could escape it, was now a growing thread knotted by multiple crises. It wasn't too much for Nilo—he'd presided over military, political, and humanitarian problems, with his Black Leaf machine awaiting his decisions—but it was slowing down the ultimate victory he sought.

Militarily, the Gomarii presented the largest obstacle. They had rallied around the damaged ship and pushed the Kublarens back far enough to allow others of their species to work with cutting torches and repulsor cranes in an attempt to replace the destroyed left-front strut done in by Nilo's sapper team. Other Gomarii went after the easier task of shoring up the other damaged struts, hoping to make them strong enough for a liftoff. Pikkek was holding the line, but they needed to regain the ground they'd lost in order to prevent the Gomarii from achieving repairs.

There were mercenaries on hand who could do exactly that, but they were engaged in holding the buyers—and their slaves—on planet. Freeing as many slaves as possible was an important factor in what Nilo hoped to achieve. His limited attack fighters had already grounded several yachts and other freighters that had attempted to test their engines against his small blockade. That had resulted in an unfortunate loss of those he sought to protect, but the ships crashing down to flames on the surface of the planet was not in vain; it made clear to the other slave buyers that any attempt to escape meant death. After that only a few desperate runners tested the Black Leaf no-fly zone, mostly those in small craft who thought they might be able to slip away undetected. None managed to get close to exiting the atmosphere.

With escape through hyperspace no longer an option, the desperate slave buyers began to work other angles. Realizing that the Kublaren force had been planted by those now patrolling the skies and seeking to bring the long slave street to order, the purchasers made the slaves themselves into bargaining chits. Banding together with other slaveowners, they threatened mass executions of those under their control.

Nilo pulled back his mercenaries, unwilling to test the resolve of these brutes. At least not yet. He could rationalize the loss of the slaves aboard the downed ships—in his mind their quick deaths were preferable to the hellish lives they would have led had their buyers escaped—but he would not suffer any more losses unless and until there was no other option.

Which meant another standstill. Nilo needed one or the other element to resolve so he could mount his combined forces against what remained. The longer the Gomarii had, the more likely they would be able to escape in their slave ship. The longer the buyers had, the more likely they would work together at a coordinated liftoff.

Nilo's blockade could stop individual strays but couldn't stop everyone in an all-out rush off-planet.

If Carter were here, he could have been trusted to clear out individual slaveowners. Nilo needed someone who could take the man's place, and soon.

As the minutes ticked by, messages came over the command channel. Powerful individuals in the world of business, both legitimate and criminal, offered deals to purchase their escape. And not just businessmen. Politicians, celebrities, and others among the rich and powerful who proved the many rumors of their excess to be true. All they wanted was a way out—and one that didn't carry with it the stain of a career-ending scandal. They offered up not only their new possessions—their slaves—but also financial payments and other considerations grand enough that even Nilo was impressed.

He considered taking some of the worst offenders up on the offer, taking control of their slaves, and then shooting the buyers out of the sky as they attempted to gain altitude. But only a fool would agree to parting with his hostages before his demands were realized. And even if Nilo found such a fool, the trick would only work once.

His primary hope now lay in Jack, an agent whose record was comparable to Carter's. If he could just open up the ship, the Kublarens would surge aboard and the nature of the fight with the Gomarii would change. They would be forced to cease their attempts at repair and instead focus on maintaining control. And once that happened, Nilo would be free to bring about the rest of his plans.

He looked through the black smoke rising from fires in the battlescape and partially obscuring the great Gomarii slave ship. The titanic vessel was easily a kilometer high and probably twice as long and wide.

A city among the stars.

"Make it happen, Jack," Nilo said to himself. "You're getting paid more than enough to do it."

The first encounter Jack's team ran into had been a surprise to both parties. The two groups met one another at the turn of a corner, the wailing of alarms sufficient to muffle each other's steps. When the Gomarii took an involuntary step backward, Jack jumped forward and opened fire in close-quarters battle.

He took down two of the slavers, and Zora sent a concentrated blast into the midsection of a third. By then Jack was at her side and had a clean shot at the fourth and final slaver.

Jack Bowie might not have had the same training as a legionnaire, but when it came to shooting, he was expert qualified, nonetheless. He put four bolts into the chest of the final Gomarii, with the third and fourth punching through the armor and killing the wicked slaver.

"That went well," Jack said dryly. He looked to Leenah and motioned his head toward the dead. "Grab a rifle for yourself. Same goes for you, Garret. If you don't know how to shoot, or won't shoot, then just hand them to me or Zora when ours run dry."

Leenah picked up one blaster and handed another to Garret. She slung a second over her shoulder. Garret did likewise. "I can shoot if I have to," she said.

"Yeah, me too," said Garret. "Or at least I can make whoever's on the receiving end think I can. Buy you time."

"Good enough," said Jack. "Because judging by the number of holocams these sket-bags have installed, some seeing eye just saw the whole thing." He pointed up to a small cam above them that was set up to observe the blind corner. "If we were tagged as a minor concern before because of the larger crisis outside, let's assume that's changed now. Next squad that comes our way will be looking for us. So, let's not let it be us who's surprised."

Leenah checked the charge pack on her weapon and wiped away some of its former owner's blood on the small bits of clothing she possessed. "I remember this level. And I remember the level above. There were a lot of prisoners in the cells."

"Anyone who might help us?" Zora asked.

"Perhaps. They're dangerous enough to cause some harm. Hools, Drusics… species like that."

"They took you down level by level?" Jack asked. He was having difficulty determining how much trust he should be putting in the Endurian. Another pretty face in a convenient place. Just like Honey.

"Speedlift would've been faster," added Zora. Perhaps she was suspicious of Leenah as well. Certainly, the reaction of the Gomarii was less than they had anticipated. That had a way of spooking you.

"Don't know what to tell you," Leenah said with a shrug, "but that's how it went. I don't think the guards were in a hurry to get back to whatever their duty was. Or maybe they just liked how hard it was for me to make the journey. I was in pretty bad shape, physically and emotionally."

"They probably appreciated tasting it then," said Garret.

"My point is," said Leenah, "that we may be able to release some of those prisoners and use their escape to our advantage."

"Not the way it works in real life," said Jack. "Those species you mentioned handle stress differently than a little Endurian princess. You get a bunch of Drusics sick of being locked up against their will, then when they get out, that's going to be a highly volatile situation. They aren't too discerning when they start raging. Won't be pretty for anyone that gets on the business end of those boulder-sized fists unless they got some serious body armor. And most of us," Jack let his eyes drift down Leenah's figure, "don't."

"He's right," said Zora. "My father used to go on about that quite a bit. That's why the Legion never opened its ranks to anyone but humans."

"And here I thought it was because they're all irredeemable bigots and speciesists," said Jack.

Garret cut in. "Okay, I know I'm a novice at this assaulting a giant ship thing," he said, "but I can't picture Captain Keel just standing around bantering instead of moving."

"He wouldn't," Leenah agreed. "Are we ready?"

"Not yet," said Jack. "What you two call banter I call hanging back in a defensible position where we can see whatever Gomarii hit squad is coming well before they get to us."

Zora looked down both of the long corridors that met at the blind corner. "So, we're just passing the time while we have a clear view in both directions?"

"That's about it," Jack said, unconcerned. "See, if you're going to rub us out, best place to do it is when we're halfway down the corridor in either direction. Gives us a really nasty choice. Charge whoever's shooting at us from the nearest bulkhead or turn around to fall back and in the process give them a nice long time to take careful shots of our pretty little exposed backs."

Leenah shook her head, a disapproving look on her face. "You mean we just wait?"

"Pretty much."

"For how long?"

Jack shrugged. "Well, there's a fight still happening outside. They're all tryin' to deal with that. But at least one team is gonna be sent to deal with us before they get to go help the clan outside too. Every second that goes by, they ain't helpin' the clan defend the ship. Which, to them, is a problem. So, it stands to reason that they won't be patient. Pretty soon they'll decide they can't wait any longer to make the hit, and then we catch them between corridors."

"Or they don't know we're here at all," said Zora, "and we'll be waiting forever, wasting time."

"Ain't a waste if you're still alive at the end of it, Z. Nice to have a kill team at our back, but we don't, so I prefer to wait until the bad guys come to me or give me a clear sign that they're interested. It's worked for me more than once."

"So we wait," Garret said, not sounding at all thrilled at this outcome.

Jack smiled and rubbed the stubble across his chin. "It's a free galaxy. If any of you wanna go on ahead, I won't stop ya."

30

"Well, that was ten minutes of my life I'll never get back," Zora said.

They had moved down the corridor they'd been watching. No sign of Gomarii slavers moving to intercept them had ever come. Now they were traversing a new corridor that was filled with holding cells. As Leenah had recalled, it was full of Hools, Drusics, Lahursian snake-men, zhee, and other notably dangerous species of the galaxy.

"You're alive, aren't you?" Jack said to Zora. "Okay, maybe my hunch was off, but just as likely whoever was after us figured we weren't going anywhere and didn't bother to divert any resources from the main fight. From the sound of it, it's a big one."

Indeed, the explosions outside continued on unabated, loud enough to reach the innards of the great ship.

"Look at all this," Garret said as they moved cautiously down the corridor. "I thought Mr. Nilo said that everything that came on the last day was going to be more like Leenah. You know, really pretty or really strong."

"Drusics aren't strong enough for you?" asked Jack. "Because they sure ain't pretty. Especially these."

Certainly, the furry, primate-like species they passed was quite large when compared to a human, but these particular Drusics looked scrawny, malnourished. Many had bald patches in their fur, and all had dull, dead eyes.

Only the subtle motion of their breathing indicated that they weren't dead on their feet.

"I get your point though," Jack continued. "These aren't in any condition for sale. Look at this one."

He pointed out a Drusic missing an arm and one eye. The top half of its skull appeared to be missing entirely. It stared dumbly at the ray shield as a trickle of drool dripped from its open mouth, wet its fur, and pooled at its feet. The prisoners of the other species were similarly damaged.

"Were they experimenting on these or something?" Zora asked. "I didn't know Gomarii did that kind of thing."

Jack shrugged a shoulder. "Maybe not for themselves, but if someone paid 'em enough, they'd do it."

"I don't remember them being in this kind of shape the first time I went by," said Leenah. She rubbed her bare arms, either from the chill she had to feel in her skimpy attire or the condition of the prisoners.

"So, add torture and mutilation to the list of these slavers' crimes, and let's keep moving," said Jack.

It was at that moment that the overdue Gomarii warriors sent to deal with the loose element finally arrived. They came storming through a blast door thirty meters ahead of Jack's party, already firing. Zora and Leenah leapt to either side of the corridor, taking cover behind the edges of a thick bulkhead that housed an emergency blast door, one of many positioned throughout the corridor to contain a hull breach as swiftly as possible. Jack dove onto his knees and slid to a stop behind Leenah, ready to fire from his low position while enjoying the same cover as the Endurian. He reached out and grabbed the slower-moving Garret by the collar and yanked the kid behind him.

"Lay down flat and hug the wall!"

Blaster bolts shot straight down the middle of the corridor or crashed into the bulkheads, sending sparks flying down below and causing the defenders to squint and grit their teeth. The Gomarii moved rapidly along the corridor, trying to make themselves small as they ran at a low crouch. The large slavers were still big targets, and Jack and Zora picked off the lead attackers, but those behind them pushed forward until they were stacked behind their own bulkheads, leaning out to exchange fire with the intruders but advancing no further.

"They stopped moving," Leenah called out after sending a volley and then ducking back behind cover.

Zora nodded, fired, and shouted back, "Trying to keep us occupied."

That was probably it. Jack checked behind them. So far it was clear, but if the Gomarii were attempting to flank them, they already had the anvil set up. He needed to act before the hammer arrived.

"Last chance to head back," Jack called. "Clear in the rear for now."

"What about opening the cells?" Garret shouted above the din of blaster fire. "I'm sure I can figure out these controls."

"Already talked about it," Jack shouted back, just missing a Gomarii that had leaned his bald blue head out a little too far. "We'd just be the first meal for those things. Rather take my chances with the slavers."

"We've got to do something!" shouted Leenah.

There was little that could be done from Jack's perspective beyond falling back and reengaging from a superior fighting position. Zora could perform the maneuver, but the others were likely to get shot in the process. He found himself wishing that the slavers had carried something like a flashbang, but their kits had been built around controlling the slaves. Ener-chains, blasters with significant stun capabilities, and the torturous whips that made the nerve endings they touched dance and writhe in agony. A painful corrective that left no outward signs of damage on the valuable commodities they were used against.

Jack had taken one of those whips from the last pack of Gomarii they'd dealt with, carefully wrapping its carrier around his waist.

"What the hell," he muttered, pulling it free.

He caught Zora's attention, tapped Leenah on the back of her thigh, and shouted, "I'm gonna need you and Zora to cover me."

Zora nodded at the whip in his hand. "What do you think you're gonna do with that thing?"

"If it works we'll both see at the same time. Ready?"

Zora and Leenah said that they were. So did Garret, who had yet to fire his weapon but was now taking aim from his prone position on the floor. The sight didn't exactly fill Jack with confidence. The code slicer seemed just as likely to shoot Jack in the back as keep the Gomarii's heads down. But no turning back now. His reputation was on the line here.

"Go!" he shouted.

The others increased their rate of fire, and Jack rolled out into the corridor and ran toward the Gomarii. The slavers were waiting for the assault, clued in by the sudden uptick in blaster fire. One of them in the rear leaned out in an attempt to get a clean shot on Jack but was struck just below the armor protecting the neck by one of the shooters at Jack's back—probably Zora. The Gomarii fell sideways, clutching the burning wound where the neck met the shoulder as it crashed into the middle of the corridor.

Jack was committed now. He couldn't stop before reaching his destination, even as the Gomarii sent several unaimed bolts sizzling past him. If he laid up behind one of the bulkheads he passed, there was no guarantee Zora and the others would have the firepower needed to give him a second round of covering fire, let alone what it would take to handle a flanking group of attackers. That meant he had to get right up to the slavers they were currently engaging, right up against the same bulkhead they used for cover, and he had to do it *now*.

He had run up along the left side of the corridor after darting out from his place on the right. The Gomarii on the opposite side had the best visuals on him, and he would be totally exposed to them once he was right up against the bulkhead. Knowing this, Jack motioned for Zora and Leenah to cease their fire and then leapt across the corridor with the nerve whip unraveled behind him.

He slammed against the bulkhead with his shoulder and lashed the long whip in a backhand motion with his left arm, sending the electric blue cord crackling toward the Gomarii on the far side.

The whip didn't crack or look particularly sharp. In fact, it was limp like a falling piece of synth rope. But as it flopped itself across the arms and heads of the three Gomarii, it did what it was designed to do. The slavers' expressions left no doubt as to the gout of pain that had erupted where the whip touched flesh. They dropped their weapons to hang on their slings and instinctively brought their hands up to their heads, necks, and faces.

So far so good, but a job only halfway done. Then again, as Mama Bowie used to say, well begun was nearly done.

Jack whipped his arm inward to yank the lash back at the Gomarii who covered on the near side of the hall, directly on the other side of their shared bulkhead, calling for Zora to "Push up!" as he did so. He couldn't see the Gomarii he struck, but their screams told him his weapon had found them. The Gomarii could see Jack's arm plainly enough, though, and one of them sent a blaster bolt into it at close range. The shot burned its way through his ulna and radius before terminating against one of the ray shields.

Jack dropped the whip and drew his wounded arm in close to his body, the hand feeling dead and useless. But unlike the cruel taskmasters on the other side of the bulkhead, he managed to push himself through the pain. To lose momentum now would be to lose everything. He lifted his blaster rifle in his good hand and fired on the Gomarii he'd first lashed, only a few meters away and beginning to recover from the whip. He took two down before the third fired back, a blast that hit his thigh and sent him falling onto his rear.

Cursing in pain, Jack shot that one as well, leaving just the slavers directly beside him, separated by only a small partition of impervisteel.

Thankfully Zora had pushed up by then to deal with them, rushing along the opposite side of the corridor with Leenah right behind her, the Endurian bravely joining the fight despite not having anything close to the armor that the bounty hunter wore. The pair unleashed on the remaining Gomarii, and it was all over in moments. Zora took a few glancing blasts to her armor, and Leenah was untouched.

Jack struggled back to his feet, hopping on his good leg and gingerly testing the bad.

"You good?" Zora asked.

He wasn't. He couldn't put any weight on the leg he'd been shot in without feeling as though he'd collapse again. He let his blaster hang on its sling and held his wounded arm tightly against his body. "Been better."

"Watch the corridor," Zora ordered Leenah. "Garret, get up here."

As the code slicer rose from his stomach and ran to join the others, Zora applied what aid she could.

Jack didn't so much as flinch as she sealed the wounds. "Well... that worked."

"If you're talking about your charge," Zora said, inspecting the wound in Jack's leg, "then yes, it did. You were just as likely to get yourself killed, though."

"Funny how things turn out." Jack looked to the Endurian. "Hey. How much farther are we talking to get to that ship of yours? Because I'm gonna be a little bit slowed down from this point on. Nothing against you two girls, but I doubt you ladies are up to carrying me along and still firing those weapons. Even if the kid helps."

"One or two levels," Leenah answered. "Like I said, I was dazed, but I counted what levels I could. Best guess."

Jack hopped on one foot and held on to the wall for support. He attempted to put weight on the injured leg again. "All right. Numbing agent's already working. I can hop and limp my way that far. But if we run into more trouble, go ahead and leave me."

"We won't do that, Mr. Jack," said Garret.

"Trust me, won't be the first time I've had to figure my way out of a tight situation without the ability to move. Getting to be a theme as of late. Either way, let's get moving now while we still can."

31

Keel moved along the stolen Republic frigate's main access corridor. The *Defiance of Reason* might have a new name, but its layout was the same. He needed only follow this route to the auxiliary stairwell and then he'd be at the base of the bridge.

He had to fight the urge to increase his pace. He watched his surroundings, poised and ready for anyone challenging his advance, watching his six and moving smoothly through empty halls and past sealed blast doors. He had seen no one since leaving the engine rooms. Death reported no activity in the docking hangar. It was a ghost ship manned by a skeleton crew. Keel anticipated they would be gathered together, if not hiding somewhere else on the ship. He wasn't about to take the time to root them out if that's what they'd decided to do. Besides, they were most likely at the bridge. That was the most defensible spot on the ship—if one knew how to properly protect it. These points wouldn't.

He pushed up through the stairwell. His footsteps echoed against the emptiness. The sense that something was off struck him again. Before moving onto the second deck, he pinged Honey, who had locked herself in the shuttle's cockpit.

"I need a sitrep. What are you seeing?"

"Nothing. Bay is empty. Remaining Nether Ops agents went in pursuit of you. Where are you now?"

The report matched what Death had told him, except for him being chased by more Nether agents. That part was new. Keel had hoped he'd gotten them all.

"Heading toward the bridge. How many did you see go after me?"

"About a dozen. I didn't get a real good count. I was keeping low hoping they wouldn't check my shuttle."

Keel hadn't seen that many agents while he was in the hangar, but things had gone kinetic quickly and his focus had been on killing whoever was in front of him and making his way deeper into the ship to reach the target. Being pursued didn't change that, but it might delay it. He felt confident he could use the size of the ship against whoever was following and pick them off until the odds were a bit more even.

But it would be easier to simply reach the bridge ahead of them and fend them off from there. In fact, if the situation were reversed, Keel would have reinforced the bridge security to stop whoever was coming from doing any damage there, set a team to patrol, and set another team to lock down the hangar to prevent escape.

He called his bot. "Death. Are the hangar's blast doors sealed?"

The bot confirmed that they were and then beeped a few thoughts and some suggestions as to how it might help New Boss.

"Sorry, pal," Keel said. "Neither of the two ships in that hangar have strong enough guns for you to try that trick again. But yeah, stay close and keep an eye on her."

Nether Ops had at least done enough to cut off a quick escape, should Keel need it. And while there were codes hard-wired into every Republic vessel and a good number of ships and other vehicles made available to the

Republic, a docking bay's primary blast door was something that could only be controlled manually once its emergency closure was enacted. Keel would have to go direct to the source and begin the process of reopening it from there. Not impossible, but time-consuming, and if Keel had need of opening those doors, it would mean that he was no longer the most dangerous force aboard the frigate.

Things weren't to that point yet.

He continued for the bridge, hoping that he had enough of a head start to reach it even while using the stairs instead of the speedlifts. It troubled him that Honey hadn't reported his pursuers until he asked for a sitrep, though.

"I'm setting up an ambush," he told Honey, though he intended otherwise. "Gonna hit them when they try to reach the bridge. Let me know if anyone visits the docking bay."

"Why don't you lay low until I can link up with you?" suggested the Tennar. "An extra gun will help, and with all the dead legionnaires you left lying around, I'll find one no problem. Or you can pull them away and then I can hit the bridge myself while you keep the agents off my trail."

"Those aren't legionnaires. And if they reach the bridge instead of chasing me, we'll have a much tougher problem on our hands. Better to take them out now. Moving. Out."

Keel pushed up the stairwell and debated whether to leave at the second level to take the speedlift and reach the bridge more quickly. But it was only one more level, not worth gambling with his life over. A speedlift could be a death trap if you hadn't secured whatever was on the other side of its doors once they opened.

He exploded up the grated metal risers, taking them two at a time and then activating his armor's jump jets to vault over the railing and up to the next flight, riding the momentum straight up and grimacing at the amount of jump juice he was using. Eventually, he'd need to reconnect with Garret and get a more economic source of fuel. Still, the juice gone was worth the time he'd saved himself as he entered the top deck.

Level three looked empty, but Keel would have to make his way to the midpoint of the ship to access the bridge, which sat on the very top of the frigate. A dedicated speedlift let out into a security station where crewmembers were checked out before being given access to the bridge proper. There would be no stairs to take there; the limited access was part of the ship's design. Unlike a destroyer, a Republic frigate was small enough that it could be boarded and taken by a determined group.

Keel reached the speedlift without incident. As expected, it was on lockdown as part of the general alarm. The override took him all of three seconds, and the doors opened. The lift's car, as expected, had been recalled to the top level. Thankfully, he had Rechs's armor instead of the Legion kit he wore when performing training exercises on ships like this one. It would make the job that much easier.

He stepped into the speedlift well, dropping a meter down the shaft to stand amid the shock absorbers set up to soften the car's fall should its repulsors ever fail. He looked up at the underneath of the car some five meters above him. He could cut his way through its thick plating, but if Nether Ops was still pursuing him, that might prove the delay they needed to catch up. Besides, there was no need. The Republic had left an easier way in.

Keel activated his jump jets to burst upward, activated his magnetic boots to clamp onto the underside of the car, and then reached around to grab the bottom rung of a maintenance ladder not visible from the bottom of the shaft. He knew it would be there. It was retractable, originally designed to retract from the base of the shaft all the way to the top. Whether because of engineering difficulties or out of a desire to save credits, instead of going to the top of the shaft, the ladder only retracted a little higher than the bottom of the car itself, which meant it could be reached by someone who had a good footing beneath the elevator.

With a firm grip on the bottom rung, Keel deactivated his boots and swung out, hanging from the maintenance ladder. He muscled his way up, thankful for the additional power the armor had; he felt like he was moving in PT gear.

While the bottom of the car was a half-meter-thick piece of impervisteel, the side of the car was barely a centimeter. He activated a micro-torch from his kit and began work on the car's side. This would have the added bonus of making the speedlift look untouched to anyone who followed him. At least until the doors opened and they saw the hole in the back of the car.

He kicked in a meter-tall oval slab of metal and then swung himself inside the car. The lift, secured by its magnetic locks, didn't so much as shake or shudder from his sudden arrival.

He experienced a brief moment of déjà vu. What felt like a lifetime ago, Keel and Kill Team Victory had practiced storming the bridge of an assault frigate like this one. The navy and its chosen contractor had wanted to see how well the improved security design of the bridges would fare against the best that Dark Ops had. They'd upgraded everything after an MCR warlord, more of a pirate than a revolutionary, had taken one of the frigates from the Republic out on the edge. The warlord and his boarding party had outfought a small number of marines and simply rode the speedlift to the bridge, where the ship was immediately surrendered by a stupefied point. That incident received galactic-wide attention, and an embarrassed House of Reason invested significant resources to correct the entire fleet of this flaw.

Only to leave in place another, equally exploitable flaw, one that the new contractor and the navy planners had failed to consider. One that Kill Team Victory identified immediately.

The bridge's new defense protocols involved recalling the speedlift so that it was at top level, bridge level, to avoid more pirates simply waltzing on board. However, the recalled lift's doors now aligned with the security station just outside the bridge. Which meant all a boarding party had to do now was climb beneath the car, cut their way in, and then, with the simple press of a button—or barring that, the application of a pry bar—they were where they needed to be.

Which was exactly what Kill Team Victory did.

After taking the two men at the security station by surprise, they stormed the bridge beyond, where they found a despondent point standing with mouth agape. His look of shock soon transformed to an angry suspicion that somehow Dark Ops had cheated. Ford promised that they hadn't and reminded the navy brass and the business executives on hand that they were all on the same team and wanted the same thing.

In a follow-up, Team Victory provided feedback for how to correct the security design. The thick undercarriage of the car and the retractable ladder were good starts. All that needed to happen was to provide the speedlift with a longer shaft so that the lift could be positioned at a new section just *beneath* the bridge deck. Boarders could still take Victory's approach—climb, cut through the floor, avoid getting hit by the falling slug of half-meter impervisteel, and then slip into the car. But at that point, if they forced the doors, they'd find nothing but impervisteel all around them. And if they cut through an equally thick ceiling, they would have to then climb again to the top of the shaft, somehow anchor themselves to the ceiling, wedge open the door to the bridge-level security station, and storm it from that exposed position against the hullbusters stationed there.

Keel remembered how the admiral in the room sat placidly during the entire presentation. Prior to the operation he'd expressed confidence that Ford's kill team would be unable to even reach the bridge in the ten minutes afforded them. Victory had proved the man wrong, taking the ship in under three. And now he seemed intent on "winning" the subsequent meeting.

"Son," the admiral had said. "You have any idea how much it would cost the Republic to add that much impervisteel to every single one of these here ships we've got in service?"

And that was the end of it. The navy ran with what they had. And now Keel was demonstrating that reaching the bridge was as simple as it had been way back then with Chhun, Exo, Twenties, and the others.

Not that he was complaining. If the navy had taken the team's suggestions to heart, he'd have a hell of a time getting to Captain Pemm. Now the man was just two blast doors away.

Keel pushed himself against the car's wall, out of sight once its doors opened. He could force them with the armor—it was strong enough—but then he'd stand centered for anyone waiting to take a shot. The lift's panel was active thanks to a slicer box. With an ear-popper in one hand, Keel reached out and pressed the "open door" button with the bottom of his slug thrower's grip.

The doors slid open, and Keel tossed the banger into the security station. It set off its blinding and deafening explosions and Keel stormed into the room. Instead of hullbusters, he found two navy lieutenants. Appointed officers, neither of them armed. Moments ago, they might have been sitting at the chairs behind the security console, but now they were prostate on the floor, their ears bleeding. Still, they'd managed to stretch their arms over their heads in order to show that they had no intention of repelling boarders. Keel half-wondered if they had been lying in this position before he tossed in the ear-popper.

The bridge's comm chimed overhead. "This is Captain Pemm. Tyrus Rechs, please do not kill the men before you. I have instructed them to surrender."

Warily, Keel moved toward the two lieutenants. He was going to be out of ener-chains if this kept up. He roughly applied them to the prisoners, watching both the speedlift and bridge doors as he did so. The men were quickly hogtied and shouting for him not to kill them, their loud voices showing that they had no concept of their own volume.

His slug thrower ready, Keel moved to the bridge door and pressed the manual entry button. He had another slicer box if it came down to it but cracking a bridge's door would take the device a bit longer than getting a speedlift functional.

The door failed to open.

"Thank you, Rechs," came Captain Pemm's voice again. "Please listen to me again. Please. I have programmed the bridge door to deny entry on the first request. You will not be denied on your second request. Nor will you find any resistance from myself or my crew. We surrender ourselves and this ship to you."

Keel silently swore in confusion, wondering whether the tremor in Pemm's voice was because he was afraid... or because he was surrounded by armed, angry, and dangerous Nether Ops legionnaires, telling him what to say and how to say it.

"I see your hesitation," Pemm continued. "You are visible on my monitor. I repeat: We surrender this ship to you, Tyrus Rechs."

32

Captain Pemm's words sounded inviting enough, but Keel wasn't about to enter the room on the strength of a point's promise. He readied a pair of ear-poppers and then attempted to open the bridge doors again, still debating whether they would actually open or if that claim had merely been a weak attempt to stall for time.

They opened.

As the doors snapped into their recess in the ceiling above, Keel tossed in the two ear-poppers and heard someone shout, "No!" before the devices hit the floor and detonated.

He stormed the bridge and found it packed with clean-uniformed spacers, none with a rank lower than lieutenant junior grade, and none of them with a weapon in their hands. Nor were there any Nether Ops—at least not in armor. All of the bridge crew had their arms on top of their heads and were either on their knees or lying flat on the floor, eyes shut tight against the effects of the flash bang.

Keel wouldn't pick a hard day if an easy one could be had, but he hadn't thought taking over the *Defiance of Reason* would be *this* easy. What the hell was going on?

"Bridge secure," he reported to Honey.

"But I thought—"

"Change of plans. Out."

The bridge team had preemptively disarmed themselves; their blaster pistols were laid out nearly on a weapons station console. And every officer in the room kept their distance from the table, as though the last thing they wanted was for the bounty hunter in their midst to think they were reaching for their piece. Captain Pemm seemed proud of the thoroughness with which his crew had surrendered.

"You see," he said, shaking off the effects of the banger, which had exploded far enough away from him to let him speak and hear properly, "we will not present a problem, master bounty hunter."

Pemm was of above-average height, but not a tall man. Still, he had a presence that came from his bulk. He had probably been an imposing figure when he was younger, but now, at well over three hundred pounds, his size seemed more detriment than menace. He'd no doubt used his status as a point to eschew naval fitness regulations. Keel was right to have guessed that Spindust would be the key into the man's heart and ship. He certainly looked to enjoy them.

Captain Pemm hobbled toward Keel, still blinking the stars away from his encounter with the flashbang. He walked gingerly, requiring a cane, a rare sight to behold. Usually anyone who found their knees or back in such a condition found relief through regenerative therapy or cybernetics. Keel guessed that Pemm had gone the regenerative route, but that in his time on the run he'd been denied access to the continued medical treatment required to keep the process from reversing under his great weight.

"Tyrus Rechs," Pemm said, pulling himself up straight enough to muster a decent impression of a competent naval officer. His voice at least sounded the part; points tended to get that much down. "My crew and I surrender this ship and ourselves to you with the understanding that we will be in turn handed over to Republic authorities."

"What makes you think that's why I'm here?"

Pemm swallowed and brought his hand involuntarily to his neck. "You're not here for the…" The captain's confidence eroded swiftly. He now sounded like a man immediately concerned for his life. "The bounty?"

"The other Nether Ops agents," Keel said, finding himself communicating the way he did as Wraith more than what he remembered of Tyrus Rechs. Cold, direct, and not quite to the point. Always leaving room for the hearer to guess what, exactly, he was asking. He found they gave up far more information that way than they did responding to direct questions.

"That… that was nothing we had any control over or say in." Beads of sweat formed at Pemm's sideburns and trickled down his face, running beneath his great, round double chin. "Shortly before we arranged for the cargo transfer, which I now see was a well-placed trap, we were hailed by a force claiming to be friendly to the true Republic." The captain licked his lips and quickly added, "I do not say that in defiance. That is merely how those of us who acknowledge the rule of the House of Reason refer to one another."

Keel said nothing and remained still, only staring at the man from behind the expressionless mask that was his impenetrable helmet.

"D-despite whatever you might think about my status," Pemm continued, "I do consider myself a duly appointed officer of the Republic Navy, acting in authority given to me by virtue of a House of Reason commission.

Where there are others seeking to undo the damage done to our Republic first by the Legion and then by that madman Goth Sullus, my crew and I have a duty to assist. We received a request to do just that, and found it was these Nether dogs."

"The orbital bombardment. Was that performing your duty?"

Again, the captain's hand went to his throat. "That was... not my decision. I was merely following orders. Had I known I was being instructed to fire upon innocent civilians of our Republic I would have refused the order. I was given no reason to think such a thing was occurring. My crew believed we were being fed valid military targets. I don't care what those damned bureaucrats might be telling the world—they *misled* me and my crew. Which is why I'm turning myself in. Let the record be set straight and let *them* hang for what was done. Not me!"

Pemm's confidence seemed to increase as he recited a speech he must have been rehearsing in his mind for some time. No doubt the man had laid out his eventual defense should he ever be brought in to answer for his actions.

Keel noticed the odd choice of words. *Let them hang for it.* That, combined with the way his hand continually went to his throat, had Keel thinking that the captain was aware of something about Tyrus Rechs that eluded the current owner of the bounty hunter's armor.

He decided to exploit it.

"There is no cross-examination at the end of the rope."

The effect of his words was immediate. The captain broke out into a further sweat. His fingers jittered. "That can't be why you're here. They said you were coming for the bounty. Not for me. The bounty. You can't hang me. Not like her!"

"Then tell me everything about them."

"Nether Ops? They haven't exactly been sterling guests, bounty hunter. They contacted us on our encrypted comm frequency, one I assure you is only known to those sympathetic to the true Republic. They claim that a significant action was going to be undertaken at a mid-core planet and that my ship would necessarily be a part of it. Of course, the crew and I agreed at once. However, when the Nether Ops agents came aboard, they quickly shifted focus to laying an ambush meant for you."

The captain stood as tall as he was able and straightened his uniform. "I told them that whatever troubles the Republic had with you, they were of no concern to me. I'm a military man and I have no standing orders concerning Tyrus Rechs."

"How many were there?"

"Twenty. Enough to force my hand."

Keel ran some quick numbers in his head. "The pilots sent to inspect the warehouse; they were yours?"

"They were not. As I stated, I was unwilling to help in any of this affair. You'll find that my actions are consistent with that. We have made no effort to delay you or cause you harm."

"That's the only reason you're still alive."

The captain cleared his throat uncomfortably. "Be that as it may, I would nonetheless like it stated for the record in your official report. The bridge is yours. At your order my crew will lock ourselves in quarters awaiting a formal transfer of this ship to the *acting* Republic Navy."

Those last words were said acidly, as though calling that entity the *Republic Navy*, though it was now under the command of the Legion, was personally painful to the man.

But Keel was focused on something else he had said. Twenty Nether Ops agents. He had killed at least a dozen of them in the hangar bay, including the pilot that had shuttled him in. That left about eight. Seven since Honey had eliminated her own pilot. Yet the Tennar had reported that almost twice that had gone in after him.

A comm chimed at the unattended communications station. Pemm looked over to it. "This is something coming from inside the ship."

"Answer it. I need to hear as well."

"I, um, am not properly trained to handle this particular station."

That was Pemm admitting he had no idea how anything on this ship worked beyond giving orders for others to do it. The point was a far cry from the capable captains Keel had served alongside. Officers who prided themselves on being able to functionally perform every duty under their command.

"Have your tech do it."

The captain relayed the order. A comm tech hurried over from the gallery of captives and received the call. "Call Station Six, this is Bridge. Proceed."

"Tyrus Rechs, we have your Tennar co-conspirator," came a man's voice from the comm. "And we will execute her if you fail to turn yourself in to us upon our reaching the bridge. You will stand trial before a Nether Ops tribunal for the war crimes you have committed."

"Sounds like you've already made up your mind on whether or not I'm guilty. No thanks."

Next came Honey's voice, distressed and anxious. "They're serious. I've got a blaster pointed at my head."

"They're not serious. They're bluffing."

"I assure you, Rechs, I am not bluffing," said the Nether agent. "You are to surrender your weapons to the bridge crew and then report directly to me. And if you deviate whatsoever from that plan I will execute the Tennar and send my team to take the bridge and you with it."

"Then consider this my deviation, because I'm not giving up this bounty."

A small collective gasp came up from the well-starched appointed officers corralled in the corner of the bridge.

"Do not seek to tempt me, Tyrus Rechs."

"I'm not tempting you. I'm *daring* you."

Two blaster bolts rang out. The gallery of points tightened and released their fists as they looked at one another in discomfort. Keel waited for the next word to come through at the comm.

It was no word at all but rather the signature beeps of Death, Destroyer of Worlds.

Keel motioned for the points on the bridge to keep back, and then spoke to his bot through his helmet's comm. "Good. And you're sure there aren't any more of them?"

More beeps.

"You were supposed to keep one of them alive, remember?"

The bot indicated that the Nether Ops human male was still alive but was bleeding wonderfully. It asked Keel to please be kind enough to wait for him to expire so Death could finally witness the end of a man as he bled out from a blaster wound made by its own mechanical hand.

"I can see why your old boss wouldn't give you that blaster. What about Honey?"

More excited beeps. The Tennar was definitely dead.

Keel frowned. He'd had his suspicions, but Death had found the hard proof he'd asked for. "So, what took so long?"

Death explained that despite Honey's behavior it was having a difficult time knowing whether her obvious deceit was intended to trick the Nether Ops agent or to trick New Boss. But when it saw that the Nether Ops agent who was currently bleeding out on the deck and making all sorts of hilarious groaning noises was not even holding a blaster pistol against the Tennar's head, and yet the Tennar pretended that he was, well, then its processors decided that the probability of her not being on New Boss's side was high enough for it to finally initiate its "preventative medicine" protocols. It shot the Tennar and then the agent with her before they had a chance to do harm to New Boss. All in compliance with the ethical protocol Death had agreed to obey in order for Keel to install a workable blaster pistol in the little gunnery bot—the same type that New Boss wore on his hip.

Keel thanked Death for his assistance and then ordered the enlisted men to leave their post at the drive room and report to the bridge. There he gave them blasters and instructions not to harm their prisoners unless they attempted escape. If they did, they would answer to him. The engineers escorted the full complement of appointed officers to the brig, and the other spacers who had been kept running systems against their will joined the procession to make sure that no appointed officer was unaccounted for.

That done, Keel sent a signal to a waiting Legion destroyer that jumped into the system and sent its marines to fully secure the frigate before shuttling over a replacement crew.

Keel sat on an overturned crate of Spindust in the hangar, watching as the hullbusters offloaded medical bots to begin the work of cleaning up the dead. Death hovered at his side and beeped a question.

"Not sure I'll miss her, but I wish she hadn't tried it."

Death asked Keel why she had, after so long.

"Because these were friends of hers."

Weren't the Nether Ops agents on the other stations friends?

"Not how it works with them."

Will Masters be angry?

"He probably doesn't even remember what she looked like. He'll be fine."

What did she want that drove her to betray you, New Boss?

Keel rapped on his chest. "This. She would have tried it eventually… we just gave her an opportunity to do it sooner rather than later."

The bot asked more questions, but Keel declined to answer, and eventually Death's beeps fell silent. Keel sat and watched the other bots work. He wanted to leave and get back to Zora and forget whatever Kill Team Ice was. To just leave it all behind.

But he knew he couldn't. The intel he'd gotten from G232 had told him more than he'd let Honey know. Clued him in on what the Tennar was after and why it was important. He felt as though he was being pulled in three separate directions at once, and he didn't know which was the most important.

But he knew what would come next. So, he sat, and he waited.

33

The level after their encounter with the Gomarii contained no further slaves. Leenah helped Jack hop while Zora cautiously led the way through a deck full of personal quarters, barracks, freshers, galleys, and everything else set aside on the ship for its slaver denizens. All that they saw of it was empty, yet each time they moved past a set of sealed blast doors, Zora found a sensation of dread welling up inside of her. There was no telling what sort of trouble might be on the other side.

On any other occasion, any other day, they would be right smack dab in the middle of the tyrannasquid's hole. But today, it seemed that all hands were doing what they could to defend the ship from the battle raging outside. One that Briscoe had declared as "going decently," the last time Zora checked in. Of course, most of the Gomarii had already been outside overseeing auction security to begin with—that was the only thing that had kept Zora and her team alive this long. The lone force they had encountered two levels below had nearly cost Jack his life as it was, and those weren't even Gomarii warriors. Leenah pointed out that several of them carried tools meant for starship repair—which meant that most likely, these were techs that worked the docking bay pressed into defense of the ship against a small boarding party.

They were fortunate that no one else had given them trouble since.

Yet Zora felt that *if* more fighting were to come, it would be here in their inner sanctuary, moving through the clean, steel-blue corridors, much taller than the others. This deck felt like two or three decks, with a cavernous, great hall sort of feel. A luxury among the stars, to have so much room.

They moved past a fantastically long table large enough to seat hundreds of Gomarii. Overhead, the clan banner hung at regular intervals—a black-and-red standard with eight armored fists forming a circle that faced inward to a stylized Gomarii head, tendrils elongated and reaching out like tentacles.

"Think these guys... *unh*... are a little proud of their heritage?" Jack asked, grunting from the effort. "I've been on Legion bases with fewer flags than this."

"No need for the running commentary," suggested Zora. "Sounds like it hurts for you just to speak."

"It does, but... *gah*... that's how I know I'm still alive."

Leenah pointed to a sign written in the Gomarii alphabet. "Docking bay is up that way. Over there is the speedlift that brought me down to this level. There's an access ladder not far from it."

"Jack's going to have to take the lift," said Zora.

Jack shook his head. "Death trap. How about you three take the ladder and let me worry about the lift on my own. Won't be any space to maneuver in there if I get into a fight once the doors open, so my mobility won't really be an issue."

Zora nodded. "Let's make sure it's empty."

It was, and Jack hopped inside and then leaned against the wall. "I'll give you a minute to get up first. If I hear blaster fire, I'll wait another few seconds and then try and drop whoever you're shooting once I reach the top, unless you call me back out."

That was the plan. Jack checked his watch as though he were a corporate drone in a perennial hurry as the doors closed around him.

Once Jack was out of view, Zora grabbed the bottom rung of the access ladder and pulled herself up. "Garret, after me. Leenah, call if someone comes, but otherwise be on Garret's heels."

They understood.

Zora made her way up to the docking bay, trusting Leenah to keep an eye on the cavernous deck the Gomarii called home. So far, Zora thought, Leenah had proven herself capable enough to be a reliable crewmember. It was clear why Keel valued her, even though she was no war fighter and certainly no bounty hunter. She had done what was asked of her with minimal pushback. And when the shooting had started, she didn't crack under the pressure. Whether that was because of her time spent aboard the *Indelible VI*, never a boring affair, or because she had some previous military training, Zora didn't know. But she could see that Leenah was determined—and serious about whatever she put herself into. And despite the difficult circumstances in which they'd found her, she hadn't once made the situation about her or lamented what she'd found herself caught up in.

Those qualities, Zora knew, appealed to a man like Aeson Keel. He had little time for anyone—lovers or otherwise—who viewed themselves as being at the center of the galaxy.

The first thing Zora's eyes set on upon climbing up through the docking bay's deck was the *Six*. It was twisted and had large holes missing from its once sleek body—a wreck. But Garret and Leenah were right: it was still in one piece. The techs, rather than cutting it apart for scrap, seemed to have been working to repair it. Even if it didn't look like they'd made much progress. Either that, or the *Six* was in incredibly bad shape when it was brought in.

When Zora was standing on the deck, looking for signs of Gomarii, Garret popped his head out of the manual access hatch.

"There it is!" he whispered in excitement. "I need to get to work."

"Slow down," said Zora. "Stay put behind those repulsor chests and wait for Jack to get out safely from the speedlift. When we move, we're moving together."

Zora turned to see if Leenah was proceeding as planned and found her already halfway up the ladder and moving swiftly. She was topside by the time Jack's speedlift opened. The navy spy hopped out unharmed, his blaster rifle in one arm, wrapped to it by its sling.

"Go help him," Zora ordered Garret.

The code slicer obeyed, letting his rifle hang on his sling as he jogged over to Jack. He put the larger man's arm over his thin shoulders and did what he could to lighten the load from Jack's bad leg. It had clearly been bothering him more and more as the trip went on, the pain meds fading.

Zora motioned to a place near the entry ladder, well protected by the big tool chests the techs used. "Best place for you is here, Jack. Watch for anyone coming from lift or ladder."

"Means I get to sit down again," Jack said as he eased himself onto the deck. "I ain't complaining."

Zora turned her attention to the others. "You two stick close with me. We're going to clear and secure the *Six*—and only then do you start working, Garret."

Both Garret and Leenah nodded, but something in Garret's face made Zora worry he wasn't listening.

"Hey." She waved a hand right in front of the kid. "That means no matter what little piece of tech you see that gets your blood going, you leave it until I say. Savvy?"

"Yeah, I got it."

"Okay. Let's go."

The bay was broad and housed a few other ships besides the *Six*. Zora would have felt better securing the entire space first, but its size and the need to get their task finished quickly allowed her to talk herself into just controlling the *Six*. Still, it was easy to feel like more Gomarii were hiding somewhere just out of sight of their hastily discarded tools and open-drawered repulsor chests.

"Generator is aft," Leenah pointed as they moved toward the *Six*. "We have to start with it."

Zora's eyes locked onto the snapped and twisted comms array that ran from the top of the *Six* down to the main power supply and backup generators. She led them to a side opening in the middle of the ship where the main lounge would have once been. The *Indelible VI* now had multiple entry points thanks to the amount of hull plating that was missing or had been blown open. As she pulled herself up onto the ship, Leenah and Garret covering her, she scanned the interior for any signs of ambush. But the ship was as silent and empty as the rest of the docking bay—no Gomarii hiding in any of the nooks or corners where the ultrabeam mounted to her blaster rifle swept.

Zora waved for the others to follow and motioned for them to watch this section while she pushed to the right, seeking to clear the longest angle in the space. She moved past twisted impervisteel and ducked under big strands of tangled conduit that hung down low like uncoiled entrails spilled from the metal beast that was the *Indelible VI*.

She couldn't imagine how Keel might react if he saw his beloved *Six* in such a sad state.

She followed her route to a charred and blackened partition that had had several holes punched through it from the opposite side. Each was no larger than a fist, but it was still impressive that they had blasted their way through the thick metal. It was a wonder there was anything left of the ship at all.

"Okay, clear," Zora reported, then moved to the next room. It took a moment for her to realize that the large unfamiliar area she had just swept used to be the crew quarters, fresher, galley, and main lounge. All of it had been wiped away, reduced to its structural beams, every item it once housed now lost to the swirling darkness of space.

That meant she was about to clear the area containing the power core and backup generators. The core itself was gone, either ejected or outright lost in the flight. The generators were in sorry shape, except for one that had organized wires coming out from it and splicing into another mess of wiring that seemed to travel in all directions.

Zora checked the surroundings thoroughly for any signs of occupation. The light of her ultrabeam penetrating the dark corners revealed little beyond a few greasy handprints and some discarded tools. The prints were too big to have been Leenah's or even Keel's—likely the work of the Gomarii techs who had been inside the ship. Probably their tools as well.

"Okay, we're clear back here, too," Zora told the others. "Still need to clear the cockpit unless there's another space that I'm forgetting."

"No, this is all that's left," said Leenah.

Zora cleared the cockpit and came back to find Garret already inspecting the generator.

"This is really good work," he said to himself before emerging from the area. "Okay yeah, it's working fine. But they did clip your cables to the beacons so they couldn't be traced back to here once they left hyperspace."

"Funny," Zora remarked. "I thought that was how you and Nilo found this rock."

Garret gave an uneasy laugh but didn't elaborate. "So, all I need to do is run some power from the generator to my station." He looked around. "I don't see any spools long enough to make that happen."

"There's wire all around us," said Zora.

"Not enough to run the distance," said Leenah. "It's all fused and clipped. We need to get something from their stores. I saw a couple of spools at the far end of the bay."

"That's good," said Garret. "I'd hate to have to try and pull a main line out of one of the other ships. Take forever."

"Let's not take forever," said Zora. "Garret, you can move wherever you need to *on board* the *Six*. But if you're going to go outside, I want you to tell me so I can cover you. Jack will do the same."

"Roger," said the code slicer. "So, in that case I'm telling you right now. I gotta go get that conduit running from the generator to my station before I can do anything else. Either that or... hang on." Garret peered out of the ship through one of its many new windows and slapped his forehead. "Yeah. Duh. Actually, all I need to do is grab a portable generator, fire up its repulsors, and then run its hookups direct to the station. Much easier."

"Okay, let's find one of those then," said Zora. She led Garret to the back of the ship and then watched as the code slicer hopped down from what was once a smooth, flat deck but was now a wavy rippled wreck of impervisteel only partially bonded to its support beams. "Jack, Garret's moving outside the ship. Leenah to escort. They're looking for a portable generator."

"Copy that. Think I saw a mobile generator next to that beaten-down Preyhunter on my way off the speedlift."

Zora relayed the message to Garret, who hurried off with Leenah toward the location. The Preyhunter was visible from the *Six* and looked as though it had been on the losing end of a dogfight. Blaster scorch marks ran along its fuselage and wings, providing a black powder coating that covered the Gomarii fist symbol they'd seen elsewhere on this mothership. If this little starfighter had won the battle, it was only barely.

The pair slowed as they neared the ship, and then Leenah moved ahead, rifle ready, knowing that both Jack and Zora were covering her as well. She checked behind the tool chest near the ship and reported, "All clear. And there's the generator."

"Perfect!" Garret said, hurrying forward to see it for himself. After inspecting it for a moment, he activated its repulsor jack. The circular generator rose, levitating to reach the code slicer's midsection as it hummed faintly. "Still has a fifty percent charge," he reported as he began to lead the machine away from the Preyhunter.

"Hey, kid," Jack called over the comm. "You forgot to unplug it from the ship."

Garret looked back and saw the power supply trailing from the generator to somewhere inside the Preyhunter's cockpit. "Oh, right. Sorry."

He hurried back to the small snub-nosed fighter and disconnected the generator from its internal power input. The conduit retracted itself inside the generator unit, and soon Garret was again pulling it toward the *Indelible VI*, with Leenah on overwatch.

They were halfway to the ship when the sound of a lone blaster bolt echoed through the docking bay.

Zora grunted in pain and fell off the ship. Her armor clattered hard onto the deck below.

34

Leenah didn't think when she saw Zora tumble off the *Indelible VI*. She just sprinted toward the bounty hunter. It was clear to her that Zora had been shot in the back, and though the attack wasn't fatal—Zora was already struggling onto her hands and knees—it had packed enough of a punch to dent the armor back there, now blackened and smoking.

The Endurian had spent enough time around Keel to know that likely meant one of two things. Either the shooter had fired from enough distance that the impact of the blaster bolt had been reduced, or the shooter hadn't used a particularly powerful weapon to begin with. Leenah had seen Keel punch holes in better sets of armor with his blaster pistol from close to medium range.

But whatever the reason for Zora still being alive, Leenah was glad for it.

As she got closer to the ship, her sense of self-preservation and caution began to catch up with her. Zora might have armor strong enough to withstand being shot, but Leenah certainly did not.

She wondered why the shooter hadn't already followed up with a second blast. With Zora out of the ship, perhaps she'd fallen out of their line of sight. Another lucky break if so. Leenah kept herself low, covering behind crates and scanning the *Six* and as much as she could see behind it and underneath it.

"Zora, I'm covering you. You good?"

The bounty hunter grunted and crawled her way to cover with Leenah. "I'll be okay."

"Gimme a sitrep, Z," said Jack. The spy was scanning the bay for targets, checking back for a potential attack from the lower decks. Garret had covered behind the portable generator.

"Didn't see the shooter," Zora answered. "Caught me in the small of the back."

"Someone got eyes on you through that ship? The thing has more openings than a Hool brothel. Wouldn't be hard."

"Negative," Zora grunted. "Set myself up so there was nothing but partitions and impervisteel behind me. Just didn't clear the ship as well as I thought."

Leenah had a pang of nerves at the thought that whoever shot Zora had been on the *Six* with them the entire time. Had they targeted her or Garret...

"Well let's clear it again," Jack said. "We're running out of time here. I'll come and assist."

"Stay there." Zora sounded better in control of her pain now. "For all we know whoever took that shot was just trying to distract us from a team set to move through your sector. I'll flush out whoever's in there. Armor's held up so far."

"I'll go too," said Leenah.

Zora looked at the Endurian. "You're not exactly dressed for the kind of action we know is on board right now. I can handle it."

The bounty hunter moved forward to clear the ship alone. It was neither ideal nor wise. Jack, Zora, and anyone else with half a tactical brain knew it. But the only other option was throwing Leenah or the code slicer into a situation they were neither trained nor equipped for—and they needed those two alive to get the doors open to the Gomarii vessel. That was still the mission, one that Zora and Jack couldn't do alone.

Still, the bounty hunter, like many of her trade, had been in situations like this before. Yes, there is strength in numbers. And yes, storming a room with a Legion kill team behind you is a whole hell of a lot safer than going in on your own. But a bounty paid the same regardless of how many hunters worked on it, and most of the contracts in circulation weren't high enough to afford a single partner, let alone a full team of guild members. Less backup meant more pay for yourself. It was simple economics.

"Leenah," Zora said as she paused against the *Six*, waiting to jump back up inside. "What did we miss? Where could they have been?"

The Endurian shook her head, pink hair-like tendrils swaying as she attempted to come up with an answer. And then all at once it hit her. Her eyes went wide. "Do you know the smuggling hide in the lounge?"

Zora cursed her own forgetfulness. Of course, she knew it, and of course that would be the spot where anyone who knew of it would go to hide. "I know it."

"When power is down there's a manual release," Leenah said. "So, if a smuggler is hiding himself instead of cargo, he can still get out if systems are shut down."

"That's got to be it. Or at least that's where they were. They could've moved since then."

Leenah nodded. "Or they're assuming we don't know about it and are waiting to take another free shot when we're not looking."

Zora looked up at the opening above her, ready to vault onto the ship. "I'm going to clear the ship. You keep yourself covered but watch my back. Just focus on the hide and blast anything that pops up."

Leenah nodded that she understood and covered Zora as the bounty hunter bounded up into the *Six* and moved with her rifle ready in a furious storm of action. The lack of any blaster bolts as Zora moved through the ship and re-cleared the rooms made it clear right away that whoever had been on the ship was now either hiding or had slipped away somewhere else.

Through it all, Leenah watched the smuggler's hide for signs of activity. When Zora walked by it after re-clearing the cockpit and Garret's nook where he kept his workstation, Leenah saw the hatch quietly pop open. She called out a warning as she fired her rifle.

The blaster bolt went wide of the opening hatch and exploded into a shower of sparks at the far end of the ship, but the small personal defense blaster pistol that had been sneaking its way out from the hide to take another shot at Zora darted back into its hole, and the deck sealed over top of it.

They had found their stowaway.

Zora motioned for Leenah to come aboard and help flush the intruder out. "Can whoever's in there hear us?" she asked when Leenah arrived at her side.

"Maybe if we scream. Aeson is always evasive when I ask him about the time he locked me in there."

Zora raised her eyebrow, but that story would have to be saved for another time. "Since we don't have a fragger at our disposal, our best bet is to pop open the door and empty our charge packs inside. Or we can pop it open, step back, and try to talk whoever's down there into surrendering. They have to know they're trapped."

"Let's do that," said Leenah. "See if they'll come out on their own."

Zora gave the Endurian a surprised look. This was unexpected. "You know it's a Gomarii down there, don't you? Even after all you've been through, you don't want to just dust this kelhorn?"

"No. Not unless we have to."

Zora shook her head. "You and Keel are an odd pairing."

She stomped on the panel with the heel of her heavy boot and shouted. "We're going to pop this thing open, and either you throw your blaster out and live, or you get shot down there like a slave!"

To the Gomarii, being treated like a slave was the single greatest dishonor one could experience, exceeding even being banished from a clan. But whoever was inside made no reply.

Zora moved to the front of the hatch, ready to activate it with the toe of her boot like she had seen Keel do countless times before. But Leenah waved her away and motioned for her to kneel on top of the false panel like she was.

"It's strong enough to lift both of us up with it," Leenah explained. "Those mechanical arms can do two thousand pounds easily. Even in your armor, we're well below that."

Zora joined the Endurian and then watched as she released the panel with her fingers and quickly pulled back her hand. The panel rose into the air a full meter and then slid back, giving whoever was inside a view of everything except for the top of the panel.

"Toss your blaster outside or we toss a fragger in with you and seal you in with it," called Zora.

Whether demoralized because it could not see what hunted it, or simply unable to abide the thought of its life ending in a confined space at the hands of such a cruel weapon, a blue hand slowly rose from the opening, the blaster pistol hanging by its trigger guard around an index finger.

"Toss it," Zora ordered.

The Gomarii sent the weapon sliding across the deck, where it bounced erratically on the misshapen surface before coming to a stop.

"Now climb out. Slowly."

The slaver obeyed this order too, slowly lifting himself out of the smuggler's hide and then laying himself flat on the deck. Though he wore armor, it was thin and flexible. This was one of the techs, a lower caste of Gomarii. Useful, but considered too small, too slight, and too mild to serve as a warrior or taskmaster. Necessary to the clan, but his exploits would never be passed down in lore.

"How many others are in there with you?" Zora demanded.

"Only this one," said the Gomarii, his voice forlorn and his words imprecise, spoken through the sucking of his facial tendrils. "I am the only of the clan not sent in the final defense. To my eternal shame. Now you have compounded it. You would do me an honor to kill me in battle."

"You're not fooling me any more than you're fooling yourself," Zora said. "If you wanted to die in battle all you had to do was take a shot at us from the middle of the docking bay when you first heard us coming. You hid instead."

The Gomarii laid his head face down against the deck and issued something that sounded like a sob.

"I'll get Garret so we can finish this up," said Leenah. She moved off and called for the code slicer to bring the generator to the ship.

"You're the only one they didn't send," Zora said to her new prisoner. "Why? We were loose on the ship, and we met hardly any resistance at all."

"Anyone loose on the ship can be dealt with once it returns to the stars. But the ship itself, it must not be taken. It must not be discovered. My clan mates go to stop the Animals outside. They are the immediate threat."

Zora looked warily at the Gomarii. "Why can't the ship be taken? Your clan will find no honor and no future. Its days have come to an end whether you lift off or not. None of you will survive. You will be hunted down."

"This clan does not matter. The great clan remains hidden. It is you who will be hunted. It is *you* who will not survive."

Garret reached the ship and began pulling the necessary power supply from the portable generator to his workstation. It was up and active in a moment, and soon he was affectionately rubbing his holoscreens. "I missed you," he said lovingly. "And I really need your help. So, let's see what we can find about this Gomarii ship."

His fingers begin to fly over screens, overlays and pop-ups stacking one on top of the other even as he gave voice commands to achieve other tasks. He sent ready-made programs on attack, sometimes reading their reports and other times flicking them away without so much as a glance. Whatever he was doing was lost on Zora, but she could tell the code slicer was engaging in a dance with the Gomarii system that he already knew all the steps to.

It wasn't long until Garret sat back and declared, "Okay. I got it. Doors below are opening up, door above will open any second now, and mission is accomplished."

"That fast?" Zora said incredulously.

"It is not possible," said the Gomarii.

Zora gave him a kick to let him know that his input was not desired at the moment. The blast door sealing the bay began to rumble open above them, further testifying that Garret's words had been true.

"It was actually pretty easy," the code slicer said, as though the captured slaver's defiance was an invitation to talk slicing. "You see, Gomarii-coded slave ships can be a bit tricky because it's not like there's a lot of data out there that explains how to interface with them but there's a few hypotheticals and a few algorithms I've got that can fill in the gaps when you need to, they just have to kind of start reading the code and then they go ahead and code into the code and just start attacking lines directly seeing what will be accepted or rejected—it basically starts to fill in a back end that allows you to teach the Gomarii system to learn a different style of code, only the style that you're teaching it to learn helps you instead of them—so I was going to try with that and I *did* try with that for a little bit but right away it seemed like that wasn't working and I was wondering *why* it wasn't working when I realized it wasn't Gomarii code at all! It was something else that was really old and I thought 'This is weird' but it also wasn't that foreign, like I've seen it before, and I tried to think 'Okay where have I seen this code before' because it was kind of familiar and then it dawned on me this is the same type of code that I saw with the armor and I'm like 'I guess it makes sense because Tyrus Rechs's armor is old and this is old' so it's just some old form of code, so

I start to pull out some of the data systems I had for the armor and sure enough that started talking and once it started talking it got really comfortable and once it was comfortable it let me in and really from that point the rest was easy and now it's done."

Garret sucked in a breath of air, happy with himself.

Zora shook her head slowly. But any annoyance she might have once had for the excited code slicer's tendency to speak in gigantic run-on sentences was overcome by admiration. "You really are incredible, Garret. Don't ever let anyone tell you otherwise."

A giant smile crossed Garret's face, diminished slightly by the blushing that raced across his nose and cheeks.

The display beeped. Garret looked at the screen and all at once the smile vanished. "Uh-oh."

"What?" said Zora. "What is it?"

"Good news, bad news. Good news is our Kublaren friends are inside and pushing their way up through the decks. Bad news is it looks like the Gomarii figured out what we did and those who aren't trying to hold back the boarders are on their way to get to us."

Zora turned around at once, her eyes on the speedlift and manual access. "Sket," she mumbled, and then shouted "Jack! We're going to have company!"

35

Nilo waited to hear that the first few levels of the slave ship were cleared and secure before moving in himself. Pikkek's small army of Kublarens had disengaged from the skirmish with those Gomarii defending the repair sites the moment the great doors leading up into the belly of the ship had dropped askew onto the ground. The tilt of the ship left a gap between part of the great ramp and the landing pad, requiring several koobs to hop over as they surged inside.

The slavers rallied at the sight of the Kublarens breaking off and disengaging until they realized where they were headed. Panicked at their impenetrable fortress being raided, they left the construction and focused their efforts on a push to keep the full force of Kublarens from breaching their vast cosmic home.

It would be a fight to see who would have control of the great slave ship.

The first Kublarens aboard were met with fierce resistance as a massed force of Gomarii slavers—all of them warriors—sought to repel the boarders. They had been stationed for just such a defense. Pikkek would need to rush more of his main body to overwhelm them. That seemed to be the only play.

Carter might have seen some other strategic angle of attack. At the very least, he would have worked in tandem with the other teams and waged a firefight meant to keep the warriors at bay while reinforcements took to the shuttles and inserted themselves in the docking bay. But Carter wasn't here, and Nilo had no ability to wield the Kublarens in the manner he needed, nor could he call his mercenaries away from their duty of keeping the slave buyers from escaping the planet.

So Pikkek would either succeed or fail using the same strategy that had long served the Kublarens: sending overwhelming numbers in successive wave attacks. It was an age-old tactic for the populous species; their willingness to charge into the face of certain death for the individual had often secured victory for the many. Such an approach had resulted in countless yellow phosphorescent bloodbaths between tribes, leaving Kublar's battlefields covered with swollen, bloated corpses of its native species—but it had also allowed the species to successfully repel a Savage invasion of their planet long ago. Not to mention fighting legionnaires to a standstill, and expelling zhee invaders and their traitorous supporters who resided in the Soob. The Kublaren chieftains needed only be reminded of what their species was capable of when unified. Something far too many of its leaders, and certainly the Republic itself, had worked to prevent. But Nilo had overseen a change to that, and now anxiously waited to see whether it would pay off against the slavers.

The Gomarii defenders made the initial attackers pay a heavy toll for forcing their way up the ramp and into the ship. But as each Kublaren firing his weapon fell, the one behind it moved that much closer before falling in turn. The species had no trouble bounding up and over their dead, and soon they were at the lines, vaulting over impervisteel barricades and protected firing positions to fall upon the slavers with their peculiarly sharp stone-edged tomahawks.

The hand-to-hand fight played out quickly, and always the same. The bigger, stronger Gomarii would crush skulls and parry blows and then feel the weight of the Kublarens pulling on arms and legs, followed by a literal butchering as the tomahawks came down, chopping one slaver to pieces before feasting ravenously on the next. A frenzy of blades and bodies toppling these relative giants.

This frenzy, the Kublarens with their indiscriminate swinging and firing, cost the lives of friends as well. But all that mattered was that the charge continued to push forward. Enveloping and destroying the enemy line was everything the koob warriors could think of and all they wanted.

The rapid croaking of their throat sacs filled the corridors until it was louder than the blaster fire itself.

The Kublarens were a powerful weapon in the Black Leaf arsenal—when used properly. Against the disciplined troops of the Legion, such an attack would have been disastrous—but here in an unexpected and hastily thrown together defense by an overconfident enemy, Pikkek's fighters pushed through in a rout, and the lines of Kublarens hopping aboard the slave ship grew thick even as the corridors just inside were piled high with the bodies of the fallen.

Nilo received a report from Jack and Zora that the Gomarii defense was wavering from the assault, but not entirely because of the koobs. What Pikkek had reported as the slavers running to avoid death seemed instead to be a tactical withdrawal to the higher levels of the ship, including an assault on the docking bay. Jack was wondering when they could expect reinforcements to arrive through the bay doors they'd opened. Nilo promised to work on getting that done as quickly as possible and asked for them to hold on as long as they could.

He wondered why the Gomarii didn't simply overrun the docking bay with overwhelming numbers. Perhaps shutting down Garret's ability to interface with the ship was no longer a priority, the damage already done, and with so many Kublarens raging in the lower decks they needed every fighter they could get to keep from being completely overwhelmed.

And yet, they *were* attacking the bay. The two thoughts didn't add up in Nilo's mind. Either all the Gomarii were needed to fend off the Kublarens, or they were confident enough to split their forces. He needed more information.

Up to this point, he had resisted the urge to pester Pikkek with requests for status updates. He was about to do just that when the Kublaren leader sent in his own comm transmission.

"This Pikkek."

"I hear you, Pikkek. Go for Nilo."

"Big die... k'kik... level wahn, two-uah, three. You all clear to come. Big fight now. No more blue-ones-ah... k'k. They big die and run. Now we fight slaves."

"Say again. They've released the slaves and these are fighting you instead of joining you?"

"Slaves-ah, ya ya. Strange-ee ones-ah. Many... k'kik *ollowak*," Pikkek said, using the Kublaren word for *alien*. "Not hooman *ollowak*. Other ones."

This wasn't making sense. Nilo had seen what freed slaves did to their Gomarii tormenters in the past. It wasn't this.

"What do they look like?" The question was hasty. Nilo corrected and refined. "I don't mean what sort of *ollowak*,

I mean do they have visible interfaces or armor grafted to them? Cybernetic implants or weapons that are coming out of their bodies?"

"Some... k'kik... look like machine part on outside. I cut open one for big die. Look normal inside."

"You say that levels one through three are secure?"

"Only dead ones on those lev-ahls."

"Understood. I'm coming on board, Pikkek. I'll link up with you soon."

"Find Pikkek by follow the blood," said the Kublaren.

"May it flow from your enemies as a river," replied Nilo, finishing the Kublaren phrase.

He looked around the battlefield and saw that despite the chaos at the ship the rest of the situation remained as it had been. His Black Leaf mercenary teams continued in their standoff with the slave buyers.

"Surber," he said over comm, "I need your team off the shuttle and supporting down here. Sarai can handle things while it's empty."

"We'll be down in three minutes," answered Nilo's second. "I take it there's now a change of plans."

"There is. I want you to take over negotiations with the slave buyers. Rescue as many slaves as you can, but no slaver is to make it off this planet under any condition."

"Understood."

"I'll be on the Gomarii ship. When you have the men to spare, send them into the docking bay and secure it. Our man Jack is inside putting up a fight."

"A bit tough for a Gomarii slave ship, it seems."

"Yeah," said Nilo, his voice gritty and hard. "I think this ship is one of them."

There was the slightest of pauses before the smooth and unflappable Surber answered, "That certainly does not bode well at all, now does it?"

"No. It doesn't."

"Do be careful. It would be a real shame for you to die now."

"Slavers couldn't do it the first time; I won't let them do it this time, either."

"It's not the Gomarii I'm worried about. But you knew that already."

"Garret, not to rush you, but we're going to need you to get to a more defensible position in a hurry here," said Zora.

Knowing that company was coming, the code slicer was attempting to overload the weapon system on the banged-up Preyhunter scuttled nearest the speedlift. With Zora alongside to watch his back, Jack watching the ladder, and Leenah watching the prisoner, Garret had exposed the cannon's housing using the tools on hand.

The kid cast his eyes toward the speedlift. "I got a nice locking worm set up on the lift. They'll have to spend at least some time cracking it before they can get the doors open. Then they'll have to crack a new code to get up here."

He returned to his work, cutting, soldering, and splicing, rewiring the system and rerouting processors with a mix of mechanical and programming know-how.

It was then that Jack began firing down the ladder well, carefully leaning back as return bolts zipped up through the opening, sizzling past him to strike the docking bay's shielding or showering down sparks when they hit part of the heavy crane's overhead track.

"Here we go!" he shouted. "Better hope that lock you put on the speedlift is a good one."

"Do you need me to come over and help you keep them back?" Zora asked.

"Pretty easy so far," said Jack, who leaned over the edge and then ducked back before a blaster bolt could strike him. "If they try to climb, I shoot. Otherwise, I wait. Stick with the kid."

"Roger." Zora squinted as the bright blue flashes of Garret's cutting torch made micro fusions in the Preyhunter's forward cannon.

"Yeah, this'll just about do it," the code slicer said. "Won't want to be anywhere near here."

"How big of an explosion are we talking about?"

"Pretty big. The cannon's charge just continues to cycle but the message that it's issued a sufficient charge for a blast never reaches so what happens is the blast just continually charges and just kind of runs in circles inside and eventually enough of the charge particles build up and it can't take it anymore but it also doesn't project because of the way we're wiring the sensor here so it just blows up all in one spot and that will destroy the blaster cannon plus most of the rest of the underside of the ship and send everything flying."

Zora waited patiently through this, knowing it was easier and often quicker than cutting the kid off and having to dance through all his apologies. "Will we be safe back at the *Six*?" she asked.

Garret paused as if he was only just considering this. "Oh, yeah. Yeah, I think so."

"Wonderful. Let's get a move on."

"Almost finished."

Jack had just shot another Gomarii attempting to storm the docking bay. Suicide by climbing. Eventually, those with more honor than brains would die out and the agent would run out of targets. Either that or they'd get the speedlift working again.

"Okay!" Garret shouted as he slammed the sensor panel back down over the Preyhunter's weapon system. "It's starting to overcharge."

"Now?"

"Yes. We should get away."

Zora shook her head. "I thought you'd set it off later."

"Oh, no. I'd need more parts and time to do that. It's going to take a bit to get really going, but the process has already started."

"How much time do we have?"

"Probably two minutes. It could be more if the system is choice. Or less if it's already banged up."

"Looks banged up to me," Zora said, and tried to hurry Garret away from the blast zone. But the code slicer broke off and headed to the speedlift. "What are you doing?"

Garret punched in a code on his slicer box and then ran back to Zora. "I released the lock. When this thing goes off I want it to actually hit some bad guys. I can lock it down again remotely after that... well, unless the blast takes my box out."

Zora had been hoping that the locks on the lift would last until either the Kublarens came up or Black Leaf made their way down into the hangar. But what was done was done. Hopefully Garret had made the right decision and the lift would have been operable soon anyway.

They ran over to Jack. Zora took over the man's vigil at the unpowered entrance while Garret helped Jack limp back to the *Indelible VI*. Once they were in position and set up on the wreck, they called for her to run back as well. She sent a few parting shots down the opening, hoping to keep any Gomarii from trying it again for a while, then hustled where they'd make their stand. As she ran, she cast a wary glance at the Preyhunter, hoping it didn't explode while she was still out in the open.

It didn't, but the first group of Gomarii did choose that moment to arrive from the now-functioning speedlift. Six warriors exited with blaster rifles already firing. But the shots were for shock and suppression rather than on sighted targets, and by the time the Gomarii had found the location of the defenders aboard the *Six*, the new arrivals were being cut down.

Three of them were dusted right there, the other three took cover behind the Preyhunter and the nearby tool chests. One popped back up and emptied a charge pack with suppressing fire as the other two began to hastily pull over more chests and crates, building cover for the next set of Gomarii who would come up the lift.

Zora could just see the doors open as a second lift unloaded. Now there were a total of three Gomarii suppressing the *Six* while several others continued to fortify their toehold in the bay. The strategy might have worked… had the Preyhunter's cannon not overloaded.

A third carload of six more Gomarii had just arrived when the eruption shook the entire bay. Large chunks of shrapnel zipped through the Gomarii caught in the blast, their quickly stacked cover blown apart and useless. Pieces of the Preyhunter even managed to reach the *Six*, causing metallic *tinks* and *clanks* to sound against its hull.

"Everybody okay?" Zora called out.

The others confirmed they were. The Gomarii were less fortunate. Jack and Zora picked off the few who still had the strength to crawl. Two Gomarii emerged from the ladder, hoping to use the explosion as a distraction, only to be picked off by Leenah. The odds had been evened.

"Clock is reset," Zora said. "Be ready for more."

Unfortunately, Garret reported that his slicer box hadn't withstood the blast, and he couldn't lock down the speedlift again. Another carload arrived shortly after the explosion, and its occupants were met by concentrated fire from Jack and Zora the moment its doors showed two centimeters' worth of space. As the doors opened further, two Gomarii fell forward dead, with others lying bleeding and dying behind them. By the time the speedlift doors had closed again, the only Gomarii left alive in the docking bay was crawling across the deck for cover, leaving a blood trail behind him, his dead clan mates riding back down to greet the next team waiting their turn to come up.

Zora hoped there weren't many waves left. But the size of the ship and the number of slavers it contained suggested that there were plenty of carloads to come so long as the Gomarii were committed to the fight. If even one slaver escaped their fire each time, then in only three more trips the number of attackers in the bay would match the number of defenders.

Garret recognized this problem as well. "I need to get to my station and see what I can do," he said, setting his rifle near Jack in case the man might need it.

"What you need to do is stay here and keep firing," Jack complained.

"No," said Zora. "Go, Garret." She looked at Jack. "He can do more for us there than with a rifle."

"Yeah. All right."

Garret had just brought up his screens when Nilo patched himself into the young code slicer's comm. "Garret, do you still have an entry point to the slave ship's system?"

Garret verified he did with a quick glance at his readouts. "I do. Or at least I will."

"I need you to get in there and find something for me. I'm on the sixth level with the Kublarens and we're up against something that's not Gomarii. I want to see if there's a way to shut it down remotely."

"That's where all the Drusics and Hools are!"

"It is, and they're giving us hell. Tell me what you find."

"Okay. Stand by."

Garret began his work regaining access to the slave ship. As his programs went where they didn't belong and weren't wanted, and with nothing else to do while he waited, Garret decided to see how much he could accomplish locally. He patted the power supply cable and felt the warmth that hummed through it. And then an idea struck him—a way he might better Leenah and the others' chances. It was clear from the volume of fire impacting in and around the ship that Zora, Leenah, and Jack were engaging an increasing number of targets, and there were no more Preyhunter cannons to overload. Something needed to happen if they were going to survive.

He told Nilo that he was slicing his way back in and would let him know once he had control again. Then he ran to the portable generator, grabbed a second auxiliary hookup from it, and carried the supply throughout the ship, splicing it into every system he could think of with the hopes that the restoration of power might activate some asset aboard the *Six* they could use. Of course, the ship was in no condition to fly or reposition itself, even with full power; if it were, they could fly out of the bay altogether, or simply nose the big Naseen freighter against the speedlift, disabling it completely. In fact, that might be something to try with one of the other Preyhunters on deck, if they could reach one that could move. But given the current intensity of blaster fire, that seemed unlikely. It was a good idea, too late.

And then another idea hit Garret, one he was sure he could accomplish if a blaster bolt didn't hit him.

"I'm going under the ship!" he shouted.

Both Leenah and Zora shouted for him to stay put, but the code slicer jumped down, still holding the power supply as blaster bolts danced around his feet. He wondered if the slavers were trying to pick him off at the knees or if these shots were just sprayed at the *Six* in the hopes of keeping its defenders down or scoring a lucky hit.

He felt an odd sense of calm despite being shot at. He'd had more than his fair share of the experience on Rakka with Captain Keel, and he remembered what Keel had told him. About keeping his focus and continuing to move. About deciding what to do and then doing it and not letting fear lock up his mind.

So that's what he did. He pushed back concern and worry and focused on dragging the power cable until he was at the belly turret beneath the *Six*. The turret was concealed in its housing, which was a good sign. It was supposed to retract before a jump, but Garret couldn't be certain, and had it been sitting out, it would likely be dead and ruined from some direct blast from an enemy starship. As it was, there was still a chance it could be made to work.

Except... he needed the weapon out in order to do what he had planned.

Garret hung his head and wondered what Captain Keel would do. He realized at once that Keel would do whatever he needed to do in order to complete his mission. But not before voicing his frustration.

"Why can't it ever be easy?" Garret yelled, and somehow felt better for having done it.

He left the power connector where he would ultimately need it and then retraced his steps, dodging still more blaster fire until he popped back up inside the ship.

"Leenah!" he shouted. "I need one of the servo-pryers or something else that can pop open the belly turret. I think I can get it functioning if I can just get the kelhorned thing down."

Leenah looked surprised at Garret's language; he wasn't the type to swear. She shook her head. "You don't need to pry it open. That'll ruin it. Go under the deck crawlspace past the exhaust manifold. There's a manual release you can pull. It'll drop right down."

That made sense now that he heard it. The turret was designed not to be visible on the outside. Garret had only gone to its placement because he already knew where it was. If finding it was as easy as digging a prybar into what looked like a seamless section of plating, then every port inspector with a toolbelt could nail you for having an illegal weapons package.

"Okay. Manual release… past the… manifold… uh, crawlspace."

Leenah looked at Garret for a long moment, then decided this was something she'd better do herself. She handed him his rifle. "Take this and shoot it at any Gomarii that make it past the farthest container." She pointed to the one. "There. That's my job, now it's yours. Until I get back."

Garret nodded and then went into position, prone and looking down the weapon's holographic sight display, hoping that no Gomarii made it to the point where he would become responsible for taking them down. Not because he objected to killing them, but because he doubted his ability to do it. But as he watched the world through the sights, his confidence increased. The display did all the work. The reticle was attuned to the movement of the gun and "stuck" to humanoid targets, letting Garret lead them and adjusting itself to any tremors or sudden jerks.

While the code slicer was watching for an opportunity to be helpful on the trigger, Leenah dropped herself down below what remained of the deck and began to crawl through its tight confines. She felt as comfortable and familiar there as a nettle viper in its own rocky nest. In almost no time she reached the turret's manual release, grabbed it, and pulled back. It gave a dull *clunk*, which was followed by the soft hiss of the weapon system dropping down unpowered. She couldn't see it, but she could tell the release had worked as intended.

Now to get out again.

The access tunnel was only large enough for her to move in one direction—she wasn't large and yet she couldn't come close to turning around once inside. Usually, she would continue on her path and come up from another one of the maintenance hatches, emerging on the other side of the ship the way a matnit popped up out of its many burrow openings, but after a few meters of crawling she found the path completely blocked off by a crisscrossing, scissoring maze of twisted impervisteel. There was no way out except for the way she'd come in.

Moving feet-first through the tunnel took longer than she'd hoped, and by the time she returned to recover her rifle, she saw that there were two dead Gomarii lying beyond the point of no return Garret had watched. She gently patted the code slicer's shoulder, took the rifle, and resumed her sector. Meanwhile, Jack and Zora remained heavily engaged; the Gomarii were mounting an increasingly strong attack from the speedlift.

Almost as soon as Leenah's eyes settled on the holo-sights a third Gomarii passed the line and was added to the dead who had gotten beyond that last crate. "Garret! Sooner you get the turret up and running the better!"

That was all the prompting Garret needed. He sped to the belly of the *Six*, dodging more blaster fire, and there was the turret, its cannons pointing straight down at the deck and able to swivel with the push of a hand. Garret grabbed hold of one of the thin antipersonnel blaster barrels to hold the weapon in place, then he picked up the auxiliary power cord and plugged it into the port located at the turret's base. Almost at once the weapon stiffened and came to life as if awakening from a deep sleep.

Garret let out a whoop of triumph before hurrying back aboard the *Six*. There was still more to do. Just getting the weapon system online wasn't enough—now he had to get it something to shoot at. He reached his station and heard Nilo calling for him in a tiny voice. He looked down and realized that he'd left his comm sitting there unattended. He picked it up.

"Sorry, Mr. Nilo. I forgot my comm and I had to do something."

"Have you gotten in yet!" Nilo called, shouting above a chorus of blaster fire, screams, and croaks. He didn't sound worried, but the situation did sound tense.

Garret checked his screens and found that he had obtained full access to the system. It was just waiting for him to give a command. But also waiting was the *Indelible VI*'s belly turret...

"Uh, almost. One minute."

"Only have a few of those left at our disposal before I have to start bringing in the mercs. We've got this battle won, but I don't want to let the slaves be taken off-planet!"

"Going as fast as I can," mumbled Garret as he worked through the ship's systems, all of which were now operating out of his workstation node.

With the cannon online, he merely needed to send a burst telling it what to do. He tasked it with sentry duty, which meant it would shoot any humanoid that came within thirty meters of the ship. That would prevent the guns from opening fire on any Gomarii running around behind cover—those were better handled by Jack and Zora—but ensured it would engage any who moved past the point of no return he'd briefly monitored.

All things being equal, he would rather work the gun manually and take out advancing Gomarii and lay down heavy fire on the ones from cover. The repulsor chests and other mechanical pieces wouldn't hold up against a weapon of this magnitude for long. But manual control meant he wouldn't be able to assist Nilo, who sounded like he needed it.

"I'm switching on the guns!" Garret shouted to the others. Then, as an afterthought, "Don't get off the ship or you'll get shot!"

Not five seconds later the spitting fire of the belly turret added its own noise to the war-torn hangar as a charging team of five Gomarii slavers went down. They had picked the wrong time to push up as one.

Jack shouted for joy as the other slavers jumped down behind cover, unaware that they were out of range.

They would keep their heads down for a while at least while trying to work out this latest wrinkle in their plans.

"Okay Mr. Nilo, I'm in. What am I looking for here?"

"A program. It should be called something like Pantheon or Xanadu. Look for those keywords."

Garret searched and saw numerous hits come back. "Okay, yeah. Tons of instances of it here." He squinted. "What is this? Some kind of... mind control?"

"Can you shut it down?"

Garret shook his head before answering. He was still trying to decipher what it was he was viewing. Whatever this program was, it definitely seemed to be controlling the slaves, but all he was really looking at was surface information. He still had no idea how it was being done.

"Trying," he finally answered once he became aware of the time that had elapsed since Nilo's question.

The program used a hybrid language, combining Gomarii tech language with the same tech language that Rechs's armor used to communicate. Since this was a slave-control program, Garret figured the underlying code structure was Gomarii, and some tech they'd brought on board afterward introduced the armor code language. But as he dug his way down further into the source he realized that he had it all backwards. The Gomarii code wasn't written beneath the Rechs code; it was the other way around. Which had to mean that the ship was *not* a Gomarii ship first. It had been something else *before* it was secured by the Gomarii. And whatever it was, it must have been made during the same period of civilization that produced Tyrus Rechs's legendary armor.

It was quickly apparent to Garret that he couldn't shut down whatever program was controlling the Hool and Drusic slaves—not quickly, anyway. His understanding of the armor code was too limited. But he was not about to give up. Not with Mr. Nilo in trouble and certainly not with the way the *Indelible VI* was spewing fire on what had to be an increasingly numerous and desperate enemy. There had to be something else he could do.

And then he remembered what Leenah had said the prisoner they had taken had told her. That the ship could not be taken. Maybe the Gomarii weren't trying to protect their clan, but the ship itself? Or something on board? But what could be so important that they were willing to risk the total destruction of their clan to protect it?

Given the complexity of the slave-control program he was looking at—not to mention the oddity of such code even existing on a Gomarii slave ship—one possibility immediately sprang to mind. *This* was what they were protecting. Programs. Data. Garret could be wrong about that, but something told him he wasn't. And even if he was... well, stealing it was his only move.

He quickly began to explore the rest of the ship's databanks, grabbing everything he found, large swaths of data, and copying it to his node, partitioning it to keep it separated from any of his own programs. The ship's dual-language programming slowed this down more than he'd like, but he pulled big chunks of it all the same.

Suddenly, alarms began to sound within the Gomarii vessel. Loud warning claxons that hadn't sounded throughout the entire siege.

"I've got you," Garret whispered. He pinged Nilo. "I started copying over the databases I was finding and that's when the alarm sounded. Maybe a coincidence, but I don't think so. I think these Gomarii are trying to protect this ship and the information it contains."

"I'm almost certain that you're right," said Nilo. "Grab everything you can. We're taking heavy losses, but we've cut through most of these defenders. There can't be many left beyond us, and then we'll reach the flight controls and data centers."

There was a beep at his console, and Garret saw that two things were happening. First, someone was trying to lock him out of the system. And second, some kind of eradication program was now in the process of rapidly deleting whatever it could. He passed the information on to Nilo.

"Get as much as you can, Garret. I can't begin to tell you how important it is. Everything you can get, get it. Scan with your eyes anything that your system isn't downloading and memorize it. Capture holopics. Everything. Every byte that we miss could be crucial. I'll do what we can to stop this at the source once we get there."

Garrett went back to his work, doing as Nilo had asked. He was so focused on his work that he didn't realize that Zora had come to stand beside him. She clapped him on the shoulder and called his name, causing him to jump.

"Garret!"

"Huh! Oh... sorry. What's wrong?"

"I said they stopped. They just... left."

Garret looked down at his screen. He was locked out. He looked back up to Zora and nodded. "I think... I think they were just trying to hold us up."

EPILOGUE

"You've got balls of impervisteel, Ford," said Bear as he brought Keel into his crushing grip with an enormous side hug worthy of the operator's name. Keel certainly felt like he was being pulverized by a Darkon grizzly.

Bear discreetly nodded to a team of Legion marines who were passing through the secured docking hangar of Captain Pemm's frigate. "You know, one of the hullbusters puked when he saw what you did to the Nether boys with the nose of that shuttle."

Keel raised an eyebrow. "Sure it wasn't one of the points who swapped uniforms? Doesn't sound like any hullbuster I ever met."

Bear chuckled. "Not a point. Was a staff officer though, and they ain't hullbusters. Not really."

"Did you wipe out all the Nether agents?" asked Nobes, the kill team's intelligence sergeant. He and Bombassa had joined Bear on the trip to retrieve Keel.

"One survived," Keel answered.

Bombassa nodded. "If he's in condition to speak, it would be wise of us to go to the agent first."

"Yeah," said Keel. "As I recall, if the Nether agents are going to talk, it's right at first. Give 'em too much time and they start thinking better of it. Pemm'll talk whenever you give him the opportunity. Wants to clear his name."

"Needs to answer to those people whose family he killed," said Bear. He stooped to retrieve a bag of Spindust from a partially opened carton. "This stuff ain't poisoned or anything, is it?"

"Not as far as I know," said Keel before nodding toward the open blast door leading to the rest of the ship and telling Bombassa and Nobes, "Nether is stable last I heard. In the med bay."

Bombassa seemed relieved to have something to do other than make small talk. "Let's go, Nobes. If the med bot gives trouble, I'll handle it. You work on the agent."

"Sounds good to me."

The two legionnaires headed off. When they were out of earshot, Keel said to Bear, "Hey. That captain was scared to death I was going to hang him from the rafters. You got any idea why, now that you're top operator on the team?"

"I don't have any intel that you haven't seen, if that's what you're getting at," said Bear, grinning as he chewed on the fluffy candy. "But... I heard a story once that Rechs—this was a while back—went and personally hunted down and hung a House of Reason delegate he didn't see eye to eye with. Kinda figured that was just one of those stories they made up."

Keel nodded. He hadn't heard that one. "That adds up with how Pemm was behaving. You guys tracking a network of House of Reason loyalists looking to try and carve out a place for themselves?"

"Tracking a lot of things, my man."

"Well, Pemm's a part of it. Said he got mixed in with Nether when they told him they needed his ship for a mission somewhere in the mid-core."

"Where?" asked Bear, his mouth half full.

"Didn't get around to that."

"Well, Kima looks like it's gonna go hot before long. Got a team there now—not sure which."

Keel knew that much just from watching clips from the news holos and House of Liberty briefings. "Maybe we should talk with him."

Bear became serious. "I haven't known you to care that much about what's goin' on in the galaxy, Ford. Especially when your crew isn't with you."

Keel shrugged. That was true enough. "Yeah, well, all these factions forming up seem to have it in for me personally."

"Nah. You're just the unluckiest lucky guy I ever met." Bear clapped Keel on his armored shoulder. Keel could feel the impact of his big paw despite the protection. "Nature and politics abhor a vacuum. Gonna be some scuffling before things even out. We got it handled, boss."

Keel shook his head and looked around the bay. Maintenance bots were cleaning up the grislier remains of the fight while techs used the hangar's limited crane and docking functionality to try and make room for the two wrecked shuttles and incoming and outgoing craft from the nearby destroyer.

"So how did your Tennar friend try to finish her mission?" asked Bear, balling up the finished bag of Spindust before dropping it for the maintenance bots.

"Wasn't sure she *was* going to carry it out, to be honest. Put my bot on her after we found her files in that data retrieval. Also kept the armor on just in case—you know, make it harder for her to get it if she did want it."

Bear nodded. "You shoot her?"

"More or less." Keel didn't want to get into the details of his arming a gunnery bot to fire an actual gun—a highly illegal modification, and one he'd probably keep in place for now given how well it had worked out. Unless the little bot managed to become even more eccentric.

"Oba, I don't wanna unpack that."

That was fine with Keel. He was still unpacking the events that had led him to this point and the best way to approach what came next. He had what remained of his crew isolated with an organization that Dark Ops wanted him to infiltrate and monitor. And he had a sinking feeling that his friends in the Legion were soon to be sucked into another engagement.

The little bot, Death, Destroyer of Worlds, seemed to sense all of this in Keel. It rolled over, leaving the place where Keel had instructed it to stay, and gently bumped into Keel's leg. It beeped a gentle promise that more enemies would soon be slain, and that their blood would tint the stars a glorious red.

Keel petted the little maniac despite all of that. "You get a holo of Honey?"

"Why would you want something like that?" asked Bear.

"Gonna have to prove I didn't let her go," said Keel. "Otherwise, it could be a choppy reunion with the rest of my crew. How long do you think before I can get that shuttle ride back? I need to get moving."

"Shouldn't be too long. Just need to talk to—" Bear cut himself off and held his index finger up to ask for a moment. His other hand went to the micro-comm in his ear, and he walked away, talking to whoever was online.

Keel sat on his haunches, feeling supported by the armor as though he were resting on a small stool. It felt nice to simply stop moving, at least for a while. He watched the hullbusters come and go, along with navy techs, bots, and everyone else that followed up and supported after the fighting had finished.

Then he saw Bombassa and Nobes hurrying toward the bay, their faces set and determined. Keel stood to greet them. "Quick interrogation."

"We only just started when Bear called us back," Bombassa explained.

"Something's up," said Nobes.

The three men looked to Bear, who finished his conversation and motioned for them to come speak with him in his quiet little section of the hangar bay. Death moved to follow, but Keel waved for it to stay back. The bot beeped and then obeyed.

"What's going on?" Keel asked.

Bear waited until they were drawn into a tight, small circle.

"Things just went kinetic on Kima. 131st is getting set to hit the ground—that includes all attached kill teams."

"You gonna get this ship's new captain to jump you there?" Keel asked.

Bear shook his head. "They got a sector to watch and Kima isn't close. Actually, was gonna see if you could do the honors. We need to get there *uptime.* Rest of the team is already on the way."

Keel gave a nervous chuckle while the other three legionnaires watched him. "Yeah, I mean… at this point being on time to link up with Black Leaf isn't happening."

Bear nodded his agreement. "Want you to think about staying with the team until we've got it under wraps."

"That I can't do."

The big man's eyes were serious. "Hang on, let me finish. Found out that Masters's kill team is the one who got hit in the opening salvos. No luck reaching them either."

Keel felt his stomach drop as he mentally added another name to the ever-growing list of fallen comrades. Exo. Twenties. Kags.

Masters.

"He ain't dead, Ford," said Bear. "If we get there ahead of Chhun, we'll have a free shot at pulling him out before we get tasked with other missions."

Keel shared a look with Bombassa, who stood expressionless, not willing to let his thoughts on the matter come into view of the others. But when he saw Nobes's eyes, he recognized the same sentiment he himself felt. Bear had no way of knowing what he'd just said was true. He was only telling them what he hoped—what he *wanted*—to be true.

"Gotta give me a decision, bro," said Bear, and Keel could see the torment in the big man's eyes. He wasn't pleading or begging, but the best-of-rivals bond the big man had with Masters was right there for all to see. "Hate to keep spinning your repulsor, but I gotta know so I can plan how to get us there."

Keel looked behind him to the freight shuttle and the little bot. When he turned back to the legionnaires he saw his future in Bear's face. Or at least his next stop.

"Okay," he said, giving a slow, smooth nod. Taking control. "Let's make 'em pay."

The first Kublarens to enter the docking bay Zora and the others were defending were nearly wiped out by the belly turret of the *Indelible VI*. They poured out of the speedlift and up the manual entry, overwhelming the hangar unannounced. Still, they showed incredible discipline, taking cover and not returning fire—clearly they knew that the hangar bay was friendly, even if the *Six*'s targeting system didn't know the same about them.

Garret quickly shut the system down. Leenah jumped down and sought to administer aid, unsure where to begin, but wanting to help. She ran to the nearest Kublaren who had been struck by the turret; he expired in her hands, stained yellow by his own blood.

The other Kublarens seemed not to be bothered, and were soon up and moving through the bay, checking all the corners the defenders hadn't been able to and confirming that they were empty. The koobs kept a wide berth of the *Six*, climbing atop Preyhunters and croaking to one another in tight groups, their own battle ended.

At last, a small transport shuttle entered through the top of the hangar. Jack, who was now sitting up against a twisted vertical beam aboard the *Six*, grumbled to Zora, "Better late than never, huh?"

"Yeah." Zora didn't look happy. "That's Surber's shuttle. This'll be fun."

"Been nothin' but, so far," said Jack, who then grimaced from a sudden jolt of pain he'd brought about in letting his arm drop into his lap.

The shuttle's ramp dropped, and Surber's two bodyguards moved quickly down, weapons up as though the hangar was still unsecure. Surber came down next, followed by a team of Black Leaf mercs, who spread out to provide security for the shuttle.

Surber made his way directly to the *Six*, one of the mercenaries in tow—a raven-haired human female who looked to be the team's medic.

"You all earned your pay today," Surber said. "Remind me to think better of you next time your names are suggested for something important. Garret—Mr. Nilo wants to see you on the bridge, and it's best not to make that man wait. And since you're not employed like these others, here's your 'pretty please.' Get going."

The code slicer hesitated, checked with Zora who released him with a nod, and then moved toward the speedlift.

"Hell of a job, kid," Jack called after him.

Surber looked toward Leenah, who had returned to the *Six*. "You must be our slave girl. Congratulations on your rescue. Miss Romnova here will fix up that bleeding." Surber motioned his head for the woman behind him to move forward. "Lana."

The medic jogged ahead.

"It's not my blood," Leenah said. "Endurians don't bleed yellow. She can help Jack."

But Lana had already recognized that it was the spy who needed her aid. She'd headed in his direction from the outset.

"Good for you," said Surber. "And Jack... I advised against paying your rates. Perhaps I was wrong."

"Thanks," muttered Jack. "And thanks for finally showin' up through the big door we opened up for you up here. These guys you shuttled in would've been useful thirty minutes ago."

"I was still earning my pay thirty minutes ago, Jack. We all got a job to do. I didn't realize part of yours was doing employee reviews. I was promised an extra day of vacation and use of a company sled, Jack—can you be sure to put that down?"

"Asshole," Jack grunted.

Surber either didn't hear or didn't want to continue with the banter. He turned to his bodyguards. "Get me that Gomarii so we can have a chat."

The two men unchained the captured slaver from his spot—his arms had been fastened behind his back around an impervisteel column—and marched him back toward the shuttle.

Surber glared at the slaver as he passed, then turned to Zora. "You. Bounty hunter. I need to know why your friend Wraith still isn't here despite your being paid a considerable sum for the opposite to happen. So, find me at my shuttle in ten minutes."

Zora knew better than to protest or make excuses. Not with Surber. She moved past Lana, still walking gingerly because of the shot she'd taken to her back.

"You're hurt," Lana said, looking up from checking Jack's wounds.

"I'll be fine."

Surber smiled as Zora settled down next to Leenah. "Of course you will. Tough girl, this one, Lana. Survivor. Like you. I'm sure you three will all be fast friends in no time, giggling and sharing who your crushes are this week at the next sleepover."

He left the *Six* and followed his men and the Gomarii.

Zora watched Jack and Lana as the medic applied skinpacks and new pain controllers. There was a familiarity between the two that had caught her attention. She listened, picking up their conversation while doing her best to seem like she was watching the Kublarens.

"When'd you get back?" Jack asked.

"A week ago," answered the woman. "They almost got me."

"Yeah, well, things are picking up."

"Obviously."

"Did you hear from her while you were out of action?"

"No. Not directly. From the other, though."

"And?"

"Not yet."

Jack leaned his head back against the impervisteel. "Well, it's damn well going to have to be soon."

"I know. I need to get transferred to a better team, by the way."

"I'm Big Nee's latest hero," Jack said. "I'll see if I can get you hooked up with whatever they have me do."

Zora was unable to hear anything further; Leenah had started to talk.

"Tell me how you knew Aeson," she said.

Zora raised her eyebrows and let out a sigh. "It's a long and complicated story..."

The bridge was still being cleared of Gomarii bodies when Garret arrived. He found Nilo poring over the slave ship's systems, moving through screens with a swiftness and deftness that the young code slicer recognized at once as belonging to a fellow savant. Nilo operated in a single, confined window—only one holodisplay hadn't been destroyed by the fight to take the bridge.

"You wanted to see me, Mr. Nilo?"

Nilo nodded but didn't look away from his display. "Just Nilo is fine, Garret. No need for formalities between friends."

Garret noted that the man had not instructed him to use his first name. But then perhaps for a figure such as him, the last name felt more common and natural.

"Okay. I'll try to remember." And then Garret did remember the slim data crystal that he had packed with as much intel as he could. He held it out to Nilo, waiting for the man to notice and finally saying, "Oh, I brought this, Mis—Nilo. It's less than one percent of everything that was there I think, but it's better than nothing... I hope."

Nilo took the chip gratefully. "It's going to be the best that we have. They weren't just resisting our attacks; they were ridding themselves of all evidence. What you thought was a concentrated deletion was actually a data transfer. Everything was being pulled out and sent somewhere else, with no trace left for us to follow. You have more than one copy of this, right?"

Garret said that he did and asked a question about the information transfer. "That's, uh, that's how some of the old Republic state agencies run their intelligence, isn't it?"

Nilo turned from his work, a look of mischief in his eyes. "I probably shouldn't be surprised that you know that, but yes, that's how they do it, too." He motioned around the ship. "And this is where they got the idea."

Garret looked around the bridge more closely while Nilo went to load the chip into the system. As the files Garret had copied began to present themselves to Nilo, the man followed Garret's gaze to one of the many Gomarii battle flags around the bridge.

"Does that look familiar to you, Garret?"

The code slicer shook his head. "I don't think I've ever seen it before today. But it was all over the inside of the ship. Is it a big Gomarii clan? I had some friends on the boards who were into tracing the Gomarii—always tried to guess their locations and would message the social media accounts for the Repub military to get them to try and hunt them down. Never happened.'

"In fact, it's not a Gomarii clan at all," said Nilo. "Not in the way anyone would think."

Garret waited for Nilo to say more, but the enigmatic business titan left it at that and returned to the holodisplay. Garret moved alongside him, thinking that perhaps he could be of use by guiding him to what he felt were some of the more interesting pieces that he'd managed to capture.

"So, I took a look at this while the gun people were cleaning up. Pretty sure that I recorded right up until deletion. Or, I guess, when it transferred everything out of the database. That's a really fast transfer."

Nilo nodded in agreement.

"Yeah, so, there are files and stuff like you'd expect, but they were huge and encrypted, but I came on this feed and it was like a holostream, but not from one of the security cams. At first I thought it was a bot flying over the battle because I could see the Kublarens and the slaves fighting up close, but then I manipulated it a bit and realized it was more like I was watching the fight through one of the slave's perspectives. Like the program had a neural implant and was recording what the host's eyes saw."

Garret was trying hard to speak in complete sentences, resisting the urge to let it all just come out at once because, though he was excited, he was also frightened. And he felt he needed to be calm and controlled because he wanted Nilo to hear and then see what he'd seen.

"I dug down further and activated this HUD overlay, which I guess is kind of like how legionnaires get enhanced battlefield info in their helmets, but it was different than that and on top of the whole thing when you alternate audio tracks, you get more than just the sounds of battle, there's a master that was playing music the entire time. Like old music. You know, classical. So that was weird enough but—augmented reality I mean, yeah, it's everywhere. No surprise there except right in the middle of it this totally new overlay pops up and just kind of sits there for a while and then it's gone."

"You didn't bring that one up?" asked Nilo.

"No."

"Let's see the feed. Our friend Sarai is already working on cracking whatever else is in there."

Garret gave a fractional nod and then assumed control of the workstation, feeling odd at first for taking control as if Nilo were the confused grandparent wondering why he wasn't getting his holonews stories delivered. He brought up the file and skipped it forward to the end—just enough for Nilo to see a first-person perspective of a Hool fighter wielding one of the Gomarii's blaster rifles as well as its venomous spines against Pikkek's Kublarens, who were attempting to swarm and overwhelm it.

The rate at which the Hool fired, and the accuracy of those shots, was stunning. On a level rivaled only by legionnaires. And any time a Kublaren looked as though it might escape the punishment being meted out by the projectile weapon, the Hool somehow always seemed to know it and used its toxic spines to add devastating damage. Sometimes it impaled a diminutive koob and shook it off, adding to the pile of dead. More often the Hool simply shifted its position, allowing its needle-sharp quill to slash or prick the skin and relying on the incredibly lethal neurotoxins to do their killing work.

Nilo lowered his head and then pounded one of the dead consoles. "I knew this would happen!"

He sucked in a big breath of air and calmed himself, closing his eyes as he said, "I knew it was *happening.*" He was speaking to himself and not to Garret. "But this is all too soon. It wasn't supposed to happen this fast." He looked up as though praying. "You told me there was more time."

Garret could no longer hold in his confusion—and mounting dread. "What's going on? This is more than a Gomarii slave ship, isn't it?"

"Yes and no," said Nilo with a heavy sigh. "On closer inspection this is a Gomarii slave vessel that was built over a millennium ago—perhaps four hundred years after the start of the Savage Wars. But *not* by the Gomarii. The shipwrights did a fantastic job hiding its original design. Garret, this is a Savage hulk."

The code slicer's eyes went wide. "They *stole* a hulk from the Savages?"

"Stole, received as a gift, as a bribe—I don't know. But what's on the holodisplay right now," Nilo pointed to the carnage unfolding on the screen, "is the most common operating system the typical Savage marine used in combat."

Garret squinted at the image and felt his stomach grow queasy. "But those weren't Savage marines. They were slaves."

"They were slaves that the Gomarii, or whoever controlled this clan, had turned into an ad hoc Savage marine force."

"I don't understand. Why would Drusics and Hools fight for the Savages?"

"They didn't. Not really. Sarai will need to do some research based on what we have, but my theory at this point is that whatever mind or personality was once the Hool in this video, it's either been eradicated completely, or it's been so thoroughly suppressed that it may never escape whatever dark corner of its brain it's been forced into. A prisoner in its own mind, only able to come out if it suits the programmer. We're going to need to run detailed neural scans on every slave that we rescued from here, including your friend."

Garret wanted to repeat Nilo's bombshell, just to have something to say. He was stunned. He tried to bring back what he knew of the Savage Wars and the Savages themselves. The Savage marines were essentially floating brains determined to devour whatever calories were needed to keep their brain functions alive. Floating brains operating incredibly sophisticated and lethal battle suits.

"From what I know about Savage marines... everything was efficient," Garret said. "As little organic material as possible. But this Hool... he's fully organic. So how were the Gomarii making him function as a... as a Savage warrior?"

"I don't know," Nilo said. "But thanks to you, we've got what we need to start looking into it. This accelerates everything. Still, there's so much more to do. There are some pieces of Savage technology that I've been after that we can no longer afford to do without. Garret, I need your friend Wraith, and I need him now. The way this is going I'm going to need the entire Legion."

"I can't help you with the Legion thing, but now that we have Leenah and Wraith's ship... I mean, if you can start fixing it and we can get word to him about that, I don't see how he wouldn't stop whatever he's doing to get back here."

"Consider it done. And Garret... I'd like for you to oversee all of it. Whatever that ship needs, you repair it and outfit it however you see fit. There's no amount of money that is too much to get this done. No one will bother you about it except for maybe Surber, and if he does just tell him to talk to me."

Garret could think of a number of things he could do for the *Six* with a blank checkbook, not to mention what Leenah might have in mind. Which wasn't to say that Keel couldn't have afforded these things himself, but Keel had the tendency to always be moving, and when he moved, he used the *Six*. It was never in one place long enough for a real systems overhaul to occur. But now was the perfect opportunity to do everything. On the technological side, where Garret had the most experience, and on the physical side, where he'd defer to Leenah. He knew she would make the ship a better hauler, starfighter, and jumper than it had ever been. The Naseen light freighter's ability to do all things decently would be transformed into the ability to do all things just as well as its specialized counterparts. The *Indelible VI* would be better than any other ship in the galaxy.

"Okay. I'll get started right away," Garret said, wanting nothing more than to do exactly that.

Sarai's voice sounded in his micro-comm. "I have an early analysis. And I hope you don't mind that I've included Garret in reaching out. I like him."

"What do you have?" asked Nilo.

"Evidence that this group—designated as Batch 1616—was one of many."

"On the ship?"

"Inconclusive. I did, however, find navi-coordinates for what I believe to be a live-fire test of the design. Your interaction was with a batch that appears not to have been meant for combat. At least not yet."

Garret swallowed hard. The creatures certainly seemed capable of giving Black Leaf hell.

Nilo looked back to the display, still paused where he had left it. "What are the coordinates?"

"The planet Kima."

Nilo nodded, but kept his gaze fixed on the screen. He skipped forward until the overlay at the end of the transmission that Garret had spoken about was visible. Garret crept up to look over the man's shoulder. The words on the display made more sense now that he had the context to think about them in terms of Savage marines.

Leaderboard
FIRST PLACE – Crometheus
KILL STREAK: 88
CURRENT REWARD: Track Selection (Rebel Yell)
NEXT REWARD: N/A

And beneath that, more names, and more scores.

Nilo resumed playback on the holorecording, and the classical music screamed back to life, issuing from the audio relays to fill the bridge as the singer shouted... "More, more, more!"

THE END

GALAXY'S EDGE SEASON 2 CONTINUES
NOVEMBER 2021 WITH

CONVERGENCE

FOR A FULL RELEASE SCHEDULE
AND MORE INFORMATION ABOUT
GALAXY'S EDGE, VISIT
WWW.GALAXYSEDGE.US

GE BOOKS

(CT) CONTRACTS & TERMINATIONS

(OC) ORDER OF THE CENTURION

SAVAGE WARS

01   SAVAGE WARS
02   GODS & LEGIONNAIRES
03   THE HUNDRED

RISE OF THE REPUBLIC

01   DARK OPERATOR
02   REBELLION
03   NO FAIL
04   TIN MAN
OC   **ORDER OF THE CENTURION**
CT   REQUIEM FOR MEDUSA
CT   CHASING THE DRAGON
CT   MADAME GUILLOTINE

Explore over 30+ Galaxy's Edge books and counting from the minds of Jason Anspach, Nick Cole, Doc Spears, Jonathan Yanez, Karen Traviss, and more.

LAST BATTLE OF THE REPUBLIC

- **OC** **STRYKER'S WAR**
- **OC** **IRON WOLVES**
- 01 LEGIONNAIRE
- 02 GALACTIC OUTLAWS
- 03 KILL TEAM
- **OC** **THROUGH THE NETHER**
- 04 ATTACK OF SHADOWS
- **OC** **THE RESERVIST**
- 05 SWORD OF THE LEGION
- 06 PRISONERS OF DARKNESS
- 07 TURNING POINT
- 08 MESSAGE FOR THE DEAD
- 09 RETRIBUTION
- 10 TAKEOVER

REBIRTH OF THE LEGION

- 01 LEGACIES

JOIN THE LEGION

FOR UPDATES ABOUT NEW RELEASES, EXCLUSIVE PROMOTIONS, AND SALES, VISIT INTHELEGION.COM AND SIGN UP FOR OUR VIP MAILING LIST. GRAB A SPOT IN THE NEAREST COMBAT SLED AND GET OVER THERE TO RECEIVE YOUR FREE COPY OF "TIN MAN", A GALAXY'S EDGE SHORT STORY AVAILABLE ONLY TO MAILNG LIST SUBSCRIBERS.

INTHELEGION.COM

HONOR ROLL

We would like to give our most sincere thanks and recognition to those who supported the creation of *Galaxy's Edge: Dark Victory* by supporting us at GalaxysEdge.us.

Artis Aboltins
Sam Abraham
Guido Abreu
Chancellor Adams
Myron Adams
Garion Adkins
Ryan Adwers
Elias Aguilar
Neal Albritton
Jonathan Allain
Bill Allen
Jake Altman
Justin Altman
Tony Alvarez
Joachim Andersen
Jarad Anderson
Galen Anderson
Robert Anspach
Melanie Apollo
Britton Archer
Benjamin Arguello
Thomas Armona
Jonathan Auerbach

Fritz Ausman
Sean Averill
Nicholas Avila
Albert Avilla
Matthew Bagwell
Joseph Bailey
Marvin Bailey
Nathan Ball
Kevin Bangert
Caleb Barber
John Barber
Logan Barker
Brian Barrows-Striker
Robert Battles
Eric Batzdorfer
John Baudoin
Adam Bear
Nahum Beard
Antonio Becerra
Mike Beeker
Randall Beem
Matt Beers
John Bell

Daniel Bendele	Joseph Calvey
Royce Benford	Van Cammack
Anthony Benjamin	Chris Campbell
Edward Benson	Danny Cannon
Cody Bente	Zachary Cantwell
Matthew Bergklint	Brett Carden
Carl Berglund	Jacob Carwile
Brian Berkley	Robert Cathey
David Bernatski	Brian Cave
Tim Berube	Shawn Cavitt
Justin Bielefeld	David Chor
Shannon Biggs	Tyrone Chow
Brien Birge	Isaiah Christen
Nathan Birt	James Christensen
Trevor Blasius	Bryant Christian
WJ Blood	Casey Clarkson
David Blount	Jonathan Clews
Evan Boldt	Beau Clifton
Rodney Bonner	Sean Clifton
Thomas Seth Bouchard	Jerremy Cobb
William Boucher	William Coble
Scott Bourne	Robert Collins Sr.
Brandon Bowles	Alex Collins-Gauweiler
Alex Bowling	Jerry Conard
Chester Brads	Gayler Conlin
Jordan Brann	Michael Conn
Ernest Brant	James Connolly
Geoff Brisco	Ryan Connolly
Paul Brookins	James Conyers
Raymond Brooks	Garrett Copeland
Marion Buehring	Robert Cosler
Jim Burkhardt	Ryan Coulston
Tyler Burnworth	Andrew Craig
Matthew Buzek	Adam Craig
Noel Caddell	Jonathan Culbertson
Daniel Cadwell	Phil Culpepper
Brian Callahan	Ben Curcio

Tommy Cutler	Travis Edwards
Thomas Cutler	Justin Eilenberger
Christopher Da Pra	William Ely
John Dames	Michael Emes
David Danz	Brian England
Matthew Dare	Andrew English
Brendon Darling	Stephane Escrig
Brendon Darling	Benjamin Eugster
Alister Davidson	Nicholas Fasanella
Peter Davies	Christian Faulds
Walter Davila	Steven Feily
Ashton Davis	Mike Feliciano
Nathan Davis	Meagan Ference
Ivy Davis	Brad Ferguson
Joseph Dawson	Adolfo Fernandez
Ron Deage	Ashley Finnigan
Anthony Del Villar	Matthew Fiveson
Tod Delaricheliere	Waren Fleming
Ryan Denniston	Kath Flohrs
Anerio (Wyatt) Deorma (Dent)	Daniel Flores
Douglas Deuel	Steve Forrester
Isaac Diamond	Skyla Forster
Nicholas Dieter	Kenneth Foster
Christopher DiNote	Timothy Foster
Matthew Dippel	Chad Fox
Gregory Divis	Bryant Fox
Ellis Dobbins	Doug Foxford
Brian Dobson	Mark Franceschini
Graham Doering	Greg Franz
Gerald Donovan	Bob Fulsang
Garrett Dubois	Jonathan Furney
Ray Duck	Elizabeth Gafford
Trent Duncan	David Gaither
Christopher Durrant	Seth Galarneau
Cami Dutton	Christopher Gallo
Virgil Dwyer	Richard Gallo
Brian Dye	Kyle Gannon

Phil Garcia	Mohamed Hashem
Michael Gardner	Ronald Haulman
Alphonso Garner	Joshua Hayes
Brad Gatter	Ryan Hays
Tyler Gault	Adam Hazen
Stephen George	Richard Heard
Nick Gerlach	Colin Heavens
Christopher Gesell	Jon Hedrick
Kevin Gilchrist	Jesse Heidenreich
Dylan Giles	Brenton Held
Oscar Gillott-Cain	Jason Henderson
John Giorgis	Jason Henderson
Johnny Glazebrooks	Jonathan Herbst
William Frank Godbold IV	Daniel Heron
Justin Godfrey	Kyle Hetzer
Luis Gomez	Korrey Heyder
Tyler Goodman	Matthew Hicks
Justin Gottwaltz	Anthony Higel
Mitch Greathouse	Samuel Hillman
Gordon Green	Aaron Holden
Shawn Greene	Clint Holmes
Eric Griffin	Jacob Honeter
Ronald Grisham	Charles Hood
Preston Groogan	Tyson Hopkins
Harry Gurney	William Hopsicker
Levi Haas	Jefferson Hotchkiss
Tyler Hagood	Fred Houinato
Brandon Handy	Ian House
Erik Hansen	Ken Houseal
Greg Hanson	Nathan Housley
Adam Hargest	Jeff Howard
Ian Harper	Nicholas Howser
Revan Harris	Bradley Hudson
Jordan Harris	Kirstie Hudson
Jason Harris	Mike Hull
Matthew Hartmann	Donald Humpal
Adam Hartswick	Bradley Huntoon

Bobby Hurn	Evan Kowalski
Wayne Hutton	Byl Kravetz
Antonio Iozzo	John Kukovich
Wendy Jacobson	Mitchell Kusterer
Paul Jarman	Brian Lambert
James Jeffers	Clay Lambert
Tedman Jess	Jeremy Lambert
Eric Jett	Andrew Langler
Josh Johnson	Mikey Lanning
Eric Johnson	Dave Lawrence
James Johnson	Patrick Lawrence
Cobra Johnson	Alexander Le
Nick Johnson	Jacob Leake
Randolph Johnson	Eron Lindsey
Tyler Jones	Paul Lizer
Paul Jones	Kenneth Lizotte
David Jorgenson	Andre Locker
John Josendale	Richard Long
Sunil Kakar	Oliver Longchamps
Chris Karabats	Joseph Lopez
Ron Karroll	Kyle Lorenzi
Timothy Keane	David Losey
Cody Keaton	Steven Ludtke
Brian Keeter	Andrew Luong
Noah Kelly	Jesse Lyon
Jacob Kelly	Brooke Lyons
Caleb Kenner	John M
Daniel Kimm	David MacAlpine
Zachary Kinsman	Patrick Maclary
Rhet Klaahsen	Richard Maier
Jesse Klein	Ryan Mallet
Kyle Klincko	Chris Malone
William Knapp	Brian Mansur
Marc Knapp	Robert Marchi
Andreas Kolb	Jacob Margheim
Steven Konecni	Deven Marincovich
Ethan Koska	Cory Marko

Quinn Marquard
Edward Martin
Jason Martin
Lucas Martin
Pawel Martin
Trevor Martin
Joshua Martinez
Joseph Martinez
Phillip Martinez
Tao Mason
Ashley Mateo
Michael Matsko
Justin Matsuoko
Ezekiel Matze
Mark Maurice
Simon Mayeski
Logan McCallister
Kyle McCarley
Chase McCullough
Quinn McCusker
Alan McDonald
Caleb McDonald
Jeremy McElroy
Hans McIlveen
Rachel McIntosh
Richard McKercher
Jason McMarrow
Joshua McMaster
Colin McPherson
Christopher Menkhaus
Jim Mern
Robert Mertz
Jacob Meushaw
Brady Meyer
Pete Micale
Christopher Miel
Mike Mieszcak

Ted Milker
Daniel Miller
Patrick Millon
Reimar Moeller
Ryan Mongeau
Jacob Montagne
Mitchell Moore
Matteo Morelli
Todd Moriarty
Matthew Morley
Daniel Morris
William Morris
Nathaniel Morris
Alex Morstadt
Nicholas Mukanos
Bob Murray
Vinesh Narayan
James Needham
Adam Nelson
Tyler Neuschwanger
Travis Nichols
Bennett Nickels
Trevor Nielsen
Andrew Niesent
Sean Noble
Otto (Mario) Noda
Brett Noll-Emmick
Michael Norris
Greg Nugent
Christina Nymeyer
Brian O'Connor
Matthew O'Connor
Timothy O'Connor
Sean O'Hara
Colin O'neill
Ryan O'neill
Patrick O'Rourke

Grant Odom
Conor Oehler
Max Oosten
Tyler Ornelas
Gareth Ortiz-Timpson
Jonathan Over
James Owens
Will Page
David Parker
Matthew Parker
Shawn Parrish
Eric Pastorek
Andrew Patterson
Joshua Pena
Zac Petersen
Marcus Peterson
Chad Peyton
Corey Pfleiger
Jon Phillips
Dupres Pina
Jacob Piper
Jared Plathe
Paul Polanski
Matthew Pommerening
Stephen Pompeo
Jason Pond
Nathan Poplawski
Chancey Porter
Brian Potts
Jonathaon Poulter
Chris Pourteau
Daniel Powderly
Chris Prats
Thomas Preston
Matthew Print
Aleksander Purcell
Joshua Purvis

Max Quezada
Scott Raff
Jason Randolph
T.J. Recio
Jacob Reynolds
Cody Richards
Dalton Richards
Eric Ritenour
Walt Robillard
Brian Robinson
Joshua Robinson
Daniel Robitaille
Paul Roder
Thomas Rogneby
Chris Rollini
Thomas Roman
Joyce Roth
Andrew Ruiz
Jim Rumford
John Runyan
Chad Rushing
Sterling Rutherford
RW
Mark Ryan
Greg S
Lawrence Sanchez
David Sanford
Chris Sapero
Jaysn Schaener
Landon Schaule
Shayne Schettler
Jason Schilling
Andrew Schmidt
Brian Schmidt
Kurt Schneider
Theodore Schott
Kevin Schroeder

William Schweisthal	Jeremy Spires
Anthony Scimeca	Peter Spitzer
Connor Scott	Dustin Sprick
Preston Scott	Cooper Stafford
Rylee Scott	Travis Stair
Robert Sealey	Graham Stanton
Aaron Seaman	Paul Starck
Phillip Seek	Ethan Step
Kevin Serpa	John Stephenson
Dylan Sexton	Seaver Sterling
Austin Shafer	Maggie Stewart-Grant
Timothy Sharkey	Jonathan Stidman
Christopher Shaw	John Stockley
Charles Sheehan	Rob Strachan
Wendell Shelton	Benjamin Strait
Lawrence Shewark	James Street
Vernetta Shipley	Joshua Strickland
Ian Short	William Strickler
Glenn Shotton	Shayla Striffler
Joshua Sipin	John Stuhl
Andrew Skaines	Brad Stumpp
Scott Sloan	Kevin Summers
Steven Smead	Ernest Sumner
Anthony Smith	Randall Surles
Daniel Smith	Sonny Suttles
Lawrence Smith	Aaron Sweeney
Sharroll Smith	Shayne Sweetland
Tyler Smith	Lloyd Swistara
Michael Smith	Carol Szpara
Michael Smith	Travis TadeWaldt
Timothy Smith	Daniel Tanner
Tom Snapp	Blake Tate
David Snowden	Joshua Tate
Alexander Snyder	Lawrence Tate
John Spears	Kyler Tatsch
Thomas Spencer	Justin Taylor
Troy Spencer	Robert Taylor

Tim Taylor
Jonathan Terry
Stavros Theohary
Daniel Thomas
Chris Thompson
Steven Thompson
Jonathan Thompson
William Joseph Thorpe
Beverly Tierney
Matthew Tooze
Daniel Torres
Matthew Townsend
Ian Townsend
Jameson Trauger
Cole Trueblood
Dimitrios Tsaousis
Scott Tucker
Oliver Tunnicliffe
Eric Turnbull
Brandon Turton
John Tuttle
Dylan Tuxhorn
Jalen Underwood
Matthew Utter
Barrett Utz
Paul Van Dop
Andrew Van Winkle
Patrick Van Winkle
Paden VanBuskirk
Patrick Varrassi
Daniel Vatamaniuck
Jason Vaughn
Jose Vazquez
Stephen Vea
Brian Veit
Josiah Velazquez
Daniel Venema

Marshall Verkler
Cole Vineyard
Ralph Vloemans
Anthony Wagnon
Humberto Waldheim
Christopher Walker
David Wall
Justin Wang
Andrew Ward
Scot Washam
Tyler Washburn
Christopher Waters
Zachary Waters
John Watson
William Webb
Bill Webb
Hiram Wells
Ben Wheeler
Greg Wiggins
Jack Williams
Justin Wilson
Scott Winters
Evan Wisniewski
John Wisniewski
Reese Wood
John Wooten
Bonnie Wright
Jason Wright
Ethan Yerigan
Matthew Young
John Zack
Phillip Zaragoza
Brandt Zeeh
David Zimmerman
Jordan Ziroli
Nathan Zoss

ABOUT THE MAKERS

Jason Anspach is the co-creator of Galaxy's Edge. He lives in the Pacific Northwest.

Nick Cole is the other co-creator of Galaxy's Edge. He lives in southern California with his wife, Nicole.